The Tapestry of Isabella

The Chronicles of the Children Book Two

Kimberly Glassco
& Carissa Barker-Stucky

The Tapestry of Isabella by Kimberly Glassco & Carissa Barker-Stucky

Published by Everlight Tales & Tapestries

ISBN: 979-8-9893672-3-8 (print)

ISBN: 979-8-9893672-2-1 (ebook)

Cover by Carissa Barker-Stucky

The following content is a work of fiction.

Any likeness to actual people or events is purely coincidental. Some
aspects of various cultures have been adapted within this fantasy
setting; cultural dialects, norms, fashion, etc. may not fit what you
expect based on their source.

Dedication

For my amazing mother, Pamela Glassco, and my amazing sister, Katie Sheldon. Words can't express how much your support and enthusiasm mean to me.

— Kimberly

For one of the bestest friends a girl could ask for. Erin: You're welcome, but we made you wait until the last chapter.

— Carissa

Table of Contents

Acknowledgments

Mom:
Thank you for being a wonderful mother. As always, I'm so grateful for your support and love. It means so much that you take an interest in my passions. Thank you for being willing to be my sounding board when I'm trying to figure things out, whether for writing or just life. It encourages me to hear how much you care about the characters and the story. We both appreciate the time you give to help us make this story great and promote it to others. I hope you continue to enjoy the adventure.
Kimberly

Katie:
Thank you for being an amazing sister, and for always taking an interest in my life. Thank you for giving your time to help us in our writing endeavors. We appreciate your continued support and are grateful for the enthusiasm and love you have for our characters and story. I can't wait for you to get to read the rest, and I hope you continue to love it just as much.
Kimberly

Martha:
We wanted to express how much your support has meant to us. I'm thankful I met you and Allen, and I'm so grateful for your encouragement and business advice. You give us a place to replenish our spirits with good company and a warm atmosphere. The coffee and tea are delicious bonuses.
Kimberly

Chris:
I know things haven't been easy lately, but I appreciate and love you
with every fiber of my being. Thank you for helping me sit down
and get things done, for being my rubber duck on several occasions
and my constant caretaker through all these crazy ups and downs.
The ride may be crazy at times, but I wouldn't want to be on it with
anyone else.
Carissa

Maaura:
Told you the next book wouldn't take nearly as long. ;)
Thank you for all of the support through this journey, from helping
with tech issues to making sure I ate during our longer sprees. And
making sure the fur kids ate, too. Love ya <3
Carissa

Mom:
I can still remember the days I all-but dragged you into the library,
where you patiently had to assure any new librarians 'yes, she will
read all of those.' I have you to thank for my creative genes with
writing. And don't deny it. Our styles may be different, but we have
the same love of putting words on a page.
Carissa

Biscuits:
You may never read this, since I'm not gonna warn you it's here and a
lot of people skip the front matter, but just know that your friendship
and support through this entire process has been invaluable. Thank
you for the hours of entertainment. Also, sorry, but we did it again.
You'll know what I mean when you hit the end. ;)
Carissa

BEN-GAL
REGALIA
ANDOR
Petalore
Cassiona
Lilymere
Stonecarllon
SYLVA ARAE
DOMIR MTNS
Keep Shadow Veil
Caer Talon
Thorn-Drake
NIKKO MORI
Hawk Glen
House Gale
N O C I S
Caer Albright

REGALIA
ANDOR
SYLVA ARAE
Petalore
Cassiana
Lilymere
Stonewillow
Keep Shadow Veil
Caer Talon

1. Wounded Respite

Captain Isabella MoonChild's world was awash with colors.

Threads and patterns twined around every living being, adding to the Tapestry of Time in a swirl of shades. The more skilled Weavers among the Doran could learn to view and interpret entire sections of the tapestry, but even the most novice Weaver could manipulate the smaller threads and patterns. Captain had yet to decide if her fate was a lucky one: due to her powers as the Moon Child, she could see what only the most seasoned Weavers could, yet she could barely contain her abilities or stand to see the Grand Design. Mixed in with visions of past and present, a myriad of futures twirled through her mind when she used the Sight. Some, she could prevent. Others, she could cause. Still more, she had no say and could only prepare herself to stand by those affected when the time came.

Captain Isabella MoonChild's world was awash with colors— and she was drowning.

A cursed, red light pulsed through her mind alongside a vibrant crystal. A dark talisman hovered at the edge of her awareness, but she didn't follow the thread yet. Chaos and blood were her companions in the vision of the past. She hadn't even acknowledged Amaya's arrival and transformation aside from a slight smirk, her legs crossed and her eyes closed as she pieced together what had taken place in the keep. Her mind was already racing ahead— where to go next, what to do now. It would only be a matter of time before the survivors spread word of the castle's demise, perhaps even pulling Jeremiah out to investigate. Threads spun, and stories wove, but where would theirs fit? What should come next? The Star Child was living-dead, the Sun Child was shattered, and they were still within enemy territory. They had failed to protect Arianna from Tsukuyomi, though Captain at least knew now how he had managed to reach the girl. Her fate would have been the same in the forest, but that didn't help the guilt and sadness weighing on her heart. Finally, she opened her eyes, turning to watch Amaya and the fallout from the woman's reveal.

Solomon was unsurprised, though he would never out his knowledge being Captain's fault. She had still been learning to control her Sight and occasionally would speak what she saw or knew. The rest of their party was a different story. There had been a beat of silence, shock, some mouths hanging open. The crew, especially, found themselves uprooted after years of service. They had known Captain was the Moon Child, had known Solomon was from the Order, but Amaya...she had always been the first mate. Captain's guardian and friend. They had never known nor guessed there was more than a formidable pirate beneath those ebony locks. Zatook seemed as stoic and impassive as ever, maintaining his stance at the edge of camp; he had, at least, been convinced to sit down and let someone try and mend his clothing while he wore the shadows.

Jabez wearily studied Amaya from where he now lay on a bedroll as he recovered from his fight with Marilyn the blood mage. Calculations laced his memories of Amaya. She had never been afraid of him even when he relapsed at times during their travels together. He recalled how she seemed unfazed by StormShaper when he fought with Zatook in their camp more recently. How the lightning never reached any of their supplies or crew. Had it all been her? Instead of asking questions, Jabez decided to listen as others did the interrogating. His body ached terribly, and he felt so tired. And then there was the grief— the all too familiar sense of failure. His memories shifted to the moments when Arianna trailed after Amaya, and the woman's interactions with the child. Jabez's heart weighed heavily. He lacked any special gifts that gave him more knowledge than what he himself could discern, so he didn't know how the little girl had perished so silently under their watch. Jabez closed his eyes and tried to focus on his breathing. And yet the thoughts refused to be silent. They failed Arianna. They failed Tristan. They failed Rose. *Jabez* failed.

For his part, Alconai remained silent for a moment, his mind taking a similar path of deduction as his brother's. The entertainer stayed near Jabez and Lancelot to keep an eye on both men. Alconai's best friend and Alconai's brother had been through a lot in the last few hours, and then there was Captain's silence. Being a storyteller, Alconai learned how to observe everything and everyone around him. And yet, even with the hints, he'd only suspected that there was more to Amaya than met the eye. Oi yosh, had that been an underestimation.

Still, as his gaze shifted to look over Rose and Tristan lying unconscious and broken in ways he couldn't even begin to fathom, Alconai asked the one question that kept echoing through his mind: "Why did ye nae intervene sooner?" His voice held no accusation, just quiet confusion.

"By order of the Celestial King, we're not allowed to intervene or interfere with the goings-on with this plane," Amaya said dryly, her tone attesting to her opinion on such a law. She moved to a pack and retrieved some bandages. She then started wrapping her arms, hiding the darkened coloration along her hands and part way up her forearms. In contrast to the discoloration, the rest of her complexion appeared paler than usual. Amaya continued to speak as though everything was the same, "My family's one of few who tend to bend the rules quite a bit to help where we can." She gestured back the way they came. "We only outright break them when absolutely necessary. It's why we haven't been wrangled back to the Celestial Realm." Amaya's gaze softened as it shifted to Tristan. "As for why I waited 'til I did to join the fray, I had business to conduct that couldn't wait. That's all I can say for now."

"The Sistas be t'e same," Captain noted softly. "Lady Death an' t'e All Mother. Tha's why t'ey healed us an' helped Rose but havenae shown t'emselves much aside from tha'. T'ey be contendin' wit' a... stubborn king." Zatook snorted softly enough that only a few heard him. He knew much of stubborn kings deserving of other titles. Captain reached up to rub her forehead. "An' tha's why we be workin' wit' the assumption t'ey cannae 'elp. I's a blessing an' a surprise when t'ey do."

Lancelot ran a hand through his hair. Celestials, Chosen Children, kings...He was trying to keep everything straight. "Could someone please explain just what is going on? What does any of this have to do with the keep exploding?"

Captain sighed, lowering her hand. "T'ere's a lo' ye need ta be caught up on," she noted with a subtle laugh. She gestured to Alconai. "Ye, too, t'ough ye be kennin' more t'an yer friend." She shook her head. "I only ken wha' I been shown," she cautioned. "But Tris o'er t'ere is in charge o' guardin' some'in' very dangerous, some sorta talisman. I donnae ken anythin' about it ot'er t'an it's bad. An' his dad be t'e kin' o' person he's gotta keep it from. His mum hid him an' Anna away in a Shaddai-Blessed forest an' even poured 'er life force inna second protection spell until 'e was old 'nuff ta protect 'er on 'is own. As her extra protection started ta fade, I started ta See more abou' me fellow Chosen." She gestured at Solomon. "I wager ye ken more about 'ow t'is affects Nocis."

Solomon shook his head. "Little. The Order is aware that Nocis and Andor are on the cusp of war, but I do not know how this talisman or High Lord Tsukuyomi tie in."

Captain nodded wearily, then she startled when Rose spoke. "Jeremiah." The others were looking at the Half-Drow now, the woman who should by no means be the first awake. "Marilyn works for Jeremiah. She's... one of his most trusted mages. She's the missing link. I just don't see... what she's linking..." Her voice faltered towards the end, and she closed her eyes again. Captain looked thoughtful as she watched the woman.

"We 'ave a lot we be needin' ta figure out," she noted softly. "Especially wit' Rose bein' dead." She ran her hands over her face. "An' we be needin' a place safer'n t'e middle of a field ta figure it all out."

Alconai stared at her in shock. "Wha'?" The entertainer noticed that Amaya appeared unfazed by the news. She seemed to take everything Captain said in quiet contemplation. "Is t'is some gif' o' Lady Death, then? I cannae imagine T'e Lady jus' lettin' t'e Star Child roam undead. Or anyone for tha' matter."

"Wha', 'ad ye nae noticed?" Captain matched his surprise. Then she shook her head, sighing. "No, tha's nae tha' surprisin'. A lot's 'appened." She grimaced. "No one coulda survived wha' she went through when Tris'an beat 'er ta a pulp under Marilyn's control." Her gaze shifted back to the Star Child, watching her carefully. "She's 'ad Lady Rin's power clingin' ta her ever since. An' Rin mentioned somethin' abou' a boon when she came ta camp."

Zatook sighed, looking away. What deal had been struck, he wondered? Based on the Lady's appearance after Arianna slipped away, it had something to do with taking down Tsukuyomi and saving Tristan. He glanced back at Tristan, not aware of Solomon looking that way, as well. Both men knew a loss similar to the lad's, and both were wondering how best to aid the Sun Child through what was to come and what had already passed.

Zatook, for his part, shifted his gaze to Captain. She blinked when she felt him reach for her mind, meeting his gaze as she let him in. "Ye wan' us ta go ta Andor?" she asked aloud, letting the others in on the conversation. Solomon hesitated but then sighed.

"It would be the safest from Jeremiah and Tsukuyomi," he conceded. "As much as Nocis and Andor are at each other's throats, the Nocium army doesn't yet have a way to cross the border. Even if they do, we would be ahead of them and potentially safe in the capital."

Now Amaya's demeanor stiffened, and she wrinkled her nose in distaste. "I can travel with ye there, but I can't enter the kingdom. The King and I had a...disagreement, and he forbade me from crossing their borders again," she explained.

"We cannae even sneak ye in?" questioned Alconai. His expression showed how much he disliked the idea of separating from their Celestial ally. With all the powerful enemies coming after them, the group needed all the help they could get.

Amaya shook her head. "'Fraid it's not that simple. I can't physically enter, stealth or no. The king set up wards against me beyond Andor's usual defenses. 'Sides, Captain and Sol are right. It'll be harder for Tsukuyomi to get to you if you're in Andor. Don't worry, ye'll still have Sol and Shadow to look after you, and I'll make sure you get there and inside."

"Wha' did ye do to piss off the king so badly?" Alconai inquired with an incredulous look.

Amaya remained quiet for a long moment. Then she shrugged. "I took issue with the way he treats his family, and he took issue with me being friends with certain members of his family. Least that's what it boils down to."

Zatook was now staring at Amaya, this time in actually apparent confusion. He wasn't surprised she had history in Andor, seeing as how she had sung to Arianna in the language— more that she had gone against the king and gotten away with it. Banishment was uncharacteristic of the king; Traiborn wasn't one to let his enemies wander, mythical beings or not. Even Solomon was staring at her now in surprise.

"Would they really harbor all of us?" Lance asked carefully to pull some of the attention off of Amaya, since she didn't seem keen on discussing the matter. "To be fair, I was part of that Nocium army until… well, now, I guess." He reached up to rub the back of his head as he glanced at Alconai.

Captain stretched, standing. "Oh, aye, 'specially since ye're technically a deserter. Andor's also go' t'eir own legends abou' us, so t'at should 'elp our case. Though, it wouldnae 'urt to be sure?" She glanced at Zatook, who nodded, then clapped her hands together. "Well t'en, tha' settles it. We best ge' wha' sleep we can, an' I'll brew up some more healin' potions in case we need 'em."

"We might also consider sending the men back to the ship," Solomon pointed out softly. Captain pulled a face.

"Aye…we probl'y shouldnae be marchin' a band o' pirates through Andor. We can 'andle tha' after we've gotten some rest, 'owever. I be pre'y sure we all need i' at this point." As if to prove her point, the girl yawned behind her hand. "An' Zattie? Lemme ken wha' 'e says after." With the dark warrior's nod, Captain turned and ducked into one of the tents the group had set up.

***

As night came and went, activity slowly woke in the clearing. Captain rose with the sun, yawning and stretching as she exited the tent and surveyed her crew and the additional souls with them. She was only slightly surprised to see Lancelot exiting the tent he had shared with Jabez and Alconai, the knight nodding in her direction before heading off to check on the other encampment that housed the staff and soldiers Tsukuyomi had abandoned. Solomon had set out her cookpot during his turn on watch, and the older man was currently working to get a fire started.

"Oi, Sol, i's as if ye ken me," she teased lightly.

"Shocking, I am aware," the bronze man teased in turn, bending to blow on the kindling. "Zatook left to fetch some water; there wasn't really a good place nearby."

Captain grimaced. "Ta be fair, 'e probl'y wan'ed someplace a bi' more secluded ta reach out ta ye-ken-'ho." She plopped herself down by the growing fire, rubbing her hands together. She didn't take her eyes off the flames. "Are ye gonna be good?" she asked softly. Solomon was quiet, the silence stretching between them.

"In time," he finally answered. "I must admit, I had not planned to return. I should not be surprised you learned of matters." He smirked subtly at the sheepish grin that broke the girl's solemn expression. "I made a vow, Isabella," he ignored the shift to a scowl and then a resigned shake of the head, "and I intend to keep it. I go where you need me. Even if that path lay in Andor." The pair fell into a companionable silence as the rest of the camp slowly began to stir. Unsurprisingly, her crew were among the first to wake. After all, they had only really had to scuffle with a few soldiers. A few minor scrapes and bruises, easily tended and not even requiring a Concoction. Captain checked in with them all to be sure while Solomon pulled out some rations for breakfast. He couldn't help a slight smile at Captain fussing over 'her boys' before sitting them all down to break the news that she was sending them back to the ship no matter where their little party wound up traveling next.

"An' I donnae wanna be hearin' any complaints. We be needin' ta lay low, an' ye ken Nugge' an' t'e ot'ers could use t'e company. I trust you lot ta keep an eye on t'e ship fer us, aye?"

There was a reluctant round of 'aye's in response, but the men knew better than to bicker. Instead, she set them to breakfast. It wasn't much longer before Zatook returned to camp, shadows rising from the ground before falling away to reveal him. He had taken what looked to be a small tree across his shoulders to hold four water buckets, grabbing extra so that they could have fresh water with their breakfast and to wash and rebandage the wounded. By now, the rest of the party had started to join Solomon and Captain around the fire.

Amaya stayed at the edge of the camp at first. Slowly, she walked the perimeter as she kept an eye out for any enemies. Once she felt satisfied they were safe for the moment, she moved to take a couple of the water buckets from Zatook. "Thank you," she told him softly. Her demeanor remained quiet and contemplative as she carried the two buckets to the campfire. Her eyes strayed first to the tent where Rose and Tristan resided and then to the one where Jabez still slept.

Alconai considered catching up with Lancelot to check on the other camp, reluctant to let his newly freed friend out of his sight. Then again, he hesitated to leave his wounded brother. Finally, he moved to join everyone by the fire. As he settled down, he felt the sorrow permeating the camp like a tangible ache. He hadn't gotten to know Arianna or interact with her much. Still, even he felt the weight of her absence. Finally he greeted the others with a soft but warm, "Good mornin'. Wha's fer breakfas'?"

"A wonderful selection of jerky, cheese, and dry biscuits," Solomon answered, the hint of a smile tugging at his mouth. He handed a portion to Amaya and Zatook as the pair dropped off the water, one bucket of which Captain snatched up and poured into her pot before rifling through her packs for ingredients. "Not much, but we figured simple was best this morning."

Alconai grinned at Solomon's answer. "T'e feast o' 'umble trav'lers," he agreed. "Sometimes simple be jus' wha' people need."

"We shouldnae linger too long," Captain added as she started sorting out herbs and what looked like dried fruits. "I'll be brewin' a small batch ta ge' us started on t'e road, but I donnae doubt in t'e leas' tha' t'ere'll be people 'eaded 'ere. Between t'e massive ou'burst o' magic an' t'e refugees headin' ta town, i's only a ma'er of time."

Amaya didn't bother to sit, too antsy with the coming travel and potential dangers. She managed to keep her bandaged hands steady as she ate. "I'll help the boys pack and get underway. Then I'll help with the invalids we'll be taking with us. We need to make sure the injured get fed and tended before we start jostling them."

"I can help," Alconai volunteered. "I ken a thing or two 'bou' treatin' wounds."

Solomon nodded. "Then I shall leave it to you both. I will check in with the other camp and make sure they have something to eat and drink."

Captain tilted her head towards Zatook for a moment. "Mm. We be good ta head for Andor," she confirmed for the others. "We be gettin' an audience, a' least. I wager Zattie can give t'e boys a head start ta shore an' us t'e border. I donnae t'ink 'e should take us all t'e way." Solomon gave her a knowing look but didn't speak on it. Of course the girl would want to delay having to leave Amaya. Her capture and the jaunt to Keep Shadow Veil were probably the longest the pair had ever been apart.

"Sounds like a plan," Amaya agreed. She finished her food before moving to help the pirates pack camp. She ruffled Captain's hair as she passed, the girl leaning into the touch.

"Do ye need any 'elp, Captain?" Alconai asked as he stood from finishing his own meal.

"Nah, I'll be good," Captain assured him, throwing a few things into the pot. "Go ahead an' see ta Jabie. 'e should ge' some new bandages 'fore we 'ead ou'."

Alconai nodded. He took some of the rations and ducked into the tent. He wasn't surprised to find his brother still sleeping. Sitting beside Jabez, Alconai simply watched him for a moment. So much had happened in thirteen years and then in the last few days. Alconai had finally found his brother only to nearly lose him again. That thought tugged sharply at Alconai's chest. His eyes took in what he could see of Jabez's features, the mask and cowl still in place to hide everything below and above Jabez's eyes. He still looked young, if world-worn. Alconai honestly had no idea how Jabez didn't feel like he was suffocating with the fabric over his mouth and nose. Finally, Alconai touched his brother's shoulder to wake him. He froze when Jabez's eyes snapped open and stared uncomprehending for a moment at the tent ceiling. Alconai slowly retracted his hand and gave his brother a moment to fully wake. He watched ice blue eyes take in details of the tent before finally landing on the minstrel. Though his eyes still looked a bit distant, Jabez's gaze softened.

"Mornin', Nai," hoarsely greeted Jabez. Alconai smiled at him.

"Mornin', Jabie. Ye feel up ta eatin'? We be movin' ou' soon."

"Makes sense," Jabez agreed. He considered for a moment. "I think I can handle eating. Might need help sitting up."

"That I can do," Alconai told him. Carefully, he helped Jabez sit up and handed him the rations. Alconai didn't think much of the situation until Jabez started to reach for his mask and hesitated. It took a moment for Alconai to understand. He had yet to see Jabez actually eat. And yet, considering Jabez's history of recovery, there had to be people who had seen the man maskless. But how many people had seen Jabez's face by his choice? Alconai felt a pang of regret and hurt that he wasn't one of those people. Still, he couldn't hold it against his brother. It had been thirteen years. "Here," Alconai encouraged. He shifted his brother's makeshift pillow and sat in its place, pressing his back to Jabez's. After a moment, his brother relaxed against him.

"I'm sorry," Jabez's voice sounded so small as it reached Alconai. Instead of answering, Alconai reached back and found his brother's wrist, giving it a reassuring squeeze.

"Eat and get yer strength up," Alconai encouraged him. "Like I said, we be movin' soon. T'ough, ye donnae be walkin' on yer own if ye be walkin' at all." They lapsed into silence for a moment where Alconai assumed Jabez was obeying his advice. "I was thinkin' o' checkin' the lands and speakin' with t'e farmers in t'e area ta see if we can get some easier food for our more out o' it patients."

"That's a good idea. There's only so much we can do with rations, and it'd be best if we can manage to make them some broth. Easier to eat in their states," Jabez said. Alconai felt warmth bloom in his heart with his brother's praise. The warmth grew when he felt Jabez lean against him more heavily and touch the back of his head to Alconai's shoulder. "Fair warning, if I sit like this for much longer, I'm going back to sleep."

Alconai laughed, though he tried to be careful not to jostle his brother too badly. "Oi, I gotta change yer bandages and then we gotta go."

"I ken, I ken," Jabez murmured. Alconai couldn't help smiling wider with Jabez's slip into his old dialect. As much as they enjoyed the moment, Jabez let Alconai know when he had his face covered again. Cleaning and tending Jabez's wounds reminded Alconai of his brother's part in the recent skirmishes and how Alconai himself had come away mostly unscathed. "You've gotten good at this," Jabez praised.

"Like I said, I been takin' lessons from Lady Hoshiko," Alconai remarked easily. He finished applying the fresh bandages. "Come on ye." He helped his brother get ready to leave.

By the time the brothers exited the tent together, the pirates were no longer in the camp. Captain was bottling up her brew, Solomon sitting nearby and staring pensively into the flames of the dwindling fire. He glanced up when he noticed Lancelot returning to camp. The knight waved when he passed Alconai, but he continued on to Captain and Sol.

"They're set for now," he informed them. "And they don't plan to leave until after the heat of the day. It's a bit of a walk, and some of the servants are on the older side."

Captain nodded. "Tha' buys us some time, t'en. Bu' I'd rather nae dilly-dally."

Alconai helped Jabez sit on the ground for now. "Lance, ye mind helpin' me pack our bedrolls and tent?" he called to the knight as he moved to do just that.

Amaya emerged from the tent sheltering Tristan and Rose. She'd managed to soften the cheese and dry biscuits with a few drops of water and got the two Chosen Children awake enough to eat the improvised mush. She moved over to Zatook and touched his shoulder. "Would you mind helping me move our sleepers? We need to break down the remaining tents," she requested gently. "I know keeping busy helps put me at ease when something's coming that I'm dreading."

Zatook glanced at Amaya. His expression was inscrutable once more, but he turned to help with her request. Captain put a stopper in the last vial and carefully packed it into a bag with the rest. She stood, brushing herself off and looking over the party. The camp was mostly packed, Lance and Alconai working on their tent while Amaya and Zatook worked on the last one. She turned her gaze to the horizon, mulling over the different paths that lay before them. The threads of her companions danced tantalizingly in her peripheral, but she didn't attempt any visions for now. She wanted to have her wits about her, especially with three of their party down.

***

As the time to leave drew near, Zatook vanished in his shadows for a short while before returning with a small cart. He had padded the bottom with straw and cloth. It would make walking a bit slower, but they wouldn't have to carry and bump around the injured, and they could load up their packs.

Amaya and Alconai helped to situate the packs and equipment in a way to stabilize and cushion their wounded comrades as much as possible. Jabez started to open his mouth to convince them to let him walk so he wouldn't crowd their charges, but before he could get a word out, he found himself lifted and gently deposited into the cart by Solomon. Jabez gave the man a flat look even as Solomon made sure the younger man would be as comfortable as possible for the long trek. Jabez then shot his scowl at Amaya when the woman ruffled his cowl with a laugh.

"Rest, Jabez. You're allowed to be cared for," she told him. Instead of arguing, Jabez settled in. He knew when he was beaten.

2. First Steps Forward

When the shadows pulled away from the group, they no longer stood in open field— rather, they were now in a forest. The dense foliage surrounded Andor for miles, but there were roads cut through at each cardinal point. After ensuring they wouldn't run into an army, Zatook had taken them to the southern road within Nocis, as it was the nearest and the easiest to travel without interruption. The western road lay within the kingdom of Regalia, while the eastern road connected to the forest of Sylva Arae. The northern road passed through neutral territory into the desert that held Ben-Gal.

The group's cart also held a few extra sacks now. Captain had lent Alconai some of their gold to negotiate with the farmers near Tsukuyomi's destroyed estate to get a fresh supply of food, including ingredients for a broth as he had hoped. Zatook had taken charge of pulling the cart, his shadows wrapped around the wheels to shift them through any rough patches without jostling the passengers. Solomon walked alongside the cart in case either Rose or Tristan woke or Jabez needed anything. Lancelot and Alconai were to the other side, the entertainer working to catch his friend up on the who, what, when, and why of their journey.

"I ne'er in me wildest imaginin's would have thought I'd see Celestials. What next, eh? Dragons, faeries, mermaids?" Alconai positively gushed with excitement. He'd proven to be just as lively and charismatic a storyteller as he had been when Lancelot and he were younger, even with an audience of one. Alconai shook his head. "I suppose me excitement might be inappropriate considerin' things, but I cannae help it."

"I'll be honest, I didn't think they were real," Lance confessed. "I just thought they were nice stories. But now I've seen one with my own eyes…and you say you've met two…It's kinda hard to believe, but how can you not?"

"All t'e best stories be unbelievable," Alconai remarked with a grin. His smile slipped a little as he recalled the appearance of the Lady of Death. "Aye, two. Amaya and Lady Death. The Lady came ta take Tristan's little sister after the high lord murdered her." Alconai fell quiet for a moment, staring ahead as they walked. Lancelot didn't press him. While he hadn't met Arianna, he could tell she had quite an impact on his friend. Neither man was a stranger to death, but the death of children always hit the hardest. After a few moments, Alconai piped up again. "I think what needs ta be remembered with people in stories and with powers is that they be people. People are not invincible. I suppose what Amaya be sayin' about them nae interferin' makes sense. Nae everyone takes kindly ta stronger, more powerful people. Mayhap t'e Celestial King be tryin' ta protect his people," Alconai mused quietly.

Lance snorted. "Judging how Amaya explained the rule? I doubt it," he noted with a slight laugh. "Though I suppose it is fair that it could have started that way."

Alconai turned to look at Lancelot as he asked, "How ye holdin' up? Lot o' information ta take in. And yer recovering from t'e blood mage's influence."

Lance sobered. "It's... a lot to take in," he echoed sheepishly. "I won't lie. And ever since you've told me about Finnegan, I cannot help but notice gaps in my memory and wonder what he made me do."

Alconai reached up and shifted his hat a little as he considered. "Tryin' ta figure it out won't change much. Ye'll just frustrate yerself and get depressed." He reached over and squeezed Lancelot's shoulder. Retracting his hand, Alconai added, "Nowhere ta go but forwards, aye? I ken that's probably nae helpful or encouragin'."

"Mm. Not really, but that doesn't make it any less true." Lance reached up to run his hand through his hair, his helmet currently tucked under his other arm. "I get the feeling we will have more to try and process before this is all done. Legends are coming to life, and we're literally walking beside them."

"Oi, oi, nae too loud. We need Jabie's head ta still fit in t'e cart," Alconai joked. The corner of his mouth lifted in a slight grin when he heard a quiet snort from the direction of his older brother. Alconai's eyes then trailed to the inside of the cart and at the sleeping, young faces of the Chosen Children. He considered Lancelot's words and remarked more seriously, "The legends be literal children. That's a lot o' weight ta carry."

"That's why the Order exists. They try to help shoulder the burden as much as possible," Jabez piped up.

"Oi, who invited ye ta this conversation?" snarked Alconai.

"Yer supposed ta be sleepin'."

"Little hard to sleep when I've got this killer headache from my head getting so big. I might need to leave the cart. A walk should humble me right back down to normal size again."

"Ye even try gettin' out o' that cart and I'll sit on ye."

"For shame, Nai. You'd get violent with a healing patient? What would Lady Hoshiko say?"

Alconai snorted. "Lady Hoshiko isnae here. But Sol is. He'd probably just pick ye up like ye be a baby and carry ye."

"I wouldn't want to put out Solomon's back. He's getting rather old, couldn't you tell?" Jabez smoothly returned.

Now it was Solomon's turn to snort. "I am not infirm. I am still quite capable of carrying you or sitting on you. Though I would likely settle for some rope and just tie you down."

"And I am not a child," piped up a groggy Rose, although she sounded more amused than anything.

"My apologies for waking you, Lady Rose." Lance suddenly looked abashed. Jabez, at least, had already been awake for longer than breakfast.

"I am simply tired of sleeping," she assured him. "And just 'Rose' is fine."

"As far as Solomon is concerned, we're all children," Jabez remarked dryly. He opened his eyes and studied Rose. "How do you feel?" he asked her.

Solomon chuckled, but he didn't deny it. Rose was watching the sky trail by.

"Heavy. Tired. The boon for our mission is gone, and yet I've grown rather used to the pain."

"Your wounds aren't healing," Jabez agreed. "At Keep Shadow Veil, Tristan was trying to heal you but nothing happened. I thought at first that it was just his fatigue that was hindering him." He noted Alconai's concerned expression in his periphery.

"I doubt they will heal," Rose confessed as she closed her eyes again. "I'm not sure I actually need to eat, either."

Lance frowned. Even having heard it from Captain, it was hard to imagine someone being both alive and dead. He couldn't imagine what the Drow woman was going through. "Do you think physically binding the wounds more would help? Stitches and the like? I know most people these days try for potions or healers, but I was trained in non-magical wound care."

"It would certainly be worth a try. I would rather hate to bleed all over the Andorian capital. Assuming I still bleed."

"Well, we'll know soon enough," Solomon noted. "We should change everyone's bandages around midday."

Alconai nodded. "I can help, too, if need be. I be no surgeon or healer, but I ken some techniques and herbs," he offered. Like Lancelot, Alconai couldn't imagine what Rose was going through with being only half alive. And then there was Tristan. So far, the young man slept deeply, but Alconai worried. He hoped the sleep was just for recovery and not a sign of Tristan's lack of will to live without his sister. Surely Captain would have said something if they needed to be more concerned. "Anything we can do for ye in t'e meantime?" Alconai asked Rose.

"You needn't fuss over me too much. I'm quite comfortable for now." She slid her hand over to find Tristan's. "How far out are we from Andor?"

Lancelot glanced ahead of them. "We should reach the border tomorrow. Zatook placed us a little ways out to give Captain and Amaya time."

"Time?"

"Amaya cannot cross the border."

Rose's eyes opened, and she quirked an eyebrow. "I imagine I have missed quite the conversation."

Solomon chuckled dryly. "I'll let Alconai fill you in." He glanced back to check on Amaya and Captain, steadily keeping watch on their little party so the others could focus elsewhere. He had no doubt Zatook was doing the same in his own way.

***

Captain and Amaya walked a short way behind the rest of the party, the younger girl twining her hand with her caretaker's. Amaya squeezed Captain's hand and gave it a jiggle. "What's all this then? Shouldn't you be overjoyed that you're going to have one less person supervising you? It's the dream of all youth, aye?" she teased with a smile and a wink.

Captain snorted, sidestepping to bump Amaya with her shoulder. "Oh, sure, ev'ry teen's dream," she teased back flatly. "Ne'er min' t'e fact I jus' 'ad a break from ye both an' t'en ye again."

"Not to sound like an old nanny goat, but when I was 'round your age, I joined my first pirate crew. Ran away from home— the whole ordeal," Amaya told her cheerily. She bumped her shoulder into Captain in playful retaliation. More seriously, she added, "I know the anniversary is coming up, and I wish things didn't land like they have. I'd be with you if I could, like I always have. You'll still have Sol with you and now Jabie, too. And I'll be with you in spirit."

Captain fell quiet, gaze on the road before them. She squeezed Amaya's hand. "Tris needs 'em more'n me," she finally noted softly.

"Who says they can't be there for both of you?" Amaya returned the squeeze. "We're all a little worse for wear after the last few days. But that's the point of a crew, aye? A family? We lean on each other when things are bad, draw strength from each other. That's a team," Amaya reminded her. Despite her own bandages, Amaya didn't once flinch in Captain's grip, Amaya's own hold as steadfast and reassuring as ever. "I know you just met

Tristan, but perhaps this would be a good time for the two of you to be there for each other. You've suffered similar loss, though I know they are different."

"Mine is an old grief. I ken 'ow ta work through i'. 'Sides, we donnae ken 'ow long we can rest in Andor— if a' all. We need ta do wha' we can ta help Tris fin' time ta grieve wit'ou' losin' sigh' of everyt'in' else."

Amaya nodded. "That's the tricky bit. Finding the right balance," she agreed. Looking at her ward, she added, "Still, Izzy, I know you know that grief can't be navigated in a straight line. There's no shortcut to handling it and moving forward. We have stuff to get done, yes. We might not have much time to rest and recover, as you said. But when the grief is this raw, we have to be patient, and we might be doing a lot of the shouldering for him until he can get his feet back under him." Amaya gave Captain's hand a small squeeze again. "Old grief or no, it's just as important and shouldn't be swept under a rug just because someone else is going through his own. There are people who will help you shoulder it, if you let them."

Captain sighed, leaning her head against Amaya's shoulder. "We'll see," she murmured.

Amaya touched her head to Captain's. "I'm here, Moon Sprite," Amaya told her softly. "You're a good girl, you know? I'm proud of you."

Captain pulled a face. "Oi, oi, wha' am I, five again?" she protested— yet her voice was lighter with the nickname and the praise. She closed her eyes, trusting her steps to Amaya. "I'mma miss ye, Mum," she whispered.

Amaya actually slowed to a stop, tugging Captain to stop with her. She then turned them just enough to pull Captain into a firm though slightly desperate embrace. For once, Amaya didn't complain about the title, not even teasingly. She held Captain close, blinking back tears. "You'll be fine without me, but I'll miss you all the same. I'll come back to you as soon as I'm able. Faster than lightning," Amaya promised.

Captain clung to her tightly, the slightest sniffle muffled between them. "May'ap I'll kill meself a king ta ge' ye back quicker," she teased.

"Oi, don't be taking after my temperament," Amaya remarked a little thickly, but there was a smile evident in her voice as well. "Clever as you and Jabez are, I'm sure you'll figure out how to handle the king. Even if you can't lower the wards keeping me out, I'll rejoin you as soon as you leave Andor's borders." She rubbed Captain's back and briefly tightened her embrace. Kissing the girl's head, Amaya pulled away just enough that they could resume walking, keeping one arm around Captain's shoulders.

***

When midday arrived, Solomon branched off from the road to find a secluded clearing for them to stop in. They didn't set up an entire camp, but he did put up a tent to change bandages in privacy. Solomon had taken Jabez first, since he was already awake and probably a bit restless. Captain pulled out the supplies to make stew while Zatook sat at the edge of the clearing to keep watch. The shadow warrior hadn't taken part in any conversations— he hadn't signed a word since Arianna passed.

Jabez allowed himself to be tended, the young man silent and compliant in Solomon's care. He stared at the ground thoughtfully. Captain's Concoctions could take the edge off and heal the worst of their injuries, but they weren't a cure-all. Jabez was healing, but his battle with Marilyn had left grievous wounds. And then there were the wounds that weren't physical. His mind turned to Rose and Tristan. To Arianna. Despite the pain and stiffness in his body, Jabez clenched his fist as sorrow, guilt, and frustration flashed through him and took root in his core. He failed.

"Easy, Jabez," Solomon noted softly. "We don't need you opening your wounds, being so tense. I know it is not easy now, but you should try and relax. Let your brother be a mother hen; he's rather good at it."

Jabez snorted softly. "He's owed all the mother henning he can give, considering how long he was searching for me. He'll calm down soon enough once he realizes I'm not going to fall apart like some ragdoll," he remarked quietly. "My state after the battle probably didn't help matters." Jabez grew somber as he recalled his fight with the blood mage. His gaze turned calculating even as he slowly forced his body to relax so he wouldn't aggravate his wounds. "I failed," Jabez stated almost inaudibly. The image of Arianna sleeping in Solomon's arms and other memories of the bright little girl haunted Jabez's conscience. "Tristan trusted us to protect them. Rose trusted us to have her back." His voice grew cold as he spoke, "High Lord Tsukuyomi is no human. He's no mere sorcerer either. He can't be. I've never seen the man myself outside of our most recent fight, and during that time I was focused on Marilyn. The high lord could be elven-kin, I suppose. What I want to know is how he managed to get to Arianna. She never left us. She was with you in the middle of the damn camp— how did he reach her?" As Jabez continued, he started to tense again and growled the last part in frustration.

Solomon sat alongside him, considering. "Izzy was looking yesterday," he confessed softly. "But we haven't really had a chance to discuss what she saw. Even humans can use powerful magic, but no— watching Tristan, I know Tsukuyomi is likely non-human, as well." He reached a hand up to Jabez's shoulder. "I understand your frustration, Jabez. We all want answers. But we have to realize that some things cannot be changed. We did our best, it wasn't enough, and we'll have to live with that. We did not fully understand what we were up against, but recognizing such only helps so much when the pain is raw."

Jabez took as deep a breath as he dared before forcing himself to let it out slowly. "I know," he conceded, his voice quiet and devastated. "I'm glad I was able to do something useful at least, and that we were able to get Tristan back. Chosen Child or no, I wouldn't have been able to leave him there to such a horrible fate. He's a kid. They're all just kids. What father kills one of his children to torment the other?" Jabez allowed his voice to fade. After a moment, he added quietly, "I thought I was going to die. And all I wanted in that moment was to make every decision— every strike —count before I gave out."

"I'm rather glad you didn't," Solomon noted softly. "But I really must point out that fighting Marilyn was hardly the only useful thing you've done." He teasingly reached out a hand to ruffle Jabez's hair through his cowl before he fell silent for a moment. "I cannot pretend to understand men like Tsukuyomi. All I can do is pray to Shaddai for guidance and go as He leads." His eyes slid to the tent entrance and beyond, where he knew Zatook had taken up watch at the edge of the camp. Rather than following his train of thought out loud, he instead looked back to Jabez. "Your wounds are healing well enough, but how are you healing?"

Jabez took a moment to focus on the way his body felt, fully aware of what the pirate was really asking. "I've been better, but I've been worse, too. Mostly, I'm just human," he said wryly, indicating his bandages. However, he kept his gaze averted from Solomon's. "I know how to endure, and we need to get Tristan and Rose tended."

"Jabez."

Jabez still avoided Solomon's gaze, opting to stare at the ground. After a long moment, he answered, "I can't stop seeing Arianna and thinking what I could have done differently. How perhaps I should never have gone looking for the Star Child. If it weren't for me… there's every chance Captain would have been better off fighting StormShaper if she hadn't needed to worry about protecting me. I just couldn't leave her to shoulder that fight alone. And then she was alone until Alconai joined her. Then Tristan was alone. We have no idea what Tsukuyomi did to his son as part of Tristan's punishment aside from killing a little girl who just wanted to share light and joy with people." Jabez shifted his gaze to a point near Solomon's knee. "At least you'll be there this time. You do a better job of protecting Captain. Perhaps I should break off and return to being a scout and informant. I'm a liability at the moment, and even when not injured, I'm better as a spy than a guardian of Chosen

Children with powers far beyond my ken."

"And yet, had you not been with Captain, she would not have discovered your brother or the plight of his friend. We may very well have truly fought Lancelot when the time came and been none-the-wiser." Solomon couldn't help a soft chuckle. "Izzy was practically skipping in Nikko Mori and wouldn't tell me why," he added gently. "You do a fine job, Jabez. Who's to say I would have fared any better against StormShaper or even Marilyn? We face mighty foes; it will take all of our strength together. Even we humans will have our parts to play." He squeezed Jabez's shoulder encouragingly. "If you are feeling underqualified, you could always accept my offer. The title 'Member of the Order' is one of the few things that separates you and me." Solomon smirked at Jabez, but his gaze was serious.

Jabez finally met Solomon's gaze for a moment before turning his face away again. "I'm not…" he trailed off as he recalled old arguments. This wasn't the first time Solomon had given him the offer, and every time Jabez had declined. "Why? They shouldn't want me. Not after all I've done. Why are you so convinced? Persistent? I'm broken, Solomon. I've been doing better, but I could break again. I would be a stain to the Order, not an asset. I'm a coward hiding behind a mask because I can't face my own reflection." His voice held a hint of self-loathing, breaking slightly with emotion despite his deadpan tone.

"Our trials and traumas do not define us, Jabez. Needing time is not being a coward." Sol removed his hand, letting his gaze drift. "That day at the river was the first time I had seen Zatook since my daughter died at his hands. I never thought I would see him again, never thought I could bear it. Yet here we are. Traveling together, fighting together. Returning to the land where she died." He was quiet for a moment. "You are no more a stain than the rest of us, Jabez. We are not saints. We have our darkness. But Shaddai calls us still— beyond that, He calls us His own. Accepts us as we are. And He knows where we are needed." He sighed, lifting a knee to prop his arm on as the other arm slid back to support him. "I almost resigned after Aditi died. A friend convinced me to take some time instead, to pray. And I knew where I needed to be, though I didn't understand it. But that perseverance led me to you. Then to Izzy. And now here we are, at the center of it all, just as the trial of the Children truly begins."

Jabez gave Solomon a sideways glance. "I got the feeling there was something more to you and Zatook. I sensed the tension, but I didn't feel it was my place to ask. I'm sorry about your daughter. I know it's not the same, but my mother's absence was part of why it was so hard for me to go home. Still, I can't imagine how hard this must be for you. And now Amaya won't be there. I know the two of you seem to have become confidants. Then again, maybe it's a blessing in disguise that she won't be there to punch the king when he allegedly acts like a jerk." A bit of mirth twinkled in Jabez's eyes. They sobered again as he considered what Solomon said about his offer. "I don't know the first thing about helping the Chosen Children or protecting them. I spent most of my time with Captain clammed up in the shell of my own mind. I'm still coming out of that shell, and it's taking everything in me not to retreat back into it. I understand grief, but even in this moment, I don't know what to say to encourage or comfort you, much less a grieving Chosen Child."

"You think I have a speech prepared in my back pocket

for the boy?" Sol teased gently. "You put us on a pedestal that we do not deserve, and you throw yourself into a pit that *you* do not deserve. Being an Order member isn't about knowing the perfect thing to do or say. It's about committing yourself to the command of the Sacreds and assisting the Children how they need. For some members, like your mother, that meant spreading the Teachings as they spread their healing arts. For others, like myself, staying in a country and seeking information. Some never leave Ben-Gal, studying the scrolls and prophecies. There is no 'right way' to serve the Order, Jabez. You just serve. And Izzy has grown. It isn't about hiding her and protecting her anymore. It's about following the Children's path. And knowing Izzy, giving her someone to talk to."

"Members will object. I don't want my presence to cause dissent among the Order," Jabez protested quietly. He remembered some of the Order members making no effort to hide their dislike of Jabez's presence. Some had outright protested his involvement with the Moon Child. Even as the doubts whispered in his mind, he recalled other members of the Order who had been patient with him and seemed glad to have him. Captain herself had welcomed his company— even being excited to see him by Solomon's account of her venture into Nikko Mori. Then again, perhaps she'd just been excited to meet another Chosen Child. "And what happens if I..." Jabez stopped when fear choked his voice. He gripped his hand into a fist as memories of a darker, chaotic time assaulted him. "If I relapse into the madness I was in when you found me, I'll be more than a hindrance: I'll be a danger. I'm not arrogant enough to think any of you couldn't beat me, but I...I don't want Captain to see me like that. I don't want her to have to fight me. Rose would probably have no problem with dispatching me if it came to it. Tristan's been through a lot already, and then there's Alconai." Jabez's hand started to shake from clenching his fist so hard. "And what happens if my abductors catch up with us? Not all of them are human or mortal. I should leave. I should have never–"

Solomon's hand gently landed on Jabez's wrist. "Life is full of what-ifs and fears. And that is why Shaddai puts certain people in our midst. You would not be facing any of this alone, Jabez. Whether here or at Ben-Gal. I shouldn't need to tell you how much Izzy adores you. And Alconai is glad to have found his brother. They know you, Jabez. And they know you wouldn't mean it. When you do not trust yourself, place your trust in Shaddai and your friends. Your family." He shook his head, sighing. "The Order will always hit its snags here and there, but any who protest would know better than to let their bias interrupt their work. We have the leadership hierarchy because we are imperfect. The wisest among us do their best to guide our ways. And they already gave their blessings to asking you to join. They've seen the good work you've done, Jabez. And they've seen how the Moon Child favors you, if I'm to be fully honest. They see the wisdom in my choice."

Gradually, Jabez unclenched his hand as he calmed with Solomon's reassurances. "With the way you carry on, I didn't think you were ready for retirement so soon, Sol," Jabez teased to lighten the mood and drag his mind from dark memories. "Captain seems taken with Alconai. He'd do better as an Order member to help keep up her spirits. He's always been like that. Charismatic and brave with a ready smile or story." Jabez shifted his gaze to the tent entrance as he thought about his own future. "I want to do what I can to help. I wanted to follow in my mother's footsteps, but I don't know if I can. You may believe and trust in me, but I don't hold any belief or trust in myself. The Order has done so much for me. *You've* done so much for me. I just want to be someone you and my mother can be proud of. I want to be someone Shaddai can be proud of."

"You already are, Jabez," Solomon pointed out softly. "I've been proud of you for a long time now. I try not to speak for the Sacreds, but I have little doubt that They are, as well." He chuckled slightly. "I don't have to retire for you to join, you know. If that's what you're waiting on, I guess the Order will be waiting for quite a while."

"Captain needs you," Jabez remarked. He chuckled softly before adding, "Don't tell Amaya I said this, but I think she needs you, too." Despite Solomon's encouragement, doubt lingered in Jabez's ice blue eyes. "Captain doesn't need three Order members following her around. She's a handful, but like you said, she's grown. And she's still growing. For what it's worth, I think she sees you as a father figure. She's always happy to see you and Amaya. I am, too, even if I don't always show it."

"And she sees you like a brother. Quite the family we make, eh?" Solomon winked at him before sighing. "I won't force you to stay, Jabez– frankly, I don't think I could. But promise me this at least: stay with us in Andor. Heal up good and proper before you make up your mind. Deal?"

Jabez gave him a flat look. "Deal. Though I'm sure by the time we leave Andor, you and Captain will have convinced me to stay like you two always do. With Alconai backing you up as well, I'm a goner already." Once he was sure

Solomon was done with him, Jabez stood, allowing the chuckling man to help him out of the tent.

***

Outside, Amaya left Tristan and Rose in Alconai and Lancelot's care for the moment. She moved over to Zatook and simply stood with him, her eyes watching their surroundings. She felt a storm of emotions roiling within her with no good way to release them. Not in this time and place anyhow. "I feel so tense I want to do something to work it out, but I dare not leave the group right now. Otherwise, I'd ask you to spar with me," Amaya finally intoned softly. "I imagine you've got your own feelings to work out, too."

Zatook shrugged a shoulder in response, his expression unchanging. He folded his arms as he leaned back against the tree. Captain glanced their way but didn't say anything. As reluctant as she was to leave Amaya, she could only wonder what waited for Zatook returning home. She wasn't even sure he had left with permission from the king, though the queen herself had sent him.

"I appreciate you reaching out to the king about giving the group an audience. Can't be easy interacting with that…piece of work." Amaya recalled her conversation with Solomon regarding the shadow warrior. She wanted to inquire if Zatook would be alright going to Andor, but she had a feeling she already knew the answer to that question given the man's demeanor. Amaya studied his eyes for a moment. She then lightly touched his shoulder; he looked at her hand and then back at her. "I wish I knew how to break your chains, Shadow," she intoned quietly, giving his shoulder a squeeze. "Maybe the Chosen

Children can help you with that, but I know not all chains are physical or magical." She let go and shifted to lean beside him against the same tree. Taking the cue to return to watch, he dropped his gaze back to his arms.

Amaya glanced at him before remarking somewhat jokingly, "You watch that way. I'll watch this way." When his only response was an honest nod, Amaya flashed him a cheeky smile and poked him in the ribs. At his raised eyebrow, she raised one of her own to playfully mirror his expression. Zatook simply looked away again. The woman was a mystery; he still wasn't sure why she bothered with him, other than her grudge against the king. Amaya's smirk widened a little. "I was mostly joking, you know," she finally explained. "Trying to find something to lighten the somber mood, even if just a little." She leaned her head back against the tree and watched the canopy above her. "By the way, I thought your more gargoyle form was rather impressive. What I saw of it anyway. I was a little too preoccupied to get a good look. Would you mind letting me see it sometime?"

Zatook was rather glad the woman wasn't looking at him now, lest she realize she actually got a bit of a reaction with that. Pure surprise painted his face before he quickly looked away, pushing down the feeling. He didn't answer her. He wasn't really sure what to say. Would they even meet again, once the king realized his shadow had been hanging around a sworn enemy? And he was really only allowed to use that form when the situation called for it; being asked was not calling for it. And still, despite the shadow warrior's silence and now refusal to look at Amaya, he felt his cheeks warm.

"I understand if you're not comfortable with someone

seeing. Transforming for battle is one thing, but I know I can feel self-conscious in my Celestial form outside of a fight," Amaya told him. After a glance at the camp to make sure she wasn't needed, she pushed off the trunk and stepped farther into the trees. She kept her back to the group, but she stayed near Zatook. Now, Amaya stood studying her wrappings. So far, she hadn't flinched when she used her bandaged arms and hands, seemingly unaffected by the phenomenon plaguing them. However, her hands trembled subtly as she started unwrapping the linen. While the blackened coloring didn't look as angry as before, it also wasn't going away. Amaya stared at the discolored flesh of her hands and forearms, allowing herself a tiny wince when she tried squeezing one hand into a fist. "I don't want them to see or to know. I don't want them worrying when there's nothing we can do to fix it right now. I'm not even sure where to start," Amaya confessed quietly.

Zatook watched her calmly, but at her confession he looked back towards the camp. Partially to give her privacy and to ensure the others didn't break it unnecessarily. He hesitated as she kept speaking before finally placing a hand on the ground. Shadows slipped around his fingers before sliding in front of her and spelling out on the ground, *They could check the Archives while in Andor if they knew.*

"They're going to have plenty to deal with in Andor," countered Amaya. However, she said, "I do have people I can see about this. Some leads I can follow. It's just enduring it while we travel." She reached into a pack she'd brought over with her and started working to wrap clean bandages around each finger and her palms. She made sure nothing showed before starting on her forearms.

"It hurts," she admitted softly. "Feels tight and tense and wrong. Sick. And if that power did this to me in my *Celestial* form, then what is it doing to Tristan inside him where we can't see?"

Zatook shook his head; he didn't have an answer. *Only he can say,* the shadows wrote.

"Hopefully, he'll be willing to open up," Amaya agreed. She found it interesting that Zatook was talking to her at all. Normally, he tended to be rather reserved. Amaya had half-expected him to ignore her rambling. Rather than bring attention to the writing, Amaya finished wrapping her hands and moved back to lean against the tree. "Thank you for keeping watch." Zatook lifted his hand from the ground, folding his arms once more and simply nodding.

***

After Solomon and Jabez left the tent, Alconai had carried Rose in next, Lance just behind to see what they could do to make her more comfortable. Upon washing her wounds, they discovered that she no longer bled. Alconai and Lance worked to treat her wounds with numbing poultices in hopes of helping her with the pain, at least, before rebandaging them to protect them and make movement a little easier for her. By the time Alconai carried her back to the cart, everyone could smell the stew Captain was working on. She divided the dish, letting the wounded have simple yet nutritious broth while the rest of the camp had a more hearty meal for their travels.

Amaya enlisted Captain's aid in waking Tristan and Rose just enough for the pirates to help them drink the broth.

Once they were tended, Amaya joined the others and ate her own share of the stew. She sat with Captain and pulled the group into telling stories of adventures they'd had throughout their travels. Jabez stayed quiet, but Alconai had plenty of stories to tell.

As with every meal, Zatook did not join in on the revelry and conversing. Thus far, only Tristan and Rose had ever seen him eat. Instead, he simply took his bowl and returned to his tree, sitting on the side opposite the others. Captain didn't say anything about it, instead prompting Alconai to go into more detail on something from his adventures to keep the others from asking. Solomon was a bit quiet as well, but he did chuckle at a few of Alconai's tales.

While Alconai and Lancelot were engrossed in the tales, Jabez sat with his back against Amaya's back this time as he carefully ate his portion. Amaya never judged him or made him feel like a coward for hiding his face, and she easily held his weight. Once Jabez finished his food, he once more replaced his mask and sat still, enjoying the group's company. It wasn't long before Amaya felt the ninja leaning more heavily against her as Jabez slumped down a little farther. She caught Solomon's eye with a small, knowing smile and a nod towards her back.

Solomon smirked in turn, setting aside his bowl and moving to collect the sleeping Jabez and carry him back to the cart. Zatook wasn't long in returning, and he worked to pack up the patient tent while the others finished their lunches.

Once everything was packed and settled, Amaya nudged Captain to walk with Alconai and Lancelot for a bit. The minstrel lowered his voice to keep from disturbing the sleeping patients, but he continued telling his stories. Some were ones he'd experienced himself, and others were tales he'd heard during his travels. Amaya smiled at the trio, grateful to the young man for bringing some levity in the face of so much sorrow. As they traveled, she fell into step with Solomon. Amaya didn't say anything at first, simply walking with her comrade. "I'm here for now," she finally said just loud enough for Solomon alone to hear. It was the usual way she offered her support.

"Traiborn is a dark man, but not a stupid one. I doubt he will bring up matters," Solomon noted softly in turn. "I more have to be ready to see his face than anything." He hesitated before calmly amending, "see his face and not stab it. Too much is hinging on a safe stay."

Amaya chuckled dryly. "I don't know that I would have the same restraint if I were to face him again. Silver lining of my absence," she commented with a roll of her eyes. "I tend to make a mess of diplomatic situations." Amaya grew quiet as her gaze shifted from one Chosen Child to the next and then to Zatook and eventually to Jabez. "I know I don't really need to ask this— and it's a rather unfair request given your history," she started before looking at Solomon. Her confident demeanor slipped a little as she continued very seriously, "Look after them, aye?"

Solomon chuckled despite himself. "Of course," he assured her softly. Then he smirked. "And I suppose I'll have a greeting to pass on to Queen Corianne?" he added, glancing at her. "Secretly, of course."

Amaya grinned and gave him a conspiratorial wink. "No

one usually believes me when I tell them I happen to be best friends with the Queen of Andor," she told him with her more familiar cheekiness. Then her mood shifted to a more somber one again. "She might already know, but best to keep in mind all the same," she told him, "Queen Corianne was close with Reina, too: Tristan's mum." Her gaze landed on the unconscious young man again, Amaya's expression soft and sad.

Solomon was quiet for a moment. "A greeting and potentially a bit of bad news, then," he noted gently. "If I even get the chance." His gaze found Captain at the head of their little group, speaking animatedly with Alconai about something— from what words he could catch, they were discussing her potion brewing now. Ahead, he knew the border to Andor drew closer, alongside its greatest protector aside from Zatook.

Amaya followed Solomon's gaze to Captain. "She's certainly growing into her own," remarked Amaya as she watched Captain's interactions with Alconai. "I daresay she's gotten rather attached to a certain minstrel, as well. Probably doesn't even need me anymore." Amaya's tone was joking, though her eyes were still solemn. "Ye'll all be fine." She lifted her gaze to the sky, a sense of resigned determination about the woman.

Solomon couldn't help a snort. "I daresay she's too young for *that*," he teased about the potential relationship budding before them. "And I highly doubt she will outgrow either of us." Yet his own gaze didn't leave the girl as he considered what lay ahead. Amaya lapsed into companionable silence beside him, the pair watching over their wards and wondering what lay in store for them.

Alconai kept the group fairly entertained during their journey until the sky started to stain pink.

"Zattie, can ye fin' us a good spot ta camp?" Captain called over to the silent shadow, whose only response was a nod. Solomon caught up to Captain.

"A little early to call it a night, isn't it?" he prompted gently.

"Oh, aye, if'n we be worried abou' efficiency e'ry day. Bu' we be reachin' t'e border sometime t'morrow, aye? A full suppeh an' a good nigh's rest'll do us all some good."

Solomon nodded. He had a feeling there was a bit more to it than that, but he didn't argue. After a little while, Zatook pulled the cart off of the road again and led them to a subtle camping spot. It was far enough from the road to risk another fire, so Captain and Amaya started on dinner while the others got camp ready.

Alconai worked with Lancelot to get the tents set up. He then helped to unload the carts and get Tristan and Rose settled in one of the tents. Jabez roused at some point during the transfer and stared blearily at the camp. This time he managed to exit the cart before anyone could try to scoop him up, but he made his way to Captain and Amaya, carefully taking a seat with his back against a tree.

"What's on your mind, Sprite?" Amaya questioned Captain as they worked. "You're not stalling to keep me around longer, are ye?" She winked at the girl.

"Oh, tha's certainly par' o' it," she confessed unabashedly.

Then her voice softened as she added, "Bu' I t'ink qui'e a few of us would rat'er like a li'l extra time 'fore we reach Andor." Her gaze found Solomon and then Zatook.

Amaya nodded in understanding. Her gaze strayed to the tent housing Rose and Tristan. Would the young man wake before they reached the border? No doubt the lad was exhausted from his ordeal, and while his physical wounds weren't as bad as the others, Amaya knew from experience that wounds of the mind and heart could be just as grievous. "I won't complain to a full stomach and a full night of rest," Amaya agreed. "Too bad we need to lay low, or else I'd suggest we sing a few shanties to lighten the mood. Our new entertainer might be running out of stories to tell."

Captain snorted. "I donnae t'ink a single day be enough ta drain tha' reservoir," she teased.

"Considering his knack for outright storytelling, no," Jabez piped up from his spot. He watched his brother fondly for a moment. "Even when we were children, he was always telling stories to brighten peoples' days. He'd tell them to scare people, too."

"Oi, Lubella deserved it after what she did ta poor Miss Viola," defended Alconai incredulously as he moved to join them. "And if'n I hadnae told t'e kids about t'e tree yeti what lived in t'e woods, ye ken t'ey would have kept tryin' ta cross that stream on a rotten log 'til it broke with one o' them on it." Jabez simply gestured to Alconai as though to prove his own point.

"'e also tells stories wha' ge' 'im in trouble," Captain teased, remembering his plan to get thrown in jail to

43

figure out what was happening to Lance.

"Doesnae take talent ta tell a truth no one wants ta hear," Alconai remarked dismissively.

"Why am I not surprised? Is that what you were doing in jail?" Jabez questioned dryly.

Alconai waved him off. "I got information, aye? And I met Cap'n. It all worked out."

"Lad after my own heart," Amaya praised with a wry smile.

"So you're both trouble, noted," Lance teased as he joined them around the fire. "Is that the only time you've gotten yourself arrested on purpose, Nai? I can't remember," he joked to the entertainer.

"Jail's nae so bad. Roof o'er me head, some nice stale bread and crusty water, it be a right good ol' time," Alconai joked right back. As he settled down by the fire, he asked, "Now, come on, ye pirates. Certainly ye have some tales o' yer own ta tell."

"Oh, aye, a few. T'ough I'm sure 'Maya an' Sol 'ave more'n me."

"All right, all right. I've got one," Amaya said. As she and Captain dished out dinner to the group, the first mate went into a tale of her time at sea before she met the Moon Child. She soon proved that Alconai wasn't the only one good at regaling crowds. Between Alconai and Amaya telling tales, a sense of levity overcame the group, banishing the dread of impending circumstances for a little longer.

3. Echoing Silence

Tristan's consciousness returned slowly, his body feeling leaden like it did when he woke from a deep sleep. And then he wished he hadn't woken at all. Instantly, he felt the weight of wrongness— reality crashing into him like an icy tidal wave. He tried his best to ignore it, but even as he attempted to force the memories from his mind, the feeling of Arianna's life force disappearing haunted him. Images of his father's torture session clouded his vision. Finally, Tristan could take it no more. Opening his eyes, he sought to escape the pain and despair only to be confronted with a hammer strike to his heart. As Tristan's senses caught up with his wakefulness, the silence of Arianna's absence sounded more deafening than the cacophony of the camp surrounding him.

Tristan's mind refused to comprehend the sight of Rose beside him in the tent as the death of his sister consumed him in crushing heartache, squeezing the tears from his eyes. Lifting a shaky hand, Tristan covered his mouth to stifle the sobs wrung out of him. And yet, there was still work to be done. His responsibilities as a Chosen Child couldn't wait. His father needed to be stopped. Grief would have to come later. Even as his world shattered with the cold left in the wake of his sister's warm presence, Tristan swallowed back his sobs and eased himself up, wincing with the stiffness plaguing his body. Tristan hadn't even realized someone aside from Rose was with him until he felt firm hands grip his shoulders gently. Blearily glancing up, his gaze met Amaya's silver eyes.

"Easy, Tris, easy," she coaxed him. She looked as though she wanted to say more, but she remained silent for now.

"W-Where are we? Th-the people at the castle...Rose...my father," Tristan murmured distractedly, his voice choked with his continued efforts to silence his pain. He wiped the tears from his eyes and fought to keep them in check.

"We're nearing Andor's border. You'll go there and have an audience with King Traiborn. He's lower than dirt, but try not to punch him," Amaya answered solemnly. "As for the people in your father's castle, they all got out. Thanks to you."

"It's because of me they needed to be rescued in the first place," the young man bit out tiredly. "I felt such rage...I didn't think. I was stupid."

"Yeah, you were. You were also thoroughly exhausted in every sense of the word. Running on fumes...it easily ignites into an emotional inferno that burns more than we intend. And we're all guilty of doing it at some point in our lives," the pirate intoned. "But you helped rescue them; that counts for a lot, Tristan. You pushed yourself past your limits to save them, and you did it."

Tristan released a shaky breath as he felt his eyes still stinging. As his grief tried to crush him, he struggled to force his emotions down. Once more wiping his eyes with his hand, Tristan eased himself to his feet. Instead of protesting like he expected her to, Amaya helped him with steady hands gripping his biceps. However, a glance at her face showed her expression to be one of wary concern. Still, Amaya aided him in leaving the tent. Once outside, Tristan motioned to her that he would be okay, and she released him, though she stood behind him. Surveying the camp, Tristan noted the forest surrounding the space and the absence of the pirate crew save for Solomon, Captain, and Amaya herself. The young man refrained from meeting anyone's gaze, not wanting to risk seeing pity or sympathy. They needed him to be strong, to do what he was meant to do. He couldn't be vulnerable right now, no matter how much he wanted to crumble.

He kept expecting to hear footsteps pattering towards him moments before feeling a warm bundle of love and light barrel into his legs with such strength she would probably take him to ground. His subconscious reached out to feel Arianna's joyful presence that always stayed near him. The lack of these things left him cold and aching. Breathing deeply, Tristan pushed through the pain and stared out blankly. "What is our plan when we reach Andor?" he asked with a strength he didn't feel.

"Hell no," Amaya's voice sounded sharp behind him just before Tristan found himself spun around and into her strong arms. One hand tucked his head under her chin while the other arm held him to her; she cradled him the way his mother used to, the memory bringing a fresh wave of grief. In a softer voice, Amaya spoke soothingly against his ear but with just as much resolve, "No one expects you to be okay right now or anytime soon. You need to grieve, Tristan. Yes, there are things still to do, but you are allowed to grieve. So, grieve." She held him more tightly as she spoke. Tristan felt despair and heartache swelling in his chest, choking his breaths even as he continued to resist in his shock. Amaya continued, "No one here is a stranger to loss. We've all felt it. And no one is going to judge you. So let it out."

Gradually, Tristan lifted his arms and clutched Amaya as he shook with quiet sobs. Once he started, he couldn't stop, the fragile dam shattering. "I failed her," he choked out. "I was supposed to protect her...and I failed."

"No, Tris. This is your father's fault, not yours," Amaya told him firmly. "You should have been able to turn to him for protection. You should have been able to trust him. You should have no shadow of a doubt that he loves you. Instead, your father has done the exact opposite of what fathers should be and do. You have every right to be upset." Tears spilled down Tristan's cheeks as his sobs grew louder. He tried to keep them quiet enough that any pursuers wouldn't hear him, but the grief crushing his chest wrung the cries from his lungs.

From where he sat once more against a tree, Jabez watched solemnly as the young man unraveled in Amaya's arms. After a moment, Jabez averted his gaze. He recalled nights when Amaya held him through nightmares and grief, when the world closed in around him and shame burned him. Hearing Tristan, Jabez felt anew the pain of his own losses: his blood father and his mother. Kouta was his father and a great one, but that didn't mean Jabez didn't miss his birth parents. Glancing at Alconai, the ninja knew his brother was remembering the same pain. Alconai stared at the flames of the fire he sat near, giving Tristan some semblance of privacy but unable to tune out the young man's anguish. If Amaya weren't already holding Tristan, Alconai would be. No one should have to grieve alone or feel that they couldn't mourn.

Lance had slipped into the tent behind the pair to keep an eye on the Drow maiden. Solomon calmly tended the fire, his gaze distant even as he subtly took over the cooking for Captain. The pirate girl had slipped away shortly after Amaya had spun Tristan around, sliding into the shadows of the trees. Solomon kept his senses tuned to her, but he knew all too well what this sort of sorrow awoke for the girl. She didn't venture far from the camp, not wanting any of her guardians to feel the need to follow, but far enough away for her own sake. Her emerald eye studied the skies beyond the tree canopy as the rays from the sun slowly vanished.

Zatook watched this all with a stoic expression. Despite wondering for the past few days how best to help the Sun Child, he found himself woefully unprepared. It had been so long since he dealt with his own grief, and longer still since he was in a position to offer someone comfort. He straightened, running a hand through his hair. If only he had a voice…He considered shifting but decided against it. No use wasting energy and causing himself pain for something that probably wouldn't help anyway. *Zatook, you doubt yourself overly much.* He paused, looking up at the sky as a warm presence filled him.

The warm presence did not leave, instead spreading to fill the others before the All Mother focused on Tristan. *It is unfortunate that grief is a part of life…but there is also joy. And Arianna was a fountain of joy. Take comfort that your sister has found peace with her mother, and always remember the warmth she brought to your life. Do not dwell on blame; Amaya is right— your father is the one responsible. You did not kill your sister. You were given a very difficult choice, Tristan. I know it may not feel like it now, but your choice saved her much suffering by allowing her to die in a time where she was at peace, rather than murdering her yourself under your father's control. You protected your sister's happiness to the end. That took much courage.*

Normally Tristan would have started at the sudden voice in his head, but grief left him staring dully at the flames of the campfire even as Amaya continued to hold him. This voice didn't sound like the one from before that had helped him at the castle. And yet the tone was similar. *Who are you?* he questioned wearily. After his fight with his father and the emotional strain he had endured, Tristan knew he lacked the fortitude for a mental battle. *Great protector I turned out to be,* he protested weakly. More tears slipped down his face. *Arianna deserved so much better. I should have done better for her.* Tristan buried his face against Amaya's shoulder. *I...I should have been able to protect her. My decisions killed Arianna. If only I'd never left the forest...If I hadn't let her wander off...she would have never...*but if Arianna hadn't wandered off into the forest that day, they never would have met Rose. But then, perhaps that would have been a good thing. Tristan's mind flashed to his fight against the Drow while he was under the blood mage's control. *Rose...how is she alive? I felt...I saw...I killed her.* The tears flowed more with the memory, his breath hitching as he sobbed.

The warmth blossomed a little more as if to comfort him. *My name is Mythril. And you did not kill Rose— Marilyn did. Rose survives through the power of my sister, Rin. A time will come when my sister will reclaim that power. Then, Rose's fate will lie with you. That is all I can say on the matter for now. It is my sister's domain.* She paused for a moment as the words sunk in. *Do not dwell on what might have been. The potential futures swirling around us are a sea of what-ifs and could-have-beens. But we have no certain knowledge of how events would have played out. You may have found yourself alone when your father found you. StormShaper may have found the grove as Reina's barrier faded. The forest was not meant to hold you forever. Those chosen by the Sacreds rarely have the luxury of simple lives. But you were granted just that to watch your sister blossom and to hone your own abilities with your mentor. And in the end, when your father did the unspeakable to his own blood, Arianna was surrounded by people who loved her.*

Tristan now cried silently into Amaya's shoulder as he tried to process everything Mythril told him. Rose's fate lay with him? What could he do? And would Rose want him to be the one to help her after what happened? Even as the thought occurred, Tristan remembered Rose fighting to free him from his father, comforting Tristan in his grief. Staying with him as his anguish ripped apart the castle around them. He didn't deserve her, but he would try his best to do right by her. He owed her that much and so much more. As his strength waned, Tristan leaned a little more heavily against Amaya, but the woman had yet to protest. Instead, she started guiding him back into the tent he had been resting in earlier. Tristan let her. However, he had her help him settle a little closer to Rose. Heartache squeezed his chest again as he took in the Drow's state. He reached out to try and heal her, but Amaya gently guided his hand away.

"It won't work. Her wounds have sealed, but they won't actually heal. Probably has something to do with her deal with Lady Death," Amaya explained. She hesitated a moment. Then her hand reached up and lightly carded through his hair. "Get some rest, Tristan. We're here for you." Amaya nodded to Lancelot before slipping from the tent. Since Tristan was awake now and could call if the pair needed anything, Lancelot followed her out to give the pair some privacy.

Tristan watched them leave for a moment before turning to Rose. He tentatively reached out to touch Rose's hand, keeping his touch as gentle as possible. He resisted trying to connect with her for now— he wanted to let her rest, but he also wanted her to know he was with her.

Rose turned her hand to hold Tristan's, squeezing it lightly to let him know she was awake as well. She peeked her eyes open, gazing up at him before letting her lids slide closed again. Everything took effort; she felt like her muscles were lead, weighing her down rather than giving her the strength needed to look around.

Tristan returned the squeeze gently. "I'm sorry," he whispered. "I never wanted anyone to get involved in my feud with my father. I'm sorry I've caused you pain. Even if I was being controlled, I remember vividly our fight and kicking you into the river. It felt like a nightmare, and I wish that had been all it was." He sighed heavily, weary from grief and sore from everything he had endured during his time with this father and the aftermath. "I know about...I know you made a deal with the Lady of Death." Tristan fell quiet as his mind turned over everything that had happened.

"I should be the one apologizing. I was unable to distract Marilyn long enough for you to break free." Rose was quiet for a moment. "There's something wrong with that mage. Aside from her appearance, which she must have hidden under a glamor before. She is not Drow, yet her powers far exceed most unnatural blood mages. And she... feels wrong. I do not know...how to explain."

Tristan nodded. "There is definitely something unhinged about her," he agreed softly. After a thoughtful silence, he added, "I wish I could talk to Clovestein, my mentor from Nikko Mori." Tristan's voice grew more grave as he remembered his old home. In all the chaos and losing Arianna and now the situation with Rose, he hadn't had a chance to think of what his father had done to the forest when Tsukuyomi acquired Arianna's pendant. "My home...my father mentioned having a confrontation with Clo. I don't even know if Clo and the elves are still alive. My mentor is a Drow, so he might have known something about this Marilyn." Despair crushing him anew, Tristan shook his head as his eyes stung again. He covered his eyes with his free hand, fighting back the tears that threatened to spill. "I have done nothing right. What good am I as a Chosen Child if I can't protect my sister? If I get the Star Child killed? Why did you put yourself through so much pain for me?"

"Perhaps Captain can answer the fate of the forest and those who dwelled there," Rose suggested softly. "What happened to Arianna... wasn't your fault. You did everything you could to protect her. The best I can offer is she felt no pain." She grimaced slightly. "I cannot pretend to understand what you went through. What you're going through. But for now, I'm here." She hesitated as she considered his last question. She thought back to that riverbank, the sand scraping against her, the cold embrace of the Lady. Her confession. Did she dare? She really didn't know how much longer she had before the Lady came. Could she really say it? Would that not simply add to the crushing guilt already weighing on his shoulders?... And what if he did not feel the same? "We promised...in the forest. We would face what comes together. I couldn't give in to rest knowing you had been taken."

"Thank you. I appreciate all you've done," Tristan told her softly. "I'm trying to be strong, to do what needs to be done, but I'm not even sure where to go from here." He lowered his hand from his eyes as he looked at Rose. He remembered that moment in the forest. Their promise. "I remember," he assured her. He remembered the way she looked when Arianna put the flowers in Rose's hair. Even with the fresh wave of pain from the memory, he recalled how beautiful Rose had looked. His mind recalled what Mythril said about Tristan being able to help Rose, but what could he do if he couldn't heal her? As if losing a new friend wasn't bad enough, Tristan knew he felt more than just friendship for the Drow. And yet, could he really say how deep those feelings went? He felt his grief burying his feelings for Rose farther down as he tried to work through all the sorrow.

Rose started to shake her head but regretted the motion when her world spun. "I do not know what comes next," she confessed. "I do not even know how long I have before the Lady comes." She forced her eyes open, focusing on Tristan. "I suppose we really must rely on Captain, at least, to figure that out. The blessing and curse of having Sight."

Tristan fell quiet as uncertainty and sadness threatened to rob him of his breath. He pushed down the emotions and tried to bury them even as they fought against the restraint. "Is there anything I can do for you in the meantime? Any way to ease your pain or discomfort?" he asked softly.

Rose gently squeezed his hand. "Nothing that I am aware."

"I'm sorry," Tristan whispered, heartbroken. Tears stung his eyes no matter how hard he tried to keep them in check. He lightly squeezed her hand in return. Finally, he slowly lowered himself to lay next to her, tucking his face near her shoulder as he let the tears fall. He kept hold of her hand, desperate to hold onto her for as long as he could.

***

Captain closed her eyes again and willed herself to remember. The specifics had faded over time. She knew she could Look, but she hadn't been able to bring herself to do so. She just…couldn't face it yet. Not like that. She sighed, opening her eye once more and fishing out a small silver disc. She made sure her eyes weren't puffy; she didn't need to worry about tear stains. She hadn't really cried about things since…well, a few years ago at least. But it gave her a few extra moments to take steadying breaths and make sure her hands held no tremors. After a few more moments, she descended from her perch and rejoined the camp, taking her portion of the food with a bright smile and sitting between Alconai and Amaya to eat.

Amaya gave Captain a knowing side-eye but refrained from saying anything. Instead, she knocked her knee good-naturedly against the girl's even as Amaya resumed eating. The woman's eyes returned to surveying their group, taking in everyone's more somber demeanors. The cooler air felt all the harsher without the little princess of light and warmth flitting in their midst. So very much like the absence of flower fragrances and heartening sunlight in winter. Despite her usual carefree attitude, Amaya's eyes now reflected the sagely gaze of one who had walked the world through years beyond average ken.

Alconai watched Captain calmly, shifting to let their shoulders touch in reassurance. Despite their travels and chatter, the underlying sadness dragged at the group's heels and hearts in different ways. He could only guess to Captain's thoughts and feelings, but he knew Arianna's passing had hit the group harder than they might like to admit. For Alconai's part, he hadn't gotten to know Arianna like the others had, but even with the little time he got to see her, he knew she had shone brightly. His eyes darted up when Jabez stood with two bowls and started to move toward the tent with Tristan and Rose. Alconai reached up and squeezed Captain's shoulder, giving her a soft smile, before he stood and intercepted Jabez. His older brother gave him a slightly perplexed look but yielded the bowls without a fuss. Food in hand, Alconai slipped into the tent while Jabez held the flap for him, letting it fall behind the minstrel once Alconai was inside.

Tristan barely looked at the food as the entertainer set the bowls beside him, the young man once more fighting back tears. Grief stole his appetite, but he knew he needed sustenance. What good would he be if he made himself weak and sick? Tristan forced himself to acknowledge the man when he felt Alconai squeeze his shoulder sympathetically.

"Not that I donnae think ye can handle it, but would ye like some help? Either o' ye?" Alconai offered indicating the food.

Tristan shook his head. "I've got it." Alconai nodded before giving both Chosen Children a reassuring look. He then left them alone in the tent once more.

"I might need that help," Rose confessed softly once the tent had closed again. "Go ahead and eat. It'll give mine time to cool."

Silently, Tristan ate as much as he could stomach, which was only about half a bowl, before he pushed it aside. He remembered how Arianna would sometimes sit in his lap to eat. The memory brought a fresh wave of heartache and a lump formed in his throat. However, he swallowed it down and helped Rose sit up just enough that she could eat a little more easily. He then helped her by gently feeding her. "I...I saw Jeremiah at my father's castle. They were talking about...I think Jeremiah might have killed Nocis's king," he told her thoughtfully. "I'm not sure how much of a hand my father actually has in all this. He said that he wanted...to remake the world into a better one. I don't know if he's delusional or just that arrogant."

Rose had a tendency to take things in stride. A soldier's calm. But when Tristan mentioned what Jeremiah had done, she actually choked on her food. "He did...what?" She cleared her throat, getting her food down before leaning against Tristan as he finished. Jeremiah killed the king? That made no sense. "Arden was like his brother," she breathed, her brow furrowed. She knew he had changed, but she never would have thought him capable of such a thing. She tried to think back, to pinpoint any moment where she noticed something different. But his change had been so subtle, she often doubted her earlier memories. And yet… she also found she was struggling to remember. She could recall her time with him as a soldier, to a point. What if his kindness towards her had just been part of his plan? And just what was his plan? She sighed, shaking her head. "What is arrogance if not a delusion in itself?" she murmured. "The world is not his to shape. It already has a Creator." Was this part of dying? Steadily losing her memories? Or had she simply never noticed before how things slipped from her mind like sand?

With her comment about the dragon knight's relationship with King Arden, Tristan thought back to Lancelot being controlled by blood magic and even his own time in Marilyn's control. "Do you know how long Marilyn has been around him? Could she control him like she did me?" asked Tristan. How many people were caught up in this mess of ambitions? Tristan almost wondered if perhaps his own father had been twisted by magic, but he knew in his heart that wasn't the case. As much as he wished it to be different— wished to believe that his father could be saved —Tristan knew he had to face a heavy truth.

Rose closed her eyes, thinking back. "I don't see how," she noted. "I have sensed her blood magic with those who were under sway. I spent almost every day with Jeremiah, I surely would have felt it. And Marilyn never used blood magic when she was around. Another reason I did not place her when we were at your father's keep. I only recognized her voice once…well, once everything was calm."

"What kind of master was Jeremiah to you?"

Rose chuckled. "Unconventional. Kind but firm. But as I grew older, he changed. It wasn't anything sudden; I cannot even pinpoint when it began." She frowned, furrowing her brow. "I find I am not remembering much," she added softer. "I know he has a wife and daughter, yet I cannot see their faces. I know Marilyn was around, and my grandmother, yet I could not tell you why they were near. It is...disconcerting."

"I wonder if that's a part of your deal with Lady Death. Or perhaps something else interferes," Tristan mused. After helping Rose finish her meal, Tristan ran a hand through his hair in slight frustration. "Nothing can have a simple answer, can it?" he groused softly. He let her lean against him for as long as she desired. "Why must visions and quests always be riddles and vague assurances?" His mind drifted once more to what Mythril said about Lady Death letting him help Rose. He wrapped his arms gently around the Drow woman, holding her for a moment.

"Simple? I suppose not. I certainly would not have minded a little 'simple' between 'fugitive' and 'zombie'." She smirked slightly, finding what humor she could in the moment. It slipped as her gaze wandered towards the tent entrance. "Have you ever been to Andor?" she asked. "Or will this be your first time?"

Tristan grew contemplative for a moment, trying to recall the neighboring kingdom. "Not that I can remember. My mother told me stories of Andor. Especially of Andor's first king, since he and my grandfather were friends," he answered. "I know Andor is more advanced in magical enhancements than Nocis due to Andor's first king being an innovator. More than that, I don't really know much, and I've never been there myself. I think my mother wanted to take me there, but we never got the chance to go. Have you been there before?”

“Not often, and only ever in my armor,” she noted calmly, closing her eyes. “It’s a beautiful country; I’ll be curious to see what the welcome is like when one is a visitor instead of a soldier escorting a diplomatic mission.” She chuckled at that. “No one really wants to talk to the other country’s champion, and I wasn’t really allowed to mingle. Now that I think on it, I do not recall seeing Zatook when we were there. But I always enjoyed looking at the architecture and the gardens. The whole capital was sung from stone. But I’ll let you see for yourself.” She shifted slightly in an attempt to get more comfortable before continuing. “Though I cannot help but worry that Captain will have her hands full if she hopes to convince the king to help us. Traiborn is a stern and stubborn man who rarely bothers with things beyond his borders.”

Tristan helped her to get comfortable on her bedroll again. “I’m curious to see it. I never got to travel much until now,” his voice grew quieter as he spoke. Arianna would have loved the gardens and seeing a new country. She and Tristan had always shared an adventurous spirit despite Tristan’s reluctance to leave Nikko Mori. “My mother was friends with Queen Corianne at one point, but it’s my understanding that King Traiborn is the reason they lost touch. I’m not sure how receptive he’ll be. I suppose that Andor is the best place for protection against my father for now, even if just as a small respite before we continue somewhere else.” Tristan’s mind wandered as he considered where they were to go from there. “We initially set out to escape my father and then to rescue Captain. Then to rescue…me…I’m not sure where to go from here. What to do.”

He reached up and rubbed his face in weariness and bafflement. As his thoughts wandered, Tristan wondered after the fates of Clo and the denizens of Nikko Mori once again. "You know…you're not alone in your exile. My mentor in Nikko Mori, Clo, I mentioned that he's Drow. Now, I wish there had been time for you to meet him. He wasn't raised by his people either, so he didn't grow up in their teachings and social mentality. I never saw him treat anyone as inferior. Rash perhaps, or naive, but never inferior." His lips ticked up slightly in amusement even as his eyes stung. "Clovestein was— is —the guardian of Nikko Mori. He had a responsibility to protect the forest and keep vigil over those residing within its borders. Even so, he always made time for Arianna and me. As Arianna got older, Clo would let me go with him to patrol the forest and help him care for it. I think he was trying to keep me from going stir crazy and to give me some respite from caring for Arianna all the time. Some elven friends would look after Arianna. Sometimes Clo's adopted parents would even visit and watch Arianna."

Tristan wiped away a tear that made its way down his cheek. "It's only been a short time since we left, and yet it feels like months. I miss it. I miss him. I miss them. I miss…" he trailed off, not wanting to sound redundant by voicing how much he missed his sister. More tears spilled down his cheeks as he added thickly, "Sometimes I felt restless and stifled. Sometimes I felt overwhelmed with trying to care for an infant sister when I was still a child myself. But I cherish it. The memories, the people, the tree we called home. All of it." He shook himself as he wiped away his tears again. "I'm sorry. I'm…I'm trying to focus, to look forward to the things that need to be done next. I just…" he trailed off as he sighed heavily.

"You have no need to apologize," Rose assured him softly. She reached a hand up to gently catch his. "Nor do you have need to hide your tears. From what you say of him, of the elves in the forest, I have little doubt they escaped your father. Perhaps Shaddai will allow your paths to cross again." She closed her eyes, sighing. "I cannot help but feel grateful to hear of other Drow who do not take after the Elders," she confessed. "Some would claim the entire race evil, but they are no more evil than the Nocium who followed Arden or the Andorians who follow Traiborn. They go by what they are taught, what they believe they know. And the Elders have no wish to change the way things are." She grimaced. "My grandmother once told me that the reason she sold me to a human was that serving an inferior race would further tarnish my existence in the eyes of the Drow. Which makes me wonder what Marilyn could have done to ingratiate herself enough to know and use her name." Her brow furrowed as her mind returned to the puzzle of a blood mage, but then she shook her head. "My thoughts are wandering, pay no mind," she murmured. How old was Marilyn? How long had she known Keeshe? Was there a connection that involved Jeremiah? Or was it a coincidence?

Tristan squeezed her hand gently in gratitude. "I don't mind hearing your thoughts. Clovestein is a gentle and wise soul. I hope I get to speak with him again. I imagine he's encountered other Drow, but I get the feeling they wouldn't have gotten along. I don't think the Drow Elders would appreciate that he called me by a Drow name or that he looked after a forest where the main denizens are elves and fae." Tristan considered what he'd seen of Marilyn and what Rose told him of her grandmother. "Perhaps the situation with King Arden and Jeremiah was something like a slow-acting poison. Administered in small doses over years rather than all at once. As for what

Marilyn did...honestly, I'm not sure she's entirely human. She's more like a nightmarish patchwork of whatever she could find that wasn't human. It could be someone vouched for her with your grandmother." Tristan watched Rose for a moment before adding, "You should rest. I think we're close to Andor, but we still have some traveling to do."

Rose sighed with a slight hum. "I do not like sitting still," she admitted with a half-smirk. "But I suppose there is little else for me to do at this point. Though Captain is outside not wishing to interrupt, so you may as well hand her the bowls," she added after a moment of silence. She squeezed Tristan's hand once more before letting go so he could deliver the dishes to Captain. The Doran girl waited patiently before taking the dishes and practically prancing over to where Lancelot and Alconai were rinsing them out.

"'Ere ye go, lads, last o' the batch," she announced cheerily. The knight thanked her quietly as he took them. He hadn't really met her eyes since she and Alconai had been catching him up on everything, but she didn't think it worth pushing yet. Let the man be embarrassed for a bit, and if he wallowed in shame then she'd smack him over the head with something. Not like he could control the part he played. That settled, she moved back to the fire and plopped herself by Amaya, leaning against the woman. "Will ye be goin' back ta t'e boys, then?" she asked quietly. "Or do ye have other plans in mind?"

Amaya gently bopped her head against Captain's in greeting. "I've got some people to talk to, but I'll mostly be keeping Tsukuyomi's minions distracted," she answered. "You don't really need me around much anymore, grown as you are. Still, I don't like leaving you to deal with Traiborn. Any of you." Despite her usual laid-back attitude, her gaze was rather somber as she watched their group. Alconai was making sure Jabez was resting properly while also making quiet small-talk with Lancelot. Amaya's gaze drifted to the tent housing Tristan and Rose. "I imagine you ken that I need to talk to Tris 'bout something important before I leave. I'm just not sure how to broach the subject." She wrapped an arm around Captain's shoulders and pulled the girl against her. "What about you? Don't think I didn't notice you slip away while I was handling Tristan. How are you doing in light of all that's happened?"

Captain was quiet for a moment. "Less thinkin' o' t'e last few days an more thinkin' what be comin' up," she noted softly. "An' tryin' ta figure out our next steps. I cannae imagine we're mean' ta laze aroun' a castle t'e rest of our days, bu' I See no paths."

Amaya held Captain a little tighter. "I'm sorry I won't be there when that time rolls around. At least you won't be with complete strangers. Solomon and Jabez are familiar with what that time means to you. They have their own days like that as well. As for what to do next, it could be that Shaddai wants you to see something in Andor before you See the next path. Maybe someone there can give advice. You don't need to be all-knowing all the time, Moon Sprite. Leave that to Shaddai and trust He'll lead you where He wants you to go. I ken that's easier said than done at times. I'm very familiar with not having all or any answers for what He's led me to do or where He's led me to go."

"I jus' 'ope any surprises comin' be less dreadful t'an the las' one," Captain grumbled as she leaned into Amaya's hold. "Le' Tris be fer tonight. 'e an' Rosie got a lo' on t'eir minds. Talk to 'im in t'e morning while I have t'e ot'ers pack up camp. Should ge' ye a chance to speak wit' 'im alone."

"We've got a bit yet before we reach Andor. It can wait a little longer," Amaya said. "Tristan's going to be out of sorts for a bit, and he's going to have a lot of questions. Considering Rose's situation, I've got a hunch of what might be coming next, but I can't say for sure." At one point, Amaya shifted and maneuvered Captain until the girl was actually sitting in her lap. She wrapped her arms around the Doran girl and held her. "You need rest, too, Izzy. You've been doin' a lot of peeking lately."

Captain grumbled a half-hearted protest, but she snuggled into Amaya's hold nonetheless. It wasn't long before her guardian recognized the steady breathing of sleep.

4. Not Alone

As morning dawned over their little camp, Captain had orders for almost everyone. First, she sent Alconai and Lancelot to find what food they could in the woods. You needed a special license to hunt in Andor, and she didn't know if they would be stopping anywhere with provisions. Best to stock up and be prepared. She sent Solomon to refresh their water supply before ordering Jabez to keep resting. Rose and Tristan didn't need that order, both still sound asleep. Zatook was sitting near where Captain was cooking up breakfast for the lot, keeping watch but also close if she needed any assistance. She shot Amaya a slight smirk, thinking back to ordering her boys around on the *Effervescence*. She didn't try to push Amaya to talk to Tristan then; the woman was probably right. He wouldn't be up for an important conversation first thing.

Amaya gave Captain a wry smile, but Amaya moved about the camp, packing what she could to help prepare for their departure. Evident to everyone was that Amaya seemed to have lost some of her vigor. She almost moved as though to stall for time. She remained quiet while she worked, contemplative. At one point, Amaya lifted her gaze in the direction the group would be traveling to reach Andor. Unease tugged at her with the prospect of the group going somewhere beyond her reach if they needed aid. She trusted Shaddai to look after them, but her concern persisted. Amaya's attention shifted back to the camp when Tristan eventually emerged from the tent he currently shared with Rose. Amaya refrained from approaching him yet, though she did give him a quiet greeting. However, once Tristan finished eating and seemed a bit more awake, Amaya caught his gaze and motioned Tristan to go with her farther into the trees. Tristan gave her a perplexed look, but he followed. Once they were out of the way and a little more private, Amaya stopped but stayed silent at first.

Tristan watched the woman for now, wondering what she wanted with him. He remembered how she'd held him as he grieved Arianna, recalled her words to him. "Thank you for the other day," he said, deciding to break the silence first. "I...I needed to hear that and to...just mourn."

"You're going to be mourning for a while, Tristan. You don't need to bottle it up or try to hide it," replied Amaya as she met his gaze with her own steady one. "Grief eases, but it's never fully gone. You'll have good days and bad days. Cherish the good days, but don't feel like you need to hide when you're having a bad day."

Tristan nodded in acknowledgment. "Sounds like you're speaking from experience." He sighed as his shoulders slumped a little. "'No one here is a stranger to loss', right?" he echoed her words back to her. "I spoke to Rose for a bit yesterday. I told her how I didn't know where to go from here or what I should do. I'm not sure how to feel about my father and what he's done. We have to stop him, but to what extent? I've lost my mother and my sister. Will I...would Shaddai really call me to kill my father?" Tears stung his eyes— not just for the thought of having to end his own father but for what his father had done to bring things to such a point. "The worst part is,

I don't think I would hesitate. I'm so angry. He's hurt our family. He killed Mum and Arianna. He tortured me. For what? Some stupid ambition that he can fix the world? Is it really worth it? I want…I want him to pay. I want revenge, but I know I shouldn't." Tristan startled slightly from his spiraling thoughts when Amaya gripped his arms firmly. His gaze had drifted to the ground as he spoke, but now he met her eyes again, her silver gaze full of determination and remorse he didn't understand.

"I can't speak for what Shaddai plans, Tristan. You're right that revenge isn't the way to go. Vengeance belongs to Shaddai, and He will see justice done even if we don't see it. Your father will have to face the consequences of his actions," Amaya told him. "Forgiving someone doesn't mean you have to have anything to do with them. It means not letting the anger and bitterness define your life. And yes, I'm speaking from experience. You're not alone in your anger and heartache, Tris. I can't even begin to fathom why my brother has chosen to hurt his family." She fell silent, watching Tristan's face closely.

For his part, Tristan stared at her in bewilderment. "Your…brother?" he all but whispered. "My father is… then you're my aunt? You're a Celestial?" New emotions roiled within him when Amaya simply nodded. He watched as she released one of his arms so she could hold her hand up between them. Electricity sparked between her bandaged fingers, the light dancing shadows across her features.

"I didn't expect you to remember me. You were just a little ankle-biter last we saw each other," the woman told him. "I'm Amaya LightningRider, Celestial of Wanderlust. Fitting title for a pirate, for sure. I told the others while you were still unconscious, though I haven't told them my connection to you and your da. Well, Captain knows, but that's no surprise given her Gift."

Tristan continued to stare at her as he tried to comprehend everything that meant. He had heard stories of his other family members from a couple who lived on the outer edge of Nikko Mori. Takumi and Feray had known Tristan's grandparents, but they hadn't told him much about his aunts. Even so, as Tristan thought back to his time traveling with the group, Amaya's interactions with Arianna and even Tristan himself started to make more sense, reminding him of the little he had heard from Takumi and Feray. He wanted to ask why Amaya had waited until now to say something, but he knew Celestials were supposed to keep low profiles when they came to this realm. "Why are you telling me this now? Why didn't you come to Nikko Mori sooner?"

Amaya sighed heavily, her gaze reflecting guilt and remorse. "I didn't say anything when we reunited because I didn't want to overwhelm you, but also because there hasn't been an opportunity for us to talk," she explained. "Still, you deserved to know, and I understand if you're angry with me. I hope you can find it in you to forgive me. As for coming to you sooner, I wanted to, but ones wiser than I told me to wait. Your aunt Hoshiko, my older sister, told me that the time wasn't right, no matter how much it hurt that I couldn't be there for you. She assured me you and your sister were in good hands, and she was right. More than that, though, you were safest in the forest with your mother's barrier, temporary as it was. And a ship was no place for a baby, much less a ship full of pirates. The lads would mean well, but the seas are treacherous even at the best of times. I also already had Izzy—

Captain—when your mother passed. Even now, Captain doesn't have full control of her powers, and she had even less control when she was younger. For that reason, I couldn't bring her to the forest. One Chosen Child can be a handful while they're learning to harness their gifts. Putting two young, emotional Chosen Children together would have been too dangerous."

Tristan listened in silence to Amaya's explanations. As much as he wanted to be mad at her and felt betrayed, he understood her reasoning. "What about Aunt Hoshiko? Why did she stay away?"

Amaya shook her head. "I don't know the details, but I know my sister. She wouldn't have left you alone if she could have helped it. Like Izzy, she has the Sight. Not in the same way, but Hoshiko perceives things beyond most people's ken. I hope for her and Izzy to meet one day since Hoshiko is probably one of the few people who would truly understand what Captain goes through with the Sight." Releasing the electricity, Amaya touched Tristan's arm again. Hesitantly, she gently pulled him.

Tristan let her, allowing himself to be enveloped in her embrace once more. "I understand. I don't like any of it, but I understand. And I forgive you. You're here now, and I'm glad to know I'm not alone."

"Oh, Tris, you were never alone. Even if we couldn't be with you physically, we tried to be there for you in what ways we could. We kept vigil over you, checked on you. Sometimes we sent things to Clovestein that we knew you and Arianna needed. That dagger of yours was a gift from me. Figured you could use one for practical uses and defense." She hesitated when he mentioned her being there now. "You're right; I'm here for you. However, I can't go with you into Andor. King Traiborn and I had a rather ugly falling out years ago, and he's sealed me out of the kingdom. I'll be outside looking after things, keeping your da off your backs and getting information. I'll meet up with you again once you leave Andor."

At the thought of her facing his father, fear gripped Tristan, his mind recalling the fight between his parents that ended in his mother's death. His grip on Amaya tightened. "Can't you...can't someone stay with you, or maybe I could—"

"Tristan, breathe, lad," Amaya interjected gently. She actually lifted a hand to stroke back his hair before using that hand to cradle his head against her shoulder. "We will see each other again. And as rash as I can be at times, I know how to be careful. I won't be alone either, and even your father knows better than to piss off certain friends of mine. As for you, lad, you need rest. I know you're mostly healed, but you need the emotional and mental rest for what you're probably going to be facing. And you should spend what time you can with Rose. I've seen how close you two have become."

Tristan sighed unhappily but resignedly. A thought occurred to him with his aunt's words. "Lady Mythril spoke to me when you were comforting me. She said something about the Lady of Death allowing me to help Rose. Do you know what she meant?" He lifted his head to look at Amaya. Her eyes said that she knew something or at least suspected, but she remained silent. Tristan started to look away, accepting that she might not be able to tell him even if she did know.

"I have a hunch. I don't know for certain because it's a rare thing, but I think I know what she's talking about. I'll see what information I can glean while you're at Andor," Amaya answered. "If it is what I think, then you'll definitely need to be at your best before you face it. Remember, you're not alone. I'll help you— we all will."

Tristan inclined his head before stepping back. "Thank you, Aunt Amaya."

The Celestial snorted. "Oh don't start that. Just call me Amaya. Aunt Amaya sounds far too formal." Even so, she couldn't help the sly grin tugging at her lips when her protest brought a small smile to Tristan's face. Reaching up, she tousled his hair. "You're a lot stronger than you think, Tris." Her hand trailed down to cup the side of his face as her expression grew somber. "I need you to promise me something."

"Okay," Tristan agreed hesitantly. Her change in demeanor sent a weight into his stomach.

Amaya lifted her other hand to hold both sides of his face. "You know Celestials aren't to be known in this realm. However, Traiborn likely already knows you're a Celestial," she said. Then more earnestly she told him, "Promise me, no matter what happens or what he may do, you will not face him alone. Don't even stay alone with him in a room."

Tristan's gaze grew steadily more perplexed. He asked, "Is the king not human?"

"Oh, he's plenty human, but he's a very old and very

powerful sorcerer. He's figured out ways to subdue Celestials," Amaya explained. She then released one side of his face to reach up and pull aside the fabric covering her left shoulder. Careful to remain modest, Amaya showed Tristan a rather brutal scar near her heart. "During my spat with Traiborn, he nearly succeeded in killing me. It's only thanks to Queen Corianne that I'm alive. She managed to get me out of Andor, and then Traiborn made sure I couldn't get back into the kingdom. Nor have I seen my friend since. Even centuries later, my wound still troubles me from time to time."

"What did he do?" Tristan asked in horror.

"The blade he used to stab me was made from materials that very specifically counter Celestials. While I recovered, I couldn't use my Celestial abilities at all. I basically lived as a human for a while. But that is a story for another time," Amaya told him.

Tristan reached up and gripped her hand still on his face. "You're making me nervous," he confessed. "I could barely fight my father, and now you're telling me that we're seeking refuge with a sorcerer who can kill Celestials?"

Amaya gave him a wry smile. "I admit I'm nervous to have any of you go into Andor without me but especially my baby Celestial nephew," she confessed. "And yet, who better to keep your father at bay than a king who can hold his own against Celestials?"

"My father at my back and a Celestial-killer at my front," Tristan murmured despairingly.

"I'll be the shield against your father," Amaya reminded, "And there are plenty in our group who can help protect you from Traiborn if he decides to be a problem. There is always the possibility that he'll decide that allying with you will be more beneficial for him than harming you." She released him fully as she spoke.

Tristan started to respond when he noticed the bandages around Amaya's hands. "What happened? Let me heal it before you leave." He caught her hand, but before he could do anything Amaya gave a flick of her wrist and the young man found her holding his hand instead.

"Save your strength, Tris. Like I said, you're going to need it," she told him. Amaya gave his hand a light squeeze and flashed him a reassuring smile. "It's just some battle wounds. I'll visit Nikko Mori to see if Takumi is up for healing them."

"Takumi and Feray spoke about you, but I didn't realize the connection until now," admitted Tristan, a bit sheepish. Tristan had met Takumi and his wife Feray not long after Tristan and Arianna first arrived in Nikko Mori. "They've known our family for several centuries. They helped me care for Arianna. I know they raised Clovestein, so for me they were more like a weird combination of grandparents and aunt and uncle given their agelessness."

"They are like an aunt and an uncle to me, but I haven't seen them in recent decades. Too busy going on my own adventures and then raising a child," Amaya answered. "I wanted to take Captain to the forest someday to meet them and you, but I needed to wait."

"I would have liked that. I still hope to go back. Perhaps

we can all go."

Amaya smiled and released his hand before nudging him back towards the main camp. "Time to go, I wager. I'll tell Uncle Tak and Aunt Feray that you send your regards. This way, too, I can check on everyone and the condition of the forest. I'll find a way to send you word if Captain doesn't beat me to it."

Tristan thanked her but paused to look back at her. "I promise to be careful in Andor, but will you please promise me you'll be careful as well?"

"It's a promise, and I swear on the pirate code that I will do all in my power to get back to you as soon as I can," Amaya affirmed. Tristan nodded with a small smile and headed back to camp.

***

True to Amaya's prediction, the camp was packed up and the others were simply waiting to head out. Rose was awake and sitting up, chatting with Captain calmly while they waited. Though Zatook was still not a fan of letting anyone in his head, he had at least let Izzy know that the first town beyond the border, Stonewillow, would have some form of transport waiting for them, though she couldn't quite understand what he was trying to describe. Still, it would be nice not to have to make him keep dragging a cart around. When the group saw Amaya and Tristan heading their way, Solomon reclaimed his pack and tossed one a piece to Lancelot and Alconai. Zatook had already claimed the largest couple of bags, and any attempt to dissuade him was met with a flat stare. Captain stood as everyone readied, stretching before greeting

Tristan with her typical grin. "Ye wanna ride wit' yer lass today, or shall I give yer spo' ta more packs? Zattie says we've go' some kinda carriage waitin' fer us thanks ta t'e king, so tha's a good sign. It'll be nice to nae be walkin' all day."

Amaya took a few of the bags without issue. She moved to walk beside the wagon to keep an eye on Rose and Jabez. At Captain's teasing, Tristan blushed. "I think I can walk. It'll be nice to stretch my legs, but if I start to slow us down, I'll get in the cart," he quietly agreed. He didn't move to collect any bags since the others seemed to have them handled. He also wanted to avoid wearing himself out too much on his first day of traveling on foot. "Captain, if it's not too much trouble, would you be able to check on Nikko Mori's guardian and the inhabitants of the forest? I realize your Gift is probably rather taxing to use, so I understand if you'd rather conserve your energy." Despite what Rose had said, Tristan almost dared not hope that they were alive.

"I'll be 'onest, I planned ta do a bit o' peekin' aroun'," Captain confessed with a slight laugh. "I'll be waitin' until we ge' t'is transpor' thingy, jus' in case I be needin' lugged aroun' next." She winked at him cheekily before spinning to face Amaya. "Joinin' us ta t'e border, then? Or ye takin' t'ose packs wit' ye?" she teased.

"I see how it is. You're eager to get rid of me," Amaya teased right back. "I'll split off from you once we reach the border. The transport will be a fun experience for you. Ignore the arse of a king, and all of Andor is sure to be an exciting adventure. High time you experienced something other than the open seas and tropical islands you know. Something better than a jail cell, too."

Captain snorted. "In person, a' least," she teased right back. She looped arms with Amaya and started their little procession towards the border. Sol fell in next to the cart, shaking his head at the Doran girl's antics but smirking nonetheless. Whether or not she had Seen anything of Andor, he knew she was excited to see things in reality, too, despite all her jokes. According to her, it just wasn't the same in visions. And the border itself was something to behold.

Though his body was stiff and sore from his ordeal, Tristan managed to walk on his own. He kept glancing at Jabez and Rose in the wagon, wanting to ease their injuries. Rose he knew he couldn't really help, but Jabez seemed to be recovering as well. Tristan had yet to ask about what happened while Rose and he fought Tsukuyomi. Still coming to terms with his grief, Tristan felt like he was living in a daze. Despite his desire to help Jabez, Tristan wasn't entirely sure about using his Child powers so soon when he was finally up and about. He lingered near Rose's side of the cart. "How are you feeling about all this?" he asked her. Part of him just wanted the distraction from his own thoughts, but he also wanted to check in with her.

"Whisked along," she confessed, watching the canopy pass overhead. "But getting fairly used to it." Honestly, she almost felt like she was back in that river, but she didn't want to pull anyone into those thoughts. Still, she couldn't help but wonder if their battle at the castle was the last time she would stand under her own power. She felt almost childish stewing at having to be carried or pulled around in wagons, but she was never one to lounge about while others were laboring. For now, she quieted her thoughts and allowed herself to be as comfortable as possible with the ever-present dull ache of her unhealing wounds.

The sun slowly rose as they made their way through the forest that separated Nocis from southern Andor. Yet as they drew nearer, the group began to suspect what Solomon and even Amaya had hinted at— there was more to the border than trees. They started to spy something bright yet solid beyond the trees, rather than a town or even open fields. A large wall waited for them beyond the forest. It appeared to be crafted from some form of metal, with embossed vines trailing around the top.

"Welcome to the Wall of Andor," Solomon announced as the group stepped free of the trees.

The Wall stretched higher than they could crane their necks and disappeared to either side. Captain ran her hand along the metal, enthralled at the cool touch and the strange vibrations beneath her palm. She took a step back to give it another long look before tilting her head to Zatook.

"So, uh…secre' password or somethin'?"

The warrior gave something almost like a snort before stepping up to the Wall and placing his hand flat against it. What was smooth and solid metal suddenly rippled like water, the waves spreading as the metal slowly drew apart to form an archway. The Wall was massive even in depth, the opening revealing a tunnel they would need to travel through before stepping into Andor proper. Captain let out a low whistle but didn't move, arm still very much looped with Amaya's. Sol gave her a knowing smirk, nodding to Amaya and patting her on the shoulder as he passed.

"I know I needn't warn you to be careful. Just be sure to check on the boys at some point and make sure they haven't burned down the ship," Sol teased softly. With that, he headed into the tunnel. He wanted to go first, to push past the apprehension that wanted to keep his feet firmly outside. A short hesitation had Lance following him, nodding to Amaya as he passed.

Jabez had been walking a bit on his own before they reached the Wall, trying to strengthen his legs. He gave Amaya a wave and started to follow after Solomon, but he quickly found himself caught by the Celestial woman. Jabez didn't resist as Amaya pulled him into a side hug with her free arm, squeezing him a moment. "You didn't really think you were escaping me, did ye?" she teased him. Touching her forehead to his she added, "Take care of yourself, Jabie. And keep them out of trouble, aye?"

"It's a promise," the young man assured her. "And don't get into too much trouble while you're roaming free."

Amaya gave him a look, mischief twinkling in her eyes. "Nothing I can't handle." She then gently pushed him towards the tunnel. She gave Tristan a hug next, holding the young man tightly. This time she lingered, her gaze shining with seriousness as she looked at the tunnel from over his shoulder. Finally, Amaya touched her lips to Tristan's brow before releasing him. "Not alone," she reminded him. "Lean on the others. Tell them what I told you about the king, so they know what to watch for." Amaya started to nudge Tristan towards the arch but instead found herself surprised when her nephew hugged her tightly again.

"Take care, Aunt Amaya," he told her softly. Amaya returned the embrace gently but firmly. It broke her heart feeling how desperate Tristan's hold was. So much so, that she didn't bother chiding him for the name.

"Easy, Tris," Amaya spoke reassuringly. "You'll see me again. It's going to be all right. Everything is going to be all right. Trust the Sacreds to watch over both of us." Despite her words, Amaya let Tristan decide when the hug was done. Eventually, he released her, and with a brave smile, he moved to head inside the tunnel. Amaya watched him head through the arch, holding Tristan's gaze when her nephew stole one more glance at her over his shoulder. Before Zatook could move far with the cart, Amaya darted her hand over the side to ruffle Rose's hood just to spite her. Amaya gave her a cheeky smirk. Then she met Zatook's gaze and flashed him an encouraging smile.

Rose made a half-hearted sound of protest, reaching up to straighten the hood. She had a feeling her braids were fine, though, considering she had practice weaving them to last. Zatook met Amaya's gaze, but unsurprisingly did not return her smile. He simply gave her a nod and started pulling the cart through. Nai had entered the tunnel with Jabez, walking alongside his brother in case he needed help. Soon enough, it was just Captain and Amaya left outside the border wall.

Slipping her arm from the teenager's grasp, Amaya gathered Captain into a firm embrace. "We won't be apart forever," the Celestial woman reassured her. "You'll probably decide you rather like me not hanging around you all the time." Amaya's smile faded slightly as she added, "Be careful of the king. Speak with Queen

Corianne, if you can. She'll help."

Captain snorted even as she returned the embrace. "Ye ken full well I willnae decide tha'," she teased right back. "I jus' donnae ken 'ow long we'll be away. An' I'm gonna miss ye somethin' fierce." For all she knew, this may end up being one of the longest times she didn't have Amaya around. Sure, the Celestial hadn't gone to rescue Tristan with them, and occasionally she would take off with Sol for something or another. But never long. "I'll see if I can find 'er wit'out causin' too much trouble," she promised. "Do ye wan' me to say anythin' to 'er for ye?"

"Probably nothing she doesn't already know. Give my regards, I guess, and let her know that her friends haven't forgotten her. For whatever that's worth," Amaya answered. "You've got Sol and Jabez with you still, so it's not all bad. I know you were missing Jabie, and you haven't really gotten much time with him lately." She brushed back Captain's hair and gently kissed her closed eye. "Be careful, Moon Sprite. Don't bite off more than you can chew." She gave the girl a stern look with that comment before smiling knowingly. "Off with you then. A new adventure awaits."

"Oh, ye ken I will," Captain teased right back even as she pulled away and turned to skip down the tunnel. She slipped her arm in with Jabie's once she caught up to him, only glancing once over her shoulder before the Wall started to close behind them.

5. The Shadow's Homecoming

As the group passed through, the Wall slowly slipped
closed behind them. It didn't force them to rush, simply
keeping pace with the last in line. Solomon paused at the
end of the tunnel, shading his eyes slightly as he stepped
back out into the sun. Stonewillow, the border town, was
just as he remembered, buildings of stone and thatch
stretching away from the Wall. The road had started to
cobble halfway through the tunnel, transitioning to a road
of smooth paving stones as they reached the town proper.
He wasn't surprised to find the streets rather bare. A
moving curtain here and a cracked door there showed
where the townspeople were. Though whether they were
nervous from the new arrivals or the escort awaiting
them, he wasn't sure.

Andorian soldiers stood nearby, alongside a contraption
he hadn't seen in ages. It boasted a few similarities to a
carriage, having rows of cushioned benches. But it lacked
a roof, wheels, or any horses, instead hovering a few
inches off of the ground.

However, it wasn't the transport or even the guards
that surprised him. A young woman stood alongside
the guards, chatting with them amicably. Her light
lavender hair was pulled into two buns, and she wore the
traditional priestess garb of a white kosode with a pair
of hakama. The blue coloration of the trousers was an

indication of her status, but he wouldn't have needed the color to know who she was. The resemblance was obvious. As she turned to smile in their direction, he immediately dipped into a respectful bow.

"M'lady."

She seemed surprised. "You needn't," she promised nonetheless. "Though I am surprised to see any of our visitors know who I am." Solomon was straightening even as the others exited. Despite her platformed sandals, the priestess went up on her tiptoes and peered over his shoulder. Despite all decorum, she let out a squeal and *ran* to Zatook as he exited, throwing her arms around him with a cry of 'Ookie!'. The man looked mildly surprised as he returned her hug before gently prying her away as if to get a good look at her. The stern gaze made her giggle. "*No*, I didn't sneak out again. I asked permission and everything. Father agreed since I offered to bring guards and reminded him you would be here."

Convinced, the warrior nodded and then gently spun her to face the others as if reminding her introductions were in order. Despite the soft 'I was getting there', the young woman faced the gathered group with a smile and curtsied. "Quite pleased to make your acquaintance and welcome you to our kingdom. I am Collette, Princess of Andor, daughter-heir to Corianne. I trust you've been taking good care of my brother?" Solomon could swear the warrior's eyes widened. Knowing Zatook and his distaste for attention, the man was likely considering heading back through the Wall that very moment. Or sinking into the shadows.

Lance had started to bow as the princess introduced

herself, but he hesitated when she mentioned her brother, straightening and looking at Zatook. The shadow fighter wouldn't meet his gaze, or that of anyone in the party, really. Solomon seemed unsurprised, so the older pirate must have known. The nearby soldiers were stone-faced, and the princess was beaming at them all, unaware of the sudden awkward revelation. The Wall slowly finished closing as Alconai, Jabez, and Captain exited. The pirate girl took one look at Zatook with the princess and instantly smiled. "Pleasure ta be makin' yer aquain'ance, t'en!" she answered warmly as they joined the others. Despite being slightly behind, there had been no missing the princess' enthusiastic greeting. Captain slipped her arm free of Jabez, pulling a dramatic curtsy. "I be Cap'n Isabella o' t'e *Effervescence,* also t'e Moon Chil'. T'is 'ere be Jabez an' Alconai, and ye go' Rose t'e Star Child in t'e cart bed. Tris'an, t'e Sun Child, is jus' beside 'er, and me guardian Solomon led t'e way in. I ken ye already me' Lance before, so he donnae need introducin'." The Doran girl didn't miss some of the tension slip from Zatook as she pulled the attention away from him.

Amusement warmed Jabez's chest as he caught Alconai's surprised expression in his periphery. Jabez felt rather taken aback as well with the revelation of Zatook being the prince, but from the man's reaction, Jabez doubted the warrior wanted them to make a fuss about it. For now, Jabez kept his focus on the princess and Captain, bowing with Alconai for the introductions. He appreciated Alconai's support though when Jabez felt his brother's hand on his back, helping him straighten again.

Tristan carefully bowed to Princess Collette, using the movement to hide his astonishment regarding Zatook. He also took the chance to regain his composure. Seeing the siblings interact had both warmed his heart as well as made it ache. He straightened, dry-eyed and calm.

If it was possible, the princess' smile grew even wider. "Excellent. Now that introductions are out of the way, please do make yourself comfortable." At this, she gestured towards the odd cart, and the soldiers moved to open doors alongside each bench. "My father hoped to ease your journey, as you have already come so far."

Captain had cast a glance back at the Wall, but she turned her attention to the…

"Wha' is tha'?" It was even stranger than she had been picturing.

"It's a TekCarriage. Most things that our engineers come up with have simple names: they just pop 'Tek' on the front, though there are a few exceptions. Depends who does the creating, really." As Collette explained, the soldiers were taking the packs from the group and piling them in one of the bench areas.

"One of those exceptions is the Wall," Solomon added.

"Yes! Apparently, its creator decided it was more imposing to just call it 'The Wall'." Collette giggled as she took Zatook's offered hand to climb onto the front bench. One guard hopped on beside her, while the other took up position on the back bench, which was also faced backward in order to keep an eye out on their surroundings. The others were left to filter in as they wished, with each bench taking up to four. Solomon clambered in before helping Jabez up; Alconai and

Lancelot also sat with them. Captain seemed to be shifting back into her element— she did ask Collette's permission first, but she hopped up on the front bench in excitement. Rose and Tristan were given a bench to themselves so the Half-Drow could stretch out. Zatook did not move to board, instead calmly closing the doors for the others. For a moment it almost looked like a sharp wind had caught his cloak before the fabric shifted to ink-stained feathers. He shook out his wings as he stepped back and then gestured the TekCarriage on.

Collette sighed after him, but then she lifted her hands. Runic circles sprang to life around her wrists in place of reins, and the TekCarriage gave a subtle shiver and started humming before lifting up a little further and gliding forward. The wind must have been somewhat shielded from the top, as it was more like a pleasant breeze without flinging everyone's hair or whisking away voices. Captain watched Collette in curiosity as the princess used hand gestures to control the transport.

"Runic magic, t'en? Is tha' wha' most Tek uses?"

"Quite a bit. It's said that our founder had many friends skilled in runic magic who were able to teach him and help create his first inventions. Some of our later pieces use embedded magic, enchanted crystals, and other such power sources. But the runic is certainly the most common. Anyone can learn the runes, even if they can't imbue them; often you'll find teams of innovators who have a mage on staff to power their inventions and help correct any incantations needed." She nodded towards the rein-like runic circles. "TekCarriages are set up so that anyone can drive them, but it always comes easier for mages. And, honestly, it's fun!" She laughed brightly, the sound carrying even to Zatook as he followed them above.

"'Ow fas' does it go?"

That got a mischievous grin, though Collette's smile smoothed before the guard glanced over with a raised eyebrow. "Some go faster than others," she explained, "but this takes what would be a month walking to the palace and trims it down to a handful of days."

Captain let out a low whistle. "Ye think t'is Tek could be applied to a ship?" She ignored Solomon's snort from behind.

"In theory, I don't see why not. In practice, good luck convincing Andorian engineers to bother with ships; we're land bound, and they're pretty focused on home."

"Wha' abou' if ye put a dagger to their throat?"

Solomon burst out laughing, but to Collette's credit, she didn't even flinch.

"I would imagine you could get quite persuasive so long as the mage doesn't walk in on you!"

"Can ye imagine flying ships? That'd be a sight," Alconai said, his eyes bright with the possibilities. "Free ta roam t'e skies like t'e seas."

"Have they tried applying the Tek to something smaller for individuals? I love horses as much as the next person, but craft like this built for one or two riders might be more plausible and marketable than flying ships," Jabez interjected. He certainly wouldn't mind having such a transport for his travels when he needed to get in and out of places quickly. He smiled beneath his mask when he caught Tristan perking up at the idea.

"So far the smallest is two benches, but that's not for lack of trying. The smaller crafts are a little harder to attune, apparently. Currently, there's a team trying for a single-seat and a double-seat style, one person per seat." Collette managed to direct her comments to them without having to crane her neck around or look away from where she was going. Trees and paths, farms and fields whizzed past to either side. "And machines that actually go up in the sky need to be tuned to the barrier." She gestured up, indicating the shimmer of magic far above even Zatook. "It's part of the Wall, so it carries the same complicated magics."

"Why does Andor have a wall?" Tristan asked, curious. "Is it because of the feud with Nocis or was there a greater danger before that?" Even as he asked, he watched the barrier above them. It reminded him of his mother's protective barrier that had been around Nikko Mori. "You have quite a lot of security."

"Honestly, I'm not sure. It was here long before my mother was coronated, though, so it's older than the current reign." She masked a grimace. "Andor tends to like its privacy…"

"And they consider most things dealing with magic sacred," Solomon noted. Collette inclined her head.

"Another reason you're hard-pressed to find a Tek team willing to share," she confessed.

"All t'ings considered, I cannae fault ye," Alconai remarked easily. "Advancements in kingdoms give ye an edge, bu' ot'er kingdoms can see ye as a threat or end up envying ye. Wars 'ave started over t'e simplest things."

For his part, Tristan was only partially listening now. As interested as he was in learning more about a place he'd never been, a slight pain had started to flare up in his chest, not unlike the ones he'd get due to the Talisman. However, he felt his body going cold. He watched as color drained from his hand, a sinking feeling settling in his stomach. It would pass, right? As bad as it could get, it always passed.

"Are you all right, lad?" Tristan's gaze snapped up at the sound of Jabez's voice. The man looked as pale as Tristan felt, but the ninja's gaze on him remained steady.

"I'm all right. Just some lingering after-effects of the battle, but I should be okay soon," the young man tried to assure him. Jabez studied his face intently for a long moment.

Just as Tristan thought that the man didn't believe him, Jabez reached over and squeezed Tristan's shoulder. "Okay." With that, the ninja turned back around and settled in for the ride. Sol had glanced back at Jabez's question, but he let the matter drop as well. Lancelot was slightly regretting sitting on the edge, practically clinging to the top of his door and looking like he might be a bit ill.

Rose opened her eyes, gazing up at him from where she lay on the bench, her head resting in his lap. *What's wrong?* Her voice slid across his mind like silk and starlight as she tapped into their mental connection.

At first Tristan considered downplaying his concern, but with his connection with Rose, he doubted he'd be able to keep it from her. *I don't know,* he answered her honestly enough. He hadn't told her or the others about the Talisman of Ruin in his possession or how it had been causing his episodes of agony. *I'm hoping it's nothing; I don't want to worry anyone. Everyone should be focusing on resting and healing, you included. Me as well.*

Let me know if it worsens. I still have my magic; perhaps I can at least ease the discomfort.

Tristan almost protested but decided against it. Instead, he nodded his agreement. Really, he wasn't sure if anything could be done at this point. He had a feeling that using the Talisman had weakened the seal used to contain its power. It was something that needed to be addressed, but Tristan wasn't sure what to say or who to tell. With everything they had gone through together, it was getting harder to remember that he'd only met them not so long ago. And yet, he hesitated to reveal this secret to them. Though with Captain's powers, it was likely they had at least a little knowledge of the Talisman. Thankfully, the pain subsided after a little longer. Despite his curiosity of the new land, the pain wiped out Tristan's energy. He soon slipped asleep.

The day slipped past the group, the two young women up front obviously fast friends while most of the party rested. Around midday, one of the guards dug out supplies for a meal, handing them to Lancelot and letting the knight wake the others and pass around the food. He did take a little for himself, his stomach slowly becoming accustomed to this odd travel. The transport proved its worth as the party rested and recovered a little more. When evening darkened the skies, the TekCarriage emitted small beams of light along their path. It was full night when Collette pulled into Lilymere, a small village along their route, and sent a guard in to book rooms at the inn. Zatook alighted with a soft *whoosh* before reaching into the carriage and gently grasping Tristan's shoulder to wake him.

Tristan woke slowly, sighing softly. Thankfully, he hadn't dreamed; he didn't think he could handle the emotions that his dreams would have dragged forward. Glancing up groggily, he nodded to Zatook in acknowledgment. His limbs a bit stiff from the long ride and the awkward sleeping angle, Tristan forced himself to his feet. He had to grab the edge of the carriage for a moment when his legs proved weaker than he was expecting, but he managed to stand on his own. Once he had her permission, Tristan lifted Rose, making sure his grip on her was steady before trying to exit the carriage.

Jabez had fallen asleep against Solomon, the ninja still recovering from his own battle. He did wake on his own when the carriage stopped though, years of being alert even in sleep ingrained in him. He gave Solomon an apologetic look and got to his feet. Since the dark pirate seemed to be watching Jabez, Alconai helped Lancelot out of the carriage. He patted his friend on the back sympathetically. Then he turned and offered a hand to Captain and Collette should they like help disembarking.

Captain easily took his hand as she hopped to the ground; the princess had come down next, graceful by instinct even though the others had recognized fairly easily she had little care for formalities. Collette softly thanked Alconai before moving to Lancelot and holding out her hand. "Here." He paused before hesitantly taking it, and a soft glow surrounded their joined hands.

"My thanks, Your Highness."

"Are unneeded, sir knight. They take some getting used to, I know." Collette assured him before donning a white cloak with golden embroidery, lifting the hood, and heading inside.

"The cloak of a priestess, but not identifying which one," Sol explained to the others as he nodded after her. "Clever, since she doesn't seem to care for royal attention."

"I had always heard from Sir Jeremiah that the queen is of a similar mind. I suppose it fair her daughter would feel the same," Lancelot noted softly. "And it makes for smoother travels, to be sure."

Solomon inclined his head. "True enough. Come on, lads, let's get everyone in and to bed."

Inside, the inn was still fairly bustling. Villagers mingled around the bar and tables with any visitors, exchanging news and rumors, tales and fables. A few had approached Collette upon seeing her priestess garb, the princess taking a few moments to heal any wounds and ask after the town without letting her true self be known. As the others dwindled inside and the second guard returned to move the TekCarriage, Zatook remained outside, the shadowed warrior staring at the inviting door before turning to walk further into the night.

Tristan paused when he noticed Zatook wandering off into the trees near the inn. As much as he wanted to stay with Rose, Tristan also felt a pang of sympathy. If Zatook really was Collette's brother, then that would make the king his stepfather at least. From what Tristan had seen and what he'd overheard the others talking about, the king didn't seem to treat Zatook very well. Once the rooms were situated, Tristan took Rose to one and helped her get settled. Despite his hesitation to leave her, he headed back downstairs and out into the night, stopping a moment to let Jabez know what he was doing. While the ninja didn't seem thrilled, he didn't try to stop Tristan either.

Soon, with the skills he'd learned living in the forest and the fact the man wasn't necessarily trying to hide his path, the Sun Child picked up Zatook's trail. He made his presence known so as not to startle the man. Zatook had been leaning with his back against a tree, staring thoughtfully at the ground. He glanced up curiously when Tristan joined him, but looked back to the ground. At first, Tristan didn't say anything, just standing with the warrior in what he hoped was companionable silence. After a moment, Tristan lifted his head, closed his eyes, and breathed deeply. The sounds of the inn faded as he drank in the sounds of the night dwellers rousing in the forest. Chirping crickets, the occasional hoot of an owl, the shrill shriek of a bat, and all manner of bustling life filled the woods with the nocturnal symphony. In this moment, Tristan felt a semblance of peace in his own stillness.

Zatook slid to sit, attentive if Tristan needed anything

from him. He had learned from the others Tristan used to live in a forest, so he assumed the lad had wanted something familiar without wandering off on his own.

Tristan let the silence stretch for a bit longer, relishing the moment to just stand still and be. Finally, he opened his eyes and met Zatook's gaze. "This is your home, but I get the sense you don't really want to be here. I've heard the others talking here and there, and then the Princess called you 'brother'. And yet, you don't seem like you've lived the life of a prince. King Traiborn isn't your father, is he?" Zatook looked away, shaking his head. The king wasn't his father, nor was he willing to fill in the role, but he wasn't sure how to convey that. Tristan's eyes shone with sympathy. "I know the situation isn't the same, but I understand at least in part. And I'm sorry that you're putting yourself through this to help us." He fell silent for a moment, thinking. Even before the words left his lips, he felt a pang in his heart with the memory, "I can...I can teach you. We can pick up where my sister...where she left off teaching you to sign."

Zatook paused, lifting his gaze back to Tristan's. He hadn't missed the hesitation. He didn't want to put the lad through more grief, but it would be convenient to learn. Finally, he nodded, but before Tristan continued, Zatook also pointed to his sword and then to the lad. Training for training seemed a fair bargain. And it might help the kid prepare for more foes like his father and the StormShaper.

The young man's gaze followed Zatook's movements. "Your style seems to be more like StormShaper's, and you wield shadows like my father. It seems fair to me," softly agreed Tristan, though he sounded uncertain. "My father was the one who initially taught me my sword skills. It was the one thing he reserved for the two of us. I never could beat him. And I never really cared for his style. I ended up tweaking it until my father finally relented and got me an instructor who knew better how to teach me that specific skill set." Tristan paused as he took in the sounds of the forest once more. So much like home and yet different. He continued, "My teacher's name was Almas. He encouraged my love of nature and exploration and taught me skills and swordsmanship that were better suited for that. He's the one who taught me about foraging and how to blend in with nature. He taught me how to hunt with the bow and arrow." A small smile tugged at his lips as Tristan spoke, his gaze growing distant in memories. The smile faded as he explained, "Almas left on a mission one day, and that was the last I saw of him. It wasn't long after that my mother fled with my sister and me." Tristan's gaze lowered to the ground as he tried to push away the memories now. "I appreciate your willingness to teach me. Hopefully, I'll get stronger so I'm not so useless in our future battles."

Zatook gestured for Tristan to sit. It was late, and the lad was tired. Their sparring could start after they had both rested. But the lad seemed to want to keep him company, at least for now, so they may as well work on the Language of the Silent.

As the woods grew darker, it became harder for Tristan to see to teach Zatook more signs. The weariness from the day and his emotional stress started to weigh more heavily on the young man. Gradually, he drifted lower and lower until he was lying curled on the ground at the base of a tree, slipping into a doze. Despite the slight chill, Tristan simply wrapped himself in his cloak and let the familiar sounds of a forest relax him. Having mentioned

Almas in the earlier conversation, the circumstances reminded Tristan of when he would camp with his teacher. Feeling safe in Almas's presence, Tristan never had trouble sleeping outside. It was one of the good memories he had of his childhood.

Zatook hesitated, though he let Tristan rest for a little while. Ultimately, he woke Tristan and ushered him back towards the inn.

Tristan groaned in protest when Zatook woke him. At first he curled up tighter, muttering about being tired. When the warrior persisted, Tristan slowly opened his eyes and took in the darker surroundings. It took him a little before clarity cleared the fog in his sleep-addled mind. Sitting up, Tristan rubbed his eyes and adjusted his cloak. Finally, he stood to head inside. When Zatook remained, however, Tristan hesitated.

"Are you staying out here? Shouldn't you get some rest in the inn, too?" the young man asked, concerned.

Zatook shook his head, motioning for Tristan to go in without him.

"Then why do I have to go in? Are you just tired of my company?" Tristan snarked softly. He understood if Zatook wanted his space, but he also felt concerned for the man staying outside alone. And Tristan didn't really want to give up the familiarity of the woods just yet.

Zatook gave him a flat look before making the sign for a rose.

"She's already settled, and it wouldn't really be appropriate for me to stay in her room," Tristan countered.

If possible, the flat look got flatter. That certainly hadn't been what Zatook was suggesting. He sighed. They were within Andor's border, but Traiborn wasn't one to watch him constantly. He decided to risk using his shadows; he held his hand out palm up, shadows darker than the night around them spelling out words.

For the morning, he clarified. *The others will be there, yes, but should you not spend what time with her you can? To add, if I am training with you before we set out tomorrow, then you need a good night's rest and an easy morning.* He waited a moment to let Tristan read before forming new words. *More than that, the soldiers will be reporting to the king on our arrival. It might seem like you are shunning his hospitality, and that could complicate matters once we are at the palace.* He hesitated before adding, *You would be wise not to appear concerned with me while we are here.*

"I can't help being concerned about my comrades. You've risked a lot already and done a lot for us," Tristan insisted. He hesitated a little longer, but he knew Zatook was right. The fact that Zatook not utilizing the inn wouldn't be seen as a slight to the hospitality was not lost on Tristan. However, he knew the situation was probably more complicated, and it wouldn't get resolved overnight. Tristan wasn't sure he really had any right to interfere at all. Still, the situation left a bitter taste in his mouth. "Fine. You win this time," the younger man replied with a defeated sigh. Then he added, softer, "Please be careful. I know we're inside the Wall, but...just...be safe. Good night, Zatook." With that Tristan returned to the inn and found the room he'd be using for the night.

***

In the inn, Alconai entertained some of the patrons with his energetic and theatrical storytelling. Normally, he might have pulled out his violin, but the instrument had been smashed when he'd been arrested. Still, the lack of instruments didn't stop Alconai from spinning grand tales. He captivated his audience with his voice and presence. He did send a wink Captain's way. Once he finished his performance for the night, Alconai moved to sit with Lancelot, not wanting the knight to feel left out or awkward.

"How's t'e sickness, Lance? Ye were lookin' a bit green when we stopped," Alconai teased, tankard in hand. He grinned at his friend.

Lance had stayed downstairs specifically to watch Alconai. It had been ages since he had a chance to watch his friend perform, and from what he could see the other lad had only gotten better with time. He lifted his own tankard when Alconai joined him before turning his gaze to the amber liquid within. "The princess helped, but I'm not really looking forward to tomorrow," he confessed. "I'm not sure which is worse: trying to reconcile what I did under Finnegan's control, or riding in that *thing*." He gave Alconai a half-hearted grin as he gestured towards the door.

"Ridin' in t'e Tek. Motion sickness be t'e worse," Alconai semi-joked. "For what it be worth, I be glad you're back. I was worried I'd lost me best friend ta blood magic, but I didnae want to give up on ye. Ye didnae deserve ta have that done ta ye. So, I'm relieved I was able ta help. Though, I'm sorry for havin' ta be a bit rough with knockin' sense inta ye." Alconai gave his friend a cheeky smirk that didn't quite reach his eyes.

Lancelot snorted. "Pretty sure I deserved worse than a grapple," he pointed out bluntly. "I have a lot to make up for, it seems. And I don't really know where to start." He glanced back up at Nai, gesturing towards him. "What about you? Found your brother, at least. And it certainly seems you found a lass." He grinned with the tease, indicating the stairs Captain had disappeared up.

Alconai choked on his drink. "Oi, donnae let dark pirate or mum pirate hear ye sayin' such," he remarked lightly. "I be likin' me head on me shoulders, thank ye. But she be a special one, cannae argue that." He flashed a self-deprecating smile into his tankard. "Probably looks like I be robbin' t'e cradle if'n I go for her."

Lance laughed. "You're not *that* old. And she doesn't seem the type to let you get away with stealing anything."

Alconai chuckled quietly. His attention strayed to where Solomon was currently guiding Jabez upstairs after Captain, the ninja going without protest. "As for me brot'er...s'more like he found me. Oi yosh, Lance, I can barely look at him in that outfit he wears. I meet his eyes 'cause I cannae bring meself ta look at t'e rest o' him. I still see me brot'er in those kind eyes, but I donnae ken how much is left o' t'e brot'er I ken. I donnae ken t'e things he's gone through. Just like I donnae ken what ye be feelin' or how ta encourage ye. I want ta help ye both, but I'm not sure how."

"The things that happen to us don't take away who we were, even if they change who we are," Lance pointed out, taking a swig of his drink. That very thought had been helping him stay sane while worrying over the type of person Finnegan had made him. "We all change, life just determines how drastically. And whatever happened to him doesn't take away the fact that you two are brothers. Besides, he seems pretty pleased to have you around. At least he didn't swat you off doting on him like I would have ten times over."

Swiftly, Alconai reached across the table and lightly cuffed Lancelot upside the head with a wry smirk. "I be allowed ta dote on me brot'er and me best friend," he remarked before adding more seriously, "It...it scared me ta see him so hurt. That's Jabie for ye. Went up against t'e Blood mage what killed Rose, and somehow held his own. But he's still a human fightin' demigods. He's still mendin' even if he looks fine." Images of Jabez appearing while slashed to bloody ribbons in the midst of the group haunted Alconai's mind. "I just got him back and almost lost him just as fast. How can I nae watch his every movement like he's going ta keel over at any moment? And yet, ye need me, too. At least Solomon's lookin' after Jabie; he's been watchin' o'er Jabie this whole time. So's Captain. And Amaya when she be here."

"We have to treasure the time we have; especially with such important events taking shape around us," Lance noted softly, staring into his drink again.

Alconai shook his head, trying to shake off some of the melancholy settling over him. Still he asked, "How'd ye get mixed up with t'e blood mage what was controllin' ye?"

Lance paused. "I…we kept getting put on the same assignments, but I don't really know when— or even how —he did it," he confessed. "I've been trying to remember, but no such luck as of yet."

Alconai nodded before clapping his friend on the shoulder. "No rush. Ye need rest, too, so donnae push yerself," he told his friend. "Circlin' back ta our talk o' ladies, any lasses catch yer eye before all this happened?" he teased with a wink.

"You think I had time for lasses?" Lance teased right back. "Sure, a few tried to win my favor, but I really haven't had much time to dwell on the idea. Even before my memory starts to fade, we were worried about war."

"I heard t'e rumors o' war," Alconai said. "Nocis and Andor be gettin' tense. It's a wonder more battles havenae broken out." His thoughts turned to the three wards in their group. For many, the Chosen Children stood as beacons of hope and protection from coming disaster. Then there were those who saw the Chosen Children as ill omens. The appearance of the Children always meant the coming of calamity. So the legends said anyway. Alconai wondered what it meant to be Chosen Children truly. If darkness was coming, what form would it take? Were they to stop the impending war? Or was there something else they needed to be doing? And then there was Rose's situation. What were any of them supposed to do about that? Silently, Alconai prayed to Shaddai for wisdom and guidance in the coming days.

Lancelot shook his head. "I don't know what King Arden is thinking," he muttered. "How he plans to get through the Wall to even try and fight. Let alone face a centuries old sorcerer-king and…well, whatever Zatook actually is."

"I be havin' me suspicions 'bout 'Ookie'," Alconai confessed. He smiled slightly when using the princess' nickname for the man. "I cannae say for sure, though." He stretched his back before taking a swig from his tankard. "They let traders and merchants through t'e Wall, aye? Always t'e possibility that someone's found a way in ta spy. One thing at a time. We be in no state ta try ta help at t'e moment."

Lance finished his drink. "Come what may with meeting the king, we'll face it better with a full night's rest. C'mon, you." He slid from his stool, playfully tugging at Alconai's sleeve until he followed towards the stairs.

6. The Strength of Virtue

As morning dawned, Lilymere began to stir. Zatook sighed as he stood, leaving his refuge in the trees and paying no mind to the villagers. Some stared, others hurried away. It was always the worst when someone dropped something or screamed, but he seemed in luck this morning. He had been tempted to wait and rejoin the party after they had left the town, but if he was going to train the Sun Child, then they would need to find times when they weren't traveling. He had found a good spot beyond the village that was close enough to the route to the castle that they could rendezvous with the TekCarriage. The chatter in the inn had gone silent as he walked through the door. Captain, seated at a table with a breakfast ready and waiting for the others, shook her head and took a drink. No use making a scene and causing trouble for the princess, but she had a mighty fine temptation to knock a few heads together. Instead, she lifted her mug of tea.

"Oi, Zatook. Come an' 'ave some breakfas' 'fore ye 'ead out wit' 'im."

The silent warrior hesitated slightly before moving to sit with her. She ignored the stares as a couple of patrons at a nearby table moved to one further away.

It wasn't long before Tristan joined them, helping Rose to the table as well. The young man looked better after a full night of sleep, his complexion not as pale as it had been. He still appeared world-weary but physically on the mend. "Good morning," he greeted both verbally and with hand signs. It had helped Arianna learn the signs better when Tristan did both while he spoke with her. However, he had gradually transitioned into just using the signs until she knew them all by heart. He hoped to do the same with Zatook; though, with them traveling with a group, he would have to speak the signs more so the others knew what he was saying to the shadow warrior.

Jabez and Alconai followed shortly, the latter getting Lancelot on their way down. Jabez was already in his usual attire with his cowl and mask in place despite sitting at the table with everyone. Alconai had freshened up a little before leaving his room so he wouldn't look quite so bedraggled. He flashed the group a bright smile. "Mornin', all."

Zatook very slightly nodded his head in greeting. It wasn't much longer before the guards came down with Collette.

Collette had once more disguised herself in the cloak and cowl, but once she reached the bottom of the stairs and saw how the villagers were acting around her brother, she swept off the hood as she greeted them all cheerfully and plopped herself right next to her brother. Zatook gave her a flat look.

"You hush," Collette quipped, dishing out her own portion. She paused a moment, tilting her head, then shook it. "I don't care."

Captain was watching curiously. "Ah, he'll talk in *yer* 'ead, eh?"

"Oh, yes, course. My apologies, I thought you knew we were in communication yesterday, as well. Oh, you must have thought me terrible not offering to heal your friend!"

Captain laughed. "Nah, I fig'red bein' a priestess, ye could tell. But 'e doesnae really like le'in' me ken wha' 'e's go' ta say."

"I would be more surprised if he let you in," Collette admitted, playfully nudging Zatook. The man simply rolled his eyes and watched the table. Despite joining the others, he did not join in their meal.

As Captain and Collette chatted, Alconai settled in at the table, taking his own share of breakfast. He'd given Jabez some space the previous night, so his brother hopefully wouldn't feel smothered. However, he'd started to doubt that decision when he'd met his brother in the hall. Even with the cowl shadowing his eyes, Alconai had noticed Jabez looked tired. His brother's movements were slower as well, as though Jabez wasn't fully awake yet, and then Jabez retrieved just a cup of tea and no food when he joined the group. Despite not wanting to pester his brother, Alconai felt his worry mounting. Even so, Alconai felt rather certain his brother still could lay someone out flat if the need arose.

Jabez stared into his mug. He'd had a rather viciously vivid nightmare the previous night and had had a difficult time getting back to sleep. Despite his lack of sleep and the raw emotional weight on him, Jabez had forced himself out of bed and down the stairs to face whatever new challenges awaited their group. He hadn't missed the way the locals reacted to Zatook's presence, but Jabez knew there wasn't much that could be done about that.

Not right now, at least. His gaze drifted to Tristan helping Rose get settled at the table before getting food for them both. Jabez's ice blue eyes tracked Tristan's movements. Even though the young man looked better, he moved a little more carefully, a little apprehensively. They needed to have a conversation, but part of Jabez hesitated to have it in front of Princess Collette. And yet, they needed to have this conversation before they reached the capital.

Despite her conversation with the princess, Captain cast an appraising eye over her current crew. A hint of concern touched her expression when she caught sight of Jabez, but she quickly masked it and pulled Lancelot and Alconai into the conversation so that Jabez wouldn't have quite so many eyes on him. 'Quite so many' included Solomon, who gently touched Jabez's shoulder as he sat next to him.

"You should eat, Jabez," he noted softly, taking advantage of Captain's louder conversation to be subtle in addressing the obviously tired ninja.

Jabez dropped his gaze back to his tea. He took a draught, careful to only lower his mask enough to drink. Replacing his mask and putting the mug back on the table, he responded quietly, "I know I should; I'm just not sure if I can." Not eating after having a bad night was a habit that both Amaya and Solomon had been trying to break him of for the last few years. Jabez had been doing better, but there were times that he still forwent food after a significantly stressful night. "Rough night. I was exhausted, but after everything that's happened…" he trailed off a moment before adding quietly, "My dreams came from jumbled memories of my time in captivity and my fight with the blood mage." Jabez refrained from voicing what else had haunted him in the night: the power Tristan had unleashed going out of control again. In the dream, Amaya wasn't there to catch the blast with her powers, and Jabez had to watch helplessly as everyone around him disintegrated. "Sol, your scimitars…how much power can they seal? What's their limit?" Jabez hoped Tristan couldn't hear him over Captain's conversation. He wanted to avoid putting more pressure on the young man right now, not before talking to him in private.

Solomon gave Jabez an appraising look, but then reached up to rub his chin. "I can't say as they've been shown to have a limit, but that doesn't mean they don't," he noted calmly. "The library in the capital might help me answer that question." He leaned his elbows on the table, looking thoughtful. "What we know of them came from what scrolls we had, but there were pieces missing. Andor is said to have an expansive library within the main palace, and rumors of an oracle to boot. I've not wanted to tax Captain with trying to look, so I was hoping we might find more there." His eyes drifted across the others at the table. "You're worried about that power." His gaze slid back to Jabez with the statement. "And you're not alone in that."

"Amaya somehow used her powers last time to contain the blast, but she's not here now. I'm trying to feel out our options if things go sideways," agreed Jabez. "I don't know the extent of Zatook's powers, and we have three humans who can't do anything against whatever that was. Rose is in no shape to try, and I get the feeling if she'd had something she could have done, she would have tried it when the castle was tearing apart. As for Captain, I don't think it would be smart to match her powers against it. The outcome could be far worse than it was at the castle." Reaching up, Jabez rubbed his brow thoughtfully. "It's a worry. I'm considering cornering Tristan in private to see what he can tell me, but this is something that the whole group should probably know. So, as much as I want to give the lad his privacy, this situation has the potential to become very dangerous very quickly." He looked up at this mentor. "What do you think?"

Solomon was quiet, but Jabez could practically hear the thoughts whirring through the older man's mind. "Captain would have to breach the seal, I think, to match. And we know how that would end. Zatook did seem to think he could brace against it before the need to do so was taken away. I'm not certain the full extent of his power when he transforms. It's an old magic, and we have no records of it in Ben-Gal." He took a bite of his own food and chewed for a moment. "If we were in the capital, the queen could aid us if she has her magic." He grimaced. "I have little doubt the king has something up his sleeve that could help, as well, but we're better off not letting him learn of it. He would likely have similar ambitions to Tristan's father, whatever those may be." He glanced at Collette's guards near the doorway, chatting sleepily. "I wouldn't bring it up near his men, and in private may be the only chance to avoid that. But you're right that the group should know." He paused when Zatook stood, the warrior moving over to tap Tristan's shoulder and motion him outside. Solomon adopted an amused look. "Apparently Zatook has a mind for some sparring with the lad," he murmured, then shook his head. "If you can bring it up around the group without the guards present, do so. Otherwise, give him a chance to confide in you. I have a feeling Rose knows more about the power than we do, since she seemed to understand what was causing him pain back in Nocis."

"I'm afraid he won't say anything to me without a push given he's avoided it so far," Jabez confided. "We can't wait for too long." He watched as Tristan checked with Rose before standing and following Zatook outside.

Tristan had donned his jerkin and leather trappings once more for travel, but he didn't draw his sword or dagger yet. He wanted to see exactly how Zatook wished to train him before drawing his weapons. He also felt concerned by the twinge in his chest, similar but not quite to the scale of the pain he'd endured the previous day. Still, he hoped it didn't return. That wasn't a conversation he was ready to have, and he didn't want to worry everyone.

Once they were outside, Zatook's shadows wrapped around the pair. Tristan had felt Zatook's teleportation previously, but this time he felt the color drain from his face when the shadows engulfed the duo. Tristan's mind instantly flashed to the fight with Tsukuyomi and being trapped in the darkness. The memories spiraled into reliving losing control of the Talisman. Tristan barely comprehended the open space around Zatook and him now or that the shadows had vanished aside from Zatook's sword.

Still reeling from the sense memories, Tristan missed Zatook's movements as the man tried to sign to him. And then Zatook rushed him with sword in hand. Instead of Zatook— his comrade —Tristan saw Tsukuyomi. Tristan found his feet moving back before the thought of retreat finished going through his mind, and rather than reaching for his sword, the Sun Child formed a shield with his twilight purple and magenta crystal. Zatook's blade pierced clean through and shattered the crystal, panic and haste leaving the shield brittle compared to others Tristan had made. Tristan didn't see Zatook's brow furrow, the hesitation and then realization flashing through his eyes. Tristan continued to back away until he lost his footing and stumbled to the ground. With wide eyes and heart racing, Tristan stared up at Zatook.

For a split second, Zatook debated trying to dodge around the lad or just grabbing him out of the way with… His shadows. It clicked. Rather than bearing down on him in an attack, Zatook used his momentum to drive his blade into the ground near the lad. He had stopped running, gazing down at Tristan with his typical calm stare. His hand left the hilt of his blade, and he slowly knelt in front of Tristan before placing a hand on Tristan's knee. And he waited.

The young man flinched with the touch as though he expected Zatook to crush his knee or throw him. Tristan's entire body trembled, the young man breathing shallowly with fear. It took a moment for Tristan to do anything aside from stare, his mind battling between staying present and getting sucked into his memories. Finally, he forced himself to breathe more deeply and focus on his actual surroundings. Tristan saw the open sky above him and felt the soil beneath his hands. He heard a slight wind rustling through the grass. A new memory filled his mind of Clovestein walking him through focusing on his senses to ground him. Now out of his initial panic, Tristan remembered having a similar reaction when he first started training with Nikko Mori's guardian after Tristan had just witnessed his father killing his mother. "I'm sorry," quietly said Tristan, his voice shaking ever so slightly. "I overreacted. I know…I shouldn't…I can't afford to do that in a real fight. Hesitation can be fatal in combat. Panic even more so."

Tristan pushed himself up into a better sitting position, but he left his leg beneath Zatook's hand, instead using the physical contact to ground himself further in the moment. "My father trapped Rose and me in his shadows. I could hear Rose and Tsukuyomi, but I couldn't see anything. Even my Child powers of sunlight did nothing to pierce the darkness. It was only with…" Tristan trailed off as he fisted his hand in the soil. "That's the point of this though, isn't it? I'm too weak to be useful. I couldn't protect anyone. I destroyed the castle and nearly killed everyone in it. I wasn't strong enough to escape the blood mage's control, and Rose died because of it," Tristan's voice shook now with frustration as he continued, "I failed to stand against my father, and Arianna died. Jabez…I didn't see the extent of his injuries, but he's still healing from them." Tristan stared at his legs. "I probably seem like such a whiny weakling to you. I don't know your history, but you're willing to brave it to help us. You look like you've been through a lot, but you're so strong."

Zatook remained still. He let the lad say what he needed to get off his chest, but the more Tristan spoke of failures, the more his brow seemed to furrow. He started to raise his hand, to sign, but thinking of all the letters got a slightly frustrated huff of air. He could write with the shadows, but then the soldiers might catch him and report it to King Traiborn. Instead, he patted Tristan's knee before removing his hand and standing to back up a few paces. He let himself transform, once more becoming the giant gargoyle-like beast. There was another boon to his transformation, after all. He lowered back to his knees, pressing a fist into the ground as his other arm rested across his raised knee.

"The success of our enemies does not mark failures

within us." He did his best to speak quietly, to keep the deep voice to a low rumble. "You only fail when you admit the final defeat." His black and purple gaze held Tristan's. "The ninja was wounded in a fight he chose, to aid his allies and the destined ones. His injuries are not your fault. The Star Child did not know the extent of her enemy. That lack of information is not a fault for blame, but a weak point to be strengthened. When the walls of the castle crumble, we do not walk away and let it fall. We build. As you will. With time." He hesitated before sighing. "I have had that time. You have not."

Tristan stared in awe of Zatook's new form. He had been inside the castle when the warrior had changed for the fight, so he hadn't seen the man in his transformed state. Instead of feeling fear toward the gargoyle-like appearance, Tristan instead studied Zatook with fascination. Even so, the man's words registered in his mind, and while he knew Zatook was right, Tristan couldn't help feeling doubt. The wonder faded, and he lowered his gaze as he spoke, "Sometimes I wish I could be anyone but me. I'm…I shouldn't be a Chosen Child. I'm a curse. I've done nothing but bring pain and suffering to those around me." Then realization dawned. "Your voice… you can talk in this form but not the other?"

Zatook paused at the lad's question, grimacing. "That is not what this discussion is about," the monstrous man pointed out flatly. "You are the Chosen of Shaddai. He does not choose wrongly. Between the pair of us, I am not the one to be admired." He straightened, back tall, and crossed his arm across his chest. "It is my duty to protect and aid you during this journey; even if this aid is to help you overcome your battles and realize your own strengths."

"What strength? What is there to admire about me? I don't know what I'm doing or what I'm meant to do. For all we know, I'm leading you all to your deaths! My father made it abundantly clear that he's not above murdering everyone around me to get what he wants," Tristan persisted, despaired. "And there's more than just him. He's in alliance with Jeremiah, the dragon knight. They did something— they did something to King Arden, and now he's dead. There's StormShaper, and Marilyn the blood mage, and who knows who else." Tristan faltered more with the next admission, the young man feeling defeated, "I don't know if…as much as I want to hate him…I don't know if I'm strong enough to kill my father should things come to that end."

"And this is why you have allies, same as them. Even if your strength alone would not suffice, you have ours as well. But strength is not merely physical prowess, Tristan. It is living in the woods for years and raising a young child. It is guarding a sanctuary forest. It is accepting when fate guides you to leave. It is rescuing a pirate lass you have only just met. It is facing what comes, as it comes, and doing your best." He hesitated for a moment. "You faced him head on and denied him, knowing the cost. Despite everything, you have shown us your trust. I was unable to protect you or your sister or the Star Child, yet still you seek to teach me. And from what I can tell, you carry a far greater burden than even the other Children understand. Though I do not know that burden's true form, I felt its power. I know it is what pains you."

Instinctually, Tristan reached up to grip his jerkin over his chest. Rather than the occasional discomfort it used to be, the pain now remained a constant dull ache. He knew he should tell the group; they deserved to know, especially if the Talisman got out of control again. "It's something my mother entrusted to me when she died. I'm supposed to safeguard it, but I was so desperate in my fight against my father that I used the power instead of leaving it sealed. It would hurt before, but it would always eventually fade. Now I feel it constantly at varying degrees. I think when I used it, the seal weakened." Tristan gave a humorless chuckle. "I'm the deadliest liability we could have right now." Finally, he pushed himself to his feet but didn't meet Zatook's gaze as he stood before the transformed man. "How can I get past my hesitation?"

Zatook watched him for a moment. He reached a hand down to the lad's chin before guiding him to lift his gaze. "You face what is coming. And we start with swords." Satisfied, he shifted back down into his human form and reclaimed his blade.

The interaction felt so nostalgic for Tristan, his mind echoing memories of his lessons with Almas and Clovestein. Recalling their wisdom imparted to him and Zatook's words now, Tristan took a deep breath before lowering into his own stance. He drew his sword. Crystal raced along his blade's edge, Tristan coating the sword to make it stronger. When Zatook attacked, Tristan forced himself to face the man. His heart hammered painfully against his ribcage as fear warred within him. However, this time he managed to parry the warrior's blade before shifting to counter with his own.

Zatook started slow and simple, parries and swings, while Tristan found his rhythm again. Once the lad seemed to finish grounding himself, Zatook increased the strength and speed of his attacks. Soon they were moving at the same speed StormShaper had used fighting Zatook.

Through what he had seen of the lad's skill, he knew
Tristan could keep the same pace. True to his word, he
stuck to swordplay for now. His blade evenly matched
Tristan's crystal, so he wasn't worried about needing to
reinforce it with his own powers. A plan was forming in
his mind. First, he would prepare the lad for StormShaper.
A step, rather than an immediate leap. He had centuries
on the kid; he should not have expected him to dive in
immediately after the last battle.

As he got back into the rhythm of battle, Tristan's own
swordsmanship began to shine through, though it was
obvious he relied more on speed than strength in his
fighting. He danced with Zatook much like he had with
StormShaper, but this time he wasn't exhausted from
running and there wasn't blood raining down on them.
Since Zatook was sticking with swords for now, Tristan
did as well, but he did use his crystal like a buckler now
and again to ward off the shadow wielder's attacks.
Every so often, Tristan hesitated as he fought back
the memories of his fight with his father and even the
memories of Marilyn using Tristan to fight Rose. He
fought his way through the trauma plaguing him and
managed to continue training. He had to if he was going
to be any help to Rose or be able to fight his father or
even Jeremiah again.

7. Tumultuous Truths

Captain stretched in the rising sunlight as she waited for the others to finish up their breakfast. Collette was inside convincing the innkeeper to take her money, and the soldiers had gone around back to claim the TekCarriage. But the Doran girl was watching the village. Since 'the King's Shadow' had left, as she had overheard the villagers referring to Zatook in deep whispers, Lilymere had slipped back into its usual routine— aside from the curious eyes trying to get a look at the princess. Children ran through the street, laughing and tossing a ball between them, as a few watchful adults sat nearby with their sewing and chatter. Every villager seemed to have a task, not just the farmers who had set out to work hours ago. Some were sweeping stoops and the smooth pavers that formed a road through the village. Aside from the sewers mending clothes, Captain could smell a tanner's nearby and the leather and hides they worked. For all their nonsense with her silent guardian, the townsfolk seemed happy enough. Content, rather.

Captain shifted away from the inn towards the edge of town, curious. The town didn't appear to have a blacksmith or these 'engineers' Collette spoke of, but they had several textile workers. She watched a collection of weavers as they tended their looms. The walls of their building were strips tied with cords, so they had been rolled up and tied away in the eaves of the roof while the weavers worked. Captain admired the patterns even as she watched their movements. Weaving. That was the name of her magic, though her threads were not of cloth. But she was finding she could use and interact with them, and she hoped watching the weavers would give her ideas.

She had already learned how to isolate a person's thread and use it to Watch them. If she held them just right and pulled, she could even teleport them— though the last time she tried to pull more than one, she flung herself halfway across Nocis and into captivity. She wasn't eager to try again.

The looms and clacking dowels were loud enough that the nearby workers didn't hear her, but she was able to tap one on the shoulder before gesturing in question if she could walk around and watch. The woman gave her a warm smile and a nod, so Captain started meandering through the open building. She needed to learn more. She needed to grow stronger. She needed to understand her powers. But she didn't have anyone to train her. She hesitated near one of the weavers, watching a pattern come to life on their loom. Unlike some of the more practical projects around, this was obviously meant to be decorative. An idyllic forest, prancing animals, a caravan of Doran. Captain stared at the brightly colored carts and wagons, the people dancing along the road, and her mind remembered the pain. It was only a flash, but she quickly stepped away and spun, walking a little faster than she needed to get out of the building. She didn't really pay any mind where she was walking, trying to leave the noise behind. The flashes of color. The blinding lights, the burning pain… yet the quiet was worse. So much worse. Captain took off at a run. She needed cover. Trees. Something. She clenched her hands as the warmth tried to force itself out of her control, out of her memories, and she ran. She ran until she was out of the village and deep into the surrounding trees before she stopped and dropped to her knees, hugging herself and shaking. She needed to stop it. She needed to stay in control. Captain closed her eyes and tried to ground herself, to remember Solomon's advice. She wasn't sure how long she knelt in the grass, but she knew when he joined her. Of course he did. Solomon always knew when she needed him, when her powers were fighting her again.

"It's alright, Isabella," he soothed, gathering her into his arms as he worked to strengthen the seal. He waited until the girl's breathing had steadied and the lights had faded from her eyes before he asked: "What happened?"

"I wen' ta fin' t'e weavers," she murmured. She told him about the pattern, the Doran. "I couldnae stop rememberin'. I felt i' all over again."

Solomon rocked her gently as he calmed her. "You're safe. And so is the village," he assured her, standing and cradling her. "We can wait out here for the others, I'm sure." He set her down gently, helping her brush off the twigs and debris from the woodland floor before guiding her back towards the road.

"'Ow am I s'posed ta save t'e world if I cannae even 'andle me own powers? We donnae even ken why I cannae. Tris and Rosie donnae seem ta lose control o' t'eirs."

"No, we do not. Though I half wonder if I might find an answer as to why while here in Andor." He turned towards her. "Even still. You have made immense progress, Isabella. You are coming into them. We simply let the seal slack too far, and now it's refreshed."

The girl scoffed. "Tha' would be well an' good if we were fightin' regular ol' humans," she noted sourly. Solomon arched an eyebrow at her expectantly. "C'mon, Sol, ye ken I ainnae a match fer some Celes'ial! An' 'ho kens if I can 'andle t'e maste' blood mage. Surely I'm nae 'ere jus' ta order people aroun', eh?"

"It's… hard to say. You have spent several years now learning how to be a leader and instruct your team. To make the utmost use of their abilities. It may be that you are *not* meant to be the one fighting. At least not alone. Though, from what Jabez said, you gave StormShaper a decent run once you tapped into your powers."

"Nae decen' enough. An' ye' I donnae dare train wit' t'e king's goons aroun'. I donnae want'em ta ken wha' I can do. We donnae need anot'er Lance gettin' interested in me abilities." She sighed, running her hands through her hair. "A' leas' Zattie can ge' Trissie out o' town ta train 'im. An Rosie's nae really worried abou' figh'in', since fer all she kens…well." Captain cleared her throat. "Wha' am *I* s'posed ta do?"

Solomon sighed. "I don't have the answers," he reminded her gently. "But perhaps something will present itself once we reach the castle. It seems everything is pointing us that way for now, including your lack of visions." Captain sighed but nodded. Solomon had already warned Jabez that he would be with Captain outside of town before taking off from the inn, so the crew found them easily enough once the TekCarriage was running. Solomon quietly helped her onto the bench with Jabez and Alconai, instead taking the spot where she had sat the day before.

"Zatook and Tristan will be waiting for us along the road," Collette informed them brightly after a concerned look after the russet-haired girl. Once Captain was seated—and had flopped her head against Jabez's shoulder —the princess started the carriage moving again. Solomon struck up a conversation with Collette about Andor, asking after the villages near where he had lived before.

Jabez shifted until he could free his arm from between his body and Captain. Then he wrapped his arm around her and pulled her against him, resting his head on hers. He had an idea what happened, but even if he didn't, he usually wouldn't press. His mind mulled over Solomon's words to him that morning. If the dark pirate hadn't been there, what would Jabez have been able to do to help or ease Captain when her powers gave her trouble? If Zatook hadn't been there, what would Jabez have done to help Tristan train? He knew it was useless thinking about 'what if's, but the questions tugged at his mind all the same. At one point, he caught Alconai watching him and Captain with an amused though sad expression. Reaching over, Jabez gave Alconai's arm a squeeze, the gesture bringing more of a smile to his younger brother's face.

By the time the group met back up with Tristan and Zatook, the younger man of the two looked exhausted and a bit pale. The pain in his chest had intensified during the training, but Tristan had persevered. He gratefully took a seat in the wagon after thanking Zatook and tried to get his muscles to relax. He did check on Rose to see how she was faring.

"Gee, Ookie, you don't normally try to murder your sparring partners," Collette teased as her brother joined them. He arched an eyebrow at her. "I know, I know, 'what sparring partners'," she teased. "Are you riding or flying?" Zatook hesitated before moving to climb in with Rose and Tristan. The former had been sitting upright this time, currently assuring Tristan that she was all right. Once the pair were settled, Collette started the Tek moving again. Zatook glanced back at Captain in concern, but he left her to Jabez and Alconai for now. Lance, unfortunately, was still trying to adjust to the movement of their transport and wouldn't be good for too much conversation. 'Practice makes perfect,' he had noted grimly to Alconai before hauling himself up into the bench to leave the inn.

How was training? Rose asked curiously, leaning gently against Tristan as they moved.

I'm working through some things. Namely my hesitation to fight someone with similar powers as my father; but, it seems even without the shadows, I'm falling prey to my own memories while trying to fight, Tristan answered her. *He's helping a lot.* He subtly indicated Zatook. *Though, I wish there was something I could do for him in regards to his home. I am teaching him to sign, so communication should start to be easier with him. How has your morning been so far?*

Perhaps there will be a way we can help. Only time will tell, Rose noted, closing her eyes as the land whisked past. *I'm sitting up, so that's something,* she joked half-heartedly.

You're sitting up. I landed on my rear when Zatook first came at me. What a reversal, he teased back with a small smile. *I'm glad you're feeling a bit better.* Tristan's mind once more thought of what Mythril had told him about helping Rose. Why did he have to lose her at all? Then again, if she would be going to Paradise, what right did he have to pull her back to this realm? *Rose, would you continue to stay if you could? Or would you rather be done?*

Rose hesitated, opening her eyes and glancing up at him. The question caught her off guard, and she wasn't sure she had an answer. *I don't really know,* she confessed softly. She was tired. And she had wanted an escape. And yet... *I would stay,* the answer drifted softly across his mind after a few moments of silence. *I don't want to leave.* Her hand subtly slid to his, twining their fingers together. And yet. She didn't want to leave Tristan. She didn't want to leave their task unfinished. She wanted to experience more of the world, more of her freedom. And now, as far as she knew, she wouldn't have that chance. She had closed her eyes even as she held his hand, hoping to hide the tears that were beginning to gather.

Tristan nudged her head with his affectionately. *I'm sorry,* he told her quietly when he sensed her distress. He wasn't even sure he was allowed to say anything. Mythril hadn't said that he couldn't. *Lady Mythril, the Celestial of Life, spoke to me after I woke from the battle. She told me that I might be able to help you, but I don't know how or what she means by that. Just know that if there is a way that I can help you stay, I will.*

Rose frowned. A way to help her? *I will not pretend to understand what is meant,* she noted quietly. *But I trust you.*

Your trust is more than I deserve, all things considered, Tristan voiced between them. His gaze drifted over the group. He knew he needed to talk to everyone about the Talisman, but with the king's guards around, he wasn't sure when would be the best time. Perhaps at the next inn? He fell silent as he watched the scenery passing by the carriage. Then he shifted his gaze to Zatook. "You decided to ride with us? I doubt I wore you out during training," Tristan commented verbally along with using the hand signs.

Zatook actually snorted slightly, glancing at Tristan with amusement. He shook his head, then nodded towards his sister up front. "I did not wish to ignore her the entire trip," he signed haltingly, keeping his hands low in case either of the soldiers cast them a curious glance. He had to spell out his words that way, but at least he got his point across. Rose glanced between them, slightly surprised how open Zatook was being with Tristan. And yet, she wasn't. Rose smirked as she settled against Tristan once more, letting the pair talk.

Tristan shared Zatook's amusement even as memories of Arianna filled his heart with pain. "Little sisters tend to do that to us stoic types," he joked softly. He grew solemn for a moment as he considered. "Do you have any good memories of being here with her?"

Zatook paused for a moment, debating how to answer. He finally settled on 'Do not let the king know' as an affirmative answer. "Andor holds three havens for me. My mother, when I am allowed to see her; my sister, when she is not occupied with her duties; and Tannen, when he can step away from the forge." His hands paused before adding, "Should the king discover I am learning to sign, he will wish to impose rules on when and to whom."

Tristan glanced at the guards for a moment. His stomach turned with unease with how much the king controlled

Zatook's life. Even Tsukuyomi hadn't tried to control Tristan to that extent before Tristan's mother fled. Tristan turned his attention back to Zatook and furrowed his brow with concern. "The King won't allow you to visit your mother?" he asked. He tried to keep his own signing more discreet. "How long has it been since you last saw her?" Tristan understood the pain all too well of being separated from his mother, but at least it sounded like Zatook's mother was still alive. Even so, it couldn't be easy for the shadow warrior.

Something almost like mischief glinted in his eyes. "Shortly before I found you," he signaled. "She sent me. Before then..." he hesitated, looking uncertain. "I lost count of the years."

"I'm sorry you had to leave after finally getting to see her again," said Tristan. "The least we can do is try to make sure you get to see her again before we have to leave Andor." He considered something Zatook had signed. "Your mother is the one who knew about us. Does she have a connection with the Order?"

Zatook nodded subtly, his hand resting on the pouch that held his medallion, but he didn't comment further. Instead, he glanced at the guard up front— who quickly averted his gaze.

Tristan caught the look and fell silent for a moment. Then he lifted his hands just enough that only Zatook would see. "Does the king recognize you or your mother as a member?" he signed. He stayed alert in case the guards caught sight of him. He had a feeling they probably didn't understand signing, but there was always a possibility. He also worried about if the king caught wind of Zatook learning and then restricting the warrior's communication as Zatook had predicted.

"Me, no. My mother…" Zatook shrugged a shoulder. He doubted the man showed the queen's status any regard, but he did not truly know.

Tristan grew contemplative with that information. For a little while, he watched the landscape and the people they passed. Despite what Zatook and Amaya had told Tristan, the people seemed content, and Collette didn't seem abused. Then again, she could just be really good at hiding the abuse. And what of the queen? "How does the king treat the princess usually? And what should we expect when we meet him?" Tristan signed after turning back to Zatook.

"He dotes on her. And expect propriety." He grimaced slightly before signing. "He is a good king, if a terrible person."

Tristan grimaced. It had been seven years since he'd worried about courtly etiquette. He wondered if he could remember enough from when he lived with both his parents. "Any customs or cultural differences I should know, then?" signed Tristan.

"You would have better luck asking Solomon."

Nodding, Tristan turned his gaze back to their surroundings, taking in the kingdom. Despite his trepidation, he couldn't help his curiosity.

A good king, but a terrible person. The phrase repeated

itself in Tristan's mind when they stopped at their next town, Cassiana. This one was larger than the last, with finer buildings of differing materials and multiple roads, rather than one through the center. Music filled the air, including from the inn. Much to Collette's dismay, Zatook had jumped over the wall of the Tek while it was still moving before they arrived. She knew he was fine, apparently he did it often, but it still freaked her out when he did so. Captain wasn't surprised, really. She could imagine the music screeching to a halt if people saw the King's Shadow walk in.

"Do all t'e towns trea' 'im like t'e boogeyman?" she asked Collette as they were disembarking. Collette sighed.

"No. The effect lessens closer to Petalore. They're more used to seeing him around with father and whatnot. But the outer villages only hear rumors and stories. And father rather likes the fearsome reputation for him, so he does nothing to correct it." Captain pulled a face, but before she could press further, the guard inside ran back out and gestured for Collette. She quickly excused herself and followed him before disappearing inside the inn. A few moments passed with the group not quite sure if they should follow or not before she reappeared.

"My healing services are needed, I'm terribly sorry," she explained. "They've got rooms all set up, so please make yourselves comfortable. They won't give you any trouble." She gestured towards the door, where the innkeeper waited, before taking off down the street with her guards after a small village boy.

"The duties of a priestess," Solomon noted quietly. "Let's get inside, then." He took the lead, walking up to the innkeeper and greeting them warmly. They were shown inside, past the main room that doubled as a tavern and up a flight of stairs. Collette had arranged a private space for them to eat, a cozy little parlor. Once the innkeeper moved off to see to their food, Solomon gave the group a lookover. "So. What do you think of Andor thus far?"

"I'm not sure what to make of it," Tristan expressed. "It seems fascinating, and I would like to see more of it, but there's...I don't know how to describe it. It doesn't quite feel right."

"Ye noticed it too, eh?" Alconai voiced from where he sprawled out in a chair. "Everyone seems content, but I cannae help feelin' that's just a pretty picture."

"The people seem to like their king, if nothing else. We're looking at this with the unique perspective of having gotten to see what Zatook is like without the bias of the rumors. For the most part," Jabez remarked. "You can be a good king and still be a horrible person. It's possible the people don't ever see what their king is truly like. Even then you can be a good person and still have harsh prejudices."

Solomon nodded. "It's easy to feel something is off when we know the truth and see the reaction to falsehoods," he agreed, moving to sit. "I can tell you from experience, the people love their royal family. And they don't know Zatook's true connection to the king. He's the nightmare parents tell their children when they misbehave. Traiborn knows how to rule a kingdom. His people live normal, happy lives. But everyone fears the King's Shadow."

"What is Collette a priestess *of*?" Rose was leaning her

chin on her hand thoughtfully. "You have referred to her as such, but I see no temples or statues of deities. And I doubt a king who lets his own family suffer is following the Teachings of Shaddai."

"Ah. Yes. Andor does not have an official religion, per say, but they all revere magic. A priestess is like a scholar and a mage rolled into one. Conduits of sacred magic, they learn more advanced spells and abilities than your average mage. It's why their healing is often in demand, even as they travel. Andor has decent medical ability without magic, but priestesses outdo it all. Some priestesses will pledge themselves to a Celestial or an element, while most simply dedicate themselves to the healing arts."

"Safe to say t'e princess falls under t'e latter? Focusin' on the healin' arts?" Alconai questioned. "Or is she secretly a Follower?"

Tristan watched the exchange curiously, but he didn't want to interrupt. He did glance at Jabez a couple of times when he felt the man's eyes on him. He had an idea why. If Zatook managed to figure out something was amiss, then surely someone as perceptive as Jabez had. And they had all seen the power of the Talisman, even if they didn't understand what it was. Even once Jabez turned his gaze to Solomon and Alconai again, Tristan still felt uneasy with the impending topic of conversation. He was grateful Jabez hadn't brought it up yet, but Tristan knew he couldn't delay too much longer.

"It depends how much of her mother's influence she has," Solomon confessed. "Collette was not born when I lived here. Corianne is officially of the Order, but we lost touch with her shortly before she was coronated…

then Traiborn ascended the throne, and she all-but vanished from the public eye. We have few details around Traiborn's ascension to the throne or Corianne's current status. We know she's in the palace, we know she's alive, but we have been unable to contact her privately. She is only ever seen in Traiborn's presence. I attempted to ask Zatook for more information in the past, but Traiborn's magic prevented his answer." He paused, folding his arms. "I should warn you. Though human, Traiborn and Corianne are both ageless. Traiborn has been king for a few hundred years now— since Zatook was a child."

Rose was frowning. "Whenever we would be in Petalore for diplomatic visits, I would see the queen. She was beautiful, but she rarely spoke. I caught her staring at me a few times, but I thought it because I was a champion."

"She likely sensed who you were," Solomon noted softly, though he looked concerned.

"An' le' me guess. 'Cause t'e king be so popular, we go'a play nice when we ge' t'ere," Captain griped, folding her arms and flopping back into her chair.

"Aye. At least until we learn more." Solomon gave Captain a look. "No being a bloodthirsty pirate and getting us exiled from another kingdom," he added teasingly. Captain just huffed.

"You said Corianne was coronated and *then* Traiborn ascended the throne," Rose noted softly. Solomon nodded.

"Corianne is the true heir. Andor is traditionally passed down through daughters rather than sons. Which is amusing, considering it was founded by a man. A widowed queen set the precedent in her will, and it stuck. Which makes it even stranger that Traiborn was able to come to power."

Captain tapped her chin, frowning. "What abou' Zatook's da?" Solomon frowned at her. "Ye said he's been alive longer t'an Traiborn's been king. So where's his da?"

"...ah." Solomon hesitated, sitting back in his chair. "That's another mystery. We don't know what happened to him." He held up a hand as Captain started to ask another question. "No. I won't tell you who he was. That's Zatook's secret to share, if he chooses. If he can, even."

The discussions of fathers arrested Tristan's attention. He thought of his own reluctance when he first told the group who sired him, but he had a feeling his and Zatook's reasons for hesitancy were vastly different. Very likely the king had forbidden Zatook from speaking of his birth father, and given the king was a sorcerer, he probably enforced that forbiddance with some kind of magic. The whole scenario made Tristan's blood boil. He wasn't sure how he was going to keep his cool in front of the king if the man started mistreating Zatook in front of them. Amaya's words echoed in his head about how she and the king disagreed in regards to how the man treated his family. Did she know what had happened to Queen Corianne? Did she know about King Traiborn being Zatook's stepfather? At the same time Tristan felt anger, he also felt icy dread. Her scar and Amaya's warning came to mind. With the questions circling in his thoughts, Tristan felt Amaya's absence more sharply. His eyes studied the group, the people he was learning to trust and whom his aunt trusted. If his mother and Amaya had been best friends, did Amaya know about the Talisman? Really, it didn't matter. The situation still needed to be addressed.

"There are…some things we need to talk about," Tristan faltered as he started. He almost shrunk into his chair when all eyes landed on him. "I…" he started but stopped, his mouth suddenly dry. There was so much; where should he even start? The Talisman? Amaya's warning? Should he tell them what he overheard while in captivity? Tristan lowered his gaze to the floor as he tried to decide what to say first. He startled when a hand touched his shoulder and gave a reassuring squeeze. His eyes snapped up to meet Alconai's patient gaze.

"No rush, lad," the entertainer assured him. "Speak in yer own time."

Tristan nodded and just breathed for a moment, working to steel himself. "Well, Amaya gave me some important information before she left," he began, "She's one of my aunts. My father's sister to be exact." He studied the group's reactions as he let that information sink in with all its implications.

Jabez wiped a hand down his face, careful not to dislodge his mask, as he muttered a curse under his breath. Alconai shared his brother's sentiments in a low whistle.

"I be thinkin' Celestials arenae as rare as we be told. They be poppin' outta t'e woodwork. And t'e same family ta boot!" the entertainer remarked with an incredulous smile.

"Aye, ye'd be surprised," Captain couldn't help it. "I ken a couple o' ot'ers. Like 'Maya, t'ey try an' keep 'emselves lesser ken."

"Including Lady Rin?" asked Rose.

"Nah. Her domain is too in'erconnected ta le' t'e king lock 'er up. Her Gate Guardian tends ta stay a' t'e gate, an' she rarely leaves. But 'er messengers do, an' often."

"If Amaya's your father's sister, then he's a Celestial, as well?" Rose asked, turning the conversation back to Tristan.

Tristan nodded. "Yes. Both of my parents were full-blood Celestials," he explained. "I wasn't sure if I should tell you before, and then I didn't get the chance when it would have mattered. To that end though, Amaya warned me that King Traiborn has ways of countering Celestials' abilities. It's how he beat her in their last altercation. Amaya told me that if not for the queen's intervention, King Traiborn would have killed her." He barely met Jabez's gaze as the man watched him calmly.

"There's a lot that makes sense now. And now we know something specific to watch for," the ninja said. "Amaya didn't happen to tell you what the king used on her, did she?"

Tristan shook his head. "She didn't specify, but she showed me a scar next to her heart. I'm assuming he tried to stab her in the heart with a blade and missed. She told me that the effect was horrible, though. Amaya lost her Celestial abilities and was vulnerable for a while before she got them back."

"Ah." Now all eyes turned to Solomon. He grimaced. "It's… well, we don't really understand it. The old records called it 'Celesbane'. It seems to be some kind of mineral that can mix with other materials like metal or dissolve into liquids. All we know for certain is that it existed before the Mists were raised and that it has a devastating effect on Celestials." He shook his head. "Most of the records from that far back aren't easy to trace down. Some, we just don't know the languages anymore."

"Is it likely that Traiborn would speak these languages?" Rose asked.

"I do not know. But I believe there are others who can." Here, Solomon hesitated. "Including Zatook's father, though I do not know if he would ever be of a mind to assist…"

"I don't suppose we'd get lucky enough for there to be anything on it in Andor's archives," Jabez remarked dryly. If the substance wasn't well known, then he doubted the king would have notes on it within easy access to outsiders.

"So we be runnin' from a Celestial ta a sorcerer who can go against Celestials while also havin' a Celestial in our group," Alconai commented wryly. He winked at Tristan. "I donnae suppose ye got anything more ta add that'll complicate this further?" When Tristan looked away a little guiltily, Alconai's eyes widened in surprised concern. "I was jestin', lad. What's got ye goin' pale all o' a sudden?" He knew Tristan had said that there were a few things he needed to tell them, but Alconai was trying to lift the young man's spirit with his comment, not make him squirm.

Tristan took a moment to mull over his words. Instead of telling them about the big thing complicating matters, he said, "When I was captured, I heard my father talking to Jeremiah the dragon knight about how they used Marilyn to kill King Arden. Since the king didn't have any heirs, the council gave the throne to Jeremiah. So we have complications inside Andor and out."

Lancelot sat up. "They did *what*?" Rose shook her head.

"My reaction when he told me the same," she explained softly before looking at the others. "Jeremiah and Arden were like brothers. Something drastic must have changed, but over time."

"Oi yosh," Alconai breathed. Then he paused before sputtering, "Back up a moment. What do ye mean 'dragon knight'?" Lance hesitated as well, the word seeming to sink in even as he worked to process the murder.

Tristan ducked his head with a sheepish grimace. "Right, that hadn't come up yet. When Rose and I fought him in Nikko Mori, Jeremiah revealed himself to be a dragon."

"So all the potential problem people are nae human, got it," Alconai snarked. "And they killed the human king of Nocis. I didnae like the man, but I wasnae vyin' for his death by any means."

Rose sighed. "I've noticed I'm having trouble remembering my more recent time with Jeremiah. It might be the whole death thing, or it could be related to whatever's happened to him. I just know that he…wasn't like this. He didn't care about being king."

Lance shook his head. "King Arden and Jeremiah had a pact that their kids would get married," he added, to Rose's apparent surprise. "Like, they weren't just friends. They were closer than Alconai and I are." He frowned at Rose. "You don't suppose it affected the rest of his family, do you?"

The Half-Drow shrugged. "I do not know. I can barely recall them at this point."

Lance frowned, folding his arms. "None of this is making sense," he murmured, still reeling to hear the famed knight was a dragon and a traitor.

"What of t'e blood witch? T'e one that fought Jabez?" Alconai inquired. He looked to Lancelot. "Ye said with Finnegan, ye'd lose time and such. Would a stronger mage be able ta alter memories? Or put something on a person what makes others forget o'er enough time?"

"I don't think she could have with blood magic," Rose noted softly. "At least not without my having noticed it much sooner. She claims to have trained under…someone I know. And I've never met a Drow-kin who could affect memory." She looked to Lance. "Yours could just as easily be explained from the times you were controlled. But I hate to treat it so simply when there are other issues at play."

"Aye, but i' be possible she's usin' fell magics," Captain

pointed out glumly. "If she's cracked enough ta go fer blood magic while nae bein' a Drow, 'tis nae tha' far fetched ta think she's done ot'er rotten stuff."

"Is there a way to reverse it? If Jeremiah is being controlled, and we break whatever is controlling him, won't that fix half our problem?" Tristan asked quietly.

Jabez spoke, "We'd have to be able to get close enough, I'd wager, before we could even determine anything. And that's not something we're doing right now." He didn't mean for his tone to be firm, but he also didn't want any of the Chosen Children to get it in their heads to go confront or even spy on the new king of Nocis. He softened his voice as he added, "We can speculate and check the Andorian Archives if we can access them. We'll need to decide our next course of action, but that may be something we'll be better able to do once we reach the capital. Aside from planning, we need to focus on healing and recuperating." He studied Captain, Rose, and Tristan individually. "If our last battle taught us anything, it's that we're woefully unprepared as we are."

"Aye, what 'e said," echoed Captain. "I could prob'ly figure it ou' if I go' close enough, but 'e's 'onestly t'e leas' of our concerns righ' now. Speakin' of, I hear dinner comin', so 'ang on."

There was silence around the table, interrupted by a hesitant knock. Lancelot moved for the door, letting the innkeeper in with a cart of food and drinks. The more mobile of the group quickly helped get the cart in and unloaded, Solomon thanking the innkeeper before they left. They waited for Rose to confirm that the innkeeper's steps had receded.

As the food was being passed around and everyone started eating, Tristan mulled over the topic he'd yet to broach. He was so used to keeping this particular secret, but Jabez was right. They had been unprepared, and that was partly Tristan's fault. That lack of information could have cost them dearly and still had the potential to hurt them. Tristan became momentarily distracted when he noticed that Jabez didn't really take any food for himself. However, the man's gaze catching his brought Tristan back to task.

"The power that you saw destroy the castle," Tristan began quietly, staring intently at his plate, "You can probably guess it was my doing. A mixture of my powers as a Celestial, the Sun Child…and the current guardian of the Talisman of Ruin." The resounding silence had Tristan wishing he could sink into the floor and out of sight.

"Oi yosh," Alconai murmured, "No wonder ye been outta sorts lately."

"Tha's a mighty unpleasan' name," Captain commented brightly.

"And one I have not heard before," added Solomon.

It was Lancelot who seemed to have an inkling, the knight folding his arms and looking troubled. "It's an artifact of great destructive power," he finally noted softly. Solomon looked at him in surprise. Lancelot sighed, running his hand through his hair. "I'm a sealbreaker," he confessed softly. "I don't have any magic of my own, but I can break seals and barriers and some spells through special runes or a type of channeling. So, of course, one of the first things we learn is the seals that should not be touched.

Ever. And that includes the seal on the Talisman of Ruin. There's…not a whole lot known about it in human records, though. I don't know much beyond that." Captain subtly scooted her seat a little further away from Lancelot, flashing him a cheeky grin. Lancelot snorted. "I can't break anything on accident," he assured her with a hint of a grin. "And it's much harder to do without a blade. Only a few sealbreakers can work without one." He hadn't been wearing his bracers or greaves as they traveled, partially to keep the guards at ease.

"I heard stories, but ne'er thought I be seein' it in person," Alconai remarked semi-lightly. He watched Tristan intently. Then a thought occurred to him as he recalled Amaya's bandaged hands and arms. Just as he opened his mouth to ask, he felt a sharp rap against his foot. Snapping his gaze to the perpetrator, he found himself on the receiving end of Jabez's pointed look. So, it seemed Alconai's brother had the same thought but didn't want to voice it to Tristan just yet. A part of Alconai wanted to protest, but he also understood not wanting to heap more guilt onto the lad. Instead, he turned back to Tristan as another realization came to him, "Yer injuries have healed, but ye still move like yer in discomfort if nae pain."

Instead of outright answering, Tristan continued his explanation. "The Talisman was originally made by an evil force that used the blood of a powerful being to create it. The power is corrosive— like acid or poison — but not necessarily evil." He folded his hands together as memories brought a different pain. "My mother was the guardian before me. I'm not sure if my father ever truly loved my mother or if he married her to have better access to the Talisman. As its keeper, my mother could summon the Talisman, but she was never to use it— its power of ruin harmful even to its wielder. When my mother refused to let my father use the Talisman, he tried to force her. I think that might be why he made the pendants that contain my and Arianna's essences: to control us so he could control my mother," Tristan's voice and eyes darkened with the recollection. "But Reina, the Celestial of Order, would not be broken.

After she gave birth to my sister, she took us and fled. My father pursued us to Nikko Mori and tried to recapture us. Things escalated faster than I could stop them. I was only eleven— what could I do? I should have done...*something*. Anything. But I had to protect Arianna, and my mother protected us. Things got out of hand, and my father struck my mother down. He claims he never meant to kill her, but I don't know if the truth of that is he really cared for her or that with her death the Talisman would pass to another. He would have to spend time finding the new keeper."

Shaking his head slightly to ward away the anger and bitterness he felt towards the monster that was his father, Tristan continued in a softer voice, "My mother managed to place the barrier for us to escape, and I helped her into a nearby grove of trees. My mother poured her lifeforce into the barrier she'd made so it would last for a long while after she was gone. It stood for seven years." Tristan took a deep breath to steady himself, letting it out slowly as his eyes shone with tears. "As she lay dying, my mother named me her temporary successor for the Talisman. I was to hold onto the Talisman and guard it until Arianna was old enough or someone else came along. No one came to claim it as the new guardian, and to be honest, I don't know that I would have ever given the Talisman to

Arianna. Especially not when I started having episodes of pain lancing through my chest. I could feel the Talisman's power as though it was leaking into me. I think during the fight with my father, the seal might have weakened." Tristan's gaze lowered in shame now. "In my desperation to beat him, I used the Talisman's power to fight my father. I think when I did, I made the seal worse. I feel it like a constant discomfort that spasms into full agony now and again. Used to, it would stop entirely, but now it only recedes to a dull ache."

"Is it killing you?" Jabez asked gently.

"I don't know." Tristan slowly raised his head, unshed tears glistening in his eyes. "I think…when my father fought my mother, he attempted to take the Talisman from her or tried to force her to use it. I think that might have been what killed her. That's why he…" Tristan trailed off as the tears spilled. He buried his face in his hands as he tried in vain to stop the flow of anguish. The memories of his fight with Rose, of his meeting with his father, of his sister's death flooded his mind. The psychological torture Tsukuyomi put him through reinforced Tristan's guilt and self-loathing over the whole situation. His voice came muffled and broken as he forced himself to continue, "He gave me the ultimatum. He didn't want to lose another keeper and start all over. So, he threatened to kill all of you, one by one, until I gave him what he wanted. And then…he pulled out her pendant and told me that to save my sister I had to give him—" A sob choked his voice before he could continue. And then suddenly he found himself wrapped in a strong embrace. The plate had been removed from his lap without Tristan realizing, and now someone held him tightly.

"Shhh, easy, lad," Alconai's voice soothed as he held the young man. "Ye donnae have to relive it for us. T'e monster gave ye an impossible choice. And as much as it hurts, ye made t'e right one."

"I couldn't let my mother's death be in vain," Tristan cried softly. "My father wants to use the Talisman to remake the world. I had to measure my sister's life against possible thousands."

"Aye, an impossible choice," Alconai repeated gently. "Ye made a mistake using t'e Talisman, ye ken that. But ye listen t'e me, lad. Ye didnae make a mistake when it came to refusing yer da t'e Talisman. I ken ye've heard it already, but Anna's death be yer da's fault, nae yers. As for t'e business with this Talisman, we'll figure it out. Yer nae alone." He slowly released Tristan and helped steady the young man when the Celestial pulled back.

Tristan wiped his face and took deep breaths to calm himself, so he could continue the discussion. "I can't control it if it gets out of hand again. I understand if you—" Alconai's finger on his lips stopped Tristan's words.

"Ah, ah," the man tutted. "What did I just say?" He gave Tristan a pointed look when the young man started to protest again. Alconai retracted his hand to let him speak.

Sighing in defeat, Tristan answered, "I'm not alone."

"Right. Yer stuck with us, lad. Better get used to it." Alconai moved back to his own seat to give the young man some space now. Alconai noted his brother on the edge of his seat.

In truth, Jabez had been part way out of his chair to go to Tristan, but Alconai had beaten him to the young man. Now, Jabez settled back a bit to get comfortable again despite how pensive he felt. "We might have some options for containing the Talisman. We'll keep a look out for any texts that might talk about it. If we get access to the palace library."

"S'long as we can pu' up wit' t'e resident ass," Captain noted with a snort. Then she shook her head. "Rewin' a sec. T'ese pendants ye mentioned? I Saw t'e one yer dad used against Arianna. Ye said t'ere is one fer you?"

Drying his eyes on a cloth napkin, Tristan breathed for a moment until he was sure he could answer clearly. "Pendants that contain essences," he told them. He'd really hoped to be done talking, but he guessed he should have expected the group to pick up on that bit of information— especially Captain and Jabez. Tristan noticed the ninja focusing on him with a calculating gaze. "I can see essences, but I've never learned to manipulate them. Few can since it's a rather tricky and frankly dangerous endeavor. One mistake could severely damage the host if not kill them." Tristan thought back to his lessons with his mother. "When she was pregnant with Arianna, my mother told me about the pendant my father managed to make when I was born. Essences of newborns are easier to manipulate because they're more malleable, still in the process of separating from the mother. My mother knew my father would make a pendant for Arianna." Tristan stopped to drink some tea and give his voice a moment of rest.

Then he continued, "Essence pendants are similar to blood stones. They give more control over a person but at a higher risk. If the pendant breaks, and the person isn't nearby for the essence to return to the body, the essence will scatter and be lost. If that happens…" Despite his best efforts, here Tristan choked a little, hearing the crack and shatter of Arianna's pendant. Seeing her essence escape. Trying to save as much of it as he could, no matter how futile the attempt. Swallowing down his emotions, Tristan managed to keep going, though his voice was thick, "The person dies. Even if the person is nearby, there's a great risk the essence won't return to the body without a manipulator to guide it." Tristan fell silent as he tried to wrangle his emotions once more.

"Does your father have your pendant?" Jabez asked when Tristan seemed to be a little calmer.

"No. My mother hid my pendant years ago; I don't know where. Arianna's she took with us when we fled the castle," Tristan stated. "After my mother died, I hid Arianna's pendant in Nikko Mori. While we were racing to rescue Captain, my father invaded the forest. He said that he…that he cut down anyone who opposed him and razed the forest to the ground until he found the pendant."

Captain crossed her legs, looking thoughtful. She tapped her fingers along her arm. "We should ken t'e truth o' that soon," she piped up. "I had been plannin to try an' fin' time to take a look at some things, an' I'd rather do so before we reach t'e palace. I donnae ken 'ow much t'e king kens about our powers, so I'd rat'er try nae ta use 'em too much while we be t'ere."

Tristan lifted his gaze to Captain at that. "Thank you.

Their…wellbeing has been weighing on me." He had almost said fates, but that felt too close to implying their deaths. Until he heard otherwise, he forced himself to believe Clovestein and the others were still alive.

Captain nodded before glancing at the parlor's window. "We also need ta fin' a way ta le' Zatook ken e'ryt'ing we been talkin' about."

Jabez grew contemplative as the group finished eating. As much as he wanted to trust Zatook given everything the man had done for them, Jabez wasn't sure how deep the king's control went. "Can we tell Zatook everything?" he asked, meeting Captain's gaze meaningfully.

"Aye. I ge' yer concern, bu' if t'ere's one t'ing Zatook 'as mastered, it's omission. T'e king's been known ta fin' stuff ou' regardless, bu nae from 'im."

The ninja nodded. Forcing himself to release some of the tension in his posture, Jabez attempted to lift some of the heaviness that had settled over the group. "In the interim, we should get some rest," he suggested. "I know sleep might be difficult given the circumstances and topics of late, but we should at least give our bodies some respite." Jabez stood and ruffled Tristan's hair as he passed him, feeling a bit of relief when the gesture earned him a small smile from the young man.

8. Lullaby in a Storm

Tristan helped Alconai set the cart up with the empty dishes for the innkeeper. He then helped Rose get to her bed in the set of rooms down the hall and get settled. Tristan retired to his own room, but instead of sleeping right away, he pulled a journal and writing utensils from his pack that he had recovered from the group. The leatherbound book was one of two he kept— this one a gift from his mother. She had started getting him journals and canvases when she learned how much he enjoyed drawing and artwork. He had enjoyed drawing all kinds of things, especially when he studied nature with Almas. The second journal contained writings of the things Tristan learned about survival in the wilderness as well as pictures and entries about the things he'd seen and experienced.

The journal he now held contained his pictures that were more artistic. Many depicted people from the castle and even landscapes of the grounds. There were a couple of pages he skipped over as he flipped through the book, unable to bear the sight of his mother and his sister at the moment. Instead, he settled on a blank page and started sketching the room around him. At first, he kept the image realistic to what he saw, wanting something simple to distract him from the harrowing memories dredged up in the discussions. However, Tristan soon began to add elements, letting his imagination guide him

into a different reality. He drew faeries dancing through
the air and leaving glittering trails in their wakes. He drew
them playing across the furniture in the room. One faerie
started to grow vines through the window and along
the walls while another helped flowers bloom from the
foliage. Sketching the playful scene brought lightness to
his chest that he hadn't felt for a while now. It didn't erase
the pain of grief completely. Instead, it made him think of
Arianna and how she loved playing with the faeries. Even
as tears stung his eyes, Tristan smiled at the memory. His
head snapped up when a knock sounded at his door.

"It's Jabez," the familiar voice announced.

Tristan made sure his eyes were dry and his voice steady
before he answered. "Come in."

Jabez entered the room, silent as the ninja he was. Closing
the door behind him, the man approached Tristan's
bedside. Jabez always moved gracefully, whether walking
or fighting there was fluidity and purpose. Control and
experience. Tristan had noticed it before, but he had never
fully watched the man. "May I?" Jabez asked, gesturing to
the bed. When Tristan nodded, Jabez took a seat beside
him. The man remained silent for now, simply sitting
with Tristan. When Jabez studied the still open journal on
Tristan's lap, the younger man blushed a little, feeling a
bit self-conscious of his work. Glancing bashfully at Jabez
Tristan found the man looking at the drawing with a soft,
fond expression.

"I suppose I shouldn't be surprised by your skill given
the creative designs in your home," Jabez praised. "It's
beautiful."

"Thank you," Tristan responded quietly. "I've always liked doing creative work— whether it's drawing or carving or even with my crystal sometimes." Before the discussions, Jabez's gaze felt intent and investigative. Now, the man's demeanor exuded calm and understanding. Warmth. Tristan's heart ached as he was reminded of Almas. Jabez and Tristan's former teacher had similar temperaments and presences. Almas had always made Tristan feel safe. Right now, Tristan felt safe.

"I wanted to check on you," Jabez admitted as he looked at Tristan.

Tristan remained quiet for a moment, gathering his thoughts. "I know I needed to tell everyone, and I hope I can get through telling Zatook without breaking down," he said. Then as his eyes stung again and he looked away, he whispered, "It hurts." They sat in silence as Tristan tried to keep his emotions in check. He felt like he'd been doing nothing but breaking lately. And yet, when a sturdy arm slowly wrapped around his shoulders Tristan instantly leaned into the side embrace. Jabez held him tightly, and after a moment, his hand started rubbing Tristan's shoulder.

"I lost both my parents when I was young," Jabez told him. "My father died when Alconai was still just a toddler. My mother died when I was older but still a child." Tristan looked up at him, but Jabez's gaze seemed far off. "My mother was an Order member, and one day she answered a summons. I'll never forget the day we got the news we hoped never to hear."

When Jabez lapsed into silence, Tristan asked, "Does the pain ever go away?"

"With time it eases, but it's never completely gone," Jabez answered, focusing on Tristan once more.

"How do I push through it?"

The ninja's look grew thoughtful before he answered, "Be kind to yourself. While my stepfather grieved my mother, I did everything I could to help around the house and look after Alconai. I wanted to be there for both of them. I pushed down my own pain and focused on them and the chores. But ignoring it didn't make my grief go away; it didn't change the fact that my mother was gone. Finally, I couldn't hold it back anymore. I was in the garden trying to water and weed the plants when it truly hit me. My mother always worked in the garden, and I would help; but I wouldn't get to help her anymore. My grief overflowed until my tears watered the garden. The next thing I knew, my stepfather pulled me into his arms and cried with me."

Jabez lifted his hand from Tristan's shoulder to instead place it on the young man's head, ruffling his hair a little. "Cry all you need to, Tristan, and don't belittle yourself for it. Also don't be afraid to seek comfort. There are things that need doing, but you're allowed to ask for help. Even if it's just needing someone to be there for you while you take a moment for yourself." Tristan nodded as a couple of tears spilled. He leaned against Jabez's shoulder as the man held him. Tristan didn't sob, but he didn't try to hold back the tears either.

"My father," Tristan spoke after a bit, "is the Celestial of Reflection. One of his abilities is that he can make someone relive their memories— force them to reflect. He can turn your own mind into a living nightmare of all your mistakes— both real and not." He shuddered as he remembered the hell his father forced him to endure. "My father made me relive my memories of my mother's death, of fighting Rose, of Arianna. I already felt like it was my fault, but he showed me how it really *was* my fault. And that even if it wasn't, I still failed to protect them. I hurt Rose. I left Arianna and failed to protect her."

"Shh, Tristan," Jabez soothed. "You don't have to tell me. You've relived quite a bit already tonight." He started stroking Tristan's hair. "I'm sorry you had to endure that. Torture is horrible no matter the form it takes."

"Sounds like you're talking from experience," Tristan murmured.

"I am." The young man tried to lift his head to look at Jabez fully, but the ninja kept Tristan's head on his shoulder. "But that's not a discussion for tonight. If you need to talk, then I'm willing to listen, but don't force yourself. As for me, I have people who help me when I need them. How are you feeling?"

"Like a wrung-out piece of fabric," Tristan confessed dryly.

He heard the smile in Jabez's voice, "Sounds right. Do you think you can sleep any, or did I make that harder with our talk?"

Tristan shook his head, careful not to dislodge Jabez's hand. He enjoyed the comforting feel of someone petting his hair. "I think it helped to get it all out there. And to know that someone else understands. Not that the others don't or haven't been willing to listen. It just feels a little truer now that I've heard your story. Thank you for sharing with me."

"You're welcome. Though, you really should try to sleep."

Sighing, Tristan nodded but stayed still for a bit longer. Finally, he asked ever so softly, "Jabez?" He continued when the man hummed in acknowledgment, "Will you stay? At least until I fall asleep?"

"Of course."

Tristan put away his journal and supplies before getting comfortable under the covers. Jabez retrieved a spare blanket and lay down on top of the covers. He pulled the spare blanket over himself as the two of them settled in for the night.

***

As the others drifted to sleep, one by one, Captain watched each of their threads. She ran her fingers along them, but she did not pry into their minds or dreams. Instead, she let her gaze wander to the ceiling as she took a steadying breath. Then, she switched eyes.

Troops marched through fields; soldiers left their homes; a nation mourned a king. A woman with white hair and one green and one gold eye reached a hand towards Captain, calling something the young girl couldn't hear. Zatook sat beneath the stars, gazing at the sky. A woman with violet hair slightly darker than Lettie's stood upon a palace balcony, doing the same, her hand clutched over her heart.

A forest...

A forest spread before her, wounded but healing. Elves moved together in groups, singing more strength to the plants and tending their wounded. A Drow lay amongst them, injured but healing and wakeful. An elven woman with silvery white hair and a man dressed with a pirate's flair moved through the forest, the threads around them gleaming with power as they lent their magic to healing the forest and its inhabitants. Nikko Mori grew once more.

The white haired woman again, wearing a white gown. Thin, swirling red lines decorated her pale flesh. She sat at a small wrought iron table, serving herself tea— yet there were two cups.

The violet-haired queen, retreating to her room. Moving to a small keepsake chest and releasing a spell.

Jeremiah, bedecked in the armor of a royal, his gaze turned to Andor, an army in his wake.

Fire. Ash. Destruction. There wasn't enough time for screams. Only crying, crying and pain and bright colors and darkness and someone laughing—

Captain bolted upright, closing her eye and slamming her hand over it as if that actually helped. It made her feel better, at least. She took deep, steadying breaths. She needed to focus. Focus on what was new. Nikko Mori was not destroyed, and its guardian lived. She had seen the queen. But who was the other woman? The one who seemed to be calling her? Captain shook her head, sliding from bed and moving to pour a small glass of water from her room's pitcher. She had half a mind to pull herself out to Zatook and give him some company, honestly. But he might be enjoying the break from everyone.

Solomon would throw a fit, too. With a sigh, she moved back to bed. She hated this time of the year, and yet she never seemed able to escape the effects. But now there was the added danger of the Andorian capital looming. Could she keep her powers in check in the castle? What if she couldn't? Captain stared at the ceiling of her room. The woman kept bugging her. She was tempted to look again, see if she could learn anything. She took another deep breath and opened her eye.

***

Collette was the first in the tavern area for breakfast in the morning. She seemed a little groggy, but mostly hungry from her night of healing. Rose had actually met Tristan at her door and managed to walk down the hall, but she needed help with the stairs. One by one, everyone was gathering to eat. Except for Captain.

While Collette was the first in the tavern area, Jabez had also woken rather early. Ironically, he had had a sleep full of nightmares of his life as a shadow in Shaedra. Before Tristan had woken, Jabez had slipped away to his own room to freshen up and compose himself. He felt exhausted, and he lacked the appetite for breakfast. Still, he knew he should show up, so the others wouldn't worry. Once downstairs, Jabez quietly greeted the group, touching Tristan's shoulder as he passed the young man. Tristan gave him a grateful, small smile in acknowledgment. While everyone got settled, Jabez noted Captain's absence. The ninja waited a bit, not wanting to smother the girl and hoping he was just being paranoid. Given the month and everything that had happened, he'd be more worried if Captain didn't act a little off. Still, the lateness was unlike her. Finally, Jabez headed back up the stairs to her room. He paused only momentarily when Alconai followed him, his younger brother's eyes concerned. Instead of trying to dismiss his brother, Jabez simply continued to Captain's assigned room. He knocked firmly on her door. While he wanted to avoid scaring her, circumstances made him want to eliminate the possibility of her not hearing him. He waited long enough for her to answer if she was going to.

"Excuse me, Captain," Jabez announced just in case before opening the door and stepping inside. Alconai stayed in the hallway so as not to crowd the girl.

Captain still lay atop her bed, fully dressed, though now she was on her side and slightly curled. Her fingertips twitched occasionally as if reacting to something in sleep. But as Jabez drew closer to try and wake her, there was no mistaking the rainbow gleam beneath her eyelids. However, the colors also curled like dust around the tips of her fingers. As the dust trailed away into nothing, it slowly turned an ashy grey. Her brow was furrowed, but she made no noise or sounds of pain.

Jabez furrowed his brow as he moved over to her, kneeling beside the bed. "Captain," he called gently but firmly. Should he get Solomon? Damn. What a time for Amaya to be away. She always seemed to know how to reach the girl, but Amaya wasn't there; and Solomon was downstairs. And Jabez was right there. He took Captain's hands in his and had just enough time to hear Alconai's panicked shout before the world vanished around him.

After a moment of darkness, the world was replaced with a chaotic whirlwind of images and voices. Some, Jabez recognized from his travels with Captain. Others were of people and places he had never seen before. A prevalent scene was a stormy night filled with rainbows and ash. A person made from ash reached for him, empty mouth open in a scream, but before it could reach him a woman burst through the figure and dispersed the entire vision. She was tall and pale, her skin painted with thin, winding red lines. Her white hair slowly faded to red at the ends and was pulled back into a chignon. One green and one golden eye held his gaze. She reached out her hand to Jabez, calling something he couldn't hear. She seemed to realize her voice didn't reach him, beckoning instead.

Despite the chaos swirling around him, Jabez's experience in battle helped him remain calm. Likewise, he was no stranger to memories muddled into nightmares. As the woman beckoned him though, he hesitated. She didn't seem like a memory, or a passing vision given she was actually interacting with him. Well, he was in this far, he might as well. Carefully, he made his way to her, his eyes intent on her.

Once he neared the woman, she turned and walked through the whirlwind. The visions almost seemed to part around her as she guided him— and guide him she did. It wasn't much longer before he saw Captain, or at least her mental self. The lass was on her knees with her hands in her hair, desperately trying to block it all out. The visions, the nightmares, the Woman She Couldn't Reach. She just wanted it to stop. A pile of ash swirled around her, the dust occasionally forming screaming faces. As Jabez drew nearer, he could hear cold, deep laughter amidst the chaos.

Jabez gratefully inclined his head to the woman. Then he moved to Captain, ignoring the vortex around them except to avoid the worst parts, and knelt before her. "Captain," he called gently. His hands gripped hers carefully but firmly enough to ease them from her hair. Guiding her hands he had them grip his shirt instead and coaxed the girl into his arms, holding her tightly. "Izzy," he called again. "I'm here. It's going to be alright. Focus on me." The laughter bothered him, but he concentrated on Captain for now. He tried to think of how Amaya would reach her, what the woman would do. This was the first time he could remember Amaya being away from Captain during this month. No matter what was going on, Amaya had always made a point to be with Captain during this time. But she wasn't there. As Jabez sat with Captain now in his lap, he recalled a song he'd heard Amaya sing to her when the girl was distressed. "Come away with me, little moonlight dancer. Join me on the waves, under the stars. Dance with me where the dolphins play, round and round with bubbles in the deep. Listen not to the roll of thunder, 'tis the waves drumming. Raindrops be the sea foam spraying, lightning-schools of fish flashing. All to the rhythm of the sea," Jabez's voice as he sang sounded rough though not unpleasant, testament to the things he'd endured. He focused on comforting the girl in his arms and drowning out the cacophony around them. "Fear not for Father Ocean is watching, guarding, his children and friends of the deep. So dance with me, little moonlight emerald. Together, let's dance and sing the song of the sea."

As Jabez held her and sang, the visions around them slowly stilled, replaced by the sight of a bright beach along the ocean. The steady wind and waves washed over them, a few gulls calling through the memories. He felt Captain take a deep breath in his arms before everything faded away. And then he was back in the inn, staring into the eye of a very groggy Captain.

Jabez smiled beneath his mask and released one of her hands to comb his fingers through her hair. "Morning," he greeted softly. It was then he noticed his brother's presence a lot closer than before.

After his initial panic, Alconai had slipped into the room to watch and wait in case the exchange was nothing to worry about; though, he'd been ready to run to get Solomon if things started to look worse. Now he knelt beside Jabez, calm concern in his eyes. "Ye two be well?" he asked.

"Physically, I think so, though it seems a few of us are having rough nights as of late. Can't imagine why," Jabez added the last part in a wry tone. Then to Captain he asked, "Think you can handle breakfast? Or should I go get you some tea for now?"

Captain held up two fingers in answer. She felt exhausted, and her head was aching. Judging by how annoyingly bright it was, she wouldn't get any real sleep before they had to head out for another full day of travel.

Jabez rose from his position, giving Captain's hand a reassuring squeeze, and headed downstairs to retrieve some tea for her. His own head throbbed with pain like when he'd had the psychic connection with Captain while she was captured. He kept a hand on the wall as he walked, his legs feeling unsteady after his stroll through Captain's tempest of memories. Carefully, he made his way downstairs and caught Solomon's eye as Jabez moved through the inn and to the counter. While he waited for the tea, Jabez tried to shake off the unsteadiness in his limbs and focus past his headache.

Solomon wasn't long in joining Jabez at the counter, leaning his back against it casually and folding his arms. "What happened?" His eyes glanced over Jabez's posture, seeming to pick up he wasn't feeling fantastic at the moment.

"Captain's powers flared. She was stuck in visions all night, so she didn't get much if any sleep. I'm getting her tea for the headache she's bound to have right now," Jabez explained. "Alconai is with her at the moment." He sighed. As much as he wanted to relay the visions and the woman to Solomon, he knew it was a discussion best had away from strangers.

Solomon frowned. "That's two days now she's had trouble," he noted softly, his brow furrowing. "That's bad even for her." He glanced around to see if anyone was listening before murmuring for only Jabez to hear. "She almost lost control at the last village. I had to strengthen her seal. But I didn't feel anything this time, so the seal isn't the issue."

Jabez met his gaze levelly. That wasn't good news. "What can we do? If her power goes out of control and causes Tristan to lose control...the repercussions would be catastrophic." He quieted when the innkeeper brought the tea; Jabez took the cup with a polite nod. Once the innkeeper moved away to tend to other customers, Jabez sighed. "I'm not sure how to help either of them."

Solomon shook his head, straightening from the counter and moving with Jabez towards the stairs. "I am unsure. We cannot very well stay where we are. All signs point to the palace." He grimaced. "Perhaps I need to speak with Zatook. I don't know what all he can do with the runic magic when he transforms. Perhaps he also has a way to calm her. My seals are holding, but I cannot make them any stronger. I am, at least, still able to calm her powers if I am near."

"At least it's something," Jabez remarked. As dizziness washed over him again and the headache intensified, Jabez waited a moment to ascend the stairs, careful not to lose his balance. When the spell subsided to a more manageable level, Jabez resumed the trek. Once they were closer to the rooms, he asked Solomon, "Say, do you know anything of a white woman with red designs along her skin? Captain and I both saw her in the vision, but I don't think she was a vision."

"Red designs?" Solomon frowned, folding his arms to think as they walked. "Like ribbons? All one line?" At the man's nod, Solomon looked slightly perplexed. "That sounds like the Celestial of Time," he noted slowly. "But according to our records, she hasn't been seen in almost six hundred years."

***

Meanwhile, Alconai had stayed with Captain despite his concern for his brother. Jabez had seemed fine, but what had Alconai's brother learned to hide? Still, Alconai remembered how Captain had been after Lancelot overtaxed her eye, and this seemed a similar scenario.

"Ye gave us a bit o' a scare, lass," he told her gently. "If'n ye were feelin' nostalgic for our time in jail, I could o' just knocked Lance upside t'e head with me yo-yo again."

159

Alconai flashed her a soft smile.

Captain snorted at the joke, giggling slightly despite her headache. "Oh, aye," she mumbled, "'tis all par' o' me grea' plan ta get ye alone."

"I be nae complainin'. Worse places ta be then trapped with a pretty woman," Alconai teased her. Slowly he reached up and gently combed his fingers through her hair, giving her plenty of time to stop him or give a noise of protest. "Is there anythin' I can do ta help ye?"

Captain sighed, leaning into the touch slightly. "Nae really," she confessed. "T'ere's few 'ho can when i' ge's t'is bad. Mos'ly Sol, 'cause he controls t'e seal. Bu'...I donnae ken. Somethin' feels differen' from t'e ot'er times I havenae been able to control it. Like...somethin' else is makin' it 'ard. But I donnae ken what i' coul' possibly be."

"Does it help ta talk about them?" Alconai questioned. He couldn't imagine how scary all this must be for her. Each of the Chosen seemed to be going through something or other lately. Though, he supposed that their lives hadn't really been easy before recent events either.

"'Onestly, I couldnae really follow most of i'," she confessed. "I go' a good look a' Trissie's ol' home, an' t'en jus' a bunch of flashes. Some memories I'd rat'er forget. An' a woman I donnae ken." Her brow furrowed slightly. "She didnae seem like a vision, t'ough. I' was like she was tryin' ta ge' my attention or somethin'."

"Mayhap she be tryin' to lead ye where we be needin' to go next," Alconai suggested. "Ye might ask Jabie since he seemed to share some connection with ye. I'm sorry ye had ta see memories ye'd rather forget. I have those now and again. Mostly of when Jabez was kidnapped."

"Aye, I linked us back when I firs' go' captured by our shiny knigh' friend," Captain noted, rolling onto her back and brushing her hair away. "So 'e wound up inside me 'ead when he came ta check on me." Her gaze was far away at the mention of memories. She hesitated to tell him more, but she fully clammed up when she heard Jabez and Solomon down the hall.

Alconai refrained from pushing her. Instead, he simply sat with her to keep her company. His ears did perk up when he heard Jabez and Solomon quietly conversing outside the room's door, probably discussing what had happened with Captain. The conversation lapsed into silence before Jabez and Solomon entered the room.

Setting the tea on the nightstand beside the bed, Jabez softly asked Captain, "Can you sit up and drink, or would you like some help?"

"I'm a'ight," Captain assured him, sitting up and swinging her legs off the bed before taking the cup and blowing on it. She arched an eyebrow expectantly at Solomon.

"I hear you met Time."

She frowned, taking a sip of her tea. "Is tha' supposed ta be some kin'a vague sage-y-ness bou' me brain goin' whacky?"

"No," Solomon assured her flatly. "That's the woman you

and Jabez saw. Literally Time, a Celestial."

"A'ight. So wha's she doin' in me 'ead?"

Solomon shook his head. "I have no more knowledge of this than you, for now. Nor do I know if we can trust her," he added, looking to Jabez. "We know very little about the Celestials. The best one to ask would be Amaya, and she's not here."

"An' I donnae t'ink I coul' reach 'er a' this rate," Captain confessed softly. "T'ere's somethin'...messin' up me 'ead whenever I try an' use me powers. I's nae me."

Solomon frowned. The mysteries just kept increasing. He sighed, running a hand over his head. "We should be reaching the capital today. Do you think you'll be alright?"

Captain shrugged a shoulder. "Should be s'long as I donnae try an' See again. Or fin' somethin' tha' se's me off." Solomon hesitated.

"We don't really have a way to guarantee that..."

She grimaced. "Aye."

Alconai's eyebrows disappeared under his hat as they rose in surprise. "Time, eh? Ye be meetin' some interestin' people," he remarked to Captain. "Ye think it might be somethin' near t'e capital that's messin' with yer powers? What about Tris and his deadly Talisman? Will it mess more with t'e seal?"

Jabez shook his head. "There's no real way of knowing,

but we have to keep pressing forward. We don't have any other options at this point." He felt his body sway a little but managed to steady himself. "I'll check in with the others. See when we'll be ready to leave." He reached down and gave Captain's hand another squeeze, careful of his balance. Then Alconai and he left the room, Solomon behind them once he was sure Captain would be all right on her own.

Alconai moved down the stairs first, but Jabez hesitated a couple of steps above his brother. The stairwell suddenly swam in his vision as pain slammed into him. Every possible ache in Jabez's body flared as his strength left him. Through the agonizing haze in his brain, Jabez realized what was about to happen, and then his stomach lurched as his foot continued through open air before landing wrong on a step too far down. His legs buckled with the impact, but instead of hitting merciless wooden edges, he collided with a sturdy body, Alconai's cry muffled by the throbbing in Jabez's head. His brother's arms tightened around him even as Jabez finished collapsing.

9. A Matter of Older Brothers

Alconai's back impacted the wall as he planted his feet on the steps, trying to keep both men from tumbling the rest of the way down the stairs. Alconai's gaze snapped up to Solomon before looking to Jabez. "Jabie? Oi, Jabez," he called quietly but urgently. He knew Jabez hadn't looked well, but he hadn't wanted to pester. Alconai took some comfort in feeling Jabez's hands weakly gripping Alconai's arms and hearing a groan from his sibling.

Solomon caught up to them quickly, guiding Jabez's weight off of Alconai and hefting the ninja up in his arms. "Let Tristan or the princess know we might need some of their healing, and grab some broth for him," he noted softly to Alconai, carefully turning around and getting Jabez back up the stairs and to his room.

Despite his concern for his brother, Alconai forced himself to move calmly down the stairs and to his group's table. He touched Tristan's shoulder and leaned down to speak into the young man's ear, "We need yer help upstairs. I'll explain there." Tristan shot him a worried look but followed when Alconai headed back toward the stairs. They paused at the counter to order the broth. While they waited, Alconai told Tristan lowly, "Jabez collapsed, and Sol and me thinks he needs healin'. Sol told me ta get ye. Or t'e princess."

"What happened?" Tristan asked, concern lacing his voice.

"I donnae ken. I ken he hasnae been lookin' good, but I donnae be sure what it be." Once the broth arrived, Alconai led Tristan up the stairs.

"He fought at the castle," Tristan stated thoughtfully.

"Aye. He fought t'e blood witch," Alconai answered. He paused to look back at Tristan. "He's t'e one that broke t'e blood stone controllin' ye."

"Marilyn. She used my body to kill Rose. How bad were Jabez's injuries?" Tristan questioned. He knew Jabez had been recovering from the fight, but Tristan hadn't been awake when everyone was at their worst. Something haunted flashed across Alconai's gaze and Tristan felt his heart sink.

"Cap'n gave him her brews ta help. We thought they took care o' t'e worst of it," Alconai told him.

"Alconai, how bad?"

The minstrel sighed heavily. "If nae for Cap'n teleportin' him out, I've no doubt me bruddeh would be dead." His heart went out to Tristan at the young man's crestfallen expression. Instead of dwelling on what happened though, Tristan steeled his features and moved to Jabez's room.

By the time they made it into the room, Solomon had convinced Jabez to stay lying down, gotten him settled, and stripped the outer layer of his clothes to check his remaining wounds. Lighter wounds had already healed thanks to Captain's Concoctions, and the worst of them had closed but not fully healed, so Jabez had been continuing to apply poultices and rebandage in the mornings. Solomon was currently cleaning the area, though he stepped away when the other two arrived. "If you can take over with this, I can help him drink." His demeanor was calm and steady despite everything.

As much as it hurt to admit, Alconai understood why Solomon made the request. Sighing, he handed Solomon the broth while Alconai took his place to clean the wounds that needed it still. "He's...more comfortable with ye," Alconai acknowledged softly.

At Alconai's remark, Tristan averted his gaze from Jabez's face. He moved over to where Alconai knelt and studied Jabez's worse wounds. Tristan recalled when he practiced healing while living in the forest: animals and people. However, as Tristan reached out to hover his hands over the worse injuries, he hesitated. His mind's eye saw the red veins that had woven through his crystal, the Talisman's power twining with his own and running parallel to his Child powers. What if he couldn't control it? What if he hurt Jabez? Tristan's heart pounded painfully against his chest, making him all too aware of the ache from the Talisman's corrosion. The pounding filled his ears as he remained indecisive. A hand weakly touching his startled Tristan.

The quiet of the room returned just as a weak voice spoke, "It's okay." Tristan barely kept himself from looking up at Jabez's face as the man continued, "You don't have to, but I trust you."

"Oi, stop tryin' ta be everyone's bruddeh for a bit and let

us take care o' ye," Alconai sniped incredulously. He did give Tristan a sympathetic look. "Ifn' ye need, ye can go get t'e princess. No judgement."

"I came to help," Tristan protested weakly. "I can…do this." He knew how to heal, and the princess already had so much to do. Collette was doing so much for them. However, Tristan's hand refused to stop shaking no matter how much he willed it. His face crumpled in despair as Jabez's hand lightly squeezed his.

"It's all right," the man's voice sounded a little stronger but just as exhausted. "No one needs to spend their energy. I'll be fine in time to leave. I can rest in the carriage."

"What you can do is drink your broth," Solomon half-teased, half-encouraged, shifting Jabez to help him drink comfortably. "Tristan. You're alright. There is no battle here, no warring destructive magics." Jabez recognized the calm in Solomon's voice. The tone the man had used many a time to draw Jabez back to himself or to calm Captain. "You are stronger than you give yourself credit for. One mistake, especially one in the heat of the moment, does not erase years of practice and control. There is no danger here to disrupt your thoughts." He was careful not to drown Jabez even as he spoke to the troubled Celestial. "The choice, in the end, is yours. You will overcome this at your own pace. But I have full confidence in you."

Tristan thought back to his training with Zatook and the man's assurance that he would overcome those trials. They had no reason to, but these people trusted him— had confidence in him. Now he just needed to have confidence and trust in himself and in Shaddai's choice to give him this power.

Closing his eyes, Tristan thought about his lessons with Clovestein and even his lessons with Almas. Both men taught him ways of healing, and Tristan used knowledge from both to determine the right way to heal a wound or ailment. He imagined the warmth of the sunlight and rustling of leaves to help calm him. He thought of how he liked to help people, animals, and plants. Healing was about helping restore. He felt the warmth accumulate in his hands, stretching from his palms to his fingertips. Opening his eyes, he saw the golden light illuminating the back of his hand where the symbol of a fiery sun appeared. The tongues of flame from the symbol disappeared beneath his sleeve where they twisted and spiraled up his arm to his shoulder. Tristan gave Jabez's hand a reassuring squeeze before letting go. He hovered his hands above the worse injuries and focused his Sun Child powers to start stitching the wounds closed. He went slow and careful, conscious of the Talisman but able to heal without interruption. He healed the wounds until they were the same as the surface ones. Not wanting to exhaust himself, Tristan left the surface injuries to heal on their own.

"As I live and breathe," Alconai whispered, grinning in awe. "That was spectacular ta see."

Tristan blushed as he retracted his hands. "Thank you. All of you," he told them. "I appreciate your encouragement and patience."

"Of course. We are all in this together," Solomon assured him. He had helped Jabez finish drinking the broth while

Tristan focused. "The pair of you should get breakfast. I can handle things from here. I'm sure the others are wondering where you've gotten off to."

Alconai reached around Tristan to grip Jabez's arm reassuringly. Then he moved to leave, squeezing Tristan's shoulder as he went. Once Alconai was gone and before he himself left, Tristan's eyes studied Jabez's wounds once more.

"What happened? The wounds were healing slowly but surely. There was no infection," Tristan told them. "Your body was strained— overworked."

"I've been trying to do mundane things like walking on my own. Apparently, my body doesn't agree with me on how much it can handle when," Jabez commented. He moved his mask back into place and let Solomon help him with his outer layers. "Thank you for the healing. It'll help a lot."

Tristan nodded. "Let me know if you need any more, and I'll take a look. Though, you should still take it easy. I didn't heal them all the way because I want to pace myself, but I can take the edge off if need be."

"I'll keep you in mind, but I don't want you to wear yourself out either. We've got poultices and the like for pain management. Still, I'll let you know if it worsens beyond those," Jabez agreed. He watched as Tristan left to get breakfast. Once Jabez was sure that the young man was out of earshot, he said to Solomon, "I don't suppose there's any way to keep this from Captain, is there? She'll note the timing and probably blame herself." He moved to swing his legs off the bed, determined to be up and about despite how sore he still felt. The healing really did help him move a lot better though. "I'm thinking whatever has Captain's powers acting up might be rippling out across our connection a bit."

"I do not know. She hadn't left her room yet by the time I carried you back," Solomon noted, keeping an eye on his ward's steadiness. "But she tends to discover things whether we tell her or not. And we do not know what all she saw before you were able to calm her."

"I just don't want her to feel guilty for something out of her control. I chose to reach out to her and let her reach out to me. I don't want her to become afraid of doing that," admitted Jabez guiltily.

"Indeed. It is something for us to keep an eye on, and discuss with her if need be," Solomon agreed. "For now, we should join our companions and see what today has in store."

***

By the time Solomon and Jabez returned downstairs, Tristan had left to train with Zatook and Collette was getting the TekCarriage ready. Captain once more slid into the bench with Jabez, Alconai, and Lance, but this time it was Alconai's shoulder she leaned against to get some sleep. She got Rose's attention before telling her telepathically what she had seen of Nikko Mori so that the Half-Drow could fill Tristan in later.

Once again, they met Zatook and Tristan outside of town, and once again, poor Tristan looked exhausted— though not nearly as much as he had the day previous. This time, Zatook motioned for Solomon to sit with Rose and Tristan so that he could sit with his sister. Captain was fast asleep by this point.

Captain told me what she saw, Rose informed Tristan. *Clo is alive, and the forest is being regrown. It definitely took some damage, and there are injuries, but everything is healing.* She touched her hand to Tristan's encouragingly. *They will be well.*

Tristan sighed heavily with relief. *I'm glad to hear it.* He felt an immense weight lift from him with the news. They were going to be okay. He still felt guilty that hiding his sister's pendant in the forest had brought such danger to the denizens, but it was one less thing to occupy his mind. *I told Zatook about the Talisman. The only one who doesn't know is Amaya, but I have a feeling she knew more than she let on with us.* Tristan glanced at Rose as he asked, *How are you feeling today?*

I'm well enough, all things considered. Solomon says we'll reach the capital today. We should rest while we can. I get the feeling we're all going to need to be in top shape to deal with the king.

***

True to Solomon's word, they approached the capital city of Petalore as the sun was setting. The first sign that they were getting closer came when the road remained paved after they left a town. Then the towns became closer together, and soon the city loomed on the horizon.

171

The first thing they noticed was the wall. It wasn't nearly as large as the one encompassing the kingdom, but it was impressive in its own right. The city wall was made of elven-sung stone. It reached up in an overlapping style, forming what looked like lotus petals; the stone of the wall was even a soft pink. Just inside the wall, the city began— and like the wall, everything had been sung from stone. The city itself was built in a circle, with magnificent buildings that slowly rose higher as one approached the center. Another, larger petal wall surrounded the palace. And still the palace stretched above it all.

The stones that made up the different buildings in the city were solid and brightly colored, with shingled roofs of varying colors, some a single color and others sporting multicolored shingles on a single roof. All the windows had glass within, even a few stained at the palace. Collette kept the TekCarriage moving, though at a much slower pace as they made their way through the city. The streets were laid out like a spider web, all main roads leading towards the palace wall while smaller roads created circles within the city limits. As they passed through the streets, the citizens would stop and bow or curtsey until the carriage was gone, all eyes on Collette as she drove.

The palace itself put the rest of the city to shame. Gleaming pearlescent walls shone in the lowering sun, reflecting a myriad of colors. It almost looked like the castle was made from shell lining rather than stone. Eight grand towers stretched towards the sky, each with a different colored roof to represent one of the main elements of magic: earth, wind, water, fire, ice, lightning, light, and dark. A ninth tower rose in the center of them all, with a rainbow crystalline roof to represent the power of Aether.

Collette finally pulled to a stop just outside of an archway that led beneath the lotus wall surrounding the palace. The guards and Zatook hopped off first before helping the others. A gaggle of servants came out to collect what luggage they had, while Collette let the party gather themselves and straighten their clothes.

"We will be stopping by the forge first to drop off any weapons or armor you might like to have repaired," Collette explained. "Then we'll be off to an introduction audience with Father. It shouldn't take long, it's just a formality. Our seneschal will then take you to the guest tower so you can get settled." Once the others were ready, Collette led them through the arch. Gardens stretched to either side of the walkway that led up to the castle's main entrance. They could now see the palace had a few layers. The first layer was set out a bit, so that the large double entrance was in the shadows of large walls. This stretched to either side, with several openings. On the right, one opening led to the forge, where the blacksmiths were hard at work. To the left was a stable, with a low front wall that had a barrier in the open space above to protect the animals within from the elements if it were to grow cold or rain. Then was the layer with the eight towers, which was level with the main door. Another circular tier filled the space between the eight towers and the large column tower in the center.

"I's like t'e fancies' cake e'er made," Captain whispered to Alconai and the others.

"Look at all the details. This must have taken a long time to sing," Rose added.

"It certainly wasn't done all at once," Solomon noted.

"From what we know of Andor's founding king, he wasn't one for grandeur. But as the years passed and the pride in Andor grew, they slowly started expanding the palace. Some of the original craftsman did not live to see its completion, but it was a source of pride to be chosen to work on it."

While they were admiring the castle, Zatook started for the forge. Another set of servants were waiting, these offering to take any weapons or armor to have looked over by the smith that hadn't been with their luggage.

"Well, Rosie, s'pose i's a good t'ing I kept yer swords," Captain noted with a grin. Rose looked at her in surprise.

"Have you been carting them around this whole time?" she asked incredulously. The pirate girl merely touched the side of her nose and winked.

Tristan stared in awe of the city, his eyes darting from place to place to take in as many details as he could. It was the most alive and attentive he'd been since waking after the battle with his father. Already, his hands itched to grab his journal and sketch, but he refrained for now. His eyes studied the palace with fascination. His attention snapped to Zatook separating from the group, but Tristan recalled the man mentioning a friend who worked in the forge. Forcing himself not to ogle at the palace, Tristan offered Rose his hand to help her out of the carriage before walking with her. Still, his eyes darted everywhere to take in the whole picture. Tristan almost missed the request for his weapons and armor, but he handed them over once the servant caught his attention.

Jabez handed over his sickle and chain to be looked over

since it'd been through a fight with a powerful blood mage. The group also saw him remove his shirt and pieces of armor that had blended with his clothes. Similar leather reinforcements were sown inside the shirt to give him hidden protection while maximizing his mobility. Stripped of the armor, he simply wore a black sleeveless shirt, his muscled arms now on display, and pants with his boots and pouches. His cowl and mask remained firmly in place.

For his part, Alconai handed them his yo-yo. He winked at the servant who gave him a confused look. "It's been through a lot lately," he commented cheekily.

"They're blacksmiths, not toymakers."

"This yo-yo has shed blood. It's all grown up, nae a toy anymore." The servant gave him a look but took the yo-yo and put it with the rest of the weapons and armor to take to the forge.

Lance handed over his greaves and bracers, though he kept the main portion of his armor. Partially because he wanted to look presentable, but also because his armor was pretty unique, and he didn't like letting it out of his sight. While Alconai had been arguing for his yo-yo, Captain had dug out a series of daggers from the layers of her skirt— enough that the servant's eyebrows had steadily risen higher.

Solomon had merely shaken his head when asked after his scimitars.

"Sir, you cannot go armed into the great hall."

"I have permission."

"Sir, no one—"

"It's not completely unheard of," Lancelot noted calmly to the servant. "When we visited with King Arden, we were allowed to remain armed."

"Y-yes, sir, exceptions are made for the protection of esteemed guests."

"And we're esteemed guests," Lance added. "Surely you would not deny a member of the Order tools to protect his charge?"

The servant stared at him, open mouthed.

"It's alright. They do all have permission, given the circumstances," interjected Collette as she approached. The servant's eyes snapped to her and then widened as he gave a hasty bow.

"Y-yes, Highness, of course. My apologies." He quickly scurried away. Collette shook her head.

"Well, at least that means not everyone knows who you are," she offered with a soft smile. "Don't be too hard on them. They're just doing their jobs."

"Of course, Highness." Lance gave a slight bow. Collette nodded before turning to Rose.

"You won't have to try and walk the entire way to the

throne room," she explained. "Our medics are sending over a special chair for you. It uses hovering and maneuvering Tek, though not as complicated as the carriage; not good for travel, but it will let you move around the palace easily."

Rose nodded her head in thanks.

Tristan listened with curiosity when Collette told Rose about the chair. He'd seen magic used in various ways and even more so since arriving in Andor. As if to remind him of his own ailment, pain flared in his chest a moment, but Tristan managed to school his features. Thankfully, it wasn't too bad, so he ascertained he would be able to walk. Tristan looked at Jabez as he remembered the man's collapse that morning. Jabez caught his look and held up his hands placatingly.

"I'm all right to walk," the ninja assured. "I'll take it slow and careful, I promise."

Sol caught the exchange, as well, though Tristan beat him to checking with Jabez. He smirked slightly at the lad. Between Alconai and Tristan, he wondered if he would find himself out of a guardian position in regards to Jabez. That got a soft chuckle as the man shook his head before patting Jabez on the shoulder.

"Come, then. We best not keep the king waiting." He turned his attention to Collette, who nodded and moved to lead the way.

While the main doors were quite large, they were also currently closed. Instead, Collette walked right up to them and knocked. A smaller door opened at the base, the seams having been unseen when it was closed. A servant stepped back and bowed to let them all through.

"Normally the main doors are only open during certain hours," Collette was explaining as they entered. "They open for daily petitions and formal diplomatic visits, mostly."

Despite his curiosity about the palace, Tristan felt a bit of unease settle like a stone in his stomach. The last time he'd been in a castle was in his father's keep, and the tall, grand structure suddenly reminded him of everything that happened. Still, he followed, helping Rose where she needed it until they could get her to the chair Collette had mentioned.

The chair was waiting for them just inside the doors. Rose took Tristan's proferred hand gratefully as she moved to sit, and Collette ran her through the one-handed motions to control it. Captain was examining their surroundings, giving out a low whistle. The inside was just as grand. High, arched ceilings, tapestries and treasures, polished marble floors and columns. Glimmering chandeliers, using the same magic crystals the elves had given Tristan for his cabin in Nikko Mori, lit the halls. The castle spoke to the prosperity of its kingdom and to a rich history. It was a good thing Captain wasn't here as a pirate, because these would be missed quickly. While the hallways branched in several directions, the main hall cut through the center to directly approach the large double doors that would lead to the Great Hall. Collette had not been concerned for nothing— it was a long walk, even though they could see the double doors looming closer.

Tristan tried to carry himself with the posture he'd learned when he still lived in his father's castle: shoulders back and head held high. Even so, he eyed Rose's chair with fascination, his curiosity getting the better of him a little.

Jabez walked more toward the back of their group for now. True to his word, he moved carefully and used the position to walk more slowly than the others. The last thing they needed was him collapsing again, especially before the king. He kept his senses alert for any threats—force of habit. At one point, Jabez glanced over at Captain and Alconai, the latter having offered his arm to the girl for the walk.

Captain's arm was looped through Alconai's, but her eyes were everywhere. A long blue rug with silver embroidery along the sides was guiding their path, a similar shade to Collette's hakama. Despite Captain's sleepless night, the sprightly girl was as vibrant as ever and ready to take charge. Rose was more calm; this wasn't her first time in the palace, even if it was the first time out of her armor. Lancelot had taken to the rear of the group, straight-backed and chin up as the knight he was. Only Solomon betrayed even the slightest hint of wariness to Jabez's gaze, a wariness that few others knew him well enough to spot.

The double doors leading into the Great Hall were not quite as large as the main gates, but they were still grand. Vine and flower designs decorated the stone, which melded so closely that the door's seams could barely be seen. Collette turned to give everyone a once over, straightening a tunic here or a skirt there before brushing off her own clothing and nodding to the seneschal. He dipped into a bow before slipping through the doors, but they could hear his voice echoing through the hall.

"Her Royal Highness, Princess Collette, Daughter-Heir; her esteemed guests; and their entourage."

The doors swung wide, giving the group their first glimpse of the Great Hall. Vaulted ceilings reached high above them, with tiled marble making up the floor. Columns of twisting, decorated stone shone with the glimmer of precious gem veins. Everything was polished smooth and looked as new as the day it had been sung. Another, more embellished long blue carpet with silver filigree stretched before them. Pairs of guards stood across from each other between each set of columns, and nobles milled about the room— though many paused to peer at the guests. The carpet continued to the base of a marble dais, two intricate thrones perched atop. As the group approached, it became clear that only one throne was currently occupied. The man seated was stern in appearance, with bold features and a furrowed brow. His hair was tones of grey, long and swept back, and a silver crown sat upon his head. The king's outfit was entirely blues and silvers, though the hue was darker and bolder than the hakama that marked Collette as Daughter-Heir. As the man turned to face the group from a whispered conversation with a servant, his features softened as his grey eyes landed on his daughter. Traiborn stood, walking to the edge of the dais and spreading his arms.

"Collette. Welcome home. The city has well felt your absence," he greeted warmly. Collette subtly motioned for the others to stay at the base before ascending to accept her father's embrace and then turning to gesture at the party below.

"Father, may I present Captain Isabella MoonChild; Tristan Nightshade, the Sun Child; and Crimson Rose, the Star Child. Alongside them, Sir Lancelot of Nocis, Solomon of the Order, and guardians Jabez ShadowDancer and Alconai FoxFeet."

Traiborn eyed each of them in turn as she listed their names, showing perhaps an unsurprising familiarity with who was who. And yet his gaze seemed to linger a little longer on Rose, then Tristan, then Solomon. "We are honored to shelter the Children of Legend. But your journey has been long and tiresome. Please." He gestured to one of the servants nearby, who bowed. "Kenneth will show you where you will be staying. What things did not need the attention of our smiths will be waiting for you. I am sure we have much to discuss once you are rested. I do hope you will be able to join us for dinner."

"T'ank ye kindly, Yer Majes'y. We appreciate t'e 'ospitality," Captain answered politely, giving another little curtsy. She could behave when she needed to. Usually.

At Traiborn's nod, the group turned to follow the servant through the more winding halls of the palace. The grey-roofed tower marked for the element of wind held the guest quarters. At entrance level was a wide, open parlor, with a columned patio overlooking an enclosed courtyard. The courtyard itself was split between a garden and a small training area; it also boasted a small hot spring in the corner. Opposite the entrance to the parlor was the door to the stairwell. As Kenneth explained, each landing up the stairwell would let into a suite.

"And you needn't worry about the stairs, miss," he added

to Rose. "The TekChair can handle them smoothly."
He then motioned over to their packs sitting beside
the door. "Some of your linens have been taken to our
textile workers, and the smiths still have your weapons.
Everything else has been accounted for, but we did not
wish to assume what went to who."

"Thank you, Kenneth. And please pass on our thanks to
the others," Rose requested. Kenneth bowed.

"If you have any further need of us, there is a small bell
atop the mantle," he informed her, gesturing to a small
fireplace. "It's enchanted, so you need only ring it and
someone will be by." With the final instructions parted, he
bowed and took his leave.

Tristan had managed to be polite toward the king, but
he wasn't sure how long that would last. Still, when they
reached the tower with their guest quarters, he couldn't
resist exploring the area. Tristan smiled softly and felt
grateful when Rose used her new chair to join him. After
looking at the rooms and the eating hall, they made their
way outside to the training area. Tristan was tempted to
go to the hot spring, but he didn't know if they had time
before dinner. So for now, he enjoyed nature and Rose's
company while also trying his best to prepare himself for
what might be a rather awkward dinner.

Jabez kept his eyes and ears alert. He checked over the
rooms and halls, looking for anything that might be used
to spy on them or any tricks the king might have set up
for them. After years in the shadows he couldn't help his
wariness of them.

Alconai stayed with Captain for the time being and

chatted with her. He still felt concerned for her considering what she had been going through lately. "How are ye, Cap'n?" he asked at one point when they were away from the rest of the group.

"Ach, I'm righ' as rain fer now," Captain assured him with a slight smirk. "I t'ink I'm startin' ta ge' used ta t'is place. 'Sides, someone's go'a keep t'is group ship-shape until we can figure ou' wha's goin' on. If'n I take t'e talkin', t'ey donnae go'a play polite aside from a smile." She grinned at him mischievously, wrinkling her nose. Then she sighed, sobering slightly. "An' I ge' t'e feelin' we willnae be seein' much of Zattie while we're 'ere. Migh' as well keep e'ryone's minds off i' until t'ere's somethin' we can do."

"I suppose it's part o' bein' t'e 'Demon of Andor'?" Alconai remarked dryly after her comment on Zatook. Despite his snark, he felt concerned for the warrior after seeing the people's reception of their champion. "Will he be comin' with us on t'e next leg o' our journey? Whate'er that be." Where indeed would the next part of their adventure take them? Alconai hoped they would at least have time to see more of the capital before they needed to leave.

Captain shook her head. "I donnae ken. I havenae been able to see wha' our nex' steps shoul' be, an' I donnae dare be lookin' righ' now."

10. *Friends in the Wings*

Given the forge was inside the palace grounds, it was a good structure with all the amenities that a blacksmith would need. The sounds of hammers honing metal on anvils echoed throughout the smithy. Bent over one particular anvil, a young elf with charcoal gray skin worked on a sword, his arm muscles bulging slightly, his swings precise as he focused on his task. Beneath a neutral-colored bandana strands of blue green hair peeked out to rest against his forehead. His clothes were simple and neutral in color, beige and browns and blacks to hide the tarnishes of working with fire and soot. Near him, in complete contrast, a girl worked the fire for this particular part of the forge. However, instead of using bellows, the fire leapt from her and swirled around her fingers and arms before filling the forge, casting a golden glow along her pale skin. She looked to be in her early to mid-teens, though really she could have easily been five hundred years old or more. Bright, multi-colored wings glimmered like the stained glass of the palace, protruding from her back to show off her fey heritage. Her thick, wavy ebony hair was cut in a short, tousled style with a purple band holding the strands back from her face. She wore a sleeveless, purple dress, the skirt just short enough to stay out of the way of her feet. A golden anklet graced her right leg. Her vibrant eyes shimmered like the golden embers in the forge.

As Zatook split off from the party to walk through the forge, almost everyone ignored him. The servant's eyes passed right over him, the blacksmiths did not acknowledge his passing. Yet once he reached the elven smith he had named as Tannen and the fey girl, Zatook seemed to relax. He paid no mind to the heat and ash of the forge, walking right up to the faerie and flicking the back of her head teasingly on his way to the smith. He had summoned his sword, rapping a hand on Tannen's workspace to get his attention before handing it over personally.

The girl whipped around when Zatook first flicked her, her eyes blazing like the fire lacing her fingers. However, once she saw him, she beamed quite literally. "Zatook!" she yelled before running up to him. Her mastery over her fire nature proved itself when the flames continued in the forge even without her actively working them. She excitedly but gently hugged Zatook from behind. "Look, Tannen! Friend Zatook is back!"

The blacksmith's violet eyes lit up as he lifted his head to see his friend. "So he let me know, Halia," Tannen teased her. After taking the sword from Zatook, Tannen set aside his hammer and clasped hands with the man. "It's good to see you, friend. And you don't look too worse for wear this time. Good." Even with the warm greeting, Tannen's gaze studied Zatook's blade for any nicks or fractures that needed repair. "I heard talk of a strange group moving through Andor with the princess, and that you were traveling with them. Comrades-in-arms or dare I hope you've managed to make some friends beyond the Wall?" He gave Zatook a teasing smile.

Zatook hesitated with the question, glancing over his

shoulder at the group currently handing weapons over to the servants, Collette flitting around them. That was a complicated question. He wasn't entirely sure himself. Especially since there were still some things the group did not know. So for now, he shrugged a shoulder.

"That's as good as a 'yes' from you," Halia teased the warrior. She finally released him so she could take the finished sword from Tannen while the blacksmith went to work repairing and sharpening Zatook's sword.

"As always, your blade tells the story of battle," Tannen commented. He gave his friend a sad smile. Oftentimes, Zatook returned from missions only to collapse in the forge from weariness or injuries. "At least if you have friends or even comrades, you're more likely to come back alive and relatively unscathed from the look of you."

Zatook touched a hand to Tannen's anvil, shadows tracing letters along the surface. *Much has happened,* he confessed. Tannen knew not to pull attention when Zatook wrote to him. Technically, he wasn't allowed to write without permission. But Tannen was one of the few with whom he risked it. He wanted his friend to know of current events, and he wasn't sure how much time he would have to tell him.

Technically, he had run away to find the Chosen Children at his mother's request. When Traiborn finally made time for him, he would be furious.

Tannen set aside the sword for now and motioned Zatook to follow him into one of the courtyards. "I could use some fresh air," he commented. "Halia, make sure the forge doesn't burn down, please."

"Will do! It was good to see you, Zatook. Don't be a stranger, now."

The blacksmith smiled as he left the forge with Zatook following him like the shadow he was. While outside, Tannen pulled off his bandana and shook out his short-cropped blue green hair. He looked rather young, and truthfully, he was younger than Zatook. Once they reached a part of the courtyard that was currently empty, Tannen slowed and glanced at his friend. "Seems like you've been having quite the adventure. I just wish there was something I could do about the repercussions of you leaving without permission."

Zatook shook his head. It was what it was at this point. And he had been needed. Once they were away from prying eyes, he used his shadow spelling to fill Tannen in on everything that had come to pass since he found the pirates canoeing upriver. He had not been exaggerating with his claim that much had happened.

Tannen watched patiently as his friend relayed his story. When Zatook finished, the blacksmith nodded thoughtfully. "You weren't kidding. At least you managed to find all three Chosen Children, though it sounds like you're losing one. Will you journey, you think, to find the new Star Child or is there a way to save her?" He had a feeling the reason Zatook told him everything was so Tannen could keep an eye on the Children and the rest of the group while the Shadow endured his punishment. "I'll keep an eye on them as best I can, and you know you have a solace in my part of the forge. Or come to my apartment if that would be better. No one will bother you."

Zatook shook his head. *Much is uncertain. Lady Mythril*

mentioned something to Tristan about saving her, but she gave no details. And there is no guarantee I will be allowed to continue accompanying them. He hesitated before adding, *I plan to take Tristan to the oracle. If anyone knows what they should do next, it will be her.* He grimaced. *With luck, I can get him there before the king bothers to acknowledge my presence. If not, I will take him when I return.* He shook his head, changing the subject. *I could introduce you, if you wish. They have likely been shown to the tower by now.*

"Perhaps the oracle will be able to tell you how to get out to go with them too," Tannen suggested. He hated when Zatook got punished, especially for things that were for the good of all. It was hardest not being able to see his friend while he knew Zatook was enduring torture. Tannen just hoped that perhaps the Chosen Children could finally free the Shadow of his shackles. Tannen hadn't been able to do it. He'd only been able to try and keep the man's spirits up through the years. "Perhaps they can finally knock the usurper off his throne. You might as well introduce us so they know I'm a friend and not one of the king's lackeys trying to spy on them. You can get the young man while you're at it."

Zatook paused, glancing up at the sky and gauging the time. *They are likely preparing for dinner,* he noted.

"True," Tannen agreed. "Feel free to join Halia and me for dinner if you're not needed. I think your group would understand if you wanted to be with some familiar faces for a bit." Zatook nodded, moving to follow Tannen and rejoin Halia.

Tannen led the man to his lodgings. The servants and

workers resided in another building along the outer layer inside the palace grounds. The building housed different sized units for the residents depending on their needs. As a boon from the queen, Tannen and Halia lived in a family unit despite not being related. While the queen had a kind soul, Tannen speculated that she had also wanted to give Zatook a place of sanctuary as well. Inside, the apartment was spacious enough to suit the trio's needs but still emanated a cozy atmosphere. Tannen illuminated the main room and kitchen areas with the light crystal fixtures. He motioned for Zatook to sit on the sofa while Tannen started preparing dinner. Halia soon joined them once she had closed down the forge for the night. Energetically she helped Tannen fix the food while also pestering Zatook with questions about the new group he had brought. Zatook answered what he could while they worked, though sometimes he sent the shadows to write the words where they could more easily see them.

"Alas, now that you have new friends, we'll probably see even less of you," Halia teased Zatook as she set the table for them.

"They're his charges, Hali. He'll be doing what he can to protect them, same as he does for you and the princess," Tannen lightly chided. He ruffled her hair before setting the food out for them. "Honestly, I think training your kin will be good for you," he added to Zatook. "I've heard it said that in teaching we learn, and it sounds like he'll need the most support from you: the one person in the group who will understand him best. Not that the other Chosen Children don't need support, mind you, but from what you've told me, I'd wager you and the Sun Child have a lot in common."

Zatook had snorted at Halia's comment, but he inclined his head to Tannen. *More than he knows,* he agreed. *Though I doubt the knowledge will elude him much longer.*

Tannen studied Zatook for a moment while the group ate. He barely hid a soft smile, glad that his friend seemed to be finding connections outside their little circle.

"Can you tell us more about the Drow or the Doran girl?" Halia asked, excitedly. "I've never met one of the nomadic folk, or other Drow-kin. And you said that the Sun Child came from Nikko Mori. Does he know any of the fae folk that live there?"

I do not know much more than what has been said, Zatook confessed. *We have been fairly busy.* That and Zatook wasn't usually one to just…chat. *Though Captain has not been with the Clans.*

"She's been running around as a pirate, right?" questioned Halia. "Must be fun— though I don't know how I'd feel being surrounded by water. Sure she's not a water fae? She looked like she's got the energy of one."

Tannen chuckled and remarked, "Like you're one to talk." Halia playfully wrinkled her nose at him. He smiled at her but then grew serious. "Sun, Moon, and Star. I understand they needed refuge, but I'm concerned. I'm sure you are as well," Tannen addressed Zatook.

Zatook grimaced. *Hopefully their status as the Children of Legend will protect them from the darker aspects of the palace,* he finally noted. *The Chosen are almost as revered as the Royal Line.*

"If they're revered, then why the concern?" Halia asked, curious.

Tannen sat back in his chair as he answered, "The king has some prejudices that could override his sense of reverence for the legends. As well as the stress from the encroaching war with Nocis. The smithies have been on notice, and more armor and weapons have been pushing through the forges lately." Tannen met Zatook's gaze. "Do you think the king will try to have the Chosen fight for Andor?"

Andor reveres them. No telling the king's personal thoughts. He already disrespects the Order. He paused at Tannen's question, shaking his head. *I do not know. He may be satisfied that they will not fight for Nocis.*

"I suppose we'll just have to keep an eye out and see how things go. Hopefully, they'll survive dinner at least," Tannen said the last part with a teasing smile. Halia snorted into her drink.

"I'd much rather be eating here than with stuffy people. Too many manners to worry about and talking nonsense that no one actually cares about just to be polite. Too much pretending," the fae girl griped. "Still, I'd like to meet them if we have time."

I am sure you will get along with them quite well.

***

As Zatook and Tannen had been walking through the garden, Collette was on her way to the guest wing

191

to discuss the plans for dinner. She waved as she approached the parlor with Captain and Alconai.

"I forgot about dinner," she confessed with a light blush. "Don't be too weirded out, but there will be some clothes brought by for you all. I've been sent to get your measurements with a spell. You'll have a little while to rest before the clothes are delivered, so I'll send some refreshments to tide you over."

Captain smiled. "Tha' soun's good ta me. Go ahead an' start wit' Nai, I'll go ge' t'e ot'ers."

Alconai spun in a flourish as he presented himself to the princess. "Shiny new garb, eh? I suppose we be lookin' a bit rough after days o' travel and battle. It'll be nice ta get clean and have some clean clothes."

"Something about dining with a king and all that," Collette joked right back, drawing a quick rune in the air above his head. A light chill ran down his spine and then was gone. "The seamsters will spruce up your regular clothes while we're at dinner. They work quick."

"Much appreciated," Alconai told her sincerely. He looked over when the Chosen Children joined them. "It be yer turns now." He noticed Jabez standing back from the group. Alconai moved over to his brother and lightly bumped his shoulder in greeting. Jabez gave him a nod before turning his gaze back to their charges.

Collette smirked after him before repeating the process. Jabez and Solomon didn't escape either, and by the time she was through with them, Lance had rejoined the party.

"That should do it," the princess chimed as she finished the rune over the knight's head. "Refreshments will be here soon, so you probably don't want to wander too far. Kenneth will be by with the clothes when they are done, and then I'll return to guide you to the dining hall."

"Your help is as appreciated as ever, Highness," Solomon remarked, giving her a bow as she left.

"You can use my name when it's just us," she informed him in return, waving over her shoulder at them before exiting the hall. The Order member shook his head.

"If there was any doubt she was her mother's daughter, it's all gone," he teased.

"That makes me more curious about the queen then. If the king is managing to keep the people content, wouldn't he at least let the queen be seen if for no other reason than to have her as a figurehead?" Tristan questioned. "And yet, she wasn't there to greet us. Should we expect to see her at dinner?"

"The official story is that the queen is in poor health," Lancelot noted, folding his arms and leaning back against the parlor wall. "But she does make appearances."

"I wouldn't dismiss it as a story," Rose added softly. "The last time I was in Andor, she did not look well."

Tristan grew quiet at the thought. He remembered how his mother had been more reserved as Tristan had gotten older and things with his father had become more tense. While Reina never grew ill, Tristan's heart went out to the queen for having to endure poor health in her circumstances. "I take it that the princess' attitude toward Zatook is due to their mother," he commented. Tristan felt glad that despite his situation, Zatook had some friends and an adoring sister.

"More than likely," Solomon concurred with Tristan's assessment. "From what I gathered during our ride, Collette is the same age as Captain." He paused a moment. "It seems he has a friend in one of the blacksmiths, as well, which is moderately surprising."

Lance frowned over at Solomon. "Is he truly that despised? Most of the servants just...ignored him."

Solomon was quiet, though Jabez could see his grip tighten on his arms. Before he could answer, there was a knock at the parlor door, and a servant came in with the promised refreshments. Solomon continued to stare at the table, arms folded and gaze lost in memories. He didn't say anything until the servant was gone. "When I lived in Andor, no one openly showed him kindness aside from one young woman. The king ordered him to kill her."

Alconai's expression darkened with the reveal, but he remained quiet. Jabez kept his demeanor neutral; though, he did subtly touch Solomon's shoulder in sympathy. Tristan stared at Solomon, mortified.

"It's not just a matter of being terrified from the stories," he continued. "Befriending him is a risk. And with the royal family as loved as they are...obviously if they treat someone as a monster, then said person must be a monster indeed." He shook his head. "It is what they know. What has been for generations. And the questions slowly died away." He glanced up to watch the others. "With Collette's actions, things may slowly start to change. But it's hard to say; one kind-hearted princess against some five hundred years of tradition."

Tristan mouthed the number in surprise. He almost asked if Zatook was a Celestial but thought better of it, Amaya's warning coming to mind. "I take it the people don't see how the queen treats him then," Tristan asked. "Is…is there anything we can do to help him?"

Solomon sighed. "It's complicated," he acquiesced. "They know the queen has a soft spot for him, but they also were led to believe she was tricked by a monster into bearing him. Remember, he was a child when Traiborn came to power, and we don't fully know the details around that day. They fear him, yet they believe he would never harm the queen and somewhat accept her affections for him."

Tristan ran a hand through his hair with a frustrated sigh. "And we have to play nice to this king?"

"If we don't want to get kicked out, then yes," Jabez piped up. "Politics is always messy, and as much as we want to change things, we best not go shaking things up until we know we have a solid place to land in the aftermath."

"In t'e meantime, we be enjoyin' every luxury t'e king be bestowin' upon us. Stick it ta him by nae showin' we be bothered. I ken tis easier said than done. But do we shall," Alconai told them cheekily.

"As much as we hate it, Zattie kenned wha' bringin' us 'ere

would mean fer 'im," Captain noted. "So we ainnae goin' ta le' tha' be in vain."

"Indeed. I hope to gain access to the Archives so we can start looking into matters," Solomon noted. "Perhaps there will be an opening to ask at dinner."

"Too bad we need to make a good impression, I'm tempted to sit in the banquet hall in my battle rags and bandages," Rose teased softly.

Tristan gave her a half-smile at the joke, his heart too heavy with recent events and the conversation to give her a full one. "I'm sure that would annoy him. I could dress to match in my forest attire. The Scarlet Swordsman and the rugged woodland dweller." That actually got a laugh out of Alconai, the man pleasantly surprised to hear the Star Child and the Sun Child joking.

"Oh, I be certain it be a riot, in more ways than one," the minstrel remarked with a smile.

It wasn't much longer before Kenneth arrived with the new attire for the evening's dinner. After taking the clothes meant for them, the group dispersed to freshen up in their rooms.

Jabez stared at the outfit Kenneth had brought for him. The tailors had decided to go with colors reminiscent of Ben-Gal. Jabez had a feeling Collette noticed his connection with Solomon as well as Jabez's introduction as a guardian. The tailors had chosen a slim-fitting, fashionable crimson jacket with cream fabric draping the shoulders in a small mantle. Golden yellow slim-fitting, stylish pants complimented the jacket. Tan trim all throughout the outfit as well as matching tan boots and belt brought everything together.

Feeling self-conscious in so many ways, Jabez hesitated to change into the clothes. A sense of unworthiness still plagued him, compounded by being verbally acknowledged as a guardian— official or no. His fingers hovered near a red fabric mask as he stared into the distance. The designer copied his face covering to go with his new outfit, but there was no cowl to hide the rest of his head. The group was going to have dinner with royalty; Jabez needed to present himself in appropriate attire to make a good impression as an associate for the Chosen Children. He needed to step up out of his comfort zone, out of the shell he'd hidden inside for years, to better support them. Yet, he faltered.

Jabez had gotten so used to wearing the garb of his captors that the clothes had become the physical manifestation of his figurative shields. Sure, he had stripped to bathe and to clean his clothes, but even that felt like stripping himself of the only armor he had against the harsh reality of what had happened to him and because of him. There were a select few who had seen Jabez out of his ninja garb, most of whom had been caring for him in Ben-Gal or torturing him while he was with Shaedra.

Pushing through the unpleasant memories, Jabez forced his fingers to move, bypassing his mask and shoving the cowl back. The fabric pulled his short, light auburn hair back, the strands flattened from wearing the cowl for so long. He forewent shaking his hair out, choosing to focus on getting his trembling fingers to remove the rest of his clothes. It was slow going and tedious, but he managed to dress in the red and gold attire for dinner. That just left his mask. Jabez's fingers hovered over the fabric once again, a lead weight sinking into his stomach simply with the notion of removing the garment. He felt the color drain from his face and sweat start to form on his brow. Cold chills ran through him as he felt physically ill from the stress. He needed to do this. He had to do this. He *couldn't* do this. Such a small thing, and yet it caused him so much anxiety. He couldn't even face his own reflection.

"Jabez," a familiar voice spoke softly. Yet, the sound jolted Jabez violently from the vortex of his thoughts and emotions. Alconai stood a few steps in the room, his golden hazel gaze watching Jabez with sympathetic understanding. "Ye donnae have ta."

It took Jabez a moment to find his voice. "I don't know why. I just...I can't..." he trailed off as he struggled to explain. He watched a bit fearfully as Aloncai approached him. His younger brother gently guided Jabez's hand away from the mask.

"Jabez," Alconai spoke again, reassuringly, "ye donnae have ta." He shifted his grip to hold Jabez's hand while his free one squeezed his older brother's shoulder. "Ye've been through a lot, and ye've got a lot o' unpleasant memories and experiences ta deal with. Sometimes trauma causes responses that cannae be explained. They just are. I've watched ye pushin' yerself fer t'e sake o' t'e Chosen Children, and I be so proud of ye, Jabie. But ye donnae need ta rush. Ye'll be ready when ye're ready. And ye'll always have me and Sol and Cap'n ta help ye when ye need us. Ye are strong, Jabie. Ye've always been me stronger, older bruddeh, and that hasnae changed."

Jabez finally released the breath he hadn't realized he was holding, his body relaxing as he felt his chest lighten with the acceptance from his sibling. "I don't feel very strong most days," he quietly confessed.

"Ye are. I ken it be nae t'e same, but is Tristan weak for havin' trouble facin' a world without his sister? For bein' afraid o' his da?"

"Never. He's been through so much in just the past seven years and then—" Jabez stopped when his brother gave him a pointed look. Jabez sighed heavily, caught in his own double-standard. "Right. Then why should it be different for me, aye?" Alconai nodded. "It's the same unexplainable thing as my anxiety with removing my mask. I wager all three Chosen Children have their own traumas they're dealing with."

"That donnae mean ye cannae, Jabie. Zatook, Sol, probably even Amaya have their share too. Lance as well." Jabez simply dipped his head in acknowledgment. Giving another squeeze, Alconai reached over and retrieved the red fabric mask. When he handed the mask to Jabez, Alconai reminded, "Nothin' ta be ashamed of. Now, I better get me own garb sorted before dinner. If'n ye need me, I be just in t'e other room."

"Nai," Jabez called before his brother could slip out the door. When his younger sibling looked back at him, he continued, "thank you."

"Anytime, bruddeh." Alconai gave him a reassuring smile before disappearing out of the room.

***

While Jabez and Alconai were talking, the others had
started to prepare for dinner as well. Solomon and
Captain had traded in their pirate gear, though the latter
had grumbled the entire time Rose did her hair. Solomon
also wore colors reminiscent of Ben-Gal, with a mix of
deep reds and oranges accented with beige and grey.
He wore a jabot shirt tucked into a patterned waistband
and a pair of comfortable trousers with a skirt of fabric
hanging almost like the bottom of a coat around his waist
to his knees. He still insisted on sandals.

Lance was dressed fit for a knight, in a tabard with boots.
However, instead of the heraldry and colors of Nocis, this
combination was white lined in dusty gray, dusty gray
leggings, and a gentle purple for the undershirt and boots.
He had been surprised at the colors, but they made more
sense after he saw the Star and Moon Children.

Rose had been gifted a gown fit for a noble. The shirt-like
top beneath was a deep satin crimson in recognition of
her heritage with silver undersleeves, while the bodice
was a deep purple with silver accents and the skirt was
also purple with a wrapping of silver. She had let down
her hair and brushed it out before taking two braids from
each side and joining them together into one large braid
in the back with the rest of her hair. She had also painted
her face, with a dark blush accenting her cheeks, deep red
lines around her eyes, and her lips fading from a silver
fill to a crimson outline. She kept her earrings, though the
teal beads and maroon wooden feathers were more visible
than they had been beneath her cloak.

Captain was perhaps the most dramatic change. Gone

were the vibrant colors of the Doran, free-flowing hair, and bare feet. Instead, she wore a sleeveless top that was white with pink accents of varying shades. Her bottoms consisted of gauzy layered legwear with decorative tassels, a chain, and rope. The trousers beneath were dusty gray, while the skirt-like wraparound was white with purple trim. The tassels and ropes were pink. She was pleased to find that they had brought her sandals, even if they were a pale pink with purple bottoms. She wore bangles of pink, purples, and silver, and a necklace with a silver chain and pink gemstone. Silver hoops adorned her ears and could actually be seen since she let Rose put her hair in a twist. She had also painted her face, with a light blush and pale pink eyeliner and lipstick. She did not, however, opt to cover her freckles with skin-colored cream.

"It's traditional," Collette was explaining to Captain with a soft laugh. The princess had come to check on their preparations when she found the pirate lass grumbling. "We've always associated the Children of Legend with their respective colors. Purple for the Star Child, golden for the Sun Child, and pink for the Moon Child."

"Wha' about t'e moon makes ye t'ink *pink*? Donnae ge' me wrong, I ainnae agains' t'e color on its own…but a' leas' make it bold an' brigh', nae t'is baby powder color!"

"It's pink because the symbol for things related to the moon in Andor is the lotus flower. And they have a rather gentle shade, you must admit." Collette hesitated before adding, "That and our founder's sister was a Moon Child. I believe she was rather fond of the color."

Captain sighed, flopping into a chair. "One dinner," she

conceded.

"Shame it's just t'e one dinner. Ye look righ' lovely, Cap'n," Alconai praised as he joined the group. He wore a green and lavender doublet with a pair of gray pants and brown leather boots. Hearing he was an entertainer, the tailors had provided a hat that was a bit fancier than his usual one: leather similar to the boots and a vibrant pink feather sticking up from the band. When Collette had left earlier, Alconai requested his coat be returned in time for dinner. Thankfully, the staff managed to clean the rather dirty garment. Now, Alconai wore it but reversed. With the brown now on the inside, the outside of the coat was a midnight blue with silver sparkles giving the illusion of the night sky across the fabric. He stepped aside to let Jabez show off his outfit, the older brother giving a slight bow. "Are we ready ta charm t'e pants off some royals?" Alconai teased.

At that moment, Tristan stepped out of his room as well and descended the stairs. Those that had seen pictures of Reina now saw her in her son. Tristan stood tall with his back straight and shoulders back. He'd combed his hair to tidy up the tousled, medium brown layers. He wore a vibrant white and gold brocade doublet with dark gray pants. He looked every bit the noble as he joined them. Even as he presented his outfit, Tristan's thoughts turned to the impending dinner followed by memories of the lessons he'd had as a child about nobility and etiquette. A part of him feared playing the part of the noble would force him to shoulder the role his father wanted him to fulfill. Being a noble, Tsukuyomi knew his way around diplomats and royalty and imparted his knowledge to his son. Mentally shaking himself from his musings, Tristan offered his arm to Rose. "You look beautiful," he told her softly.

"Flatterer," Rose teased Tristan lightly, grateful it was harder to discern a blush from her grey skin. She felt a pang of sadness remembering one of her last conversations with Arianna. The young girl's insistence that warriors could be pretty after she braided flowers into Rose's hair. She looped a hand around his arm so neither had to stretch uncomfortably while she was seated. "You look every bit the part of a noble," she mused. "Not the forest rat I met before." She winked to show she was teasing.

"I'm not sure how to feel about it," Tristan told her honestly. "I much prefer our normal clothes, but… I'm realizing that in order to do my best to help people, I'll have to start embracing my roots more. Estranged from my father or no, I'm still the heir to House Shadow Veil. I'm not sure how much longer it'll matter, but I feel I should do what I can while I have some form of influence. And I can channel what I learned from my mother and my father into my role as the Sun Child." Tristan looked up when Alconai spoke to the group.

"Well, donnae we all clean up nicely," Alconai remarked easily. He held his arm out to Captain. "Shall we?" Captain took Alconai's arm, walking near the front of the group.

"I be perfec'ly clean in me normal clothes," the Doran girl half-grumbled. Solomon chuckled behind her.

"Dressing up once in a while for diplomacy isn't the worst thing in the world, Captain," he reminded her lightly.

"Says a man," she snarked back, resisting the urge to reach up and mess with her hair. "An' a bald one a' that. No face gunk or twistin' hair ta give ye a headache."

"Says a member of the Order, who's gotten used to wearing different styles for different occasions. I once had to wear a powdered wig in Regalia."

Alconai couldn't help laughing as he imagined Solomon in some ridiculous getup and a powdered wig. "I wish I could have seen it," he commented, wiping a tear from his eye.

Jabez shook his head, but even with a mask it was obvious he was smiling. With a bow, he offered his arm to Collette. "Shall we, Your Highness?"

"You laugh, but if we end up going there, it's a thing all men must wear to formal events," Solomon pointed out with a grin as the princess took Jabez's arm and headed for the front of the line. "You may yet get the chance to see it *and* have to mimic it." Captain was snickering.

"I t'ink I ken wha' to look fer in t'e past once we're outta Andor," she teased. Solomon just shook his head.

11. *Veiled Intentions*

Once they had all lined up, Lancelot bringing up the rear of the group with Jabez and Collette at the head, the princess led them through the winding halls of the palace to the great banquet hall. She left them outside the double doors with instructions to wait for the seneschal to announce them before heading down the halls to a different door to join her parents.

The announcement wasn't long in coming, and the double doors were opened to reveal the grand room. Glistening chandeliers of crystal hung from the ceiling, and highly polished cedarwood tables graced the marbled floors. Many of the tables were clear, only the head table bearing a long table runner, candelabras, and place settings.

The runner itself was blue with silver embroidery. Matching chair covers draped from the back of the three chairs at the head, right of the head, and left of the head. Traiborn sat at the head, with Collette taking the seat to his left. To Solomon's surprise, the right seat was also occupied— the queen was there. There was no doubt in her identity, if for no other reason than her violet hair, a few shades darker than her daughter's. Unlike Collette, she did not wear the clothing of a priestess. Instead, she wore something closer in style to Traiborn's waistcoat, though far more tailored and fitted. Her hair was pulled up and back in a twist, with a large crown of blue metal adorning the top of her head. As she stood with her family to greet their guests, Solomon noted what Rose must have the last time she was here: the queen's eyes were shadowed despite her make-up, and her skin tone was far paler than Collette's. Her smile was tired but as warm as the stories claimed.

As Captain had guessed, Zatook was nowhere to be seen.

The seneschal directed the group to approach the table; one of the chairs had been pulled away to accommodate for Rose's transport. Alconai pulled out Captain's chair. Traiborn sat then, Corianne and Collette following suit. Once they were seated with chairs pushed in, the group followed.

"Despite the protocol of being announced, please feel free to relax," King Traiborn informed them. "This is hardly a banquet, presence of royalty or no."

"I apologize for my absence upon your arrival," Queen Corianne noted softly as the nearby servants began placing down salads for everyone. "I was otherwise occupied and could not leave my task."

"Perfectly understandable, Your Majesty," Solomon answered smoothly. "I am sure the pair of you are incredibly busy on even the simplest of days."

"From what reports I've gathered, your party have been fairly busy themselves," Traiborn noted, swirling his goblet a moment before taking a sip of wine. "It is not every day a Nocium high lord's keep explodes."

Captain was proud that she did *not* choke on her bite of salad. "Oh, aye. Quite a sigh' tha'," she noted lightly. "Jus' goes ta show ye can ne'er be too careful dealin' wit' powerful magics."

Traiborn eyed her appraisingly with a soft 'indeed'. "So, tell me. How do a band of pirates, two knights of Nocis, a bard, and a runaway noble come to meet? Did you already know each other and your purposes? It does seem quite the coincidence."

"Nae all of us," Captain answered easily. "Me bo— er, me crew 'ad always ken me secret, and I ken t'ere be two ot'ers. When I learned 'ho an' where, I wen' ta find 'em so we could figure out wha' we were meant ta do. We me' Alconai an' Lance during our travels."

"Travels which led back to the runaway noble's home along with its destruction?" Traiborn arched an eyebrow, but Captain merely graced him with a smile.

"Jus' goes ta show ye can ne'er be too careful dealin' wit' powerful magics," she repeated brightly, even as she met his gaze and sipped her tea. From what she had spied of the table when sitting, only Traiborn had wine. Shame. She could use a drink.

Collette was watching the exchange with a hint of amusement. "Forgive me, Father, but would it not be more polite to discuss lighter topics over dinner?"

Traiborn smiled at her, reaching to pat her hand. "No forgiveness required. You are still learning. No, it is best to understand now, so that wayward words do not plant seeds of worry. Audiences are, more often than not, formalities somewhat planned ahead of time. The more I understand of our guests, the more acutely I can guide our more public interactions."

It really was astounding. The switch from prying noble to warm, doting father. Captain was careful not to grip her teacup too tightly. She could only guess to Zatook's current whereabouts.

"Then am I to assume dinner will not be as casual as proclaimed?" Solomon asked softly. Traiborn waved a hand.

"Formality is excused, but topics are of import."

The Order member inclined his head. "Then ask, and we shall answer what we can. We needn't dance around each other's words or attempt to catch each other off guard."

Traiborn chuckled warmly. "Fair enough. Wise words from a seasoned Andorian." Solomon took a sip of his water as Traiborn addressed the others. "As I am sure you are aware, tensions between Andor and Nocis have reached a breaking point. The fact that I have harbored fugitives from at least Keep Shadow Veil will not go unnoticed. So I would hear your sides of the tale that unfolded to best prepare." He leaned forward, resting his elbows on the table as the waitstaff started setting out entrees. "Sheltering you is increasing Andor's risk. I need to be able to assure my people that we are on the right side of the legends. And the more you can help me prepare for Nocis' advancements, the better I can shore our defenses— if that's even needed. I am turning to you in trust. As a king, yes. But on behalf of my people."

"You speak of two knights. Shall I assume my true identity is known, then?" Rose asked softly. Traiborn turned to look at her, chuckling softly.

"I have other ways to identify a person than sight and name," he noted. "I knew what you were even in that armor, though the addition 'Star Child' came as a surprise."

Captain took another sip of her tea. How was the man coming across so sincerely? She had expected twisted words, glib taunts, and a touch of arrogance. But so far he seemed to be addressing them in honesty.

"Then it will come as little surprise to you that I was hunted after deserting the army," Rose was explaining. "I learned of King Arden's original plan to undermine the current peace and his plans for my abilities. So I left. Unfortunately, I have little else to say. With King Jeremiah's ascendance and my desertion, I do not know what they plan to do."

"Ah, yes. Another puzzle piece. Since when has Jeremiah sought such power?"

Rose blinked in surprise at hearing her own thoughts echoed in Traiborn's words, her gaze saddening slightly. She had found herself wishing more and more of late for how Jeremiah had been. "Would that I knew," she murmured.

Lancelot spoke up next, to pull the attention from Rose. "I have little else to share, either. Anything I had learned was while I was under the control of an unnatural blood mage." He could swear Traiborn's eye just twitched. "I could see them attempting to use my skill as a sealbreaker, but now I have left as well."

"A blood mage?" It was Corianne who spoke, her sharp green gaze turned to Rose for confirmation. "In Nocis? Openly?"

Rose nodded. "Yes. Two, as the one handling Lancelot was an apprentice."

Traiborn looked to Corianne, who had lifted a hand to her chin in thought.

"This does not solve the puzzle of Jeremiah," the queen murmured. "But it does add clarification elsewhere. Such as Arden's death and the recent movements of some Drowic Elders." Rose rather hoped they hadn't caught her flinch.

Even if their hosts failed to see Rose's reaction, Tristan caught it. Under the table, he lightly touched her hand in reassurance, opening his in offering. He gave her hand a soft squeeze when she took his. He felt his own unease with his silence, but he wasn't sure what he could say without giving away too much. He needed to act the part of the heir to House Shadow Veil since his father had yet to formally renounce him; however, the notion made Tristan's skin crawl.

Despite casually eating and drinking, Alconai followed the conversation closely. Years of gathering intel in taverns and public spaces trained him to hear beyond words spoken. He knew what Traiborn was doing.

Though staying mostly cordial, the king was pushing buttons— testing their patience. Such as the lack of wine for the guests. If he truly knew everyone's identities and recognized Tristan as a noble, then the king knew full well the lapse in decorum for not offering the beverage. Alconai also noted Queen Corianne's gaze lingering on Tristan more than once. Alconai shared a subtle look with Jabez, the two men tracking the same details.

For now, Jabez sat silently. There wasn't much he could contribute to the conversation, but he listened closely and observed the expressions of their hosts. He also kept his eyes and ears open for any funny business should the king try anything more underhanded. Jabez felt a little surprised that Alconai wasn't taking the chance to talk as much, but then it seemed Captain and the others had a handle on the conversation.

"So, then. We are up against two blood mages—"

"One."

Traiborn paused at the interruption, glancing at Captain. She calmly sipped her tea.

"One blood mage," he continued. "So tell me, champions of Nocis and Children of Legend: what else are we up against?"

"Well, I can tell you Jeremiah is a dragon," Rose offered lightly, reaching to sip her water. "As is his wife," she added, tilting her head slightly at the fact. "And he has a powerful enchantress under his watch." She paused, considering, but it was actually Captain who spoke up next.

"Actually, ye migh' be able ta 'elp wit' our own li'l puzzle," she noted.

"Oh?" Traiborn raised an eyebrow at her.

"T'ere be somethin' wrong wit' t'at blood mage. T'ough Rosie'd be be'er at tellin' ye wha'."

Traiborn's brow furrowed as he turned to Rose. The Half-Drow hesitated.

"She doesn't look human. At least, not anymore. Grey skin, tainted eyes, mangled ears."

"Marilyn?"

Now all eyes were on the queen.

"Ye ken 'er, Yer Majes'y?"

"More than I wish. Yes, I could see why she puzzles you. Few Drow-kin know the ritual she used, let alone rogue blood mages or kingdom knights."

Captain didn't miss Traiborn's eyes darkening, or the soft 'ah.'

"And what ritual would you be referring to?" Lance asked curiously.

"She drank someone's blood," Corianne answered softly.

"Particularly, the blood of an Elder Drow Matriarch. A few decades ago, at least."

This time, Captain *did* choke on her drink, but so did Collette.

"She did *what?*" Collette reached for her napkin to stifle her coughing.

"It is an old, dark ritual," the queen explained. "Typically, the Drow do not accept unnatural blood mages, though there have been exceptions in the past. It has little to do with the manner in which these mages acquire their abilities, and more to do with the fact that they are not Drow. One of the ways into their...graces, so to speak, is to best a powerful Drow and drink their blood in a special ritual that makes it part of the caster's own."

Rose let out a breath, shaking her head. "Drow revere the Elder Matriarchs," she noted softly. "They would want the power of her bloodline to continue, whether in an inferior host or no." So that was how Marilyn had met her grandmother. Keeshe must have been tasked with teaching her.

"And that means she is far more dangerous than you have realized," Corianne added with a nod. "A blood mage with Drow training. Access to spells and knowledge long lost to other people."

"Is the blood responsible for her..." Rose gestured to her own face, and Corianne laughed softly.

"Partially. Her pallor, yes. Her own corruption affected

her eyes, and her hair is a choice. As are the ears." She grimaced slightly. "She renounced humanity long ago, but she also seemed to disappear." She lifted her gaze to meet Solomon's, knowing at least he would understand the weight of her next words. "She is older than even I."

"What would be the best way to counter her?" Tristan questioned politely. He remembered the blood rain and his time under Marilyn's control. If she was more powerful than that still, what other dangerous things could she do? "Jeremiah introduced her to my father. She's working with both of them for now."

Corianne opened her mouth as though to answer, but Traiborn interrupted.

"How do you fight any mage? You train yourself to be powerful, as well," he noted calmly, arching an eyebrow at Tristan. "A powerful mage is not immune to harm, simply harder to hurt. All mages have their weaknesses, and all magics as well. It's a matter of finding them."

"I would imagine light magics would be especially effective?" Collette offered, but Traiborn shook his head.

"Light in and of itself, not necessarily. Powerful light? Yes. But those spells are difficult."

"For a mage, perhaps. But I believe the Children of Legend could find a way through their own talents," Corianne noted gently. "Further in the castle is Andor's main library and archives. There are many legends and folktales about Children of the past and various lesser known magics. You may very well find something there."

"Yes, of course. You would be welcome to access the tomes within our library during your stay," Traiborn added.

"We appreciate the invitation," Solomon noted, his expression and tone calm. "I am sure there is much we could glean from such a vast archive." He caught Jabez's gaze knowingly— this would also let them try and look into the runes on his scimitars.

Captain was still following the conversation, though her eyes seemed far away. Something tugged at the edge of her senses, but she couldn't place it. She didn't dare Look, especially not in the midst of dinner. But it felt like something was calling to her. Her mind thought to the Celestial of Time. Was there something in the castle that was amplifying the woman's call? Was that what was causing her own magic to go off? And how could she find it?

"Nae ta change t'e subject, bu' all this talkin' of magic reminds me. Does yer archive 'ave anything in it about t'e Celestial o' Time?" she asked curiously. Traiborn's gaze trained on her, level and suddenly rather masked.

"That is a curious question," he noted slowly. Rose could practically see the gears in his head turning to create an answer. But he surprised her with the simplicity: "Why?"

Captain shrugged as she finished her bite of food. "We be hittin' a bi' of a brick wall wit' wha' we're mean' ta be doin', and I ken some Doran caravans would speak wit' 'er for guidance."

"Would you not know more of that than I, then?"

Something passed across Captain's expression, but it was gone as quickly as it came. Solomon was quick to answer, drawing Traiborn's attention away.

"Captain was separated from her people at a young age. We do not currently know the whereabouts of other clans. It was safer to raise her myself."

"'Safer'?"

"Are you going to deny that there are those who would seek the Chosen Children for their own purposes?" Solomon countered levelly, meeting Traiborn's gaze. Captain hadn't looked up from her plate, her expression hidden though she was obviously tenser than she had been, at least to her comrades. Traiborn and Solomon stared each other down.

Beneath the table, Alconai's hand touched Captain's, silently offering comfort and encouragement. When she didn't pull away, he took her hand and held it gently. From what Solomon had told him, Alconai could guess Captain's past was a sensitive subject. "Who safer ta be with than an Order dedicated ta t'e survival and trainin' o' t'e Chosen, eh?" Alconai commented easily. "A neutral party nae driven by greed or ambition ta bend t'e Children ta their wills. Or so I be understandin'."

Traiborn's appraising gaze was on him next, but he merely nodded. "Fair enough. So, a power-hungry dragon, his family, an enchantress, and a fell mage." He leaned back in his chair, folding his arms again. "That does not explain why I felt my shadow use his full power at length."

Corianne hesitated in her bite but quickly masked it. Collette was not so subtle, both eyebrows up. The queen sighed.

"You want to know about Lord Shadow Veil. We already *know* about Lord Shadow Veil," she noted with a restrained gentleness.

"I was rather hoping to hear it from them."

"With all due respect, this has all been fairly recent. And we only just found sanctuary behind your wall," Rose spoke up, gently gripping Tristan's hand. "Not all of us are battle-trained soldiers. And many of the wounds from events are still fresh."

Traiborn seemed to give everyone at the table another appraising glance. Then he sighed. "You are right, of course. My apologies. I allowed myself to be carried away by the threats at hand. But we do need to figure out what to say at the audience tomorrow. I do not wish to overly worry the people, especially given *King* Jeremiah appears to have need of a new plan."

"If I may?" Solomon ventured, and Traiborn nodded to him. "The Children are aware of Andor's connection to magic and the legend. They have come to hone their skills away from those who would misuse them." Traiborn considered, nodding.

"That will do. But we will need to discuss the truth in more detail in private."

"Of course, Your Majesty. We just request a few days rest before we get into details."

"By then I should also have my shadow's full report. Very well, then." He sat up straighter when a servant walked towards the table and hesitated, the king motioning for the man to come forward. The servant bent to whisper in his ear, and Traiborn frowned. "Well. Please, do not rush on our account. It seems we have business to attend." He stood, offering his arm to Corianne. Taking the cue, she stood as well and looped arms before curtseying to their guests, and the pair swept away.

The table was silent until he was gone, but it was Collette who broke it by stabbing her fork in her steak. She lifted a hand, and runes swirled through the air around them.

"No one is listening," she announced after a moment, lowering her hand. Captain let out a breath.

Tristan squeezed Rose's hand. "Thank you," he intoned quietly, gratefully. Amaya's warning and seeing the scar that nearly ended her life ran through Tristan's mind again. They would have to be careful what they revealed to the king regarding Tristan's father. "Do you know what they meant about what they already know about Keep Shadow Veil?" he asked Collette.

"Something about Lord Tsukuyomi, but I don't know details myself," she confessed, shrugging a shoulder. "I'm not terribly involved in politics yet. I mostly focus on my own duties and learning. I've started being trained in some things, mind, just not really intel. I hadn't known you got to see Ookie's powers."

"Only a little," Rose confessed. "He stayed transformed to fight StormShaper, but he only used that strange magic to open the keep."

Collette nodded. "I'm not surprised. He's not really supposed to use it much."

"Is that your father's rule?" Solomon asked curiously. Collette shook her head as she chewed, waiting to answer.

"No, not completely. It's Mother's, too. Though that's another bit of information I'm not privy to: why."

Tristan thought back to his training with Zatook and how the man had used the form to speak to him. He almost said nothing, but the princess had assured them no was listening; and she seemed to be on Zatook's side. "When Zatook started training me, he used a different form at one point so he could talk to me; big and more gargoyle-like. I'm assuming that's the form he used at the keep?" he asked.

"Oi, he can talk?" Alconai questioned, surprised.

"In that form, yes. In exchange for training, I've been teaching him to sign," Tristan answered hesitantly.

"Sign? As in the Language of the Silent?" Collette asked curiously. "He's actually letting you teach him something?"

Rose chuckled softly, but she also answered Tristan. "Yes, that's the form he used. But he also called on some sort of magic."

"Yes...?" Tristan answered Collette, a little taken aback by her question. "I know he's not usually very open, but is it that strange? Then again, his openness is probably due to my sister. She started teaching him while we traveled. The only magic I've seen him use is his shadows."

Collette hesitated, but it was Solomon who answered.

"Zatook is slow to trust, and hesitant to open enough to learn. As you have seen," he explained softly.

Collette nodded. "I've only ever known him to open up to Tannen. He even tries to keep *me* at a distance," she explained. "Unfortunately for him, I can be just as stubborn. But it took time. And you haven't exactly had a lot of that." She hesitated. "I'm sorry," she added softly in regards to his sister. Zatook had told her of the little one's loss.

"Thank you," Tristan replied softly to the condolences. "I'm glad I can repay Zatook in some way, and I hope he'll have an easier time communicating with people. At least, with people who know the language."

"Mayhap ye could teach me, so I ken what he says," Alconai encouraged gently. "Give me a project in me down time."

"I'd be happy to teach anyone who wants to learn," Tristan agreed. "I know Rose already knows the language." He looked to the rest of the group.

"I've learned it as well," Jabez answered, "but I appreciate the offer all the same."

"I have been trained, but I would encourage Captain to learn," noted Solomon. Said girl was currently twirling her fork through her food with half-lidded eyes, having lost track of the conversation. She hadn't really taken a bite since Alconai took her hand. "Though for now, I might need to get her to bed," he added, watching her. Poor girl looked like she wanted to curl under the table until everyone was gone. He turned back to the others. "It has been a long day. The best thing for now is to get some rest. We can start searching through the archives tomorrow and deal with the show pony audience when it comes." He stood, moving to gently back Captain's chair away from the table. A quick glance from Solomon to Alconai let the entertainer know he could go with them if he wished, but Solomon was getting her out of the awkward situation. She numbly took his proffered hand, murmuring something before letting him lead her back towards the guest quarters. Rose glanced up to watch the pair leave; a concerned frown twitched at the edge of her lips.

After receiving a reassuring nod from Jabez, Alconai followed Solomon and Captain from the room. He stayed silent for the trek, letting Solomon handle things. Alconai had noticed Captain seeming out of sorts but had attributed it to Amaya's absence and the loss of Arianna. The audience with the king hadn't helped matters. However, Alconai wondered if there was more to it. He recalled what happened between Captain and Jabez at the inn.

Solomon took Captain to her suite in the tower. Each room had a bed, a washroom, and a small sitting space; he walked her to the small lounge sofa and guided her to sit, stepping away and letting Alconai join her. Since she wouldn't be alone, he moved back downstairs to ring the servant's bell in the parlor to request some calming tea.

Alconai sat with Captain, but he stayed silent. He simply tried to be a comforting presence. He would let Captain speak in her own time.

Captain let herself slide sideways until she was leaning against his shoulder, half-heartedly fiddling with her bangles. She was silent for a while, but finally Alconai heard her softly explain, "T'e anniversary o' me clan's death is comin' up."

"I wondered," Alconai said softly. "Ye donnae need ta tell me if'n ye arenae ready. Take yer time." He touched his head to hers, his hat tilting slightly up with the gesture.

"It was my faul'," she confessed, staring at her hands. "I was jus' a tot. Donnae really remember it. Jus' bits an' pieces. My powers destroyed everyt'in'. Jus' left a bunch of ash. An t'ey havenae worked righ' since."

"If'n ye were only a tot, then ye had little ta no control o'er t'e situation. Great powers be difficult ta control—next ta impossible fer a child with no trainin'. I ken that's small comfort," Alconai told her gently. "I donnae think they blame ye." He considered his next question. "If'n ye donnae mind me askin', how did ye survive?"

"'Maya foun' me. Her sistah told 'er where ta go, an' she raised me."

"Ye take after her spirit," Alconai said with a soft smile. "Ye miss her, aye? Is there anythin' I can do ta help ye feel better?"

"She's basic'ly me mum," Captain confirmed. Then she sighed and shook her head. "It would be be'er if we coul' figure ou' wha's makin' me powers go wonky-doodle," she muttered crossly. "Tha's makin' i' worse. Bu' I donnae t'ink we should push t'ings jus' ye'." She paused, glancing over when Solomon entered with a small tea tray.

"There is more downstairs, as well as some treats the kitchen included. The others should be returning soon, so I left the rest in the parlor."

Captain hummed, staring at her cup of tea, but she looked up when something in the threads caught her eye. She reached out to run her fingers down a few strands. "Well, I guess i's a good t'ing t'ere's extras. Seems Zattie's plannin' ta pay us a visi' tonight, an' he'll be bringin' someone wit' him." She let go of the thread as she felt her powers pulling at her, not wanting to risk being drawn in. She closed her eyes and took in a deep breath, pausing when Solomon touched her shoulder.

"Take your time, Izzy. You can join us when you're ready." He nodded to Alconai before returning to the parlor.

12. Tightening Chains

Back in the dining hall, Jabez had stayed with the rest of the group. Despite his concern, he didn't want to crowd Captain, and he knew Solomon and Alconai were more than capable of looking after her. He turned his attention back to the conversation.

"Will Zatook be able to come with us when we leave?" Tristan asked Collette. "Is there any way the king would allow it?"

Collette hesitated a second before her straight-backed demeanor faded. She placed her elbow on the table and her chin in her hands, her expression downright depressed. "I do not know. I have been attempting to have him placed on my personal guard, but even Father's favoritism towards me does not sway him. If I inferred correctly, Zatook is growing more defiant since traveling with you. Glad as I am to hear it, it rather does hurt his chances to leave again. I do not fully understand all of the magics binding him. I'm fairly certain I'm being prevented from discovering them, as well." She grimaced. "He could certainly try, but if Father disallows it…he would have to return."

Tristan clenched his free hand around his silverware before forcing himself to place the utensil on the table. His heart went out to Zatook. Even if Tsukuyomi hadn't been as horrible, Tristan sympathized with having his freedom stolen and his family threatened. At least Traiborn seemed to dote on Collette. Hopefully, that meant he would never kill her to get to Zatook. As a brother, Tristan knew he would have taken any form of pain and punishment if it meant his father let his sister live free and happy. "At least he has you and your mother," Tristan voiced softly. He knew it was probably little comfort. "Maybe…maybe I can try. I'm not sure what I can really do, but I want to try if Zatook will let me."

Collette sighed, sitting up and moving to leave the table. "I shall attempt to convince Father for now. It helps that you are not set to leave immediately." She glanced to the group. "Do not be surprised if Zatook does not come around often while you are here, however. Father keeps him busy even in peaceful times. It is not uncommon for him to be gone for days at a time." The group had stood as she did out of respect. Lance sat back down as she left.

Tristan returned to his seat more reluctantly. He wanted to leave and have some space. His mind swirled with thoughts of Zatook, Rose, Arianna, and Amaya. He considered the rest of the group and what everyone had been through— what they were still to go through. Throwing decorum to the winds, Tristan set his elbows on the table and propped his head up on his hands, pressing his fists against his forehead to hide his face for a moment.

"We can go back to our quarters if you're all ready," Jabez prompted. "This might not be the best place to hold discussions even with the Princess' ward." His eyes looked over Rose, Lancelot, and Tristan. The Sun Child kept his head lowered.

Rose touched a hand to Tristan's arm even as she responded to Jabez. "True. And we need to decide how to approach tomorrow. We should include the others in that conversation."

Finally lifting his head, Tristan nodded. He stood and offered his hand to Rose once she guided her chair from the table. He remained quiet as the group walked. Even without an audience, Tristan kept his posture just in case they passed anyone. "Biting back retorts and keeping up decorum and peaceful relations feels like trying to swallow nails," he remarked for the group's ears only. "The king seemed cordial enough, but something about some of his remarks…" he trailed off, unsure how to express his thoughts.

"They felt a little too intentionally wrong to be an accident?" Jabez offered. "I noticed too. The joys of politics." When it looked like Tristan might say more, the ninja caught his eye and gave a subtle shake of his head: not here. Once they reached the guest tower, the group found the tea and desserts that had been set out for them. While Tristan helped Rose retrieve food and refreshments, Jabez checked the area for any signs of magic that would let someone spy on them. Because he knew enough of magic and runes to know what to look for, Jabez found the markings etched subtly around the guest quarters. However, rather than used for spying, these runes provided protection from such intentions. His mind went to Princess Collette. Satisfied they would be able to speak freely, Jabez returned to the parlor where the rest of the group had settled. "The guest quarters have been warded to keep prying eyes and ears from gathering information," he told them.

"Traiborn made very sure to let us know he knew who and what we all were," Rose noted.

"Do you think it's safe to assume that he knows about me?" questioned Tristan. Jabez ran his fingers through his auburn hair, the movement and color catching Tristan's curiosity. Tristan managed to keep from staring, but now that the group wasn't under intense scrutiny, he had a chance to really take in the rare sight of the ninja without his cowl. Tristan added, "Aunt Amaya said that he might already know."

"Probably. I imagine that might be what he was getting at when he mentioned Keep Shadow Veil," Jabez agreed.

"If he already knows, then why does he want us to give him answers?" Tristan wondered aloud.

Jabez sat on one of the sofas before answering, "He's giving us a chance to answer him of our own volition. The king is using intimidation tactics to wear us down, so he can get the information he wants. Intentional lapses in decorum, remarks just this side of too intentional not to be direct barbs, giving us a 'chance' to demonstrate our trust. They're all mind games. He wants us to know that we have no secrets here. That he has power and control, and that we are at his mercy. And he'll make sure we know that all while smiling and politely extending to us his hospitality."

"It won't just be him, either," Lancelot noted softly. "Not completely. Aside from the princess and Zatook, most people we speak to here may play at similar word games. It's all politics to them. I believe Traiborn is the only one who can put weight to his intimidation tactics, however."

"A solid reminder to watch what you say while we are in Andor," noted Solomon as he joined them. "It is hard to know what someone really knows."

"How is Captain?" Rose quickly asked him.

"She'll be alright. Alconai is keeping her company for the moment. She will join us again when she is ready, but I have to ask you not bring up her quietness."

"I imagine it has something to do with her lack of clan?"

Solomon hesitated, but he did nod.

"Then I shall hold my queries. I can sympathize."

Jabez looked up when Zatook entered the parlor from the tower's main door. With him was a young man with charcoal gray skin and blue green hair. The newcomer smiled when he saw the group. "Hello there, I'm Tannen StoneHeart, blacksmith in the royal forge and friend to Zatook. If you hear someone use the name ShadowCursed, they are referring to me— though they'd never call me that to my face." He noted Tristan's glance at Zatook with the name. "I don't really let most Andorians know that I'm aware of the moniker with which they've bequeathed me. I take the name to be a testament to my friendship with the 'Demon of Andor'."

Tristan stood and bowed in greeting as he studied the blacksmith. "It's an honor to meet you. I'm Tristan Nightshade," he replied. A bit reluctantly he added, "The Sun Child." He still felt undeserving of the title and strange introducing himself as such.

"Ah, the one training with Zatook. I'm glad he has someone to keep him company while he's out and about. And I think it's good for him to have someone to teach." Tannen gave Tristan a bright smile. He grew solemn again as he studied the young man, noticing the burden of loss and responsibility he usually recognized in his friend. Considering what Zatook told him, Tannen had a feeling these two might form a lasting bond through their similar experiences with terrible fathers. "Zatook told me about your sister. I'm sorry for your loss." Tristan simply nodded and quietly thanked him. Tannen added, "I know all of this must feel like a lot to deal with right now, but know you are in good hands where Zatook is concerned."

Tristan inclined his head in acknowledgement as he said, "He's been very supportive and has been helping me work through some insecurities that would affect future confrontations." The Sun Child considered this blacksmith. Zatook must really trust the man to have told him so much, and Tannen seemed genuine. Tristan couldn't help feeling curious about him, given the man's unusual hair and eye color. "I hope I'm not being too forward in asking this, but I've never met an elf-kin with hair and eyes like yours. Then again, the princess has lavender hair, so does it have to do with being Andorian?" Tannen surprised him by laughing.

"No, no. I'm not Andor born," answered the smith. "I came here to expand my craft as a blacksmith a few years ago. In truth, my hair and eyes come from my mother who is dragon-kin."

Tristan regarded the man with renewed fascination. "Dragon? Your mother's side? Am I right in thinking then that you are not a full-blood dragon?"

"You are correct, though I pass off much of my other half as being part of my dragon heritage." He smiled kindly at Tristan's inquisitive look. Tannen turned his gaze to Rose as he added, "I will say that from what Zatook tells me I have kinship in common with you." He watched in amusement as the Sun Child and the Star Child processed that idea, saw the realization click into place in Tristan's vibrant eyes.

"I had wondered if what I sensed was true," Rose confessed, softly accepting his greeting. She smiled at Tristan. "Very rarely will a Drow not sense another; the more diluted the blood, the more subtle it may be," she explained. "I have never felt another halfling before to be sure of the sensation."

To Tristan, Tannen said, "Zatook's also told me about a unique ability of yours that I would like to discuss with you later. For now, I should finish introductions with the rest of your group."

"Of course," Tristan said.

Jabez inclined his head to Tannen and shook the man's proffered hand as Jabez quietly introduced himself. "We can speak freely here. The princess left some gifts for us," Jabez explained.

"Ah. That does sound like her," Tannen commented with a grin.

Smirking subtly at news of his sister's antics, Zatook had glanced around the table to see if everyone else was there; he hesitated when he saw Solomon step around to shake Tannen's hand. The Ben-Galian did not address the hesitation. However, with Zatook's reaction, he couldn't help but wonder if Tannen knew about Aditi and what had happened between them. Then again, that had been twenty years ago.

"A blacksmith, you say?" asked Lancelot as he offered his own hand. "We'll likely see more of each other, then. Loathe as I am to admit it, I can't exactly keep up my armor on my own. But I'm a little overprotective and tend to stay in the forge when it's being worked on." He rubbed the back of his head sheepishly.

Tannen shook Lancelot's hand. When the knight mentioned Tannen's blacksmith skills, Tannen replied, "I'd be happy to help. With smithing or anything else you can think of. I understand any mistrust you may have, but please believe I am your ally alongside Zatook." Returning his attention to Rose, Tannen added, "It is as you sense, my kin. I was born of a union between Drow and dragon. The king does not take kindly to our people. With my mother being a black dragon, I have been able to pass my coloration off as part of my heritage on her side. Though, I am glad to meet another like me given how...pretentious the elders and leaders of our people can be."

"My former mentor was a Drow. He mentioned how he's considered an outcast because he wasn't raised in Drow culture," Tristan piped up. He recalled what Rose had told him of her grandmother. "Is it a similar situation for you being half Drow?"

"Yes. Though, the prejudice comes mostly from our elders and leaders, not the people as a whole. My father is a good example," Tannen answered. He took some tea when Jabez offered him some. After sipping the beverage a moment, Tannen continued, "Due to my mother being a black dragon, my father originally mistook her for Drow. For her part, my mother believed he realized and was different from his kin. I'm sure you can imagine the falling out they had when he learned the truth. It almost ruined their courtship." Tannen smiled with the recounting of the tale. "However, my father couldn't ignore the feelings that had been genuine between them, and he began to doubt the teachings of our elders. Gradually, he concluded that they were wrong and chose to leave his kin in order to settle down with my mother. They live together outside Andor and the Valley of Dragons."

"What made you decide to come to Andor?" Tristan questioned, helping himself to his own tea and dessert.

Casually, Tannen explained, "I've always had a fascination and passion for working with metal and unique materials. So originally, it was to take an apprenticeship and hone my craft as a blacksmith. Then I met Zatook. It took time, but we found a kindred spirit in each other, both outcasts and alone. Never allowed to truly be ourselves in the public eye thanks to the king. I suspect the main reason I was able to rise to a position in the royal forge had more to do with the queen wanting her son to have an ally than my skills as a blacksmith." Tannen gave Zatook a wry smirk.

Zatook rolled his eyes, signing to Tristan, "More like they finally found a smith who could handle working on my blade." He had taken up his usual spot on the wall, arms folded as the others got to know his friend. Tristan's mouth twitched in lieu of a smile.

"How long have you been in Andor, then?" Solomon asked. He paused when Captain and Alconai came down. "Ah, Captain." He held out his hand so she would join them. "This is Tannen. He's a friend of Zatook's."

She gave Tannen a bit of a mock bow and winked at him like an old friend sharing a joke. "Cap'n Izzy, a' yer service," she announced happily.

"It's a pleasure to meet you, Captain," Tannen greeted warmly. He shook Alconai's hand when the minstrel introduced himself. In answer to Solomon's question, Tannen said, "Fifteen years. I came to Andor when I was seventeen. I'll let you do the math, though I am considered quite young for both my heritages."

"Ye donnae look ta be much older than me," Alconai agreed easily. "Jabie, whadda ye ken, yer nae ta oldest anymore." He grinned at his brother when Jabez rolled his eyes.

"Technically, I was never the oldest in the group," the ninja snarked, nodding towards Solomon. Then he reconsidered. "Actually, I think that title might go to Zatook."

Solomon laughed. "Aside from a certain Andorian, yes, I'm cursed to be the eldest in our ventures," he teased. He knew from her tales that Amaya was older, but he was still wary about mentioning Celestials even with the princess's wards.

Tristan smiled at the brothers' bantering. However, he sobered when Zatook drew his attention. He watched

Zatook sign, "I have something to show you, if you aren't against leaving the conversation. I know it is late, but I am uncertain when else we shall find the time."

Tristan glanced at Jabez and Solomon and then Rose. Deciding to demonstrate his trust in Zatook, Tristan nodded his consent and moved to follow the man.

Zatook led Tristan away from the tower, into the palace proper. Any servants or passing guards paid them no mind, continuing about their business. Walking with Zatook showed Tristan that the palace was as large as it had looked; they even traveled up a few flights of stairs before finally reaching a room with large, worn doors. The old wood was covered in carvings, but Zatook didn't pause to let him look as he pressed inside.

As he followed, Tristan found them surrounded by books and scrolls. The library was massive, full of towering shelves filled to the brim with tomes ancient and new. The room stretched to either side and back as far as Tristan could see. But Zatook was not done leading him. He motioned Tristan to continue following as he walked straight to the back and then to one of the corners.

All of the tomes and scrolls here were ancient and weathered, some even covered in dust though others were still obviously accessed. Zatook reached for one of the dustier volumes and tipped it down slightly. In response, a section of the bookshelf slid back and to the side, revealing a stone corridor with a staircase leading down.

Tristan had been staring in awe of all the books and scrolls, his eyes lit up with curiosity. He yearned to browse the shelves and find a tome to curl up with— to

escape into a different world for just a bit. The library
at his father's castle was one of the few things he'd
missed while living in the forest, so he had often gone to
the elven village to find books for Arianna and himself.
Before his thoughts could slip him into depression with
the memory of his sister, the new passageway caught
Tristan's attention.

"It wouldn't be a castle without at least one of these,"
softly joked Tristan to Zatook. "I used to scour my
father's castle for secret corridors and the like as a child.
I found several and would play in them quite a bit. I never
really thought about their significance until my mother
used one to sneak Arianna and me out of the castle."
Tristan peered into the darkened interior for a moment
before motioning to Zatook that he would follow him.

"I would not advise trying to explore these on your own,"
Zatook confessed. "I do not know all the traps the king
has laid. But the path we take is safe." He stepped inside
and waited for Tristan to follow before touching a stone
in the wall so the door slid shut. Hopefully, they wouldn't
be found. He reached up to claim a torch that was burning
in a sconce before leading down the twisted stairs. At
one point, a corridor branched off, but Zatook walked
straight past it and further down. Based on the amount of
time they were walking, Tristan estimated that they had
reached the main floor of the palace, yet still they went
down. Down until the stairwell opened up to a cavern.

A massive ceiling was stretched before them. Light
seemed to filter in the cavern from somewhere— looking
closer, Tristan could see small crystals embedded in the
walls. The ground dropped off to either side but stretched
to meet an intricate stone bridge that arched over an

expansive chasm before meeting a column of land in the middle. The edges of the small island were sheer drops, yet the scene atop was picturesque. A garden. Flowers. A brook that seemed to bubble up from the column before running over the top and off the edge. And centered on the brook's source was a stone gazebo housing a pedestal and a whitish-grey orb. Zatook stepped to the side of the entrance and gestured Tristan forward, to the orb.

Tristan studied the details of the cavern, mesmerized by it. All this was under the palace? He wondered what kind of flowers made up the garden for them not to need sunlight. Or perhaps magic was at play here, or even more of the Tek. He hesitated when Zatook gestured him inside. Carefully, Tristan made his way across the bridge to the gazebo, taking in the details of the garden and the brook and the structure. Finally, he stood before the orb and stared at its smooth surface. Uncertain, Tristan glanced back at Zatook to see what the man wanted him to do. When the man motioned for him to touch the orb, Tristan stretched out his hand and gingerly let his fingers rest upon its surface.

Red strands seemed to whirl into existence in the center of the orb, as if swimming through a fog. They reached towards the edge, lining the area where Tristan's hand was. And then the cavern fell away.

A woman in white, with red designs patterned along her skin, cupped his face in her hands and smiled. The sky stretched before him, the sun sliding across quickly and gaining speed. One...two... three, four, and on— forty-five day and night cycles sped past Tristan before the scene panned down to the castle. In through the roof, down the corridors to the guest tower. To Rose's room. The Drow was standing, speaking with a woman of flesh and shadows. Lady Rin. Tristan was asleep nearby. While Rose moved to kiss his temple in farewell, the Lady placed a small scroll on Tristan's pillow. Rose rejoined her, taking the Lady's hand and vanishing into shadows.

It changed.

Jeremiah sat on a throne, elbows on the armrests, hands templed before him and eyes thoughtful. A woman stood near him, with skin a dark golden brown, deeper than Solomon's, and hair of ebony. A dark crystal was set in her brow. She touched a hand to Jeremiah's shoulder, smiling gently and bending to pull him from his thoughts into a kiss.

It changed.

Tristan found himself overlooking a large valley, fully encircled by mountains. Dragons flew through the air and traipsed through the trees. A smaller circle of mountains was in the center, with an opening between nine peaks to let in travelers.

It changed.

A hallway in the palace, a tapestry between two sets of armor blowing in the wind.

It changed.

A sword, brightly gleaming, hanging from the hip of Traiborn's armor.

The changes were coming faster now.

The Talisman of Ruin clasped in a man's hand and dripping a strange, pink liquid.

Almas, gripping something in his hand as he took one last look towards Keep Shadow Veil.

Zatook flying through a battlefield, surrounded by ash and smoke.

Traiborn admiring an intricate dagger with bright purple metal interwoven with the steel.

The group, in the guest tower, speaking with Tannen. Captain clutching her eye, hollering, falling.

The woman in white wrapped her arms around him, pulling him into an embrace. And Tristan realized he knew her. "Grandmother?" After the barrage of visions, Tristan's voice sounded loud in the stillness. As the scene began to fade, Tristan returned the hug tightly. "Wait. Where do I find you?" The woman gave him a soft smile, but before she could answer, the scene faded away.

Tristan found himself back in the cavern as the red vines receded. His hand slipped from the orb to the pedestal as his mind and body worked to reorient themselves. Vaguely, he wondered if that was how Captain saw things when she used her gift. Even now, Tristan wasn't sure what to make of any of it. Why would the orb show him his grandmother? Was she in Andor? Tristan stared at the orb. His grandmother had disappeared centuries ago. Was the orb connected to her? Even as he contemplated his grandmother's appearance, another scene stood out in his mind: Rose and Lady Rin. Forty-five days and Rose would have to leave, but what was the scroll? It was probably Lady Rin's instruction for what he needed to do to help Rose. Even as hope flickered in him, Tristan also felt the pressure like a great weight, his shoulders sagging.

And what of the vision of Jeremiah? Considering what Rose had told them, Tristan wondered if the woman had been Jeremiah's wife. And then the sword at Traiborn's hip. The dagger with the odd metal— Tristan thought of Amaya's warning about Traiborn having a metal to counter Celestials. Tristan had a feeling the valley he'd seen might be the Valley of Dragons, though he'd only heard stories and read about it, especially from his childhood as a Nocium noble's son. Who was the man with the Talisman? Was it a vision of its origin or someone tampering with it? Why had Tristan seen a vision of Almas? And of Zatook? What did it all mean? His mind reeling, Tristan tried to parse through the images and commit them to memory as best he could. So many questions without answers.

His mind went back to his grandmother hugging him. He wondered if it was supposed to be an apology for overwhelming his mind with visions or perhaps in comfort for what was to come. Or maybe for an entirely different reason. No matter the reason, Tristan found himself wishing the embrace had lasted longer. He wanted to talk to her— to any of his family who might know and understand things beyond him. Then Tristan's mind recalled the vision of the group with Tannen. Of Captain in pain. *Rose, is Captain all right?* Tristan asked through their connection.

Her powers flared suddenly, but Solomon took her to her room. He says it's not her powers causing the issue, but something else triggering them. How did you know?

Tristan barely had time to process the question before he heard someone clear their throat behind him. He turned. Back across the bridge, Zatook was on his knees with his hands in front of him, a guard to either side with hands tightly gripping his shoulders and spears crossed in front of his throat. He was glaring at the king. Traiborn stood on the bridge proper, arms folded and face cross.

"You are trespassing on sacred ground," he growled.

It took every ounce of self-control for Tristan to keep his expression neutral, biting back several responses he knew wouldn't help the situation. He cast his gaze in Zatook's direction but had to look away as his blood boiled at the sight of the man's treatment. Silently, Tristan prayed to Shaddai to guide his words. Then he met Traiborn's gaze levelly. "I must ask that you unhand Zatook. He was aiding me as one would for one of the Chosen Children of Legend. The information I needed to progress lay here, so though I meant no offense in coming to this place, I will not apologize for furthering my Shaddai-given mission," Tristan responded calmly despite the heat blazing in his chest. He stood tall once again, embodying the noble his father had raised him to be— as much as he hated to. Tristan remembered what Zatook had said regarding the king's acknowledgement of Zatook's status as an Order member, and Tristan doubted his own standing as a Chosen Child would mean much to a king who didn't follow Shaddai. And yet, the Chosen Children were revered here, so he had to try.

Traiborn was quiet while Tristan spoke, his face stoic and stern. Tristan could just see the two guards warily exchange glances. After a few beats of silence, Traiborn sighed. "Though your coming here was... unorthodox, I suppose it speaks to your claim that the oracle was willing to show you her visions. For this, I shall grant you a pass. But know that this cavern is open only to myself and the queen. And do not return here unless it is with our permission and presence." He jerked his chin to the soldiers, who hauled Zatook to stand. "As for the Shadow: no. He has many things for which to answer, let alone this latest trespass. Had he wanted you to meet the oracle, he should have petitioned properly rather than take it upon himself."

"As if you would have allowed us down here even had he petitioned you— likely because it came from him. You have no right to treat a living person the way you treat him, much less your own stepson," Tristan countered, a slight growl slipping into his voice. His mind flashed to the things he'd had to endure from his own father, and that had hurt him immensely. From what little he understood of Zatook's situation and seeing the interaction now, Zatook had probably faced much worse at the hands of the man who was supposed to see him as a son. Tristan's hands clenched at his sides as he fought to rein in his anger, but he was tired of feeling powerless to help the people around him.

Traiborn's eyes had been narrowing even as Zatook's widened, the Shadow watching Tristan incredulously. Traiborn let out a long sigh, unfolding his arms and moving to the edge of the bridge. He pointed to the stairs. "*Out.* And be glad I only mean this cavern," he growled. Zatook glanced at the guards to ensure they weren't looking before signing to Tristan: "I will be fine. Go."

Tristan sent Zatook a perplexed look that said he knew better, but Tristan refrained from arguing further. Instead, he held his head high and kept his back straight with his shoulders back as he passed Traiborn on the bridge. Tristan gave one last apologetic look to Zatook as he went by the man before heading up the stairs. Tristan didn't stop even once he entered the library. His pace remained brisk as he made his way back towards the guest wing, his anger rising with each step. Finally, he stopped in one of the hallways, glanced around to make sure no one was there, and then raked his fingers through his hair as he let loose a frustrated growl. Why couldn't he help the people he cared about? Suddenly tired, Tristan slumped against the wall and stared almost unseeing down the hall. Tempted, he considered wandering the grounds to take some time for himself, but then he recalled Amaya's warning again. He also remembered his vision about Captain. Pushing from the wall, Tristan walked back to the guest wing.

By the time he returned to the parlor, most of the others had dispersed. Rose and Lancelot sat with Solomon before the fireplace, quietly discussing the latest the two knights were aware of Andorian court etiquette. Rose looked up when Tristan entered. She started to smile, but paused when she caught his expression. She excused herself from the other two and made her way over to touch his hand.

"What happened?"

Tristan took her hand in his if only to keep himself under control. He appreciated her support and concern all the same. "A lot," he answered wearily. He wondered if he should talk when everyone was there or go ahead and tell Rose first. With a heavy sigh, he elaborated, "I...Zatook took me to see the oracle. Apparently, that's a trespass, and now he's being punished for going behind the king's back." Tristan looked away, feeling shame for letting his emotions get the better of him. "I snapped at the king about how he was treating Zatook." Tristan moved to one of the sofas and sank onto it. He noticed Jabez asleep on the other sofa. The man had changed back into his original garb sans the long sleeves and armor bits. Since Alconai wasn't in the room, Tristan surmised the entertainer had gone to bed.

Rose shifted from the special chair so she could curl up next to him on the sofa. She leaned her head on his shoulder as he vented, her eyes on the fire crackling nearby. "I know it does not make it any easier, but he had to have known what he was doing," she noted softly. She couldn't help a dry chuckle. "I wish we did not need to worry so much over what the king thinks. Hopefully this will not affect tomorrow's audience." She sighed, closing her eyes. After a moment of silence, she spoke again. "Was this oracle a person? Or an artifact of some kind?"

Tristan touched his head to hers, appreciating the comfort and contact. "Both? I touched an orb that seemed to have magical properties, but when I was pulled into the visions, I saw my grandmother. She hugged me. I don't know if she was showing me the visions or if the orb was showing me her. Maybe the orb is like a conduit?" Tristan explained as best he could.

Rose frowned at him. "Your grandmother...?" she trailed off, then shook her head. One thing at a time. "It is possible the orb is a conduit," she mused. "I cannot say that I have heard of a conduit acting without its mage present, but I have not experienced all the magic in Aviyah."

"Perhaps the mage is inside somehow? But then that begs the question if the mage is my grandmother or someone connected to her. Or maybe I'm tired enough that I'm grasping at straws and thinking they're giving me the answers to the universe," Tristan teased, giving Rose a slight smile. "Whatever the answers, we should rest. I won't be getting back in to see the orb— not without inciting the king's wrath further." Tristan looked over at Jabez's sleeping form before addressing Solomon, "I think we're heading to bed. Should we wake Jabez or let him sleep out here?"

Solomon glanced up from his conversation with Lance, but his look softened when it fell on Jabez. "Let him sleep. I'll get him to bed here in a bit," he assured the lad.

Tristan nodded and helped Rose into her chair. "Do you want help getting settled?" he asked, not wanting to overstep but not wanting to abandon her either.

"I'll be alright," she assured him. "This Tek stuff certainly makes it easier."

"Let me know if you need anything. Good night," Tristan told her. He repeated his parting to Solomon and Lancelot before Tristan retired to his room.

***

Jabez opened his eyes and sat up, staring at the crackling

fire. Only Solomon remained in the parlor, the firelight lower than it had been when Jabez had first drifted off. Jabez sat still, a nameless dread filling him and making his limbs feel heavy. No thoughts came to him. There was no danger, but still unease sank deep into his bones. He heard Solomon speak his name, a question. Jabez knew he should answer, so the man would know Jabez was awake and aware. Jabez's mouth stayed shut; his voice remained silent. Aware yet unable to do anything but sit and stare. He hated waking like this.

Solomon had been on his way to collect the sleeping man. He closed the distance and knelt, keeping his hands to himself for now but staying where Jabez could see him. "Easy, Jabie. You're safe."

He needed to answer, Jabez knew he did, but his body refused to cooperate. His eyes remained on the fire even as the light hurt his eyes. His mind stayed blank, and his voice stayed buried in his chest. He needed to snap out of this. From his words and tone, Solomon probably thought Jabez was having an episode. Was he? Finally, Jabez shifted his gaze to his legs, relieving his eyes of the strain from looking into the fire. Pushing through the stagnation, Jabez slowly forced his legs over the side of the sofa, repositioning into sitting properly. Lifting his hand, Jabez dazedly reached for Solomon, a silent plea for an anchor. The older man took it, clasping his hand and continuing to wait.

Jabez stayed still for a moment longer as he continued pushing through the trance. He started to lean forward in lieu of rising but instead touched his forehead to Solomon's shoulder and leaned into the contact. Just as Jabez convinced his body to try and stand, he felt

Solomon's hand on his back and remained still. The weight behind the touch brought life back to Jabez's body and mind, finally breaking through the stupor. Jabez sank into the hold more heavily as Solomon's strong arms wrapped around him in a full hug. Forcing himself to breathe deeply, Jabez mentally shook off the cobwebs. "This happens sometimes. I don't know why," spoke Jabez softly. His whispers sounded loud to his own ears, but he felt the need to explain. Timidly, he wrapped his arms around Solomon's torso, returning the embrace.

"It could be stress. Today has not been the simplest, to be sure," Solomon noted, gently patting Jabez's back. "And you have been under a lot of it prior to throwing politics into the mix. Though I will ease some and assure you Tristan returned. He spoke with Rose a short time and then headed for bed."

"Zatook?" Jabez noticed Solomon didn't mention the man, so he had his suspicions. The princess had warned them.

"Was not with him. I know naught else, as I was speaking with Lancelot at the time."

Jabez sighed deeply. "The princess warned that the king might pull Zatook away. We don't know that he'll be allowed to travel with us when we leave," he mused. He continued hugging Solomon, finding solace. "We've barely been here a day, and we're falling apart. It's only going to get worse. We're going against a Celestial. We have the Talisman of Ruin to contend with. We've lost one and soon to be two of ours. We're seeking refuge with a king who holds prejudices against two if not all three Chosen Children," Jabez quietly spoke. His grip tightened a moment before loosening as he sagged in weary dejection. "We're not really safe, and yet this is the safest we can be. I feel like I should be doing more to help with everything, but I don't know what. I comforted Tristan at the inn and told him about my parents." Jabez grew quiet for a moment before stating, "We need Amaya. Captain needs her mum, and Tristan needs his aunt. But Amaya can't be here, so who will fill her place? I don't think I've shown enough gratitude for everything you and she do to support us. And now you're trying to shoulder this while dealing with your own feelings. And I'm sitting here lost in my own head and whining about things instead of figuring out how to help ease the load." Jabez pulled from the embrace as he forced himself to sit up despite how much he still wanted to curl up in comfort and safety.

"Jabez," Solomon chided softly. "Do not ignore your own burdens trying to hold the rest of the world. Need I remind you that you almost died as well? No one is expecting you to have all the answers, least of all while you are recovering. I would not even hold myself to that standard. Shaddai sent us to these halls for a reason. We simply have yet to discover why. We stand with the Children; there was bound to be trials and dangers. Times when we cannot find safety. That is what it means to support their mission, even if we do not yet fully understand what all that mission entails."

"I knew I couldn't beat Marilyn," Jabez remarked. "I'm just a man without any way to thwart blood magic, but I needed to do something. For all their power, the Chosen Children are children. Children being hurt and pressured and broken." Jabez balled his hands into fists as the memory of the fight with Marilyn came to him. He thought of the king taking Zatook away. Of Amaya being forced to leave the group. Of Rose giving her everything. Captain pushing through exhaustion and pain. Tristan barely holding himself together. "I'm scared," Jabez confessed softly. "I have knowledge and skills that could help, maybe. I've been using my experience for the positive and good, but I'm scared I'll slip. I don't want to go back to being a faceless body. I feel it here though— in this place with these kinds of people. The more I think I need to be seen to be a shield, the more tempted I am to slip behind the mask of who I was in that place with those people." Jabez's hands began to shake with how hard he clenched them.

As Solomon listened, he shifted up onto the sofa to sit next to Jabez, keeping his arm around the man and rubbing his back soothingly. "Most skills and knowledge are not evil on their own," he pointed out softly. "It is how we wield them that defines us. You are not in that place, Jabez. You are not with those people. You do not need to be them to turn their tactics to the Children's advantage. You have only to tame yourself, and that will take time. Even I still learn control." He hesitated for a moment. "Being human does not take away your ability to handle stronger opponents. It simply means you need better tools. When we learn more about those we face, we better prepare. And now we know just how far Marilyn has fallen, just how powerful she has become. Perhaps we can find a better way to counter her magics."

Jabez fell silent as he mulled over Solomon's words. "You seem to control yourself rather well," he finally commented, half-heartedly teasing. "Hopefully the audience will go well, and we'll be able to learn something from the archives."

Solomon chuckled. "Not as well as I could. I had to hide

behind my water lest I deck a king." He stood before offering Jabez his hand.

"You're not the only one," admitted Jabez. He took the proffered hand and stood. "Sleep well, Sol." Jabez moved to his own room to try and return to sleep.

13. Radiant Requiem

As morning broke over the palace, Captain could be found in the parlor. Servants had brought breakfast for the group, soft domes of magic helping dishes stay warm or cool as needed until they were served. Captain had started with a mug of tea, moving over to the open-columned wall that led to the courtyard and admiring the flowers even as she mulled over the past few days and visions. She was back in her Doran attire, the outfit fresh and clean once more, but she had changed her hair. Rather than hanging loose, the russet locks were pulled into a myriad of tiny braids that had been decorated with small beads and ribbons. Most were brightly colored, but one braid near her temple was twined with a simple black ribbon and four beads near the end. It had taken her hours, but she hadn't woken Rose or Jabez to help her. She rarely woke anyone for the braids now that she was old enough to do them herself. Amaya had helped when Captain was young yet old enough to know she wanted to, and Jabez a few times. While the hairstyle itself wasn't anything special, she usually only wore it around the anniversary of her clan's death. The black ribbon was a sign of mourning among the Doran, and the beads were for each family member she knew she had lost in her life. She didn't really know if she had any siblings. One day, she would Look. But she wasn't there yet.

Tristan entered the parlor, looking fresher than he had

the last few days: better rested and clean. He felt some surprise not seeing Rose or Jabez yet, but then they were both still recovering. Let them sleep as long as they could. Tristan prepared and retrieved his own mug of tea before joining Captain. He stayed quiet, not wanting to intrude. He watched the flowers and savored the crisp morning air. A part of him wanted to ask about Captain's new hairstyle, but Tristan didn't want to offend by prying.

"I would offer ta give ye a ribbon an' a couple o' beads, too, but I donnae t'ink yer 'air be long enough for braids," Captain mused, a slight twinkle in her eye. Her grin slipped a bit. "I... I havenae really said anyt'in' ta ya yet. I'm sorry. I jus'... I'm nae tha' great wit' grief meself. An' even t'ough I ken we couldnae do anyt'in' against tha' magic, I still cannae 'elp bu' feel like it was our faul'. I promised ye, an' t'en I couldnae keep tha' promise." She let out a breath before sipping her tea. "I lost me clan when I was li'l," she admitted quietly. "Whatever 'appened ta make me powers grow beyond my control...it wiped 'em out. Did ya ken tha' Doran mourn fer a week? An' t'en e'ry year after, t'ey se' aside one week ta remember all t'ey lost. Normally t'e week varies by clan, so I pick t'e week I lost 'em all." She kept her eyes on the flowers. "I feel like such a coward. I could look back an' See what 'appened. Migh' even figure ou' wha's wrong wit' me. Bu' I cannae bare t'e thought. So I'm nae really one ta help ot'ers through t'eir grief. I'm nae any good at me own."

Tristan listened as he nursed his own mug. When Captain finished speaking, Tristan responded, "I don't blame any of you for what happened with Arianna. If anything, I'm the one who broke my promise to her. She was my responsibility. I should have hidden her pendant better or not been captured." He sighed heavily and gave her a sympathetic glance. "Thank you for sharing. I don't think you're a coward. Even after seven years, losing my mother still hurts like a knife to the chest. And now in the wake of losing my sister, I feel like I'm drowning. Both times though, I've had people who kept me afloat. Clovestein helped after my mother's passing, and I had Arianna to raise. Now, this group is helping me find the way forward while not shaming me for grieving. I have a couple of pictures I drew of my mother and my sister, but I can't bring myself to look at them," Tristan told her. He held the mug in his hands, feeling the warmth seep into his palms and fingers. "When my father destroyed her pendant, I managed to push through enough to gather some of Arianna's essence into a crystal. I haven't pulled it out, though. I don't think I can look at it yet."

Captain was quiet for a few moments, lapsing into companionable silence. She chewed on her lip slightly, trying to find a way to phrase what she wanted to say. "I ken ye said 'Maya be yer aunt," she started softly. "An' she's basically me mum. Which be makin' us sorta cousins, aye?" She hesitated, gauging his reaction. She didn't want to upset him or seem overly cavalier. "Would ye min' if I be addin' a bead fer Arianna?"

Tears stung Tristan's eyes as he smiled bravely. "I think she would be honored," he told her. Then a bit shyly he asked, "If we're cousins— I know my hair's a bit short but...would you mind if I tried adding a couple beads to my hair? My mother, Arianna, and your parents?"

Captain didn't trust herself at first, simply nodding and sipping her tea. After she knew her voice was steady, she noted, "If t'e hair nae be workin, I could make ye somethin' ta wear instead. Ye donnae strike me as an earrin' guy, but I could make ye an ear cuff or a bracele' or somethin'."

"I wouldn't mind an ear cuff," Tristan agreed. "Thank you. Does Amaya wear the beads? Or anyone else on your crew?"

"Aye, 'Maya does. Sol doesnae, bu' 'e's got 'is own way o' honorin' t'e dead. Jabie's go' a necklace I made 'im." She reached up to touch the third and fourth black bead. "T'ese be fer his mum and firs' da."

"Thank you for sharing this with me," Tristan told her again. He considered a moment before asking, "If Amaya is your mum, do you see Solomon as your father? What about Jabez? If you don't mind my asking. It's just that Jabez didn't seem all that happy to see you all at first, so I wasn't entirely sure what relationship you have."

Captain laughed at that, long and hard. "Oi, yosh, tha's cuz he went an' got caught ou'," she teased. "Jabie's like a brudda ta me. He jus' wen' runnin' off on 'is own some time ago an' hadnae kept in touch much."

"He is rather reserved, though he's reached out to me a bit to check on me and share some of his past," commented Tristan. "Was he with you when you became captain? How did that happen?"

Captain snorted in her tea. "Aye, he was t'ere. I was ten. We sailed a lo' 'cause it kept us movin' and Maya jus' likes bein' a' sea. Funnily enough, we go' raided." She paused to finish her cup, moving for a refill. "We werenae t'e firs' target, but we go' taken on t'eir ship. Maya was abou' ready ta fry 'em, but I ken t'ere was somethin' on t'e ship we were supposed ta get— just nae wha'." Fresh cup in hand, she returned to the columns. "T'eir captain was… somethin'. Donnae ask me how he go' a crew an' kept it. T'ey were sloppy, both in 'andlin' t'eir ship an' in tryin' ta loot. I kid ye nae, storm hits an t'ey donnae even tie up t'eir sails. So I start yellin' at 'em, an' by t'e time t'ey're lookin' a wee bi' annoyed, Sol an' Maya an' Jabie are out o' t'eir ropes behin' me. Maya jus' starts movin' ta brace t'e ship, Sol pulls ou' his blades, an' t'ey all start listenin' righ' quick." She snickered with the memory. "Next port, we booted t'e cap'n, le' anyone off 'ho wanted off, an' kept t'e res' ta work t'e ship wit' us." She grinned at him. "'Parran'ly t'e t'ing we be needin' was t'e crew wha' stuck wit' us. Nugget was in tha' batch, I 'member."

Tristan laughed, the sound rich and warm. "That sounds like you lot," he agreed. "Your crew certainly seems to prefer you. I'm a little surprised they let a kid become the new captain. It's impressive." As he thought about her story, something caught his attention. "How long have you known about Amaya?"

Captain paused, considering. "Mm. I donnae really ken when I foun' out. I le' slip a' one point ta Sol durin' a flare, but 'e ne'er brought it up. I wasnae always so tigh'-lipped durin' me visions, so I'm sure t'ey bot' learned a fair few t'ings." She blushed slightly.

"I imagine it can be hard to keep things to yourself when everyone's business flashes through your mind," Tristan sympathized. "From what I understand and somewhat recall, I have an aunt who sees visions, but I don't know the extent of her powers." He paused as his thoughts wandered back to the previous day. "I got a taste of what it might feel like, I think. Zatook took me to see the oracle. It was an orb, and when I touched it, I saw visions. It was hard to decipher them all because they flew by so fast. Then at the end my grandmother hugged me, but I don't know if it was really her or just another part of the visions."

Captain arched an eyebrow, turning to look at him. "Ye saw yer grandmum in a bunch of visions? An' she hugged ye? In a vision, or…?"

Tristan rubbed the back of his head before taking another sip of his tea. Finally, he tried to explain, "More like I saw her, then a bunch of visions, and then she hugged me. But I was looking into an orb, so I don't know if she or someone else was using the orb to reach out to me. If someone else was doing it, why show me my grandmother? If it was my grandmother, why didn't she tell me where to find her or how to help her?" Tristan looked at Captain as he added, "My grandmother disappeared centuries ago. I only know what she looks like because some friends in Nikko Mori knew her and showed me sketches of her and my grandfather done by another friend of theirs."

Captain considered this, sipping her tea. "Yer grandmum…Who is she? Wha' does she look like?"

"Grandma Aria has white hair, heterochromatic eyes, and a pale complexion. She also has red markings along her skin," answered Tristan, tracing his fingers over his face as if to demonstrate the markings. "As far as I know, she's still the Celestial of Time. There hasn't been another Celestial named to replace her. Why?"

Captain's frown deepened. "Ok. Answers bu' more questions. I've been seein' yer grandmum in me visions, too." She pursed her lips, frowning. "If Andor's go' an orb tha' channels t'e Celestial o' Time, tha' migh' explain why t'ings been more outta whack t'an usual wit' me powers."

"How so?" Tristan questioned, curious. He finished and refilled his own tea before rejoining Captain to hear her explanation. "Why would the Celestial of Time have influence on your powers?"

"Because she be t'e Celestial behin' Weavin'." Captain paused, considering how to explain. While she thought, Rose came downstairs. She was back in the strange silver outfit and her cloak, but she left her head uncovered and kept the fancier braids. Captain let Rose join them before continuing. "A'ight, so my Chil' powers play inta magic I would 'ave regardless," she started. "Weavin' is a type o' magic specific ta t'e Doran. My powers strengthen my ability ta See t'rough Weavin', an' t'ey give me visions that are nae connected ta threads I can access. I can also destroy t'ings, bu' tha's nae our curren' topic. T'e Celestial of Time is said ta have given us Weavin' an' taugh' us how ta use it. But i's less I t'ink she is affectin' me powers an' more wha'ever artifact is strong enough ta channel her powers— if'n tha' makes sense?"

"I think so. Do you think it's been going on for years, then? You mentioned that you get flares. Do you mean like what happened with Jabez in the forest?" Tristan inquired.

Captain considered, taking a sip of tea. "I donnae think it's behin' everyt'in'. Bu' I think i' may 'ave been makin' t'ings worse since we crossed t'e Wall. Sol said t'e la'est issues werenae me, bu' somethin' else." She watched her tea for a moment. "Tha' power ye saw t'rough Jabie. Tha's supposed ta be me actual Child power. But it doesnae work like i's s'posed ta. T'ere's three levels, I guess ye could say, ta me pow'rs. Firs' is t'e Weavin', where I can see an' affect t'e Tapestry o' Time through threads tha' only Weavers can see. Then t'ere's t'e Sight that donnae require me ta be touchin' threads. Bu' t'e ot'er one is t'e biggest problem. Wit' Weavin', I jus' go'a build up me stamina fer magic, aye? An' the physical toll it can take. T'e visions, I can ge' a splittin' headache or ge' overwhelmed. But t'e blast…I cannae control at all. I's t'e main purpose of my seal, aye?" At this, she tapped her eye. "If'n I ge' overwhelmed by Seein', I can lose control of it. Wit' Jabie, fer instance, i' was 'cause Lance had been taxin' me ot'er powers." She took a sip of tea to let them process and to catch her breath. "Me seal is supposed ta fade o'er time, as I ge' used ta my powers. But Sol 'as had ta change it o'er time instead o' lettin' it degrade because I 'ave yet ta figure ou' why I cannae control it. It doesnae seem ta be an age t'ing, ya ken?"

Tristan listened, taking in what Captain told Rose and him. "If it's a practice thing, I imagine Amaya would have dropped her guise to train you, and we don't really want to be flashing our abilities around here," he mused. He looked towards the rooms, half-expecting to see at least Jabez up and about by then. Tristan felt some concern that the man still hadn't shown. Alconai slipped into the parlor and retrieved his own tea, but he only gave the trio a smile and a wave before leaving them to their conversation.

Captain shook her head. She debated before holding out her hand and channeling just enough. Rainbow sparkles formed about her fingers and trailed into the air, but they turned to ash as they drifted. "Nae a ma'er of practice," she confirmed glumly, clenching her hand to douse the lights.

"Amaya doesn't know anything? Or the Order that Solomon is a part of?" Tristan asked, his tone thoughtful as he considered her display.

Captain shook her head again. "I'll admit, I'm a wee bit tempted ta fin' t'is orb o' yours an' see if Time can tell me." She glanced over as Lancelot joined them in the parlor. The knight was wearing the same outfit he had for dinner, but he was holding some odd silver bit of cloth she didn't remember seeing before. Her brow furrowed. "Oi, wha's t'e shiny then, eh?"

Lance blinked over at her then down at the cloth. "Would you believe me if I told you it was my armor?"

Before anyone else could respond, Alconai scoffed. "Yer pullin' me yo-yo string," he said incredulously.

Tristan stared at the cloth, intrigued. He then looked at Rose. "Does your armor look like that when you're not wearing it?" he asked her.

Rose smiled. "It can, but I have my own way to store it."

Lance, for his part, took the cloth to a chair, set it down, and ran his finger around it. It shimmered under his touch for a moment before a series of odd glyphs that looked similar to letters yet just different enough they had to be a foreign alphabet lit up around the metal-looking cloth.

Then it practically melted into a liquid that left no stain, sloshing out from where it had been and solidifying as a solid suit of armor. He gave Alconai a smug look.

"Oh, am I?" he teased.

"Cheatin'. Cheatin', I say!" Alconai snarked. "Showin' off yer fancy armor. How fast can ye get it on?"

Tristan arched an eyebrow at Rose. However, Alconai's antics pulled his attention away from the women and back to the group. He glanced around the parlor and even stepped inside some more to really look around. "Solomon and Jabez still asleep?" he queried.

"That or me bruddeh snuck off on his own," Alconai remarked dryly.

"We've been watching the courtyard for a while, and we haven't seen him."

"True. He seems ta be a bit stuck ta ye three. Hoverin' like t'e mother hen he refuses ta admit he be."

"What does that make you? The rooster of the coop?" Tristan teased.

Alconai laughed. "I certainly be loud enough."

"And rather colorful."

"First impressions make or break a performance. Ye need ta be big and loud, sometimes without sayin' a word,"

Alconai told him with a wink.

"Pretty sure that makes you a peacock, Nai, not a rooster," Lance teased.

"Peacocks just be walkin' bags o' turds and feathers," Alconai clapped back. "I nae be that snobbish. Or temperamental. Or jealous. Or territorial."

Captain snickered at the banter before turning to Tristan. "Jabie may well jus' be wan'in' a moment ta himself," she explained. "Sometimes he likes his mornin's tha' way."

Tristan nodded to Captain's comment. He understood the need for solace now and again. His attention once more shifted back to Alconai and Lancelot's banter. He stared blankly at Alconai. "That…describes every bird," Tristan quipped.

"Aye, but peacocks be extra about everythin'," the minstrel insisted teasingly. With a smile and a soft laugh, Tristan shook his head in slight exasperation.

"Says the guy who fights with a yo-yo," Lance replied flatly. "Not extra at all, are ya, Nai?"

Alconai waved his hand dismissively. "It be nae extra; it be inconspicuous. No one e'er expects a toy ta be a weapon. Yer men didnae when they threw me in t'e cell."

Lance shook his head, activating the metal to become cloth again so he could carry it easily and then tossing it over his shoulder. "Well, you birds have fun, I guess. I'm headed to the smithy." He gave a two-fingered salute as he headed for the hall.

Captain shook her head before heading back to her room. She wasn't gone long; she had added the extra beads and now brought out some supplies to work on Tristan's ear cuff. She ran into Solomon on the stairwell, who greeted the others as he approached the breakfast table. He was back in his travel clothes for now.

"Of all the things we discussed at dinner, I do not know when to expect our audience," he mused.

"I imagine they'll send a summons for us," Tristan commented. "Possibly the king neglected to tell us a meeting time in order to keep us on edge and keep us from wandering too much." He sat on one of the sofas now, curious to watch Captain work. "Last night when Zatook took me to see the oracle, the king found us. He… I know we were warned, but seeing the way he treated Zatook… I let my personal feelings get the better of me." Tristan lowered his gaze in shame and frustration. "I confronted Traiborn, and now we're on thinner ice. I apologize."

"A' least ye didnae knife 'im," Captain commented lightly, working to string the beads between twists of leather and ribbon so they could be more spread out. "Kennin' what ta expect an' seein' it in front o' ya are very differen' matters. We ken 'ow he's treated, doesnae mean we expect ta bear witness."

Tristan sighed heavily as he sat back. He finished his tea before setting the cup aside with the dirty dishes to be claimed by the staff. He did grab himself some breakfast, offering to make up plates for Rose and Captain as well.

Rose took him up on the offer, but Captain just waved him off. "Did you sleep well, Solomon?" Tristan asked conversationally. Alconai retrieved his own food before sitting back to watch Captain, fascinated. He also took note of her hair but refrained from asking for now.

"I did, thank you." Solomon took one of the empty chairs, leaning back comfortably. "I must admit, it has been nice to sleep on beds again, rather than cots or bedrolls."

"I'd rat'er be on a ship. Let i' rock me ta sleep," murmured Captain.

"That does sound temptin'," Alconai agreed with Captain. "I ne'er been on a ship before, so I donnae ken how well I'd take ta it."

"Lots of creaking from the ship and snoring from the crew, I imagine," Tristan remarked with a teasing smirk. He hadn't gotten to sleep on Captain's ship, so he really had no idea, but there had been plenty of creaking and noise outside of sleeping hours.

"Pshaw, nae when ye go' yer own quar'ers," the pirate assured him with a grin.

"They didn't snore too often, really. And you rotate sleeping, so the ship always has hands on deck," Solomon added with a chuckle. "For the worst snorers, a wad of fabric in the ears can do the trick."

"What about ye, Tristan?" Alconai asked. "How quiet be t'e forest when yer tryin' ta sleep?"

"Not at all. If it does go quiet, you know something's spooked the critters, and that's never a good sign," Tristan answered, his voice wry but fond. "I suppose noise doesn't bother you much when you've been around it all your life. I actually miss hearing the woodland nightlife. I always found the sounds calming. And you, Alconai?"

Alconai snorted. "I be mostly sleepin' in inns. Most be decent at bein' quiet for their clients. Though, there be plenty times t'e night crowds got rowdy and caused a ruckus. 'Tis why I usually be pickin' t'e inns what donnae have a bar." He winked at Tristan, grinning when the lad smiled.

Captain snickered at Alconai's joke as she tied off Tristan's ear cuff and passed it over. Tristan took the ear cuff and fastened it to his ear, showing Captain and Rose when he finished. Despite the grief the accessory represented, he felt glad to be included and to have a memento of his lost loved ones.

14. Of Caers and Kings

Jabez sat by the window in his room as he gazed out at the expanse of the city and to the horizon. On his lap lay a miniaturized version of the Scriptures of The Sacreds. Jabez had decided to take time that morning to simply be still and listen to The Counselor. With the feel of the sun's rays warming his face and hair, Jabez took the moment to remember what it felt like not to hide himself. Even in the shadows Shaddai saw him and loved him. Jabez still couldn't muster the courage to remove his mask, but the feel of sunlight kissing his hair brought him a sense of peace.

His musings were interrupted with a light knock on the door. "Jabie? You up?" Captain's voice carried through.

Jabez smiled and called, "Aye, Captain. The door is open."

When Captain entered, she had a small tray with some breakfast. "We jus' found out we be havin' t'e audience soon," she informed him, sauntering in and sliding the tray on his nightstand. "An' ye ainnae goin' in fron' of a king on an empty stomach."

Jabez chuckled. "Thank you, Captain," he told her sincerely. He set aside the Scriptures and moved to the nightstand. Taking the dish, he sat on the bed and motioned for Captain to sit behind him if she wanted.

Even though it was Captain with him, Jabez kept himself turned away from her as he reached for his mask. He knew she had probably seen his face in visions unintentionally, but like with Alconai, Jabez felt too self-conscious and vulnerable to face her without his mask. "Are you planning to go in your captain's attire, or will you present yourself to the king and the court in your new, fancy outfit? I know how much you just loved the pink," remarked Jabez, his voice dripping with light-hearted sarcasm.

Captain plopped down and leaned her back against his. She snorted at his comment. "T'ey be hostin' a captain, t'ey be gettin' a captain," she announced flatly. "S'bad enough I gotta act all diplomatic. I'm wearin' wha's comfy."

Growing quiet as he ate, Jabez mused over his own options. "You've gotten good at braiding your hair. I wouldn't have minded helping, but I understand too if you were wanting some time to yourself," he commented. "How are you? We haven't had much of a chance to talk, just the two of us."

Captain was quiet at first, though he could feel her toying with a braid or two. "Tryin' ta get in a diplomatic mood," she confessed. "Talkin' ta a king ainnae like talkin' ta t'e boys, ya ken? An' every'uns gonna be starin' at us."

"Politics is a masquerade. You wear a mask and recite lines in a performance," Jabez commented. Setting aside his empty plate, he replaced his mask but simply leaned against Captain a little more. "Speak with confidence in who you are. Act with purpose. They'll listen. If it helps, picture yourself at the bow of the *Effervescence.* You command the respect and attention of your crew; you can command the respect and attention of a crowd. You are Captain Isabella MoonChild. Make sure every person in the room damn well knows it."

"It'd be easier on a ship t'an surrounded by all t'is stone," Captain joked. She was quiet for a moment, picking at a stray thread on his bedcovers. "Say, Jabie…" She paused, putting her thoughts together. "I been thinkin'. Is it weird ta keep goin' by Captain when we're nae on t'e ship? Or really wit' t'e crew? I mean, I go' you an Sol, but it's nae really t'e same, ya ken?"

"I'm hardly one to criticize names," Jabez told her teasingly. He continued in a more serious tone, "Do you want to be called Captain? I know you don't like Isabella, but do you want to be called Izzy or something else?"

"I though' about Izzy, yeah. But I donnae ken…Captain 'as more *oomph* behin' it."

"I see nothing wrong with sticking with Captain," Jabez encouraged. He fell into thoughtful silence for a moment. "I didn't choose ShadowDancer as my name. As I fought and did my best to thwart Shaedra in the shadows, the name started getting around. I don't know who started the moniker, but I felt like it suited me. I kept the name as my surname, but I prefer to be Jabez." He hesitated as he felt his heart grow a little heavy. "In Shaedra, I had another name forced on me. A…mask. ShadowDancer reminds me of who I am becoming now that I'm not in Shaedra. Jabez reminds me of who I have always been." He shook his head to ward away the heavier thoughts and memories. "I didn't mean to start rambling. Sorry."

"Ye're nae ramblin'. We're talkin'," Captain assured him. She considered for a moment before sitting upright. Since Jabez was done eating by now, she spun on her knees and hung over his back in a hug like she often would with Amaya or Solomon. "I's a pretty badass name," she added with a grin.

Jabez smiled as he looked over his shoulder at her. "I'm glad you approve. Honestly, I think Captain sounds epic too," he told her. Reaching back, he poked her in the ribs playfully. Then he reached up and ran his fingers through his light auburn hair, shaking out the strands. "How does my hair look? Acceptable for an audience with a king and his court?"

"Ye'll put all t'em hoity-toity nobles ta shame," she confirmed. "No one'll out-'andsome me brudda."

"Oh, I don't know. I think Nai has me rather beat. He has had a knack for pulling off the handsome, roguish persona," joked Jabez. "Perhaps now people will see more of Nai and my resemblances to each other. Although, I've spent so much time hiding myself to protect both me and those associated with me that I'm feeling anxious revealing something as simple as my hair." He reached up and hooked his arm around Captain, returning her hold. "Seems we're both stepping out of our comfort."

"A' least me clothes will be comfy," she teased, turning to kiss his cheek. "On tha' note, I should go see if Rosie be needin' any help. She was gonna put tha' fancy getup back on." She slid from the bed, but paused at the door. "I really mean it, tho. Ye look good wit' yer hair out," she noted before slipping out of the room.

Jabez moved to the wash basin in the room. Using the mirror, he checked his hair himself. It was lighter than Alconai's, and Jabez had kept it cut short to be comfortable under the cowl. Still feeling uneasy but determined, Jabez straightened his outfit. His armor and reinforced tunic were still at the forge, so he opted to dress in his sleeveless shirt with the rest of his black attire. He straightened the beaded necklace he wore as part of the memorial week, his fingers lingering over the beads. Moving to the table by the window, Jabez retrieved his book and carefully tucked the little tome back into his pack, his cowl left with the book. Finally, Jabez took his used dishes and headed to the parlor.

Jabez saw Tristan and Alconai already dressed and ready for the audience with the king. Both men had decided to wear the new, fancy attire— Tristan reluctantly while Alconai seemed rather pleased with his own outfit. Jabez smiled at his brother's enthusiasm. Jabez joined them once he placed his dishes with the rest for the servants to collect. Alconai stared when he saw Jabez without the cowl, but then the minstrel broke into a grin. Jabez felt grateful for his mask when his cheeks grew warm in bashfulness. Rather than say anything, Jabez simply sat with his brother and waited for the rest of the group.

Solomon wasn't long in joining them. Like Tristan and Alconai, he had opted for the new clothes from the seamsters. Captain and Rose were the last to make it downstairs. The younger girl took a look around the room and let out a low whistle. "I ken we saw it at dinner, but ye all really do clean up nice," she teased. "Best lookin' crew I've 'ad t'e pleasure of leadin'. So let's get t'is nonsense over wit', shall we?"

No sooner had the words left her mouth than a soft knock alerted them to the arrival of a servant. The man bowed low before explaining that he would be guiding them to the throne room for their audience and that Lancelot would be waiting for them there. Captain sashayed over and instructed him to lead the way. Before long, they were standing in a side hall that connected with the entrance hall where they had arrived the day before. Currently people were milling in and out of the castle and the throne room. Lancelot was waiting in the side hall, wearing his freshly polished armor.

"Apparently, people get to leave and enter between petitions," he explained as they joined him. "We won't go in until after they've stopped letting people in." As Collette had explained, the main doors to the castle were wide open, allowing anyone and everyone to attend the petitions or seek to give one. Common petitions weren't the planned affairs that Traiborn made of larger issues like the group's visit.

Tristan stood with Captain and Rose as he watched the people, fascinated. Jabez stayed toward the back of the group, his eyes studying the people for any would-be threats or persons of interest. He also stayed alert for anyone skulking in the shadows.

"Just like a king ta summon us and make us wait," Alconai groused lightly.

"How many kings have you had an audience with?" Tristan inquired.

Alconai snorted. "Me one and only audience would have probably ended with me execution."

Lancelot chuckled softly. "This is pretty standard protocol when it comes to a planned audience. It gives us time to look our best and steel ourselves for being in front of everyone. And it means we're ready to enter as soon as it's our turn."

"Nothing like adding the pressure of a crowd when subtly interrogating us," Tristan remarked dryly.

"It should not be too bad. We did work out the approach we would take last night," Solomon assured them all softly. "He would not have gone through all the trouble at dinner if he planned to pull the rug out from under us."

As they were talking, a few guards started milling along the hall, letting people know that the chamber was about to be closed for the next petition. Slowly, the hall emptied to a trickle of activity. The servant came for the group then, leading them out to the main hall and letting them line up as they wished on the blue carpet. Solomon stepped up to arrange them. For a more formal procession, he insisted that he and Lancelot take the lead, with the three Children in the center and Alconai and Jabez behind. He also warned that he would be using full formal names. Captain grimaced but did not complain.

Ahead, they could see the throne room. Unlike the spattering of nobles from the evening before, the room was packed along the sides and around to the door, with only space for the carpet clear. Nobles stood along the far wall closer to the throne, while commoners filled the rest of the space. The guards had stepped forward to line the carpet, people filling the spaces between the columns. Captain's eye widened at the sight, though only Jabez and Alconai saw how tightly she was clasping her hands behind her back.

"Tha'…is a lo' of people," she murmured softly.

"Breathe, Isabella," Rose whispered, touching her arm comfortingly. Captain just nodded, not even commenting on the use of her full name.

The servant was tutting around the group to make sure any wrinkles were smoothed and hair straightened. Satisfied, he motioned the group to wait before moving up to the door, just off to the side. Once he heard the summons given, the servant waved for the group to proceed. As Solomon and Lancelot led them into the hall, they noticed that Traiborn and Corianne were both in attendance today. Traiborn wore the same outfit as before, and Corianne still had her matching embroidered waistcoat. However, instead of slacks and tall boots, she wore a full skirt with matching embroidery. The only part of her outfit that wasn't white, blue, or silver was a small rose gold locket hung about her neck. The royal pair stood in welcome as the group approached.

Rather than take a full knee, Solomon and Lancelot bowed at the waist and stepped to the side.

"I would present the Chosen Children," Solomon introduced, making sure to project his voice so the crowd could hear. "Tristan Nightshade, the Sun Child. Comson Cryso, the Star Child. And Captain Isabella, the Moon Child."

The three dipped, Captain in a curtsy and Tristan and Rose in partial bows.

"Andor is pleased to welcome the Children of Legend," Traiborn replied calmly, seeming at ease despite the amount of people in the room and the soft whispers that started to build with the introduction— only to taper away at his response. "Since our founding have the Three been honored." Introductions out of the way, the king and queen sat once more. Captain took a subtle breath before stepping forward slightly.

"We be thankin' ye for such a warm welcome," she stated, trying her best to speak clearly. Her hands were clasped behind her back again, the pirate girl willing all of her nerves into that grip so she could focus. "T'e rumors of Andor's great hospitality pale in comparison ta our experience."

"We are glad to hear it, Chosen." Corianne smiled gently, her glimmering eyes seeming to guess the girl's nervousness. "And we hope to continue exceeding your expectations." Captain dipped a polite curtsy, but it was Traiborn who spoke next.

"What would you request of us, Child of the Moon?"

"My comrades an' I seek ta prepare fer what migh'y task Fate shall place before us. Long 'ave the Children of Legend found safety an' solace in Andor ta hone t'eir skill. We would wish t'e same."

"And you would be welcome to it. Andor and all she has to offer are open to you."

So 'ow abou' tha' oracle, t'en, eh? Captain managed to keep her tongue still, joining Rose and Tristan in another partial bow with another spout of thanks. Blood and daggers, she really did feel like a show pony. People were craning their necks to try and catch a glimpse. She almost didn't notice Corianne was standing now, moving to the base of the dais. "Come, Chosen of Moon, Sun, and Star," she encouraged, gently cuing the three to approach her. She took each of their hands, holding all three together, before continuing. "Andor's Wall stands ready to shield you. Andor's hearths stand ready to welcome you. And Andor's magic marks you friend." Warmth passed from her hands to theirs as tendrils of light swirled around them to punctuate her welcome. While the crowd was marveling at the sign of magic, she gave the three a subtle wink, gently nudging them back to their guardians. Once they turned, she moved back up the dais as Traiborn stood.

"In honor of the Children of Legend, the palace welcomes all in attendance and beyond to gather tonight for a feast. In the interim, Chosen, please be at peace and enjoy the day." Traiborn ended his statement with a bow, Corianne curtseying beside him. Solomon and the others joined the Chosen Children in returning the gestures before the Order member and the knight beside him led them back out to the hall. The servant from before subtly dismissed them back into the cross-hall so that the guards could start letting people move around once more. Captain let out a breath she hadn't realized she was holding.

Jabez touched Captain's shoulder and gave her an approving nod. "Well done," he praised softly. Looking over the others, Jabez noticed Tristan relaxing out of a tense posture as well. Alconai seemed unfazed, right at home before an audience. Jabez felt rather exposed, now glad to be away from the center of attention. He was used to keeping in the background and in the shadows. While he had chosen his usual attire to lend moral support to Captain, Jabez knew the outfit might gain some unwanted attention.

"I t'ink I be needin' a drink," the girl groaned, thumping her forehead against Jabez's shoulder.

"Why don't we return to the parlor, then?" Rose suggested gently. She hadn't been tense at all, having sat through several audiences— albeit usually in her armor. "A light lunch, and then perhaps a starting trip to the Archives?"

"Sounds like a plan," Jabez agreed. He lightly bumped his head against Captain's in an affectionate tap. While Tristan led the way back, Jabez stayed at the rear of the group, still alert. Alconai offered his arm to Captain with a smile.

As they moved through the halls, Solomon split off to go find a servant and ask for lunch in the parlor. Captain headed out into the courtyard to enjoy some sunshine, plopping herself on one of the grassy areas and watching the sky with her arms behind her head. Rose went to change back out of the gown into her bodysuit and cloak, while Lance moved to his own room to change back into the tabard the seamsters had provided. It wouldn't do to be walking around a host's castle fully armored, but he did wear the silver cloth like a half-cape off of one shoulder in case he needed it. He had adjusted it to be a softer grey instead of a full-shiny silver.

Alconai considered following Captain but decided to give her some space. Instead, he changed back into his traveling attire and settled in the parlor. Tristan changed as well before moving to explore the courtyard and take a moment to collect his thoughts. Jabez watched the two Chosen Children, considering. They needed intel, and not all of it would be in the Archives so conveniently. However, he fought the strong urge to disappear and scout the castle.

Solomon wasn't long in joining them, clapping Jabez's arm as he entered the room and picked a place to settle. He chatted lightly with Lancelot about his capelet and armor while they waited for their food, letting everyone have their space to decompress from the audience. Rose sat near the courtyard, enough to enjoy the gardens while remaining under the shade of the columns.

Once lunch was served and the group had eaten, they adjourned to the Archives. Despite his excitement at seeing the big library the previous night, the encounter with Traiborn and Zatook's absence left a sour taste in Tristan's mouth. Still, he picked a section on Andor's history to see if their records held anything concerning the oracle or the Celestial of Time. Alconai joined him in grabbing a few tomes before sitting at a table to pore over the literature. Jabez wandered the aisles, looking for anything about Andor's magic or magic in general.

Solomon shook his head as he browsed nearby. "I have heard so many stories of this place, and yet it is still far more impressive to see firsthand," he confessed to Jabez. Captain had wandered past them further into the shelves, idly perusing the tomes. Rose followed Tristan; rather than search for information on Time, however, she wanted to read up on the Wall and see if she could guess what Jeremiah might be planning.

"It reminds me of the archives at the Order's headquarters but bigger," Jabez remarked. Other memories tugged at his mind, but he pushed those down. "It doesn't smell as strongly of ink in here, though." Jabez indicated the large open windows that let natural light and fresh airflow into the area.

Solomon chuckled. "The libraries were some of my favorite places as a trainee," he confessed. "Both the archives and the more creative works." He scanned the shelves. "All those tomes, and we still have so much to learn. Especially with the Celestials. We have had little chance to update our records since they were largely banned from interfering with our realm."

"Oi, oi, do mine ears deceive me, or did Sol jus' say t'ere's somethin' 'e did fer fun?" Captain's voice floated from between the shelves to tease him.

"Surely I am not that boring," he joked right back.

"Jabie used to read everythin' he could get his hands on," Alconai piped up from where he sat. "When we were nae playin' in t'e woods anyhow. Remember when ye fell inta t'e river goin' ta Lady Hoshiko's? Glad as I be ye didnae drown, I was also rather miffed ye broke t'e rope." Alconai gave Jabez a cheeky grin. The elder brother rolled his eyes.

"I apologize that we had to take the oh-so-inconvenient bridge from then on," the ninja snarked.

Alconai chuckled. He paused as he recalled something his brother had said when they first reunited. "Oi, Jabie, ye mentioned ye thought Lady Hoshiko was t'e one who found ye, aye?"

"I'm rather sure despite how disjointed some of those memories are," Jabez affirmed. "Her presence was the clearest thing in my mind…" he trailed off as he met Alconai's eyes, an idea forming in their minds. "You don't suppose…"

"Did she have premonitions?" Tristan suddenly asked, his expression shifting to surprise.

"T'e world cannae be that small, it'll explode," Alconai retorted in mock denial. "We didnae live across t'e river from a Celestial. She probably just had t'e Gift like Captain. Nope. I be puttin' me foot down on this one."

Tristan peered at Alconai from around a shelf. "Dark hair and eyes the color of amethyst?"

"Stop, ye gremlin! How t'e blazes would ye— nope! Donnae answer that, I donnae want ta ken." Alconai eyed him wryly, though his eyes twinkled with mischief. "Tell us later."

By this point, Captain was cracking up, her back against the shelf as she just downright laughed. It felt good to laugh. "All righ', well, he doesnae ken t'em all, aye? Unless Rin an' Mythril be 'is grans or somethin'." She paused when she thought of their conversation regarding his grandmother and then doubled over again with more laughter.

Rose arched an eyebrow at Tristan. "Or are you going to

tell us Cerberus was your childhood mate?" she teased gently.

Tristan snorted. "I don't really know anything about Lady Rin or Lady Mythril, and I've never been to the Underworld to meet Cerberus," he commented dryly. "However, I know my Aunt Hoshiko has visions of the future and can look into what's going on in the present. She can see the past too, like Captain can."

Captain managed to contain her laughter as another thought caught her attention. "Oi. Ye donnae s'pose…" She trailed off for a minute before coming out of the shelves and looking to Jabez. "Speakin' of surprise Celestials, ye donnae s'pose StormShaper is a Celestial, too, do ye? T'ere's certainly more t'an we were aware of. An' if Tsukuyomi is one, it's nae tha' far-fetched, eh?"

"It would explain StormShaper's power and speed," Jabez agreed. He fell quiet as he continued looking through books. While his eyes searched, his mind worked. If they were going to be going up against more Celestials, then they needed to be ready, and they needed their Celestial to be ready. Jabez thought about his conversation with Solomon regarding Jabez's skills he'd learned from Shaedra, the organization that had taken him all those years ago. Captain and Alconai Jabez could train himself, but Tristan needed a teacher who could handle his Celestial speed and strength. Rose was out of the question in her condition, and Amaya and Zatook were not available right now.

"If he is…" Lancelot trailed off for a moment before clearing his throat. "Well, as awkward as it is, we know there's something here that helps fight Celestials."

Sol hesitated. "We would rather have to explain how we knew to even ask after it," he noted slowly. "Granted, our alliances may already be known."

"Do we really wanna risk more people figurin' it out, t'ough? If t'ey're happy ta keep it a royal secret, I'm nae sure we should go pryin'," Captain piped up.

"I doubt the king will tell us about his anti-Celestial tools," noted Jabez. "There are other ways to fight powered beings; we just have to be smart about it and careful."

"Still, it would be nice to understand more in case we come against it," Rose mused. "I do not know that I would be willing to wield such a thing, but I doubt our enemies will have such convictions."

As the conversation turned to other possible Celestials running around in the realm, Tristan's thoughts wandered back to conversations with his father and surrogate grandparents. Tsukuyomi had wanted his son to know about their Celestial heritage. Takumi and Feray had told Tristan stories about their adventures with their friends, including Tristan's grandparents and King Zetta. Tristan knew his grandfather had already passed before Tristan was born, but— as Tristan had relayed to Captain — his grandmother had been sealed away centuries ago. Tristan's mind flashed back to his grandmother hugging him in the visions from the orb. He stared at the books in front of him, completely lost in thought. Was the Oracle of Andor his grandmother? Or had the oracle used the visage of his grandmother to connect to him? And if it was someone else, why would they have the visage hug him? Tristan felt a strong urge to find the cavern again and connect with the orb, but the group needed to be careful with how they proceeded.

Tristan listened to the conversation as he continued through the library, reading title after title. If not for their circumstances, he would feel more tempted to snag a book to read later. As he moved through the aisles, Tristan took in the details of the library's architecture and furnishings: elegant and ornate but still giving a relaxing atmosphere. Wandering, he moved to a far corner of the library, though he kept an ear out for if someone called for him. The books in that part of the library appeared older, their covers worn. Perhaps they held the histories and mysteries the group sought. Studying the books, Tristan suddenly paused. Was it his imagination, the quiet and stillness playing tricks on him? Then it came again: whispers. Tristan looked around, trying to pinpoint the source. Tristan moved in the direction he thought he heard the voices. The whispers grew louder though they remained rather quiet. *ShadowVeil,* he made out. *Friend. Ally. Kindred family.* The voices spoke as though calling to him, and Tristan followed.

As Tristan neared the far corner, the whispers grew in volume and more fervent. They became loudest where the walls of the library met. A soft glow greeted Tristan as a runic carving appeared on one of the stones making up the floor when he drew closer. Mesmerized, Tristan knelt. He recognized the rune from his studies under his father as well as his time with Clovestein. It read: Kindred ShadowVeil. From the way it was written, Tristan realized the rune wasn't referring to House Shadow Veil but instead ShadowVeil himself— Tristan's grandfather. But why would the rune react to Tristan if it was meant for his grandfather? Unless it was designed for ShadowVeil and his descendants. Reaching out, Tristan went to lightly trace the rune with his fingertips only to have his hand pass through the stone. Tristan stared in amazement when his fingers brushed against leather instead of the rough stone texture he had expected. Feeling around in the small space, Tristan grasped the object and lifted it from the compartment. In his hand he held a well-used but well-kept leatherbound journal. As soon as the book was away from the stone, the rune disappeared, and the floor looked normal again. Tristan carefully looked over the book. Silver filigree swirled in simple yet elegant designs over the leather, reminding Tristan of some of the elvish texts he had seen. The journal didn't appear to be of elven make, though. Even the leather felt different.

Hurrying back to the others, Tristan sat down at the table where Jabez now sat with Alconai while the men pored over their own books. Jabez glanced up when Tristan joined them.

"What did you find?" the ninja asked, noting Tristan's excitement.

"A secret journal," Tristan answered even as he gently opened said journal. "There was a compartment in the floor that opened when I got near it. The rune that appeared was for ShadowVeil as in my grandfather."

"Yer granddad left a journal here?" Alconai inquired, his own curiosity piqued.

"I don't think..." Tristan trailed off as he noticed the language scrawled across the pages. "This...this is written in...how?" The writing was in Celesi: the language of the Celestials. However, the first passage confirmed the journal wasn't owned by a Celestial. He looked over the first page again and read the text aloud, "The Recordings of Zetta Albright, King of Andor."

Alconai stared at him in slight exasperation. He sputtered, "Ye found what of who?"

Captain snickered nearby, having seated herself at the table with a small stack of scrolls and tomes to look through. "Well, tha's prob'ly gonna come in 'andy," she teased. "Though if'n it be mean' fer ye, I donnae s'pose we should go readin' aroun' yer shoulder."

"So first it's a secret cavern with the oracle, and now it's a journal. I am beginning to see why all signs pointed to Andor," Rose mused. While Tristan had been exploring, a cart of tea had been brought for the group.

Solomon was currently pouring himself another cup. "Zetta Albright. Isn't there a Caer Albright in Nocis?"

Lancelot nodded in response. "Which begs the question of how did an old King of Nocis end up the King of Andor."

"He wasnae king in Nocis," Captain noted calmly. Now Lance was staring at her.

"Caers are named for kings."

"Aye, t'ey are now. But nae back t'en." She hefted up the scroll she was reading. "Accordin' ta this, Nocis was founded first, but Albright an' 'is crew wanted to go further in."

"Founded first? But it's..." he hesitated at the gleam in the pirate's eye.

"T'ey came through t'e Mists— or should I say, t'e Mists werenae t'ere." Now she had Solomon and Rose's attention as well. She slid her gaze back down to the faded ink. "This doesnae go far enough back," she complained, sipping her tea. "It starts wit'em landin' on t'e new continent an' watchin' t'e world close off behind 'em. An' t'ey donnae mention it again, a' least nae yet. Tha' Zetta is mentioned in 'ere." She nodded towards Tristan.

Tristan almost spoke up in answer to Lancelot's comment, but Captain had a handle on the answer. Tristan also felt a bit self-conscious after the teasing about him knowing all the Celestials. With Captain's nod, Tristan picked up where she left off, "My mentor Clovestein was adopted and raised by a couple in Nikko Mori: a human man named Takumi WaterSong and an elven woman named Feray. Feray shared her immortality with Takumi, so they've lived for centuries. They knew my grandparents and Andor's first king personally. Feray and Takumi would tell me about their adventures, but they didn't tell me everything. I do know that the group included the Chosen Children of that cycle, and that Zetta settled Andor in the kingdom's current location because it is near Sylva Arae, another sanctuary forest."

Tristan looked down at the journal again, touching the pages with careful reverence. He felt a mix of excitement and nerves fluttering inside his stomach. Finally, Tristan began to read aloud, "'To my friend, be it ShadowVeil or his kin, these words are for you. Within these pages, you'll find my research into the dreaded Celesbane that formed the catalyst for when our Celestial comrade split the continent. While I hope you'll never encounter the crystal that was developed to be the bane of your people, I am not naïve enough to believe that people will not give in to fear and spite. I refuse to watch helplessly again as the blood of Celestials soaks the earth while the ungrateful spit on their sacrifices." Tristan switched to reading silently for a moment as he combed over the passages. Jabez and Alconai watched him intently, both brothers looking more somber with the implications of the words. Tristan noted, "He goes more into a war that he refers to as 'The Purge' that broke out. The Mists were formed as a barrier around the continent of Aviyah to keep the other side from pursuing. Takumi and Feray never went into detail about the war, but as much as I want to read it, I'll leave that for later. Here:

'With RuneSage's assistance and my own experiences in the war, I learned that Celesbane is a crystal that is not naturally occurring, and the crystal has anti-magic properties with even more devastating effects on Celestials. Celesbane is difficult to learn to make, and the process is delicate. As such, it tends to be passed down in trade, and not many can make it— our friend RuneSage being one of the rare few. While he is willing to impart the knowledge to me, RuneSage swore off making any more after allying with the Celestials it was made to kill. During The Purge, our enemies learned how to get the Celesbane to adapt to any soil or metal it's introduced to. Celesbane is made through a mix of crystal that is used to create magical items, a crafted poison that corrupts the crystal, and runes. Despite its anti-magic properties, there are a few natural and divine magics that can draw it out. Drowic blood magic and Sylvarin healing magic as well as the divine healing from the Chosen Children and Shaddai's Blessed can draw out the Celesbane like drawing poison or shards from a wound.'"

Captain was quiet, though her eyes had stopped scanning her own texts. She was tempted— oh, was she tempted. But trying to look back that far now could be disastrous with the orb or whatever interfering with her visions. It was Rose who finally spoke.

"Well. Good to know we already have what is needed to defend against it, then," she mused to break the silence.

Jabez nodded. "The knowledge gives some comfort, yes," he agreed.

"There are some sketches of the crystal in here, but I don't see anything referencing something that was made with it during King Zetta's reign," Tristan added.

"Considerin' how he feels about Celestials, I be imaginin' that King Zetta would have gotten rid o' it," Alconai put in, "Sounds like t'e king was close with yer granddad, Tris."

"Yeah. Uncle Zetta mentions my grandmother too," Tristan told them. "'I feel truly blessed that two of my greatest friends lived through The Purge and are here with me even as their kin have gone. It means I get to share life's joys with them. Such as their union in marriage. I can't think of a more fitting pair than the Celestial of Time and the Celestial of Virtue. Perhaps I'll live long enough to see Trystan and Aria's children, though Celestials tend to have their children rather far apart at times. What are a few hundred years to beings who live thousands?'" Tristan glanced up at the group and immediately noticed Alconai giving him a flat look.

"Tris, me dear, sweet lad," the minstrel started evenly, "just when were ye going ta tell us that yer grandmum be t'e Celestial o' Time? T'e same Celestial o' Time we be tryin' ta find information on?" His tone became incredulous by the end of the spiel.

"I wanted to be sure before I brought it up with everyone. I've never met my grandmother," Tristan countered, a bit flustered. "I know she was sealed away as a punishment for a rebellion she'd been a part of in the Celestial Realm. No one knows where she was sealed, and it's been centuries. My grandfather was the Celestial of Virtue, and I know he's dead. Another Celestial hasn't been named for Virtue, though. I thought the same might have been the case with my grandmother, but then I saw her when I saw the visions in the orb."

"When did your grandfather pass?" Jabez questioned calmly.

Tristan shrugged before he answered, "He died before my grandmother was sealed. It's the one topic my father didn't really like to talk about and neither did Takumi and Feray. I know Trystan ShadowVeil died during the rebellion and that my father named our House after him. As for my grandmother, even Takumi and Feray don't know what happened to her after the sealing."

"I be guessin' mum didnae ken eit'er, t'en," Captain noted softly, folding up her current scroll. She didn't name Amaya since they weren't in the warded guest tower. She glanced at Solomon when the man stood and moved for the door, but he gestured he would only be a moment. She turned back to Tristan and the others. "An' I donnae 'ave a way ta tell 'er, fer now." Solomon was not long in rejoining them.

"We have permission to take most of the items in the Archives to our tower, but not the older scrolls," he explained softly as he sat. "Specifically, there's a section of scrolls that have carpeted shelves. Those have to stay in here." He gestured to Captain's pile. "Those should be fine."

"Then I recommend we adjourn to our shared parlor," Rose mused. "I would hate to keep others from feeling like they could spend time here." She also knew they could speak more openly there; she just didn't want to speak openly about hiding things. "That also allows us to take breaks in the courtyard as needed."

Lance closed his current tome. "I noticed there is an empty area in the courtyard we could use for training, as well."

"As of yet, we do not have a timeline for how long we are staying," Solomon noted. "For now, I would suggest we take advantage of the provided amenities. Rest, train, study. We should not push ourselves while we do not need to."

15. *Masks and Memories*

Jabez and Alconai helped gather some of the books and scrolls they were allowed to take. Tristan discreetly tucked the journal under his arm so it looked like an ordinary book or like one of his sketchbooks. He followed the others as the group returned to the tower. His mind felt abuzz with the information they had garnered. As they walked, Tristan tried to look for the tapestry he'd seen in the vision. He doubted finding it would be that easy, but he wanted to try while the group had an excuse to be outside the tower.

Rose was more than happy to stack a bunch of books on her lap for the others to transport them. Once they were back in the parlor, the group sorted out the different items before scattering. Captain chose to read out in the sun, with Alconai joining her nearby. Solomon, Lance, and Jabez followed them to the courtyard, but they moved beyond the gardens to the area Lancelot had mentioned as a potential training ground.

The space was small but bare; there were no plants or anything that they would disturb. The dirt was worn a bit, hinting that the space had been used for sparring before.

"It makes sense they would provide a private area for guests to practice without being ogled," Lancelot remarked, standing from where he had been examining the ground. "Though, we might still need to worry about containing powers if the Chosen wish to practice."

Solomon nodded. "I may send a missive to the princess asking if she has any ideas. They may be able to tie off a barrier for us, but then we still have the issue of training Tristan. I am not a Celestial. I could help in some instances, but I feel he would quickly outpace me."

"I can spar with him if I wear my full armor," Lance pointed out. "Though, it would be better if I could use an actual blade rather than my greaves. And I do not know how long I could keep up with him. But I vaguely remember facing him in Thorn-Drake, and I helped spar with the Scarlet Swordsman. Granted, Drow-kin are not Celestials, but it is a start."

"I had also considered asking Tannen," Solomon confessed. "Being half dragon-kin, he may be able to keep up. And Zatook seems to trust him quite deeply."

"I had similar thoughts about Tannen," affirmed Jabez, "However, Tannen has his work with the forge during the day, so he would have to train with Tristan in the evening." Jabez surveyed the area as he recalled his times training in Ben-Gal and in Shaedra. He didn't look at either man as he crossed his arms over his chest. "I can work with Tristan," Jabez finally remarked. Even with keeping his eyes staring ahead, Jabez felt Solomon aim the flattest of all flat looks at him. "Don't give me that," Jabez retorted. "I can at least help. Despite my encounters with StormShaper and Marilyn, I was trained to fight opponents with innate magical abilities and physical advantages over me."

"I very well shall," Solomon quipped right back. Lancelot hesitated at the exchange, though he chalked it up to Solomon's concern regarding Jabez's own recovery.

"I don't mind," Lance assured them both. "My armor should keep up with him at least until Tannen can join us. I wish I could tell you how it does what it does, but it's stronger than it looks." He turned to Jabez. "And last I heard, you were still healing. Not even a Nocium general would push an injured soldier, let alone one who fought a blood mage as powerful as Marilyn."

Jabez continued to stare at the vacant area for a bit before finally releasing a heavy sigh. Uncrossing and lowering his arms to his sides, he turned to Solomon. "I am healing, and honestly, I could probably do with some training myself." To Lancelot, Jabez added lightly but sincerely, "I wouldn't mind sparring with you. See if I can hold my own against a famed knight of Nocis." Finally, once more to Solomon, Jabez softened his voice as he tried to persuade, "I want to use my experience and skills to help." His words harkened back to his conversation with Solomon the previous night. Jabez then gave a nonchalant shrug. "Besides, Tristan can practice healing." He hoped to lighten the mood with a bit of snark.

"Help, yes. More so if healed," Solomon relented, unfolding his arms. "For now, though, it seems the others are content to be on their own. We can work out time for training." He paused, considering. "I doubt Captain will wish to join in. For this week, at least. But she had been working with me and Amaya. A few of the crew have sparred with her, as well."

"We don't know if we have the luxury of time," Jabez

calmly insisted. "These aren't like most opponents we've faced before, and we all need to be as prepared as possible." He rubbed the back of his neck, looking worn despite his protests.

"We do not know that we do not," Solomon pointed out. "I meant what I said. Until we know otherwise, we should not push ourselves too hard. Shaddai has seen fit to grant us respite, and we should take it with thanks."

Jabez started to say something but then stopped, keeping his thoughts to himself. Instead, he nodded his concession and stepped away from the two men. He considered wandering the lawn to look at the fountains and flowers but knew he felt too anxious to enjoy it. Instead, he moved back inside the tower and to his room, though he noted Solomon following him. Jabez stepped into his room and pondered what he wanted to do. His skin crawled along his back with a familiar anxiety, and his feet moved him to a corner where he turned and pressed his back against the wall. The uncomfortable feeling eased, and Jabez slid to sit on the floor. Bending one knee in the air, Jabez propped his arm on it and tilted his head to rest against the wall as he waited. He knew how Solomon might perceive his persistence and then sudden lack thereof. Standing before a crowd and being announced as a guardian left Jabez feeling wrong-footed. He felt himself wanting to sink back into old habits, slipping back into the shadows both physically and metaphorically.

Solomon leaned against the doorframe, watching Jabez calmly. "What's on your mind, Jabie?"

Jabez sat silently for a long moment. He reached up and

tangled his fingers in his hair as he tried to think how best to articulate the tumultuous thoughts spinning in his skull. Finally, he shook his head. His eyes stared into the middle distance, barely aware of his surroundings as his mind took him somewhere else in a different time. "I apologize. I don't know what came over me. I overstepped and was argumentative," Jabez's voice sounded flat when he spoke but not dry or sarcastic. His fingers gripped his hair, and Jabez shook his head again as he closed his eyes. No, he was allowed to have opinions and to push back when he didn't agree. The group didn't have time for him to be like this. And yet, speaking felt like trying to talk with a mouth full of sand, his instincts telling him to be quiet and compliant while his rational mind pushed back against the conditioning. Jabez longed to fade back into obscurity. Being out in the open physically and figuratively felt like existing with a knife to his neck.

Solomon straightened from the door frame, letting the door close behind him as he moved to sit near the younger man. He placed a hand on Jabez's knee, grounding him with his touch even as he let him focus himself.

"I doubt I truly need to tell you that you did not and were not," he noted. "But I shall voice it all the same."

Jabez shifted both of his hands to grip his head, fingers entangled in his hair. "The more I try to push forward and out, the more I feel like I'm running in circles. I thought I was getting better, but now I think I might have just been giving myself too much credit. Despite my earlier points, I'm really not the best to be trying to lead or guide the others in anything," he said the confession softly, almost whispering. "I'm best at intel gathering and staying in the background, but even that's not going to be an option anymore. My attire is made for life in the shadows but wearing it while in the group makes me more conspicuous. Draws attention we don't want. Puts another target on us." Again, Jabez considered leaving and helping the group the way he had been helping Alconai and the Order previously.

Solomon gently pried Jabez's hands free, letting him grip the older pirate's hands instead of pulling his hair out at the roots. "You've been doing incredibly well, Jabez. With everything. And the Chosen obviously respect your opinion. You have many strengths, with your skills in subterfuge being among them." He paused, letting his words sink in even as he considered his next carefully. "I would like to add to them, however. I would like to train you in the sealing blades."

Instinctively, Jabez's hands jerked a little in Solomon's grasp with the mention of learning to use the blades. Doing so would mark Jabez as Solomon's successor to the Order. Despite his initial protests, Jabez knew Solomon wanted them to be prepared just as Jabez had insisted earlier in the courtyard. This was one way. Still, Jabez released a tiny, exasperated laugh, ducking his head to indicate his own trembling hands. He kept his eyes averted even as he spoke, "I would be a waste. I can barely keep myself together as it is. What good am I if I keep going backwards?" Even as the words left his mouth, Jabez thought of Tristan shaking as the young Celestial tried to heal. Of Captain curling up in pain every time her powers flared. Of Rose vulnerable in the wake of her deal with Lady Rin. However, those were different circumstances from Jabez's situation. Weren't they? "I ran away from you. All of you. I thought I was protecting you by staying away, and now I'm going to bring Shaedra's gaze to our group. If I come out of the woodwork, so will they."

"We cannot force you to cling to our coattails forever, Jabez. The time would come when you wanted to strike out and try things on your own. Captain assured us you were on your path." He squeezed Jabez's hands. "You are young, Jabez. And learning. And healing— not simply from your battle with Marilyn. These things take time and growth. Do you think I was not a nervous fledgling when I first attuned with the blades? You would be sorely mistaken. Were it not for Pushpa, I doubt I would have been confident to take the role in Andor. I would have sat in the library, poring over texts and doing nothing with them— I am no scholar. But this is why Shaddai has granted us the companions He has. To help us grow. As you have and continue to do."

"What happened to me resting and not training because I need to heal?" dryly retorted Jabez. "Besides, with training everyone else and reading through a bunch of scrolls, when are you going to have time to train me?" He was deflecting, but Jabez couldn't help it. As much as he knew Solomon was right, and he wanted to trust the man's judgment, unease curdled Jabez's insides.

"What happened to having time and using it wisely?" Solomon countered. "We have the time, for now. You can heal and then train. I can read and then teach."

Jabez stared at their hands as he mulled over the conversation. "I know this is the best course of action given what we'll likely be encountering, but," he trailed off for a moment, reluctant, before he finished, "let me think on it? We have a feast to get through first."

"Very well." Solomon did not move from sitting with Jabez and holding his hands, but he did not press the matter. He sat with the younger man until Jabez had calmed his thoughts before moving to his own chamber to read until it was time to get ready for the feast.

***

Back in the parlor, Rose was beginning to notice that she had read the same line at least five times now. She sighed and closed her current tome, rubbing at her eyes before glancing out to the courtyard. "I would wager we have a few hours yet before dinner," she mused to Tristan. "Do you want to keep reading, or shall we explore the palace for a little while?"

Tristan considered for a moment. "I'm tempted to keep reading since we have King Zetta's journal, but I'm also both curious about the castle and wanting to see if I can find the tapestry from the vision. Though, I don't want to cause trouble for the group if we wander into something that'll stir King Traiborn's ire even more," he confessed.

"I doubt we will stir anything just looking around," Rose assured him gently. "If we find it, then you can mark where it is for now and find a better time to investigate. I will admit, I am feeling a mite stir crazy. And I cannot exactly spar with Lancelot." She smirked at him.

Tristan dragged his fingers through his hair. "Talk of training has me concerned," he admitted, "I know Lancelot can keep up with me to a point, but he was being controlled at the time. I'm not sure how much of that fight was him, and how much of it was pushing him past what he could actually do. Amaya's not here and neither is Zatook. And as much as I'd love to test my mettle against you, the circumstances aren't ideal." Tristan's eyes grew sad as he added, "Though, you may not want to spar against me after what happened. I wouldn't blame you if you wanted to stay away. I don't know how you can stand to look at me after what I did, controlled or no."

"You said it yourself. You were being controlled," Rose pointed out gently. "You have even less reason to be ashamed if she truly has reached the power of an Elder. I would have no qualms sparring with you. In truth, it may help if we run into such a situation again." She sighed, leaning back in her chair. "But no. Not until we figure out what you are supposed to do after I leave, at least. Assuming being allowed to return also means I will be back to full strength." She paused, considering. "There is Tannen. He did offer to help however needed."

"I hate to impose on the blacksmith, but he might be the best option if he's willing," Tristan agreed. "Give me a minute." He jogged up the stairs to his room and tucked the journal into his pack before joining Rose once more in the parlor. "Shall we?" Before they actually left, Tristan said softly, "Thank you for everything. I'm glad we met, and I'm grateful that you have stuck by me through all of this." Rose smiled softly, reaching up and taking his hand.

Tristan returned the smile and gently squeezed her hand. Walking through the halls felt a bit like walking through Keep Shadow Veil, different as the structures were. Tristan knew Arianna would have loved exploring the palace, looking for fun secrets and nooks. Even as he felt a pang in his heart, Tristan pushed it down and watched for any tapestries that might be from the vision he had seen.

The palace was as large as it looked from the outside, offering level upon level, floor upon floor to explore. The bottom floor had all of the public areas, including the large dining hall and ballroom where the feast was being prepared. They found workshops for Tek Engineers and various rooms for testing inventions. There was a schoolroom where the palace workers' children learned their letters and more. Some of the servant classes like the seamsters had workshops inside the palace, though places like the forge and tanners were along the outer building since they needed access to the open air. They found people dipping new candles for the feast, another team of servants washing the dining linens, and a small museum of Andor's history, both the country and the royal lines.

Tristan looked through the museum with fascination. He wanted to see how much of the history would match what the group had learned about Andor and its royal line as well as what Feray and Takumi had told him. He looked for anything about King Zetta, too, wanting to know more about the man who had known Tristan's grandfather and friends. Within the section giving details on the royal line, Tristan came across a portrait of a rather young-looking king. Dressed in regal clothes of Andor's colors, the young man stood beside a large fireplace with one hand touching the mantle and the other resting on an elegant sword at his hip. An ornate bookshelf stood to either side of the fireplace, the flames casting a warm and cozy light on the king and the books. The man's snow-white hair was cropped short and neat, and his gentle, brown eyes regarded the world with kind authority. The plaque for the portrait read: *Zetta Albright, First King of Andor.* Tristan studied the man's face again. "This is him," he softly said to Rose. "He doesn't look older than his twenties, but he was human."

"His position likely had something to do with the war he mentioned," Rose mused. "His sister looks even younger." She nodded to another portrait. The young woman within shared her brother's hazel eyes, but her own hair was a light brown, short on one side with the rest medium short and swooped to the side. Unlike the royal blues of her brother, she was dressed in a pink gown. The portrait was more casual, as well; she wasn't standing and staring at the artist, rather she was next to a pond in a garden, delicately cupping a lotus in her hands. A small selection of items beside her showed that she had been tending the garden. The gown she wore was slightly off the shoulders. Something rainbow was reaching just into view along the back of her shoulder. Rose didn't touch the painting, but she ran her finger in the air to the signature. "Looks like the same artist for a while," she noted warmly. "I wonder what other paintings they have."

Tristan looked through some of the other pictures until he found one with the painter's name written out fully. "Aster," he read aloud. "One of the king's friends. Takumi and Feray have some of her pictures she sketched of their group. She did a portrait of my grandparents." Tristan studied the pictures, admiring their beauty and realism. "I've never tried my hand at painting, but I wish I had half of Aster's skill." He stopped to look more closely at a picture of the sword the king carried in most of the pictures. Elegant in design, the sword appeared to be made of glittering glass with tiny, pink flower petals encased in the blade. Iridescent runes had been etched between and around the petals down the blade. The sword's guard twisted and curled like tree branches or swirls of magic. The picture of the sword had a little more detail on the plaque. "Starlight Sakura: a relic of the kingdom," Tristan told Rose. "Legend says that the sword cut through darkness and shone with divine light. It was lost shortly before King Zetta died, though some theorize that the king hid the blade to keep it out of the hands of the unworthy." Tristan straightened as he sighed. "I remember Takumi mentioning the sword in his stories, but he never said where it ended up after King Zetta died. Sounds like something that would have come in handy," he muttered dryly to Rose.

"Well, you've already found one hidden artifact," Rose teased. "Who is to say we shan't find the other?"

Tristan snorted but smiled and winked at her. "Well, I doubt the current king would be happy if we found all the kingdom's secrets," he joked. He looked through the rest of the museum before they continued their exploration of the castle. As they wandered, Tristan admitted, "Being here reminds me a little of Keep Shadow Veil. It's not the same, but the atmosphere is similar."

"I am honestly surprised how different it is from Caer Albright," Rose noted. "The port's fort seems not to have retained as much of the founder's influence as Andor has."

"Perhaps he didn't stay long, or maybe it wasn't just his people there," Tristan speculated. "You've been all over Nocis, haven't you?" he teased. "Honestly, I wish I could have seen more. I wish I could have gone places with Arianna, shown her more than just the forest she'd seen all her life. At least she got to see some, and she seemed to be enjoying it; although, she would have enjoyed it more, I'm sure, without the scary people targeting us." Tristan smiled fondly as he thought of his sister. He still felt the pain, but in that moment, he felt warmth with the memories.

"I do not know if I would say *all* over. But I have seen much," Rose confessed, though she fell quiet at talk of Arianna. "She seemed fond of the pirates, though I dare say she favored Solomon. And Amaya, somewhat."

"I think she was partial to you," Tristan remarked with a small grin. "After all, she did put flowers in your hair. I didn't see her doing that for anyone else."

Rose blushed, looking away when he reminded her of the flowers. "I did not give her much chance to play shadow," she confessed. "I was still— am still, really —getting used to matters…People seeing me. Wanting to speak with me. Wanting to set me up with their brother." She slid a mischievous grin towards Tristan before resuming her meticulous study of whatever the artifact she was currently facing was.

Tristan felt his face warm even as he laughed. "She never was all that shy," he agreed. He turned back to studying the castle as they explored. He considered his relationship with Rose and her circumstances. Should they pursue anything deeper before things were resolved? He refrained from talking to her about it in public. For now, he simply enjoyed her company.

16. Fairytale of Glass

Rose and Tristan eventually made their way back to join the others in preparing for the feast, the Half-Drow once more 'cornering' Captain in her room to help her get fancied up. She did not make the girl change her hairstyle, though she did pull most of the braids up and together in a special type of bun. She left the braids around Captain's face to hang free, including the Memory Braid. Aside from that, she simply repeated what they had done for dinner with the royal family for the both of them.

When she entered the parlor, she found Lance and Solomon had mostly done the same. The knight retained the shoulder cape to keep his armor near.

Alconai, Tristan, and Jabez dressed as they had for dinner the previous night. Once more Jabez let Captain lead the way when they were summoned while Jabez fell to the rear of the group. He remained alert, but he seemed more subdued. Alconai gave his brother a concerned look. However, he refrained from bringing it up right before they were to dine with and schmooze the court.

Captain fiddled with the rope accents of her dress. At least at a feast, people had things to distract them and not all of the attention would be on them. Still, the low rumble of conversation coming through the doors told her there were a lot of people. The threads would be too dense to see through if she focused on them, like looking in a bin of loose yarn all tossed in by children. She closed her eyes while they had a moment in the hall, taking the chance to breathe and practice 'hiding' the threads.

Is there a way I might help? Rose's voice brushed through her mind.

I'll be fine. Jus' gotta be careful wit' me own magic aroun' so many people.

Rose nodded in her peripheral, lightlytouching Captain's wrist in support before gently adjusting her own skirts. From what they could hear, the nobles were currently being introduced. The servant that led them had noted that they would be last as the guests of honor.

"The tables will be set differently, as well," the man was explaining to the group. "Their Majesties will be seated at the center of the table so they can overlook the hall; the heads of the noble houses will be to their left, and you will be to their right. The large wall that closed off the room beforehand will not be present, as the ballroom will be connected. You will remain seated while Their Majesties welcome everyone, but beyond that, you are welcome to wander as you please. Simply set your cutlery diagonal on your plate if you wish it to be cleared in your absence. There is no set time to serve courses, we simply replace empty or marked dishes. Dessert is not served, however; there will be a few small tables between the banquet hall and the dance floor, with individually plated treats. And you are always welcome to hail the staff by simply raising your hand."

"An' is t'ere any…er, 'who's who' we need ta ken?" Captain

asked.

The servant paused, considering. "You have already met with the royal family and the King's Shadow, and they are the only ones not expected to introduce themselves when meeting you."

"Zatook has been allowed to attend, then?" Rose smiled at the news. They had yet to see the man since he absconded with Tristan the previous evening.

"In a professional sense, yes. He attends to guard the family, but he rarely partakes in the festivities. I cannot speak to whether the king would allow him considering the…particular circumstances."

"I am surprised to hear 'rarely'. He never was one for dancing," Solomon noted absently. The servant actually smiled.

"The princess can be rather insistent. The king denies her nothing."

Tristan suppressed a smile at the thought of Collette dragging Zatook into a dance. He felt glad to have the chance to see Zatook, but he felt some concern of what might be hidden from their eyes. Nerves also tingled through him with the notion of being in a crowd of nobles. Even if they would be distracted, Tristan felt exposed. Subconsciously, his eyes sought out Jabez for support. Jabez caught Tristan's gaze and gave him a slight nod of reassurance. Smiling gratefully, Tristan turned his focus on the task at hand.

For Jabez, the Sun Child looking to him took him aback. His conversation with Solomon came to the forefront of Jabez's mind. Was he really so valued? Subtly moving closer to Captain, Jabez reached forward and lightly tickled her side, hoping to help with any nervousness. If confidence and ease were things he could give the Chosen Children, then he would.

Captain giggled, jerking slightly with an 'oi' as she released her tassels and caught his hand. Rather than pull away, she leaned back against him and hugged his arm slightly before letting go. She didn't do more or try to prod him back as the servant had straightened and moved up closer to the door, meaning it was about time for them to go in. Captain sighed, moving to the front again with Tristan and Rose while Solomon slipped back behind them. Unlike the audience, where the protectors flanked them, the Chosen would lead the procession to their table. Another servant joined the first, each taking a handle so they could remain unseen when they opened the doors to let them through. Unlike the nobles and royal family, who entered near the head table, the guests of honor got to walk the whole room from the far end to reach the table.

As the doors swung open, the sea of faces weren't the first things Captain noticed. It was the chandeliers, massive and bright, shining against the ceiling. She took a deep breath as the seneschal finished their names, walking in alongside her fellow Chosen. The crowd, at least, were ringing their own tables, so they weren't all clumped together like at the audience. There was a clear line of sight to Traiborn, Corianne, and Collette at the head table, and she could just make out Zatook in the shadowed alcove behind them. She paced herself by how Tristan was walking, grateful he had at least some experience with this nonsense. Pomp and circumstance were certainly not for her, though she was finding she could put up with it in spurts. It also helped that she had friends behind her and at least two ahead. As they neared the table, she got a closer look at one of the said friends.

Zatook had been cleaned up for the event, too. Some of his hair still fell stubbornly about his face, but the rest was styled and swept back. His clothes were finer, still mostly black but featuring silver hems, buttons, and embroidery. His sword was nowhere to be seen, but Captain knew all too well that meant nothing in regards to how quickly he could be holding it. Zatook kept his expression impassive, but when he caught her nervous gaze, he actually winked at her subtly. He still wore a black undershirt to cover the lower half of his face and his wrists, but it seemed more satin-like, shimmering slightly in the lights from the room even as he tucked himself as far into the shadows as he dared. Even his gloves and boots were styled.

Corianne once more wore the full gown from the audience, but Collette was still dressed as a priestess. The sight actually helped Captain's nerves a bit, the girl appreciating the small amount of normalcy. They were finally at the dais with the head table. Captain was fairly proud that she didn't trip on her way up or around the table. She stood next to Collette, the princess reaching a subtle hand over and squeezing hers behind the table. Captain squeezed back gratefully.

Tristan kept his posture as straight as possible and tried to give off an air of importance while still hopefully seeming approachable. A fine balance he hadn't had to practice in years. And yet, his mind wandered to thoughts of how much Arianna would have enjoyed all the fancy clothes and dressing up with Captain and Rose. Tristan wasn't sure how long she would have been able to stay still given her energetic nature, but she had often surprised him with her understanding of certain things. Then again, she might have foregone all decorum and chosen to eat in the alcove with Zatook so the man wouldn't be alone. The thought of his sister causing an adorable though mortifying ruckus made Tristan fight back a smile and settled his nerves.

Once more Alconai seemed the most at ease considering his profession of being a performer. He smiled at everyone and politely inclined his head in acknowledgment. Jabez was the picture of proper etiquette despite his life outside the courts of palaces. Having been trained to blend into any environment, Jabez forced down his unease at having any attention on him at all and put up a reserved but confident front.

Once they were all behind the table and at their spots, Collette motioned that they could sit as the nobles did so. Only Corianne and Traiborn remained standing as the rest of the guests slid into their own places. The servants currently lined the wall, standing at attention, and Zatook did not move from his spot. Traiborn lifted his hand, and the chatter that had swelled with the seating slowly died down.

"It is with a heart full of warmth and arms open in welcome that I express my deepest gratitude to each and every one of you for joining us this fine evening as we welcome the Children of Legend. To our esteemed guests, I say: let the beauty of Andor embrace you, its stories inspire you, and its people enfold you with the kind of hospitality that is the hallmark of our great land.

Tonight, as we break bread together, let us forge new friendships that will withstand the tests of time, celebrate the bonds that unite us, and dream of a future bright with the promise of peace, prosperity, and mutual respect. May the harmony of this gathering ripple through the ages, a testament to what we can achieve when hearts are open and hands are joined in a common purpose.

Let the music play, the laughter ring out, and the feasting begin! Together, let us raise a toast to the enduring spirit of friendship and to a night that will shine as a beacon of hope and camaraderie in the annals of our history. Long live the bonds that bring us together this evening, and long may they prosper!" Traiborn lifted his glass, and the rest of the room followed suit. After everyone had cheered and taken their drink, Traiborn lowered himself into his chair.

As the king and queen sat, a small group of musicians shifted into the space between the dance floor and the tables, across from where the desserts would be served, and filled the air with light music. The servants also started moving into the kitchen and back out to serve the first plates. A dedicated staff was assigned to the head table, while the rest split the floor tables among them.

Collette leaned over enough that the three Chosen could hear her. "I don't suppose any of you are dancers?" Captain laughed.

"Oh, I love a good dance. But nae ta this kin'a music," she joked. "I donnae t'ink me pirate antics will go over tha' well."

Collette gave her a mischievous look. "Oh, I bet we could make it work," she joked right back. "We had only to bribe the players."

"Why bribe them when we can just throw Alconai into their midst?" commented Tristan with a grin. "Supposedly he can play, but we haven't had the chance to hear him." He started when he felt fingers quickly tweak his ear before disappearing. Tristan glanced over his shoulder to see Jabez.

"Don't make me sick Solomon on you three," Jabez lightly chided. Then he bowed to Captain as he held out his hand. "May I have this dance, Captain?"

Captain blinked in surprise at Jabez, but she grinned and took his hand. "Oh, I s'pose," she teased. "Jus' keep a good lead an' watch yer toes, aye?"

"I know just enough to make it look like I know exactly what I'm doing," Jabez remarked to Captain with a subtle wink. He led her from her seat and out to the dance floor. True to his word, he subtly guided Captain into the correct starting position and then smoothly began leading her through the steps. He moved with surprising grace even for a ninja. As they danced, he asked, "How are you doing?"

"It's a lot o' people," she confessed softly. "An' a lot o' threads. I'm nae very good at nae lookin' at'em…"

"Would it help to concentrate on our threads or even just one? Or does that narrow your perception too much?" Jabez suggested.

"It 'elps tha' ye're nae connected ta most of t'e people here aside from location. Nothin' says practice like jumpin' inta t'e fire, aye?"

Jabez guided Captain through a twirl and a few steps. "Likewise. I wasn't expecting to be traveling with a group, much less helping the Chosen Children. I was doing better, but I confess since coming to Andor, I've felt on edge," he admitted. He led her through a few more moves before adding, "Solomon wants to train me with the scimitars."

Captain squeezed his hand with the confession, but she focused on the movements with him rather than saying something. At his second statement, she gave quite the ladylike snort. "Oh, t'ere's a shocker," she teased, grinning up at him. "I donnae need me powers ta ken he's been wantin' ta do tha' fer a while. Our li'l adventure musta givin' 'im t'e kick in t'e pants ta bring it up."

"He's brought it up before; I always declined," confessed Jabez. "Now, I'm reconsidering, especially given the situations arising around us. We need every edge, and we need to be as prepared as we can." He studied her scar for a moment. "I want to help, to be useful." He indicated her eye with a subtle nod.

"Jabie, ye donnae need a fancy sword ta be useful," Captain pointed out gently. "But 'avin' someone else ken how ta use 'em would certainly be a good idea." She was quiet for a moment, debating. "Ye ken t'e future isnae solid. Ye've seen enough t'ings change jus' hangin' aroun' me. But t'ere is a future where ye take 'im up on it. A few, really. An' a few where ye donnae. T'e choice is always yers ta make. An' I willnae tell ye a t'ing about eit'er path unless ye decide ta ask. Though, as yer li'l sis, it is rat'er imperative I tell ye you look good wit'em," she added as a tease.

Jabez gave her a fond yet flat look. "A badass name and a striking visage? Just who am I supposed to be impressing?" he joked dryly. He twirled her again as he considered her words. He refrained from telling Captain that he felt the tug in his core that taking up the scimitars was the right call. He just felt anxious about taking that first step. "I want to ask, but at the same time, I don't want the knowledge to influence my decision. If that makes sense."

"Obviously ye're all abou' intimidatin' yer enemies," she joked right back, but she sobered at his next statement. "Aye. It does. So I'll wait until ye ken."

"I'm about as intimidating as a field mouse," Jabez retorted. He continued leading her through the moves of the dance as music and chatter filled the air. With a subtle wink, Jabez told Captain, "There is one future I've seen before you. My brother will ask you for the next dance."

Captain snickered at him. "I just 'ope he's go' steel in 'is boots," she teased in turn.

***

Collette smiled as they watched Jabez and Captain from the head table. "Those two really are like siblings, aren't they?" she noted warmly.

Tristan remarked with a smile, "They don't deny it. I'm

starting to think that Jabez is everyone's older sibling, to be honest." His gaze shifted to Alconai when the man joined the remaining trio.

"Lovely evening to ye," Alconai greeted them cheekily. Bowing and holding his hand out to Collette, he requested, "Would ye do me the honor of a dance with you, Your Majesty?"

"Always," Collette assured him, taking his hand and standing. "I'm sure Zatook would happily see me have many dance partners that aren't him," she added in a tease, shooting a grin to her half-brother as he stoically did not look at her. Rose chuckled.

While Alconai led Collette to the dance floor and seamlessly joined the dancing partners, Tristan turned to Rose. "Do you feel up to a dance, or would you rather stay and eat?" he asked.

Rose paused. She had never been allowed to dance at feasts before; in fact, the only times she remembered dancing were as a young girl with Jeremiah, back when he treated her like another daughter alongside another little girl. His daughter? If they had spent time together as children, why was she struggling to remember her now? Rose took a sip of her drink to wash away the thoughts before answering Tristan. "I could go for a dance. Might have a bit of a learning curve with this." She gestured to the TekChair. She had been getting fairly good at the controls, but a part of her also wanted to try dancing without it. To experience dancing as she had not been allowed before. However, she did not want to push herself too hard; using the chair would help preserve her energy through the night. "I will probably go for one dance without it, but not right away."

"We can make it work," Tristan assured her. He moved from the table so they could venture onto the floor. He bowed to Rose and held her hand when he could as they choreographed their own dance to enjoy the evening. Tristan smiled and laughed brightly, warm joy overflowing in him.

Rose shared his smile. After a little time with the runes, she had the magic down enough that she barely noticed directing them. It was easier than she had expected, but she also wasn't the only one using TekMobility to enjoy the dance. She picked up a few things by watching others.

Tristan allowed his guard to lower as he enjoyed the dance and spending time with Rose. He learned to accommodate the Tek as Rose and he moved to the music. For now, he let go of thoughts of the outside world and of his grief. Focusing on the music, the lights, the smells of delicious food, and Rose's company, Tristan allowed himself to be swept up in the present.

***

As the music shifted once more, Captain did not miss that Alconai found himself bereft of a dance partner. Collette was far too polite to turn down the young noble who asked after her, new friends or no.

Jabez smirked beneath his mask when Alconai approached Captain and offered his hand and inquiry. Leaving Captain with Alconai, Jabez returned to the table just as Tristan and Rose did. Jabez nudged Solomon with his shoulder. "Don't you want to dance with some fine noble lady?" he teased quietly.

"I assure you, I am quite content to watch," Solomon noted with some amusement, his gaze on his second ward and her current partner. Traiborn and Corianne had descended to join the dancers for the current song. Despite the tiredness that seemed to cling to her like a shadow, the queen was as graceful as the legends told. She moved through the dance almost like water, flowing to the music. Traiborn was a little more stiff, but a few centuries of practice meant he knew what he was doing even if he wasn't as graceful as his wife. Zatook had remained where he stood. He did not need to follow the royal family to protect them. "As I am sure *you* would much prefer the company of a certain half-elf," Solomon added, giving Jabez a sideways glance.

The young man pointedly kept his gaze on the dancers. "We haven't spoken since I left, really. I sent her some letters while we were at sea with Captain and Amaya, but I haven't sent any in recent years," Jabez admitted quietly. "We weren't like that anyway." He hadn't been in the right mentality for romance when he was in Ben-Gal or during the subsequent years.

"You could be," Solomon pointed out gently. He took a sip of his drink before adding, "She wrote to me when she couldn't reach you. She was worried. I hadn't really had a chance to bring it up since Nikko Mori."

Jabez lowered his mask just enough to take a drink, using the goblet to hide his features. The fabric was back in place by the time he lowered the beverage. "I didn't want to create a trail to her. I kept my correspondence with the Order strictly business to keep Shaedra from picking up my trail if they intercepted anything. The rest of the time, I tried to stay out of sight and mind until absolutely necessary," Jabez replied. He sighed heavily. "We both know I'm not in the right place to be pursuing romance. I don't know if I ever will be."

"Do we?" Solomon leaned back in his chair, folding his arms. "Mist is a healer, Jabez. She's seen her fair share of trauma. You don't have to be a suave adventurer to court a girl."

"It's probably a good idea to be sane for more than a year, at least," murmured Jabez dryly. He watched the royal couple and the other dancers, keeping his gaze away from Solomon. Jabez had yet to touch any food. Having dinner with the royal family had been bad enough, but at least then the attention wasn't on him; and he could eat more discreetly. Here, he felt exposed and like every eye bored into him whether they truly did or not. The longer he sat in the open, the more the crawling sensation skittered along his skin.

"Jabez…" Solomon shook his head, sighing. He wasn't going to convince the lad in a night. He smirked when Alconai dramatically dipped Captain at the end of the song, the girl laughing brightly. He jumped slightly when Zatook reached between the pair to tap Jabez's shoulder. He lifted a hand, letting shadows swirl around his fingers and arching an eyebrow at the man. Solomon smirked subtly. Zatook must have noticed Jabez wasn't eating and guessed why.

Ignoring Solomon, Jabez answered Zatook, "I don't want to impose; I can eat when we retire." As if to contradict him, he felt his stomach grumble softly. Jabez managed to keep from looking away in embarrassment— not wanting to be rude to Zatook —but he didn't move to remove his mask. "It's not…it's not my appearance that bothers me. It's the attention."

Zatook touched his hand to the table. *It is not an imposition. I do the same for myself.* The shadows spelled out along the tablecloth, the man not risking signing where the king could see.

Jabez hesitated a little longer. His eyes shifted to the crowd exiting the dance floor and the new dancers spilling onto it. Then he looked back down at the table before turning to Zatook again. "I can try," Jabez finally consented, though his voice held no confidence.

Zatook nodded, slipping back to his spot in the alcove. Despite knowing the man might not acknowledge him with the king present, Tristan still greeted Zatook subtly with a wave when he pulled away from Jabez and Solomon. The Shadow actually nodded in response. Jabez felt shadows form around his face, Zatook letting them be a bit denser so the man could feel them there.

Ironically, the shadows forming over his face caused less anxiety for Jabez than the act of pulling down his mask in public. Shaedra trained their ninjas not to fear powers and spells in case the agents were ever captured or tortured. Instinctually, Jabez kept his breathing even; he couldn't recall exactly how many times he had been smothered by one power or another for the sake of conditioning. Jabez felt grateful for Zatook's consideration in making the shadow tangible enough for him to feel it. Gradually, Jabez managed a few bites of food, finding some amusement in how it must look to outsiders, especially given his red cloth mask now looked black. Still, he focused on eating and drinking while he had the shadows and keeping up appearances in front of the nobles.

Solomon couldn't help a slight chuckle. "He really has gotten good at making that look like cloth," he noted, returning to his own food. "I doubt anyone will really notice the color."

***

As Zatook had slipped away from Jabez and Solomon, Rose and Tristan had resumed their conversation regarding the things they had found in the museum and the lack of information on the Wall thus far.

"I cannot help but wonder if any information on it has been hidden from prying eyes," she confessed. "And yet we have barely delved into the library."

"The Wall was constructed after King Zetta's reign, so there hasn't been anything in the journal about it. Considering his opinions regarding Celestials and the state of things coming into a new land, I doubt Zetta would have felt the need to erect that kind of fortification," Tristan told her. He took a bite of his food, chewing thoughtfully. Eventually, he added, "It'll take a few days, I'm sure, and some digging before we find substantial information."

Rose nodded. "Considering the jealous guarding of their Tek, something had to have happened between his reign and its creation," she agreed.

"Captain had been reading a book about Andor's history. I wonder if it says anything about the construction of the Wall or at least the reason it was built," mused Tristan.

Rose couldn't help a small chuckle at the mention of their comrade. Despite another song having started, she and Alconai had yet to pause in their dancing. "I do not think she'll be in a state to tell us tonight," she teased.

"You never know. I swear Captain has enough energy to run around the castle ten times and then still join in for a dance," Tristan joked. He smiled as he watched the minstrel and the pirate having a good time. "I'm glad she's having some fun."

"I think we all needed something to pull our attention from everything else," Rose confessed. She smirked as she caught another figure in the dancing crowd. "Lancelot seems rather popular," she noted. The knight was dancing with a young noblewoman, but a small gathering nearby suggested he had others vying for a dance as well.

Tristan laughed. "I'm just glad they aren't coming after me," he said lightheartedly. "I'm a bit out of practice for courtly small talk." He smiled when he saw a young noblewoman approach Jabez. The man spoke quietly to her and then joined her on the dance floor.

Rose laughed softly. "We might be a little obvious," she teased gently, touching her hand to his wrist. She could almost swear she heard a snort from behind them, but she paid it no mind.

Tristan's cheeks burned, but he gazed fondly at her.

Twisting his wrist, he caught her hand and held it. "Maybe," he agreed. As he studied how the light illuminated her features as her smile brightened her face and his heart, Tristan felt the urge to kiss her. However, he held back. For one, he preferred that their first kiss be done without an audience, but he also wasn't sure the timing felt right. Rose would be leaving, and even though there was supposed to be some way to get her back, Tristan felt unsure how far he should pursue. He also had no idea what he was doing— he'd never courted anyone.

Rose returned his hold, smiling gently. She turned to sip her water, unaware of the thoughts running through his mind. She watched the dancers warmly, finding herself not horribly surprised to see some of the common folk asking a few of the nobles for dances, and vice versa. *You can be a good king and still be a horrible person.* The line stuck. Andor really did seem to be a pretty good kingdom for the people living there. Sure, some of the nobles had airs about them, but it wasn't unheard of for the people to mix together and enjoy each other's company. She could remember a few feasts under Arden that were strictly for the nobles and soldiers. How Jeremiah would have to get onto some of his soldiers for treating non-soldiers poorly or downright bullying them. She even recalled he once had an argument with another of the head knights over it. And then, over time, even he stopped calling it out. Stopped smiling at the younger slaves and sneaking them treats. Was that really Jeremiah? She couldn't help recalling Tristan's concern. Maybe it was magic. Another kind. Something subtle. But who? And why?

"What's on your mind?" Tristan asked, noting the contemplative look on her face.

"What isn't?" she asked softly in turn, chuckling. She sobered as she watched the activity in the room. "Nocis. Jeremiah. The current state of Andor regardless of certain factors." She chose her words carefully, not sure if Traiborn had set up anything or was still bothering to listen in himself.

Tristan nodded. "If not for what we've seen, we wouldn't know any different, right?" he asked vaguely. He knew they couldn't speak as openly in public.

"And yet, that's what brings me back to Nocis. What I've seen. What I can recall of it, at least. Sometimes I remember more, but it's like trying to hold sand."

"Don't force it. Something Clo used to tell me was the more you chase a rabbit, the faster it'll run," replied Tristan. "It'll come to you. We have time."

Rose nodded. "At least forty-five days, from what you told me," she acquiesced.

"It sounds like a lot but also not enough," Tristan commented softly. He watched the activities even as his mind mulled over the visions he had seen. "Maybe we can find answers during our studies."

"Well, we have certainly had some luck there already. Let us pray it continues."

Tristan nodded. He fell silent as he watched Alconai laughing and dancing with Captain. Eventually Jabez returned to the table to get a drink and observe once more. Despite his cool demeanor, the ninja seemed to be having a good time. Tristan's gaze shifted over to Zatook, watching the man stand guard. He felt tempted to go talk to him; however, Tristan didn't want to cause the man anymore trouble.

Corianne also returned to the table for a break, but Traiborn didn't join her. Rather, the king had a whole gaggle of kids around him, showing some of the young men how to dance with the girls their age. His current demonstration partner was a little girl standing on his shoes as he danced with her, almost looking like a community grandfather. Collette had a new young man each dance, her cheeks starting to stain pink with her laughter and all the dancing. Tristan could tell Zatook was watching her with a mild frown. Before he decided to approach the shadow warrior, Zatook moved. He slid along the outer wall, stopping a servant to claim a tray with a goblet of water before shifting into shadow rather than push through the crowd. He caught his sister's shoulder as he came alongside her and her current dance partner— the young man let go comically fast. Zatook, however, paid him no mind as he held the goblet to his sister. Collette took it in both hands, reaching up to kiss his cheek in thanks as he placed a hand against her back and guided her from the floor for a small break. After she had drunk the water and caught her breath, he let her go back to dancing. He set the tray aside for a servant and then returned to his post.

Tristan felt his frustration mounting that a seemingly good king could hide his darker side so well. If not for knowing Zatook, Tristan would almost think Traiborn a good man. Watching the warrior, Tristan smiled at Zatook's attentiveness toward his sister. At least Zatook had a few people in his life that gave him some joy, even if the man rarely showed it. Tristan grimaced when the exchange between siblings made his eyes sting. He couldn't help recalling memories of his own sister and her bright smile. Try as he might, Tristan resigned himself to losing the battle with his emotions. Quietly, he told Rose that he needed to get some air and then slipped away from the table. He debated where to go. He knew the alcove where Zatook stood guard had a curtain, so Tristan made his way there. He managed to keep himself steady until he was behind the curtain. He barely registered the standard door the curtain hid; he only hoped no one came through it and saw him. Pressing his hand to his mouth, Tristan let the tears fall even as he worked to get his emotions back under control. He wondered how long the feast would last, and if he had the fortitude to make it to the end.

Solomon frowned when he noticed Tristan get up without Rose, whispering something before slipping away. A knowing look passed behind his gaze, the man having seen Traiborn and Zatook as well. He knew the feast was safe enough to let them be on their own, especially with Zatook on guard duty. But grief was something entirely different. He slid from the chair casually, slipping towards the door that let out into the hall, but when he neared the corner he shifted behind the curtain instead and walked back. The lad probably didn't want any attention on him, so Solomon would do his best to ensure no one saw where he went. There was a good sized gap between the curtain and the wall, with the fabric stretching all the way across the short wall. He wasn't so quiet as to startle the lad, just enough that others wouldn't catch on to people behind the curtain. His gaze was soft and understanding, his heart in a similar place— though mourning a daughter twenty-years-gone and a sister only days gone had separate challenges among the similarities. He didn't try to pull the lad into a hug right away; he wasn't sure how he would take it. So instead, he approached and placed his hand on the lad's shoulder.

Tristan tilted his head back, trying to blink back his tears. He took a few deep breaths and let them out slowly. "I know I need to get back," he said quietly, his voice just barely wavering. "I'm working on it. I promise I'll be good in a minute. Do you know how long the feast will last?"

"Take all the time you need, Tristan," Solomon encouraged softly. "The feast will wait. And it will be going on well into the night. It isn't unusual for someone to slip away and return later."

"I know I can't, but I kind of want to go back to my room and just let myself be miserable for a night. Or at least let myself recuperate mentally and emotionally," admitted Tristan.

"I wish I could say otherwise," Solomon confessed, "but you can at least take what time you need here. And tomorrow, take all the time you need to care for yourself."

"I hate politics. If not for knowing Zatook, I could almost buy the ruse of Traiborn being a good man and a good king. It's frustrating because I know the truth, and yet I can't call him out," Tristan commented levelly. He heaved a deep sigh. "I'm trying to hold myself together. Seeing Zatook with Collette, though, reminds me…" he trailed off as he fought back the anguish. "Even being in the castle brings up memories, good and bad. Both painful. And then everything with Rose and Captain and Zatook. And then Jabez being hurt. I feel like I'm failing before I've even truly begun." Tristan ran his hand through his hair, not caring about messing up the strands as stress and emotions ate at him.

"There is only failure when we give up," Solomon reminded him gently. "Jabez knew the risks when he took on Marilyn. It is our duty and our pride to serve the Children and fight against those using fell magics." He squeezed Tristan's shoulder reassuringly. "He would do it again. As would I. As many times as we must." He pushed aside his hesitation, pulling Tristan into a hug. "You face many things, Tristan, but you do not face them alone. And many understand your grief. I can assure you the memories get easier with time, and yet the sadness can come upon you like a ship caught in a storm. We simply learn to ride with it."

Tristan accepted the embrace, though he continued fighting back his emotions. "Amaya said that no one in our group was a stranger to loss. I'm guessing that means you too," he remarked quietly. "I appreciate Jabez more than I can express. I'm grateful for his calming presence and consideration. I appreciate his level-headedness and reliability. I find myself looking to him for support and to help me stay calm. I'm grateful for you, too, Solomon. Your advice and support have been invaluable. I appreciate your care and wisdom."

"That would be an accurate assumption." He did not bring up his own loss for now, more focused on helping the Sun Child. "It is my pleasure to offer guidance to those who need it, Children of Legend or no."

Tristan gently pulled back from the embrace and stepped out of the man's hold. He wiped his eyes to make sure they remained clear of tears. Looking towards the curtain,

Tristan considered what lay beyond the fabric. He could hear the music and chatter still. "My father threw some parties and expected me to behave for them. However, I was young enough that he would allow me to wander off and entertain myself if I started getting too bored. He never had me stay up past my bedtime, not even for a feast. I remember—" Tristan cut himself off as the memory hit him like a rock through a glass pane. Taking a deep breath, he shook his head to ward away the memory and tamp down on his emotions. And yet he trembled as everything hit him all over again. Tristan stared at the ground as he pressed a hand to his mouth to keep himself quiet. Finally, he pulled his hand away just enough to confess, "I don't think I can go back out there. I'm too much of a wreck. I feel guilty that everyone else is braving this, and yet every time I try to push things down, another memory catches me and weakens my composure."

"Do not push away the memory. Tell me," Solomon encouraged.

Hesitating still, Tristan stared at the curtain as he fought to keep his voice steady. Eventually, he said, "My father… wasn't always as he is now. I think that makes everything so much worse. I remember during an important but rather stuffy feast, I was trying my best to stay awake until bedtime. I don't remember why, but I know I was more tired than usual. I fell asleep at the table while people were dancing." Tristan pushed through the tears and emotions trying to choke him. "I woke just enough to realize I wasn't at the table anymore: I was in my father's arms. My father carried me with my head on his shoulder and his cloak wrapped around me through the crowd. I vaguely remember him talking to people as he passed but not what he said. At one point, he pulled his cloak over my head when the bright lights bothered me. I slipped asleep again, and the next time I woke it was to my father putting me to bed," recalled Tristan brokenly, the tears finally slipping down his cheeks. "I remember feeling safe and warm. I remember how secure I felt in his arms. I wish I could forget."

"If only the world were simple. If bad men would only do bad things, and good men only good." Solomon sighed, shaking his head. "But that is not the way of things. People's hearts are fickle things. But it does not do to hate the good. Remember it. Cherish it. Even mourn it. But never wish to forget light, even if it burns at times."

Huffing a wet, self-deprecating laugh Tristan remarked, "I'm never making it back out at this rate." Once more, he worked to compose himself and dry his tears. "So much hurts right now, and I know I'm not the only one suffering."

"There is no rush. Don't worry about anything beyond the curtain. If you keep trying to push it down, it will only boil back over. You need to let it out, Tristan. So do. There is no one here to judge."

"That's all I've been doing," retorted Tristan in quiet frustration. "I've been letting it out, but then there's always more, and it wants to hit at the worst times. I can't keep crying in peoples' arms— we have work to do and have to navigate the situation with the king."

"Have you? I know you were training with Zatook while we traveled. You have been exploring the castle, survived a dinner with royalty, kept a straight face during the audience, and have been studying the journal and the castle. Can you really say all you have done is grieve?" Solomon folded his arms, leaning against the wall. "Grief…well, I'll return to the earlier analogy. It is like the ocean. We cannot control the tides or the weather. And they are more tempestuous the fresher an event. It has not been that long, though much has happened to make it feel that way." He lifted his gaze to watch Tristan. "Captain's grief is old, yet even she must face the waves when they come. Mine is even older, yet the same is true."

"What do you do when the waves crash into you at the worst time?" Tristan asked sincerely. He kept his gaze down. He knew if he met the man's eyes, Tristan would break down again. He took several deep breaths and blinked back the rest of his tears even as he wiped away the wet trails down his face.

Solomon reached into a pocket, pulling out a handkerchief. "You ride the waves until they pass. Whether that means ducking behind a curtain at a ball or slipping into the shadows at camp."

Miserably Tristan accepted the handkerchief. Instead of dabbing at his eyes right away, Tristan let the tears fall for a bit longer, not wanting to soak the handkerchief too quickly. With a wobble in his voice he admitted, "I miss her so much. At night when we bed down, I catch myself starting to think about my nightly routine of putting Arianna to bed only to remember a split second after that I don't need to do that anymore. Because of her lack of voice, I trained myself to listen for her and to feel her presence. Every morning, I would listen and feel for her to know if she needed me or if she was awake and moving around yet. Now, the mornings are too quiet, and sometimes I panic thinking that she's run off on her own. And then I remember." Tristan stifled a sob. "I was sincerely enjoying my time dancing with Rose, but then I started thinking about how Arianna would have loved exploring the castle. She would have loved getting to dress up and go to a feast." Tristan shuddered as he voiced brokenly, "My sister is dead. She'll never get to have those experiences." Finally, Tristan pressed the handkerchief to his face and released a few shaky breaths. Slowly, he worked to regain his composure. "People are probably starting to talk with how long I'm taking," remarked Tristan, his muffled voice full of resignation and pain.

Solomon smirked subtly. "Let them talk. They will talk whether they can see you or not. Traiborn is the only one we need really concern ourselves with, and I can handle him if he tries to dig barbs later."

Gradually, Tristan steadied his breathing, finally managing to hold himself together. He cleaned his face before saying, "All the same, we should get back. I can't hide back here forever." He squared his shoulders and fixed his hair. "I can have your handkerchief washed before I return it. I doubt you want to carry it right now," he commented with a tired smile. The young man felt drained, but he put on a brave face.

"There is no rush. I make it a habit to carry a few." Solomon smirked at him. He clapped Tristan's shoulder before shifting his way back down the curtain to exit closer to the hall door.

After giving himself another minute, Tristan slipped through the curtain and back towards the group. He gave Jabez a reassuring smile when the man met his gaze. Despite his feelings, Tristan steeled himself to be friendly and polite.

Rose smiled as he joined her, touching a hand to his arm in welcome. Captain and Alconai had finally come to sit for a bite to eat, as had the princess. Collette and Captain were currently poking innocent fun at Lancelot's latest fanclub. The king and queen were out amongst the crowd, speaking with people along the floor.

Tristan gave Rose a nod and a small smile. He ate as best he could and drank some water, allowing himself a moment to calm and reintegrate into the festivities. Eventually, he offered Rose his hand, quietly asking for a dance.

Rose took his hand, moving with him down to the dance area. She found a small space by the wall where her chair could wait for when they were done before letting Tristan help her stand. She blushed slightly as they stood close, Tristan taking the lead while Rose picked up the steps fairly quickly. She had to admit, there was just something magical about dancing in a fancy dress. And yet most of her attention was on Tristan. She found she rather liked the way the magic lights from the chandeliers bounced off of his hair and made some of the threads in his doublet sparkle. The effect made his eyes look even more like gemstones.

As they glided across the floor, Tristan kept his focus on Rose. Her hair shone like starlight, and her sapphire and ruby eyes held Tristan's gaze captive. He appreciated how her dress and accents complimented her natural beauty. Completely mesmerized, Tristan touched his forehead to hers and smiled softly, genuinely. "You're beautiful," he told her.

"I feel like I am in a dream," she confessed with a smile. "Or perhaps I should be watching for the clock to strike midnight."

"I'm glad this isn't a dream or else I would never want to wake," replied Tristan lightly. "Even if the clock strikes midnight and you disappear, I will find you again. So long as you'll have me." He led her into an elegant twirl followed by a gentle spin.

"I rather like the sound of that happily ever after." Rose smiled as they came together again.

"Then Shaddai willing, I'll do all in my power to make it happen," Tristan promised her, his eyes shining with determination. "For now, let's enjoy the moment." He led her through the steps, guiding them across the floor gracefully. Tristan held Rose close so she could lean against him if she needed. When the music drew to a close, Tristan carefully dipped Rose, his grip strong but gentle. He guided her back up and bowed to her, kissing the back of her hand. He then helped her back to her chair.

***

Captain sat with her chin in her hands and her eyes on the other two Children. The pair really were quite adorable together. They hadn't even looked around once while they were dancing— if they had, they might have noticed a number of eyes on them. "T'ey look like t'ey stepped out o' one o' Maya's stories," she joked softly to Solomon.

"Just wait until people are telling stories about *you*," he noted, sipping his drink. Captain snorted.

"I be'er write it meself so t'ey donnae make me out like some noble li'l lark," she teased. "Or we coul' let Nai write it."

"I be happy to," Alconai told her brightly. "I would spin t'e tale o' t'e young and fierce Captain MoonChild. As graceful on t'e dance floor as she is with a blade in her hand." Alconai winked at her.

"Are you telling a tale of her adventures or waxing poetic?" Jabez quipped teasingly.

Alconai scoffed. "I be doin' her tale justice, is what I be," he retorted.

Captain laughed. "Oi, oi, me tale is hardly a solo adventure," she pointed out. "Ye cannae forget dashin' young Tris'an an t'e starlit Rose. But where would I be wit'out Sol an Jabie, too, eh?"

"A humble heart to boot, eh?" Alconai teased. "I can write more than one story. One 'bout ye, and one 'bout all three Children. Plus Sol and Jabie."

Jabez shook his head. "I'm fine with being left out of the tale. No one needs to know about a shadow in the background."

"Ah, but Jabie, yer shadow gives contrast to Captain's brilliance, makin' her shine all t'e more," Alconai told his brother. Jabez just shook his head again.

"Isnae a story 'bout me if it doesnae include me family," Captain pointed out flatly, though she playfully elbowed Jabez. "Though I cannae help but wonder who's goin' ta end up wit' t'e most fans by t'e time Nai's done: Zattie or Jabie."

"I'm no competition for Zatook. Ladies like the strong, silent, mysterious type. He wins hands down," Jabez replied wryly.

"Jabie, ye just described yerself," Alconai prodded.

"I talk too much to be considered the silent type. Besides, we're talking about Captain. Why do both of you keep turning the conversation on me?"

Alconai gave him his own flat look. "You be no chatterbox, and when ye do speak, ye are kind and charming. Just like Captain. No wonder people think yer siblings. She gets it from you or be you gettin' it from her?"

"Captain is the one with the charm and charisma. Always has been. It's part of her strength as a captain and a Chosen Child," answered Jabez seriously.

"There is a rather strong case of chronic underestimation among our companions," Solomon mused, his mind going back to Tristan's admission of admiring Jabez. "Well, except perhaps me. I fully recognize that I am important, just old," he added teasingly.

Alconai laughed. "Yes, ye be t'e wisest of us. Ye be t'e sage-like mentor to our young Chosen," he joked.

"More like a protective father," Jabez murmured with a huffed laugh. "What about you, Nai? What part would you give yourself?"

Alconai waved him off. "I be t'e storyteller. It would just sound downright conceited if I included meself. Besides, people will be havin' a hard enough time believin' what t'e Chosen got up to and could do," responded Alconai.

Quietly, Jabez countered, "All the best stories are unbelievable." Alconai grinned at him.

"Of course ye include yerself," Captain contested with a snort. "It lends credibility when ye're tellin' wha' ye saw firs'and."

"That be true, aye," Alconai agreed easily. His gaze shifted to Rose and Tristan as the two rejoined the table. Alconai smiled, glad everyone seemed to be having a good time even just a little. He turned back to conversing with Captain.

***

The feast stretched well beyond twilight, full of good food and good company. Collette spent more time dancing than she did eating, though Zatook made sure she ate. As the evening wore on, the crowd slowly started to dwindle. Eventually, Corianne made the rounds to say her good nights and farewells, and not long after Traiborn followed. The ballroom remained open for a time, but slowly the people took their leave to prepare for the next day, and the staff began cleaning around those who dawdled.

The group had been enjoying themselves and their time together, but it was Solomon who eventually chose to retire first, shortly after the royal pair. Zatook had remained to keep watch over his sister, but as she took her leave, he nodded to the others and made as though to slip away.

Before the man could disappear, Tristan moved after Zatook, catching the warrior's attention. Searchingly, Tristan studied his comrade, trying to see if the man was hurt at all. "I wanted to say that I'm sorry for getting you into trouble, and that I appreciate you taking the risk to help us," Tristan spoke low enough only Zatook should hear. "Is there anything we can do for you? Are you in pain?"

Something like surprise flashed across Zatook's gaze, but it didn't linger. Instead, he shook his head. After a quick cursory glance to make sure the servants weren't paying them any mind, he lifted a hand to write with the shadows like he would for Tannen. *I will be leaving to scout the Nocium forces tomorrow,* he noted. He didn't want them worrying about him since he wouldn't be able to visit. *Jeremiah has continued to gather men at Caer Talon, and sources indicate House Shadow Veil's remaining forces have joined them.*

"You're going alone? Do you think Nocis will use us as an excuse to attack Andor?" whispered Tristan, concerned. He wanted to offer to have one of their group go with Zatook, but Tristan knew that they were being too well watched for the king not to notice if one of them disappeared.

They are blaming Andor for King Arden's death and the

fall of Keep Shadow Veil. I do not know what else is known. He hesitated, wary of the king's wards, but he went ahead and added, *I may seek out Amaya in case she has learned anything from outside. I do not trust the king's sources.*

"I do remember my father and Jeremiah talking about orchestrating King Arden's death to look like an attack from Andor," Tristan affirmed. Witnessing that meeting felt so long ago, and there had been so much that had and was still happening. "I imagine Amaya could at least help you in a pinch. I don't know about her stealth skills, though." Tristan flashed Zatook a small smile with the joke.

She did manage to hide what she was, he pointed out with his own slight smirk. He sobered as he continued. *I will try to let you know what I find, as well. I do not know how often I will be at the castle.*

Tristan's smile grew slightly with Zatook's ease around him. However, the young man's expression grew a bit more somber as he said, "Be careful," Tristan hesitated to add more. "I see you as a comrade, and I'm glad I got to see you tonight. I just wish there was more I could do, but I know we have to tread carefully in our situations." Tristan kept his gaze on where Zatook had been manifesting his shadows. He didn't want to miss anything Zatook said, but he couldn't meet the man's gaze right then either.

As careful as I can, Zatook assured him, before dispersing the shadows and reaching up to clap Tristan on the shoulder. He moved to duck behind the curtain, and Tristan heard the door whisper open before clacking shut. Zatook hesitated just beyond, staring at his hand and then back at the door before vanishing into the shadows. Perhaps while he was looking for Amaya, he could check in on Nikko Mori to see how Tristan's friends were faring.

Tristan watched the curtain for a moment before joining the others. He moved to Rose's side as their group began heading back to the guest wing. He stayed quiet for the walk, thinking and simply enjoying the company. Once they reached their area, Tristan gently took Rose's hand and lightly touched his lips to the back of it. "Good night, my lady," he told her, a blush dusting his cheeks despite his bold gesture.

Rose's cheeks also tinted slightly with a blush, but she smiled at Tristan as she bade him good night in turn and slipped into her room. Captain had all-but fallen asleep while they were walking, at first leaning more and more against Alconai before being swept up into Solomon's arms so he could carry her to bed. Lancelot looked half asleep himself, waving groggily as he headed up the stairs to find his bed. He fully expected to be teased mercilessly in the following days by Alconai for dancing nearly as much as the princess had, but for now he was going to have some blissful sleep.

17. Beyond the Border

Zatook was up before the sun. He stopped to have breakfast with Tannen, as the blacksmith had a habit of rising early, before moving to leave the castle. Traiborn was strict about when and how he could use his powers, so he didn't meld into the shadows until he was beyond the castle's main wall. Then, he was one with the darkness. He felt the familiar presence of the Wall as he reached the border, the magic warm and welcoming at his approach. He swirled around Caer Talon, noting the growing number of men and tents around the fortified castle and how they stretched towards the Wall. The number was certainly growing, and he spied a cluster of tents bearing Tsukuyomi's crest. He did not, however, sense the StormShaper near. Zatook frowned, but he made what notes he needed before leaving. He headed next to the ruins of Shadow Veil. Here he found more tents, but these were craftsmen and laborers. A wooden structure was already being raised where the original keep had stood. A small group of mercenary guards had been stationed to protect them while the army gathered elsewhere.

And still no StormShaper. Zatook's frown deepened. Why would Tsukuyomi's top warrior *not* be with the army or overseeing the new keep's construction? He slipped deeper into the shadows in the ground and expanded his senses. He linked his senses across the country, at least as far as he could stretch. He was surprised to find the shadows in Nikko Mori open to him, never having access to the forest before. He didn't let himself become distracted yet, searching for the presence he had come to recognize through their battles.

He was surprised to find the shaper in Caer Albright at the coast. Frowning, he withdrew from the shadows and traveled towards the port town that surrounded Nocis' first castle. He was not surprised to find he could not access the shadows of the castle, strong magic twined through the stones. Yet the clouds above the town confirmed what he had sensed: StormShaper was at the palace. It was likely that Tsukuyomi was staying there for now, and the warrior had accompanied him. Zatook moved back towards Caer Talon; if he lingered too long, Traiborn would question him. It was easy enough to say he was attempting to confirm the High Lord's current position but could not delve further without giving himself away.

And then he was near Nikko Mori again. Zatook hesitated in his travel, debating. So lost in thought, he almost didn't feel StormShaper coming— not until the obscured figure's fist connected with the ground in an effort to seek him out. An unfamiliar magic joined the shaper's power, shooting straight for Zatook. The shadow user shifted, resurfacing in the road as the first drops of rain began to fall.

StormShaper wasn't alone. Marilyn had come with him, though he almost didn't recognize her beneath a glamor, as well as a girl he didn't recognize and a few soldiers. It was Marilyn's magic he had sensed, then. StormShaper was already running at him, so Zatook quickly drew his blade and met him. He needed to be wary of Marilyn's magic in case she tried to take advantage of their fight.

Concentrating on Marilyn and StormShaper, he almost forgot the girl…until a serpentine dragon with pearlescent pink scales slammed into him from the side. Zatook grunted in slight surprise but managed to right himself and use his wings to gain some distance. The dragon was in the air now, twirling idly above her soldiers. He had known Jeremiah had a daughter, but Shila had rarely been seen by dignitaries and common folk alike— even when in public, she chose to wear head coverings and a veil. Zatook frowned. For all the obfuscation of the man's appearance, StormShaper was looking rather miffed. So, he didn't want aid in this fight. Zatook could work with that. He landed on the road and pointed his sword at StormShaper. The dragon laughed.

"It's not his call, demon. You're too valuable to risk an escape."

Zatook lowered his sword, glancing to the side as he sensed Marilyn moving around them. So, they sought to cut him off. He reached for the shadows and found he could feel them but not meld with them.

"We knew you would get curious," Shila purred as if guessing his thoughts, diving around the trees beside the road. "You were rather predictable."

She had to be stalling him. He had wasted too much time already. He would just have to fight his way past them. He turned as if to follow Marilyn, but StormShaper appeared in front of him and swung, so Zatook had to stop and raise his blade. His eyes narrowed. StormShaper first, then; if it came to it, he could call on his other powers to break whatever the blood mage was getting up to.

Overhead, lightning flashed through the clouds. Bolts streaked sporadically at first but then started to concentrate in one area of the sky. A giant bolt of coalesced lightning shot from the clouds and down towards the troops. The soldiers braced themselves. Since one of their main allies used lightning, the soldiers were warded against such magic. They felt confident the magical shielding would hold even against such a large attack. Just as the lightning reached over their heads, the electricity twisted together and flared into a column of spiraling pure flame. The roar and force of the vortex nearly drowned out the soldiers' screams.

Right as Shila moved to defend her troops, a searing pain lanced along her side from neck to tail, blood spilling instantly. The cut was deep— deeper than should be possible for a mere blade against a dragon. Generally, magic tended to be useless as an attack against dragon scales. Before Shila could fully process the implications of the gaping wound in her side, something hit her leg with what felt like the force of a mountain landing on her. Bone snapped with a sickening crack. Another blow hit her in the side from the opposite direction and then another impacted her head, dangerously close to Shila's eye.

Below, Zatook recognized the presence: he had felt her at Keep Shadow Veil— had seen her contain what would have been a catastrophic blast. Amaya LightningRider had joined the fight.

StormShaper was slightly surprised to see a smirk under the shadow user's face covering, but he didn't give him time to focus on the reinforcements. This just meant that he got his rematch; the blood witch could see to the princess. Since Zatook had been cut off from the shadows, StormShaper wasn't using his lightning. They fought with raw strength and speed, matching each other with each blow.

Shila had hit the dirt rather harshly, anger and pain filling her dark reptilian gaze. She whipped around to snap at the force slamming into her. She felt Marilyn's magic suddenly saturate the air as the bleeding stopped, the blood mage boosting the dragon's healing from afar. As the wound healed, Shila shifted back into her human form, dropping into a crouch. Marilyn appeared before her, hand outstretched as a barrier blocked Amaya's rapid attacks for the moment. Shila reached a hand down to touch her leg, and a pearl-like stone spread from her fingers, twining around her leg like vines to help brace the bone until she could finish healing.

"Aren't they all supposed to be in Andor?" she growled at Marilyn, who merely shrugged.

"As far as we knew, but it rather appears we were misinformed," the fell witch answered calmly.

Seemingly from the very air, Amaya appeared before the barrier, staring down the blood witch and the adolescent dragon. Amaya had attacked in her human form, not bothering with her Celestial form yet. Silver gray eyes bore into Marilyn and Shila even as Amaya stood almost nonchalant before them. To Shila, she remarked, "Not so cocky now that you've had a taste of the odds being evened." Then Amaya's cold gaze settled on Marilyn. "Cut and sculpt yourself into whatever lie your deranged mind will let you believe. Doesn't change the fact that I'm going to kick your arse."

Pearlescent stone wrapped around Shila's fingers to form long, thin, sharp talons, and her skin seemed to shimmer like opal now; likely a skin covering of the same ability she had used for her leg. Marilyn had simply pulled out her dagger, twirling it casually. Her eyes, however, had moved to Amaya's wrapped arms. They narrowed and then widened in something like satisfaction, but she said nothing. Forming up against a Celestial wasn't like a measly human, so she was being more careful.

In Amaya's hands she already held dual daggers. Unlike most daggers, these held a unique design of having short, double-curved blades with knuckle guards instead of hilts. While watching her opponents ready themselves, Amaya shifted her own stance into a more battle ready one. And then there were five images of Amaya surrounding Shila and Marilyn. Her smell, presence, and the sense of her blood came from all the images, making it difficult to know which, if any or all, were real.

"Ooh, she's quick, *shocker*," Marilyn remarked, not moving. She wasn't calling on her blood magic, and yet the air around her seemed dark. The grass around her feet hissed as if burning. Shila took her own stance, spreading her makeshift talons out like fans, one hand behind her and one in front. She scowled at Marilyn's blithe attitude, but she didn't move. She was supposed to follow the blood mage's lead if things didn't go according to plan, and so she would. Unless the woman just stood there talking. However, Marilyn spun her dagger before flinging it into the ground. What was solid dirt suddenly sucked at Amaya's feet like mud, letting off a putrid smell. Shila pulled a face at the stench, but Marilyn just stepped on the hilt of her dagger and pushed it further in. The patch spread, covering a wide circle of the ground that encompassed both of the current fights. But she still didn't attack.

"I have a proposition, if you're so concerned with fair fights. Let the younglings take the demon, and you and I can dance."

Shila's eyes snapped to Marilyn in surprise. She almost got angry, thinking the mage was insulting her. Yet reason argued Andor's fighter was no lightweight. And the mage…well, she wasn't known for fighting in groups. Or ever really fighting, until the latest stint when Keep Shadow Veil fell.

The mire found no purchase where the Celestial's copies seemed to touch. In truth, Amaya's feet had left the ground as soon as the mage made the muck. Now, Amaya lived up to her name and ran along the energy in the air, using her Celestial abilities to manipulate the energy around her. She didn't need to concentrate much energy with as fast as she moved. "I'm rather certain StormShaper would be mighty cross if his one-on-one got interrupted," Amaya answered casually, her voice giving no hint of direction. To Shila she remarked, "I know how it feels to be jockeyed around because no one respects that you can stand your own ground." Her voice held equal parts sarcasm and sincerity. Still, Amaya considered the proposition. In answer, the five images converged into one before literally *bolting* at Marilyn. Blades flashing, Amaya sliced for the mage's neck, intent to take her head. Fire leapt along the steel and engulfed the blades of both weapons.

The blade was back in Marilyn's hand, though the woman hadn't stooped to grab it. She didn't so much as slide in the mire when Amaya bolted for her, dagger meeting dagger and fire flaring against the strange dark aura around the mage now. She caught Amaya's other gauntlet in her hand, grin spreading as the leather darkened like it was corroding or burning. The darkened aura around Marilyn seemed to twist and writhe like smoke, seeking any crevice to burn through faster as though trying to get to something beneath. Another tendril was stretching up as if to bypass the gauntlets all together and go for her arms. Shila had stepped back for now. She didn't move to interrupt the other fight just yet, but she was ready to join either if an opening presented itself.

Instead of backing down, Amaya planted herself on the energy coalesced beneath her feet and pushed against the mage. The blood witch holding her own in a contest of strength against an adult Celestial made Amaya grateful that Jabez had made it out of his fight with the witch alive. The fire blazing along Amaya's blades flared against the tendrils trying to reach the Celestial, burning away the magic before it reached her flesh. The flames licked along Amaya's gauntlets and arms to keep the tendrils from her. As Amaya used her Celestial strength to twist free of Marilyn's grip on her wrist, Amaya flipped the dagger in her hand to change the blade's position. She frowned when the spell Marilyn was using to protect herself stopped not only the fire on Amaya's blade but kept the blade from continuing past as well.

Taking only a millisecond to perceive and adapt, Amaya dropped the flames on her blade, satisfaction swelling in her when the cut landed this time. Amaya sliced up Marilyn's arm through magic and flesh as she followed the appendage up to the mage's neck. Right as Amaya's steel started to cut through the magic covering the mage's neck, Marilyn disconnected their daggers and took a swipe of her own. While the force of the disengage brought Amaya's cut just shy of the mage's neck, Marilyn's blade sliced Amaya just past her gauntlet. Despite her frustration of missing her mark, Amaya flashed Marilyn a smug smirk. Marilyn knew why instantly: the witch's magic connected with the blood but nothing happened. In the instant it took Marilyn to make the realization, Amaya closed the scant distance between them. Her now bare hand wrapped around Marilyn's neck. The hand glowed white hot, searing into the blood mage faster than her magic could heal: Amaya meant to incinerate the woman.

The flames died. Pain lanced through Amaya from her fingertips up her arms so suddenly a cry ripped from her. Both women shoved away from each other, landing on their feet several paces back from their positions. Blackened skin marked Marilyn's throat where Amaya's hand almost burnt through her. Cold agony wracked Amaya's arms. Her own dagger flew to Amaya, and she caught it despite the pain. Amaya readied her stance once more, but the magic flared and caused her to waver regardless of her determination.

Despite the blackened neck, Marilyn was cackling like a hyena in hysterics. She was calming her laughter and starting to taunt Amaya with something when Shila called a warning. Marilyn shut her mouth, jumping away before Zatook's blade embedded itself in the ground. The champion stood just behind it, dark eyes burning blacker than her neck. The muck did little to hinder him as he pulled the blade free and stood to his full height. His hair was drenched at this point from fighting in the rain, clinging to his face and making him glare through the strands. A bolt of lightning announced StormShaper pursuing him, but Marilyn snapped her hand out and snatched him from the bolt, gripping his arm.

"We're leaving."

If StormShaper was surprised that the woman had just pulled him from lightning, they couldn't tell. But he made no move to sheathe his blade until she glared at him and growled, "*Now.* The situation has changed."

Though they could not see his face, the way he shoved his blade in its sheath spoke volumes. But he said nothing, instead reaching his other hand to Shila and then transporting away in another bolt. Zatook stayed where he was a moment longer in case it was a ruse, but he turned and moved to Amaya, the coldness in his eyes replaced with concern.

Sheathing her own blades, it took Amaya a moment to release her grip, her hands and arms stinging and pulsing with the unexpected spike. She finally managed and let her arms hang at her sides. Noting Zatook's concern, she gave him a small smile. "I'm all right. Just caught me by surprise— not my finest moment," she joked softly. "What about you? Any injuries we should wrap?" Strands of her ebony hair clung to her face, and parts of her ponytail stuck to her neck from standing still in StormShaper's rain. A few strands of hair were twisted into braids laced with beads, reminiscent of Captain's new hairstyle. Amaya's silver eyes met Zatook's dark ones easily.

Zatook returned his blade to the shadows, casting her the flattest look he could muster while moving the wet hair from his face. He gestured for her hand, wanting to check the burns.

"I've already had it looked at, but there's not much that can be done for them," dismissed Amaya, waving off Zatook's concern and his flat look. "This actually works out, though, since I was wanting to give you something." Instead of giving him her hand, she dropped a smooth, blue crystal in his hand, the object able to fit inside his palm. As she started to lower her hand, his free hand caught hers. Amaya held still, slightly surprised but also fighting back a wince. A slight blush dusted her cheeks as she watched his hand hold hers, taken aback at his insistence and gentleness.

Zatook glanced at the crystal but tucked it in his pouch for now, pulling up the hand he had caught and calmly undoing the wrappings. Shadows coiled into the air in front of her. *You could ask Tristan when next you see him. I imagine the Sun Child's healing is more powerful than most.* He reached into his pouches, pulling out a small bottle. *The princess believes this can help soothe them,* he added. *Though, I only described it as a lingering wound from a powerful curse.* The small bottle held a cream, though he wouldn't apply it without her agreement. Checking wounds was one thing, slathering a strange concoction from the princess of Andor all over her arms was quite another.

The blackness spread under Amaya's gauntlet, and at closer inspection, had started to creep up her arm towards her elbow. "Tristan's got a lot going on right now," Amaya countered quietly. "I didn't want to pile more guilt on him." Doubting her ability to apply anything without causing herself more pain, Amaya gestured with her free hand for Zatook to continue with the cream. "The crystal is a communication crystal. You can imbue it with magic and make writing appear. While you can use it for personal use, the crystal connects to another one," she explained. Reaching into her own pouch, she pulled out an identical crystal. "I have the other crystal. They connect with our magic signatures, so we're the only ones who can use them. Keeps a stranger from leading the other person into a trap. Once they're connected to a user, if the user becomes disconnected in some way, the crystal goes dark, letting the other person know something has happened. They work over distances too— I haven't found the limit to the range yet. At first, I thought you might like having it to make communication easier and to let me know when the group leaves Andor. Although, if you're going to be coming out here regularly to fight my brother's minions and Jeremiah's lackeys, feel free to send me a message. I'm always down for a fight," Amaya told him with a wink. "Feel free to message me if you just need someone to talk to as well."

Will they work through the Wall? Zatook remained careful as he removed the rest of her wrappings to apply his sister's medicine. It did have a soothing effect, like the poultices healers would apply to burns to lessen the pain until they could heal. He hesitated in his work before the shadows spelled, *Can it be detected?* He could probably leave it with the others if need be, under his sister's wards. But he wouldn't want to put them in more danger by having them hide something for him.

Amaya allowed her gauntlets to drop to the ground once Zatook removed them to get at her arms with the cream. To his question, she shrugged as she answered, "I don't see why not. It's not the Wall that keeps me out of Andor.

Traiborn had to set up special wards against me. If those were gone, I could enter Andor without issue since the queen still sees me as a friend. As for detection, the magic used is slight enough it should go unnoticed."

Zatook nodded. As he moved to treat her other arm, he started filling her in on what he knew— the group meeting the princess, taking Tristan to the oracle (though he left out the place being forbidden to him and the king finding them), the audience, the feast, and the growing threat at Caer Talon. He knew they had gone to the Archives, but he had yet to find if they had learned anything. And, while he didn't confess this to Amaya, he wasn't sure they should tell him if they did.

"At least they're keeping busy," Amaya remarked. "I half expected to hear that Jabez had run off to spy on my brother's troops or that Captain had started scaling the castle walls for fun." She grinned at him to show she mostly jested. More seriously and genuinely she said, "Thank you for helping in the ways that you could. I have a feeling Tristan probably enjoys having a mentor who can keep up with him. And it's nice to know that there is someone being a big brother to Jabez while he's big brothering everyone else." She laughed quietly. Amaya grew serious again as she added, "As for Caer Talon, I guess that's to be expected. I'll keep my eyes open for any useful information. I do have news from Nikko Mori. No casualties. Clovestein and some friends were able to protect everyone despite the damage my brother caused and the denizens sustained. Wounded but alive."

Zatook finished rebinding the blackened skin before he bent to retrieve her gauntlets. He wasn't really sure what else to say. He had barely interacted with Jabez, but if the idea in her mind brought her comfort while separated from the others, he would leave it be. There was no harm in it, really. And he was helping where he could. *And today we learned that Marilyn is, indeed, hiding many things,* he finally noted, handing her the bottle with the rest of the cream.

Amaya strapped her gauntlets back into place before pocketing the bottle. "She's certainly a wily one," Amaya agreed. She studied her bandaged hands for a moment as she went over the fight in her mind. Why would the blood witch's power resonate with wounds left by the Talisman? That shouldn't be possible. "Maybe our group can learn more about the Talisman. I'll connect with my contacts and see if I can glean anything too."

Zatook nodded. *I shall attempt to transmit any information to the others. For now, I need to return for my report.* He took a step back from her. *If you are in need of more, I can let the princess know,* he added, gesturing to the bottle. He took another step before turning and flaring out his wings. With a gust of air, he was gone.

18. Dance of Shadows

In the weeks since the feast, the group had seen little of
Zatook. Mostly a glimpse here or there when he came
to give his reports. He had gotten Amaya's message to
Tannen so the blacksmith could let Tristan know about
his home. Between reading what they could gather from
the Archive, Solomon also got the group to start training
again, as well. Lancelot took up sparring with Tristan,
holding his own as he had during their encounter at
Thorn-Drake. He had snagged a sword from the armory,
switching between that and using his greaves and
gauntlets so both boys could practice with the different
styles. Rose would often watch them, sometimes to
give feedback and other times just to study their styles.
Though Captain currently couldn't practice working with
her Sight, she did practice her Weaving. Between the
passing of her week of mourning and the lack of having to
deal with Traiborn, she was starting to slip back into her
role of bubbly Captain.

Solomon had left research of the Talisman and the
Celestial of Time to the others for now, focusing his
own attention on the tomes regarding ancient relics
and enchanted weaponry. He had found a few entries
regarding his scimitars, but the only new information
he had gleaned was their name: the Glyphseal Sentinels.
He had yet to learn if there were better ways to tap into
their power or other abilities they may possess, let alone

if they were powerful enough to reinstate the seal on the Talisman. Solomon sighed as he calmly rolled up his current scroll and set it to the side. He reached up to remove the small-frame spectacles he wore while reading, setting them on the small end table alongside the parlor's lounge. He stood and stretched, moving to watch Captain. The girl had requested a few little targets to set up in the yard so she could practice throwing her daggers. While her accuracy was impeccable with a straight throw, she was learning to use her Weaving to change a blade's trajectory midair— these she only practiced if the yard was empty, as the blades tended to veer farther than she intended or teleport and appear somewhere random before embedding in the wall or dirt. One had even wound up in the garden area's fountain. Collette had been kind enough to work some new enchantments for the yard to ensure the daggers didn't enter the parlor or end up somewhere else entirely.

The princess came and went. Often her duties kept her away, but the group had learned she was also studying under her father and taking academic classes. Solomon had told her about his scimitars in case she came across anything in her studies, but the group was still wary in what information they shared with her. As much as the king seemed to dote on his daughter, they had little doubt he had plans in place to control her should she grow too rebellious or try to keep things from him.

While he spent as much time as he could with Rose— ever conscious of the deadline for her departure— Tristan gladly accepted the chance to train. The activity gave him a focus and a goal, so he wasn't wallowing in his grief all day. He had been studying King Zetta's journal as well, learning more of Andor's history and searching for clues the group could use.

Alconai participated in his own training to keep his skills sharp and to hone his fighting. He sparred with Lancelot when time allowed and even offered to go a few rounds with Captain.

During his recovery, Jabez followed Solomon's lead in researching the Talisman and the royal family. He made sure to rest and only do light training if any at all. When he was mostly healed, Jabez took to exploring the castle in the hopes of finding the tapestry or anything else in the visions Tristan had told them. Currently, Jabez silently moved through the castle, having waited until nightfall so the inhabitants would hopefully be asleep. Sticking to the shadows in the corridors, Jabez used his skillset once more as he blended into the darkened edges of the interior architecture. While searching, a sense of familiarity filled Jabez, reminding him of the days he'd spent information gathering for the Order. He slipped past guards as he made his way through the castle. As much as they had been trying to avoid stirring up trouble with the king, the group needed to understand the visions Tristan had seen, and they needed to gather more information than the books would have to determine their next move. It was a dangerous game. Who better to step up to the task than the slipperiest of the group? Really, Jabez was surprised he hadn't been cornered after the audience given the implications of his usual attire. Still, Jabez kept alert. Even if he failed to find anything strange, Jabez took in the details to get a lay of the castle and its important areas. Best to know in case the group needed to escape should their relations with the king go completely sour.

A while into his exploration, Jabez came across a door that gave him pause. To the passerby, it looked like a standard door, nothing spectacular about it. Since Jabez was looking for such a thing in his search, he spotted the subtle runes warding the door. From the look of the enchantments, the wards acted as alarms rather than a barrier. Now, what could need such protection behind a simple door? The area wasn't the royal wing or where any vaults would be. Jabez checked his surroundings, making sure he remained undetected. Pulling out a few tools specific for this kind of infiltration, he got to work silently and efficiently deactivating the wards, confident doing so wouldn't alert anyone to his presence. Once he deemed it safe, Jabez worked the lock next. With a soft click of the tumblers, Jabez opened the door and slipped inside, silently closing the door behind him.

The room inside appeared to be some sort of office or study. A large wooden desk stood to one side, with a comfortable yet elegant chair behind. The top of the desk was tidy despite a significant stack of papers. There was an ornate quill and inkpot as well as a lantern with magical crystals that could be set to various levels of brightness. Along one section of wall were maps of neighboring Regalia and Nocis, as well as the Jaromír Mountains to the east and the Valley of Dragons within. Another wall held a few portraits of the royal family, some decorative shelves with gifts from other nations, and a banner with the king's crest. A large window looked out across the nearest section of the gardens that ringed the palace. A second desk held a variety of instruments made of glass or metal that Jabez recognized from scholars at the Order who liked to study different effects of magic or things from the natural world around them. The rest of the walls held shelves filled with a variety of tomes and scrolls. A lectern stood near the walls where the room's occupant could set an open tome or weigh parts of an unrolled scroll for easy reading. Plush carpet softened Jabez's steps as he entered. The blue hues of the carpet and the curtains framing the window, the banner with the crest, the contents of the room— all signs pointed to this being the king's personal study.

Oh boy. Now, Jabez treaded really dangerous territory. However, he was already in this deep, so he might as well take a look. Stepping carefully around the room, Jabez passed by the desk, glancing at the papers but not touching. The last thing he needed was the king noticing someone had been in his private study. Several things spread amongst the notes on the research desk caught Jabez's attention. He moved to the desk to take a closer look. A strange, purple crystal lay among papers containing all kinds of notes. Jabez refrained from touching it just in case the crystal held some kind of strange or harmful magic. Who knew what the king was studying? As for the notes, Jabez read bits and pieces of several languages, but he also recognized the makings of a cipher. Even with the languages he knew, deciphering the notes would take time he lacked. A vial of inky black liquid caught his eye, and his mind instantly went to Zatook, remembering how the warrior bled dark. Jabez wouldn't put it past Traiborn to be studying his stepson's blood. Jabez stopped on a diagram of a sword. The writings were in the same cipher as the rest of the notes, but Jabez recognized the sketching to be of the sword King Traiborn carried. Temptation stirred in Jabez. As he debated the risks of taking anything, he ducked and spun away from the hand reaching from behind him for his neck.

The assailant followed Jabez's retreat across the room.

The all-black attire covering the man from head to toe placed him as one of Jabez's former associates from Shaedra. Special lenses in the mask kept the ninja's eyes hidden while still allowing him to see clearly. Facing off with a Shaedra ninja made Jabez feel vulnerable without his cowl. At least he still had his mask covering the lower half of his face. Even so, the man would know him. Heart racing and thoughts flying through strategies, Jabez danced around his opponent, exchanging blows when the man closed the distance. Despite his trepidations and doubts, Jabez moved with fluidity through the familiar techniques and skills. He met his opponent's strikes, parrying and countering with his own devastating precision. Confidence and determination filled him. He knew this dance. As he fought the Shaedra agent, Jabez proved how despite having no powers Shaedra considered him one of their best. He had reminded them in every encounter he had with them over the last couple of years.

The duel moved around the room as Jabez tried to edge his way to the door only to have his opponent drive him away from it time and again. Still, Jabez kept the man from fully cornering or pinning him. Snatching three throwing knives from his weapons pouch, Jabez let the blades fly at his opponent, trying to get the man to back off some in the tight space. They missed his first target— the man —but hit Jabez's second intended set of targets. Glass instruments and containers shattered, their liquid contents bleeding across the research desk and ruining the papers— all but the diagram Jabez had managed to snatch during one of his passes near the research desk. He was already made; he might as well make it worth the trouble. And with the papers ruined, Traiborn would have a harder time knowing if anything went missing during the skirmish.

Jabez finally made it to the door. Flinging it open, he quickly ducked back as another Shaedra ninja took a swipe at him. As Jabez dodged his original opponent, he realized the second man had been guarding the door while the duel took place. Now, two Shaedra operatives stood between Jabez and escape. Well, this had gone decidedly out of his favor. At least the two men seemed content to block the door for the moment, allowing Jabez a chance to regroup.

"Well met, Phoenix," the first man greeted in a deep voice. "It's good to see you still living up to your reputation."

"Rugan," Jabez identified, placing the voice. The two of them had crossed plenty of times in the past; though, Shaedra's policy of their ninjas being completely covered made it difficult to place who exactly Jabez had fought when, as intended. Jabez watched the men closely, especially now that he knew he was facing one of Shaedra's elites. "Don't tell me you followed me all the way into Andor," Jabez remarked sarcastically.

Rugan chuckled. "Yes and no. We were already here in the good king's employ. Finding you was an unforeseen benefit," answered the elite easily. "Really, what did you expect going to the audience dressed as you are? Our attire blends in with the shadows but paints a target on us in the light. I wouldn't have believed you dared to be so bold if I hadn't been there to witness the spectacle." Rugan moved in an arc toward Jabez, his gait nonchalant but loose. Jabez allowed him to get a certain distance before he circled away, keeping both men in his sights.

"I knew I couldn't hide forever," Jabez admitted.

"Guardian of the Chosen Children? Can't step more into the center of light than that," Rugan remarked. "However, we both know your new position is a façade. You're still hiding— it's just behind a title now. You're not an official member of the Order. You belong to Shaedra, and Shroud wants his elite back."

"I'm afraid he's in for a long wait then," replied Jabez coolly.

Jabez heard the smile in Rugan's voice as the man challenged, "Oh, not so long really. You may be here as a guest under the king's protection, but you're well on your way to getting him to revoke that boon. If he does, you're fair game, Phoenix. I suppose we'll see soon enough. The king is on his way now." Jabez felt his blood run cold, but he kept his reaction neutral.

"The king is here," Traiborn corrected in his normal cool voice, but Jabez didn't miss the darker tones beneath it. The man was actually in something close to casual clothes: white trousers with a blue top edged in silver embroidery. He wasn't wearing his crown, but he did have the swords strapped to his waist, including the supposedly decorative one. His stern eyes were studying the research desk to assess the damage, first going to his samples and then eyeing the broken instruments. He moved further in, picking up a piece of the glass and eying his notes. Simple enough repairs, at least.

"You and your ilk are determined to make things difficult, it would seem. First the boy's trespass into a sacred space, and now your trespass here. Skulking through the corridors in the dark. Ignoring every sign that a space is not meant for you. If one were not so aware of your current situation, one might think you were attempting to get yourselves *disavowed*." His gaze slid to Jabez. "Which, as you have discovered, has far more consequences than you were aware." He gestured to Rugan. He returned to his desk, setting a hand on the wood. Magic pulsed through the air, and the delicate instruments rebuilt themselves. The liquid cleaned itself from the surface and the carpet beneath before dissipating. He lifted the ruined notes, now dry, turning them over in his hand. Once he was sure all the ink had run, he crumpled the papers and tossed them in a nearby basket. "Tell me. What were you hoping to find?" He turned to the two men, walking closer and folding his arms. "What information would be so valuable for you to risk the safety I have offered? The risks I have taken in welcoming you. In naming you 'guest', with all benefits that entailed?"

Rugan and his comrade bowed to the king and moved to keep guard at the door. Jabez remained still where he had stopped in the room, between the research desk and the door. He considered his words carefully, knowing the ire he had stirred already with his trespass. Finally, Jabez forced his body into a more relaxed stance as he answered, "A night of restlessness drove me to take a midnight stroll. I came across a simple door in an area of little importance. And yet, the alarm wards suggested this was no simple door. Alas, curiosity got the better of me." Jabez shrugged. "Old habits. I'm sure you're aware of Shaedra's reputation for intel gathering."

"And now, here we stand. And I must decide what to do with you. Typically, if someone thinks to invade my personal space, I would make an example of them. Yet this calls for discretion, for both our sakes. I am quite sure the pair standing guard outside would be thrilled if I gave you to their master, but despite a second betrayal of trust from your group, I would rather not completely break our agreement..." He strode to his desk as he spoke, moving to sit in the chair behind. "Which begs consideration of just how much you care for your comrades. You risked much by coming here, not only for yourself. So one might think you are not as close as you wish to appear. And yet, I am not 'one'. I know more about you than you likely wish, Jabez, son of Ziv. Stepson of Kouta PeaceKeeper. Ward of Solomon SealKeeper. Brother to Alconai FoxFeet. Honorary sibling to the Moon Child. Mentor to the Sun Child. 'Former' Shaedra. The man who lost his mind and seeks to get it back." He leaned back in the chair, steepling his fingers and glaring at Jabez over them. "So, bearing that in mind, your loyalty should be deeper than words can express, unless you are truly callous. And SealKeeper isn't one to give his trust where it isn't due. What would one such as you be willing to endure to both pay for his crimes and still protect his friends and family?"

Jabez steeled himself with the revelations. Most of the king's taunts came as little surprise. The group had already speculated the man knew more than he let on. However, Jabez still felt ice run through his veins with Traiborn's knowledge of his family. Alconai the king could have deduced from watching Jabez's interactions with the minstrel, but their stepfather? Not even Kouta remembered his surname. How and why would Traiborn know about Kouta? And then there was the king's taunt about Jabez's sanity. How had the man known about Jabez's fall into madness? He met King Traiborn's gaze as he fought to keep calm. "As I said, old habits," Jabez responded evenly. "If you know me so well, then you already know the answer to your question: my loyalty is carved into my flesh. It has soaked the ground crimson, and still I will give more. I am the most expendable in the group— the shadow that disappears. They don't need me to keep moving forward."

Traiborn actually snorted. "And yet I doubt they agree," he noted rather flatly. "In that same vein, I doubt I can get away with being the reason you vanish. Though I admit, locking you away for a bit is rather tempting— a fairly fitting punishment for most who would breach that door. Yet you are not most. How long would it be, do you think, before you start to unravel? Before you started slipping back into the madness?" He chuckled to himself. "Or we could put you alongside my shadow. Test how much you truly can endure. If you could keep the secret of what happens, I might just accept the compromise. I could have you back by morning, healed so well your comrades would be none the wiser…"

"Your doubt should have extended *further*." Jabez had rarely heard Solomon angry before. Stern, yes. But rarely did he ever show actual anger. Yet there was no denying the quiet fury in the man's voice as he stepped into the study. Traiborn's gaze flicked to him and then past, wondering where the hell his guards had gone, but he let the thought pass for now. Shroud would answer for their failure later.

"Ah, Solomon. I had wondered if you would join us this evening. Alas, you have no say in the matter. The decision lies with the one who *broke into my study*." If the revelation was meant to surprise Solomon, it didn't seem to work.

"Because you have ever been so careless as to let it be entered. Watched or not," Solomon pointed out flatly.

Traiborn's eyes narrowed.

"Locks and wards are not an invitation."

"Aren't they? You know all of us so well, yet you expect us to believe you were surprised by anything that has happened tonight? You even knew I would come looking for him when his walk took longer than anticipated."

Traiborn was tightlipped now, a silent fury in his gaze. Solomon met it evenly.

"We're returning to our quarters now. Restrict our access to wander freely if you must, as that would be a subtle but effective reaction, and we shan't speak of tonight again."

"Absolutely not. Your ward broke into my private study and ruined my current research. I will not allow him to simply walk away."

"You and I both understand the precarious positions we are in. You can. You will. Because neither of us wants the consequences that would come should you not."

Both men stared levelly at each other.

Jabez fought not to blanch at the tension in the room. Solomon wasn't supposed to know Jabez had left— no one was supposed to know. That way they could deny their knowledge if Jabez got caught. Now that was out the window. Still, Jabez didn't want the group to suffer for his failure. "Solomon—" Jabez started but stopped abruptly when Solomon leveled him with a *look*. For the sake of keeping up appearances, Jabez managed to keep from averting his gaze. However, he did move to follow Solomon out of the study. Despite the tensions, Jabez shared the king's curiosity on how Solomon got past the guards.

Traiborn was obviously fuming, but he let them leave. When they left the study, Rugan wasn't anywhere to be seen, but the other guard was on the ground. Solomon didn't stop, and Jabez could guess he wasn't planning to answer any questions until they were back within the wards of the guest tower. The walk was silent, though the Order member slowly unclenched his fists as they went. By the time they reached the parlor, he had regained some calm. Some. He turned to face Jabez, folding his arms. "You have some friends in the shadows."

As they had walked, Jabez had resigned himself to receiving a lecture for his outing. Even once they reached the parlor, he couldn't bring himself to relax, dreading the inevitable conversation and feeling like a child caught sneaking out of the house after dark. However, Solomon's statement caught Jabez off guard. He stared blankly at his mentor. "What do you mean?" asked the younger man. Had Zatook alerted Solomon? Surely, the warrior wouldn't have risked it. Perhaps for one of the Children but not for Jabez.

"Someone from Shaedra found me while I was out looking for you. Led me there and then had me make it look like I caught him off guard."

Jabez gave Solomon an even more confused look. "No one in Shaedra would stick their necks out for me. At least, no one I knew," he protested softly, bewildered. "We're taught to be loyal above all else. Why would...?" he trailed off as his mind started to slip into old memories. "They'll get in trouble even faking you getting the jump on them. Maybe not as much, but Shroud has high standards."

"And yet he insisted." Solomon sighed, lowering his arms. "We can only hope Shaddai will be with him in whatever he must endure for helping us."

Jabez shook himself, trying to clear his thoughts. "I wouldn't count on his help all the time, but the man's involvement is an interesting turn," he agreed. He felt himself easing a bit as Solomon relaxed his stance a little. "I was able to get some information that I can share with the group. Not a lot. I didn't have time to dig more thoroughly, but I did manage to snatch some of Traiborn's research." Jabez started to reach for the diagram but stopped when Solomon leveled another look at him—gentler than the one he'd given Jabez in the study but a warning all the same. Sighing, Jabez asked, "What do you want me to say, Solomon? We needed more information to figure out the visions Tristan saw. So, I did what I do best and went to gather intel. I was careful, but I admit I wasn't expecting Shaedra to be guarding the study." Jabez lowered his gaze as he spoke next, "I...I was going to accept. I could have appeased the king and bought us more time and protection. It was my mistake anyway. And maybe I could have learned something about Zatook."

"He was cornering you in a way he does best, and you were going to let him," Solomon pointed out softly. "Jabez, I know you aren't a lightweight. I know you can endure more than most, and you would survive whatever he did to you. But you can't put yourself in that kind of position with him. If any of us give into his schemes, even a little, he has a claw in. And it's just a matter of time from there." He sighed, stepping forward and reaching for Jabez's shoulder. "I understand why you tried. And under other circumstances, I'm sure you would have been fine. But now we know that Shaedra *is* here, and Traiborn is trying to get to you." He met Jabez's gaze levelly. "No one should go out alone anymore. Even if stealth is needed." He let go of the man's shoulder, moving to pour himself a glass of water from a nearby pitcher. "Traiborn wanted you to accept. He expected it. And I have no doubt he had several other plans while he had you."

"Solomon, despite what happened tonight, I'm still the best shot we've got to get where he doesn't want us to go," Jabez protested. "What would Traiborn even have to gain by going after me? The group isn't going to crumble if I disappear, and he already knows what he would get out of me if anything. As for Shaedra, I know what to watch for now. This wasn't my first encounter with them, and it won't be the last." He ran a hand down his face, careful not to remove his mask. "I was looking for the tapestry from Tristan's vision. I didn't find it, but I know the lay of the castle better now, and I did find something on the sword. I probably can't decipher it, but I can tell it's more than decoration."

"Jabez." Solomon sighed, setting down his glass. "We don't know *what* he knows, that's part of the problem. We know he likely hasn't revealed everything, and he's trying to bait us into giving more information. But he also isn't omnipotent, though it can seem like it at times. We can't risk some of the information we have falling into his hands. I know you want to do what you do best. I'm not even stopping you. But you shouldn't go alone." He ran his hand over his head before continuing, "Your trouble grasping your own importance isn't going to stop others from seeing it. You're right— the group would eventually move on. They would have to. But it wouldn't be easy, and it would deal a large blow to everyone. I'm not going to let it reach that point." He met Jabez's gaze levelly. "I already lost my daughter to that man; I'm not going to lose my son, too."

Jabez stared, taken aback. Over the years, Solomon had come to be more than a mentor to Jabez, and the ninja knew Solomon put a lot of effort and patience into helping him. He recalled what Solomon had told him about Jabez being like a brother to Captain. Somehow, Jabez hadn't realized the sentiment extended to Solomon seeing him as a son. "Thank you," softly said Jabez, "For looking out for me." He wanted to argue, but he understood Solomon's point.

Jabez moved to a sofa and sat, a little surprised when he started trembling once he consciously relaxed. He hadn't realized how tense he still was. "You all were fine without me for a couple of years," he held up a hand to keep Solomon from interrupting, "However, I concede that one of us disappearing would have been a blow to the group's morale. I'm not the pillar that you and Amaya are for the group. Though, after losing Arianna and with Amaya and Zatook's absences, one of us being imprisoned would have crushed spirits and fueled tempers." Releasing a heavy breath, Jabez leaned back into the sofa and rested his head against it, looking to the ceiling as he contemplated. "I wasn't thinking beyond the moment— beyond how I could help. Be a shield and an information sponge. But he was right. You are right. How much would it have really taken to undo your hard work? How quickly would I have crumbled? Facing Rugan tonight reminded me that I can fight Shaedra, but that was never truly my doubt."

"Our group is not held up by two people," Solomon pointed out gently as he moved to sit as well. "We all have our roles; we all have our relationships with the others. And we're in a very precarious position right now, as is our host. Tensions are high." He took a sip of his water as he considered his next words. "We don't know how you would react to imprisonment or torture anymore. But I'm not willing to let you be put into that situation just to find out— especially not under Traiborn. We've already seen what his control can be like if he gets access to someone."

"You mean Zatook," Jabez voiced. He doubted Traiborn would have bothered to try to bind him like he had the shadow warrior, but Solomon was right that Jabez shouldn't put himself in the position for the possibility. "We still need answers for certain things. I don't know most of the group's skills. Tristan might be the best for stealth since he's familiar with hiding his presence. However, I hate to put him in that position if things go wrong again."

"And the queen," Solomon confirmed. "And those are the two we *know*. He's had centuries to work on his magic and his manipulation." Solomon paused, considering. "Unfortunately, Rose is in no condition to be sneaking around the castle, or I would suggest her. The same with Izzy, at least until we can find a way to shield her Sight from what is flaring it. I do not know your brother's skill with stealth."

A hint of melancholy flickered in Jabez's eyes. "I've seen Alconai work to some extent, but I never stayed near long enough to fully ascertain his skillset. I didn't want Shaedra to go after him," admitted Jabez. "Tristan is the one who saw the tapestry in the vision, but so far he hasn't said anything about seeing it during our and his ventures in the palace. It's a big castle, so I'm not sure if we've overlooked the tapestry or just haven't found it yet." Jabez rolled his head to relieve some of the tension in his neck. "Any luck in your research for finding what might be causing the flares? I know you were looking into your scimitars as well."

"Captain is fairly convinced it has something to do with the orb Tristan found when Zatook took him to meet the oracle, but we've yet to find anything concrete. I'm not even sure Andor will have records of it. We have yet to determine if it is simply an artifact that channels to wherever Time is sealed or if she is inside the orb itself." Solomon sighed, shaking his head. "What I'm finding on the scimitars seems to match what we already knew, aside from their name. I am beginning to doubt their ability to aid in a seal as strong as the one around the Talisman. They may be able to divert the energy it releases, though, as I did with StormShaper's lightning."

"Something else for us to find in places the king doesn't want us looking," Jabez remarked dryly about the orb. Thinking of the scimitars brought his mind back to his conversation with Solomon about training. Rugan's words also echoed in his mind. "I'm healed up enough to train," Jabez commented carefully. "Do you still believe I'm the best choice to learn to use the scimitars? To become an Order member?"

"I do."

Jabez weighed his thoughts and words a little longer. Finally, he spoke quietly, "I'll train with you."

Solomon smiled softly. "Then we'll start tomorrow. For now, we should both get some sleep."

Nodding, Jabez stood and moved to retreat to his room. When he reached the stairs, he paused and turned back to Solomon. "Good night, Father," he said sincerely, hoping to convey his return of Solomon's sentiment. He then ascended the stairs.

"Good night," Solmon returned. He stayed up a little longer, deep in thought, before eventually turning in himself.

***

The next morning, Solomon told the others what he had told Jabez— no more solo ventures. He didn't give them the details of what happened, but he did warn them that he and Jabez had learned there were agents of Shaedra in the castle.

Alconai's gaze darkened with the revelation, but he made no comment. He arched an eyebrow in curiosity when Jabez showed the group the diagram of the sword.

"I found a few things of interest in Traiborn's study. His notes are written in a cipher that— while I can understand the languages —I don't have a key to translate the contents," Jabez told them. "I think he's experimenting on Zatook's blood as I found a vial of black liquid. There was also a dark, purple crystal." As Jabez described the crystal he saw, Tristan confirmed it sounded like the same as the Celesbane written about in the journal. "There are still quite a few things unanswered, but some of our suspicions are now confirmed. Tristan, would you be willing to come with me through the castle to see if we can find that tapestry?"

"I tried looking for it with Rose, but we had no luck. We can cross-reference where we've all checked so far and see where we still have to look," Tristan agreed, glad to do something other than read and train for a bit. However, with the mention of Shaedra and the precautions of no soloing, he understood how dangerous their task was.

Rose nodded. "While you're working on that, Lance, Captain, and I will keep training."

"I might've found a way to fin' enchantments on people," Captain explained with a grin. "We're gonna try it wit' Rose's powers first, and t'en I'm gonna see if Collette 'as time ta help, too."

"I'll stay here and see if I can make out anythin' on t'e sword," Alconai offered. "I ken a few tales that might help me figure out somethin' on it."

Jabez nodded. "Sounds like we have a plan," he said.

Once the group had breakfast and had freshened up for the day, they dispersed to their tasks. Utilizing his skills of venturing unseen through the forest, Tristan followed Jabez closely. They had managed to figure out where in the castle they hadn't looked for the tapestry yet and stealthily made their way to those areas. Despite trying to blend with the shadows, the two men kept to a leisurely pace in case they were spotted. They managed to avoid the busier parts of the castle. Tristan couldn't help feeling a little like he was traversing Nikko Mori with Clovestein once more, moving carefully to blend with his surroundings.

The morning steadily crept onward with no sign of the tapestry. At one point, they entered a hall that looked similar to others they had checked. Tristan refrained from sighing in frustration. Then he saw it: the tapestry from the vision, blowing in a wind between two suits of armor. Nudging Jabez to get the man's attention, Tristan approached the fabric as he peered at it. The picture itself was of Traiborn during some heroic quest it seemed. If not for the vision, Tristan would have rolled his eyes and continued onward given the encounter he'd had with the man when Zatook showed Tristan the orb. However, there wasn't a window close enough for the wind to make the fabric sway. Tristan took the edge of the tapestry and lifted it away from the wall to look behind it.

The stone wall would have passed as such any other time, but light hit the wall just right as Tristan pulled away the fabric. A thin line of magic shimmered in the form of an archway. An illusion spell. A barely perceptible breeze was coming through.

Tristan hesitated and looked back at Jabez. Tristan knew they needed to tread carefully with the king, but the orb had shown him this specific tapestry as though it wanted him to find the doorway. And he didn't want Zatook to get in trouble for nothing. With determined resolve, Tristan used his other hand to test if he could pass through the illusion. As his hand came into contact with it, the magic felt strange, viscous. Slowly, he managed to push his way through the spell, the gooey texture making it a weird sensation. Once he managed to step through, he found himself on a stone staircase that spiraled up. Realizing he was in one of the towers, Tristan moved up a few steps to give Jabez enough room to enter. The man followed right behind him, taking in the hidden stairs. With a slight jerk of his head, Jabez indicated for Tristan to continue. The ninja, however, stayed behind to guard the entrance. The illusion magic allowed the duo to see out into the hall while remaining hidden in the stairwell. Tristan ventured up the steps, listening and studying the stairs as he moved.

19. The Lonely Queen

At first, there was silence broken only by the occasional breeze through the tall and skinny windows. But eventually, another sound joined: humming. As Tristan moved higher, it felt as though he passed through the occasional film of magic, though he noticed no effects. At the top of the stairwell, he found himself outside of a door; the humming came from within.

Tristan wondered who might be behind the door. Was this where the queen went when she wasn't needed? Or perhaps his grandmother was in the tower rather than the orb. It brought to question if the magic along the staircase was meant to keep people out or to keep someone in. Reaching up, Tristan knocked politely. "Hello? It's Tristan Nightshade," he called. "I was…well, I was led here by a vision given to me by the oracle." Even as the words left his mouth, he felt a bit ridiculous saying them despite them being true.

The humming had stopped when he spoke. He didn't hear footsteps, but as he finished, the door opened. Sure enough, there stood the queen. Rather than the outfit she had worn for her public appearances, she now wore priestess garb to match Collette's. The fancy updo was gone; instead, her hair was pulled into two large loops that extended from each side of the back of her head. She smiled at Tristan, touching a hand to his shoulder. "Then it seems Aria has helped you to find me," she informed him warmly before pulling him into a hug. "And I can finally express how grateful I am to learn that you are alive."

Tristan could just make out the room behind her. A large canopy bed curved with the wall on one side, while two dressers and an armoire to match did the same. Most of the wall, however, was covered in portraits— the queen with people from her life. A young Zatook and Collette at various ages; one even featured Amaya. But the portrait that drew his eye the most was the one which showed her alongside Reina, the pair smiling brightly.

Tristan felt his eyes sting as he stared at the portrait of his mother. "Your Majesty," he greeted quietly, fighting back the tears that wanted to come and swallowing down the lump that had formed in his throat. Hesitantly, he lightly returned the embrace, not sure what else to do. "I believe we have some things to discuss, if this is a safe place to do so."

"Just Corianne, please," she assured him, straightening to guide him into the room. "We are warded here, so there is no concern with being overheard." Her green eyes regarded him fondly. "You've grown so much. Until your arrival, I hadn't seen you since you were just a tot scampering around your mother's gown." A sadness entered her gaze. "I'm so sorry. I would have come if I could."

Tristan's heart ached when the queen mentioned coming to him. "You knew about my mother?" he asked, fighting to keep his voice steady. At least that was a bit of news he wouldn't have to deliver. He looked down at the floor, unable to meet her gaze or to look at the picture of his mother. "My father killed her. He killed my sister, too. Just a few weeks ago. I'm sorry I don't really remember you, but my mother told me about you; and Solomon has spoken of you." He glanced hesitantly at the portraits again. "My aunt Amaya was with us for a time; she called you her friend. She told me that you saved her life when she confronted the king." Tristan's thoughts felt scattered like leaves in the wind. "I apologize for upsetting the king. Zatook took me to the cavern with the orb. I didn't know it was sacred ground, and I touched the orb. The orb showed me visions of a lot of things, including the tapestry at the bottom of the stairs. I saw my grandmother as well. Do you know if she resides in the orb or if she uses the orb as a way to connect with people?"

Corianne tackled his questions and statements one at a time, keeping up surprisingly well for how scattered he felt. "Hoshiko reached out to me shortly after. And I told Almas, as he was here at the time. I did not know about Arianna— I wish I had met her at least once. I am sorry, Tristan. Even though words do no justice here. Hoshiko is also how I knew Amaya survived." She sighed, moving to a set of doors that let out to a balcony and gently touching the locket around her neck. "Do not fret over the king. He is often upset." She turned back to look at him, gesturing to the chairs if he wanted to sit. "You say you saw your grandmother? White hair, red designs along her skin?" At Tristan's nod, she continued, "Had I known that connection, I would have taken Amaya or even your father to the orb, regardless of the king's 'rules'... The oracle was given to us by the Celestials to guard, and we have done so ever since. I do not fully understand the seal, but I believe she is within. And like myself, Aria has been further cut off under Traiborn's reign." She sighed, moving to a chair herself. "Her orb used to be in the shrine where I, and now Collette, served. Aria and I have spent more time together since my imprisonment, but her ability to actually speak with anyone is limited because of the king's magic. She is learning to convey things through visions, but only if other visions do not need to take priority."

"Grandmother showed me things pertaining to my companions. I saw the sword at Traiborn's side, but I'm not sure if it was just a warning or something else. A dagger he held, I'm sure, is made of Celesbane. I saw the dragon knight turned king and a woman I think is his wife. I saw…" Tristan trailed off as he recalled the vision of a man clutching the Talisman. "There was a lot," he said instead.

Taking a seat in one of the chairs, Tristan added guiltily, "I'm sorry about Zatook. I tried to convince Traiborn to release him, but I failed." Tristan tried to push away the voice telling him that he'd failed so many. However, he felt the frustration and despair that had been plaguing him since he had been captured by the blood mage. His mind turned back to what she had said about his sister. "My father invaded Nikko Mori and found my sister's pendant. He couldn't find mine because my mother hid it too well. I wished she'd have been able to hide my sister's pendant instead of leaving it in my care. Then maybe Arianna would still be alive." He exhaled heavily. He had been trying to take the words to heart that had been spoken to him about his sister's death from just about everyone in the group and even those outside it, but it was hard to stop the 'what ifs' from going through his head. Especially when he felt like he was reliving it all again with Rose and Zatook. Wanting to change the subject lest he lose himself in sorrow again, Tristan asked, "Do you know where Almas went? Another vision showed me Almas leaving Keep Shadow Veil with something clutched in his hand. I know he came here on a mission for my mother, but then I never saw or heard from him again."

Corianne sighed. "Traiborn does not easily turn from his anger. This is not your failing, but his. As much as it pains me to say so, Zatook knew what he was doing." She hesitated when he mentioned Traiborn's sword. "The blade at his side is a powerful relic, much like the orb. And Traiborn knows well how to harness the powers within that blade, where others have failed. The dagger…is likely the one he used against Amaya." She stood, moving to a small chest sitting on her dresser and opening it to retrieve something. "Almas was here for a while," she confessed softly. "Usually when Reina sent him with her letters, he would stay a few days to rest before returning. But when he brought me this, she warned him to stay a while longer." She returned to her chair, opening her palms to reveal Tristan's pendant. "She had Almas bring it to me because she feared your father's plans for you. I think, in a way, she suspected what was to come. In her letter…she wanted to hide Arianna's, as well, but did not think it wise to keep them together. As for Almas, since you were hidden, I believe he decided to return home to Ben-Gal."

Tristan stared at the sapphire gleaming in the light. "Thank you for safeguarding it," he said politely. He couldn't help feeling a bit of dread now knowing its location. "Are you sure it's safe for me to know?" he asked. His father had broken him once, what if Tsukuyomi managed to pry the information from him? "I know it's a selfish thought, but part of me wishes you would destroy it, or at least get rid of it to protect you and your family. I don't want any more people getting hurt because of me." Tristan stared at the floor again as he leaned his elbows on his knees.

Corianne knelt before him, touching a hand to his knee. "As much as I dislike the man, Traiborn is more than capable of keeping your father away from Andor. And were he to perish, I would regain my magic and be just as formidable. I suspect your father may know I carry it, and for now it remains beyond his reach. It is better you know, should something happen to us both and you need to reclaim it before he can." She shook her head. "I wish I could guarantee that no one would face pain because of another. But that is not the way life goes." She had subconsciously reached up to her locket again. "There is no preventing pain and sadness. We must simply learn how to make the most of happier times."

Tristan's shoulders slumped wearily. "I'm trying, but every good memory hurts right now. I know I need to be strong and push forward— that I have responsibilities even if I don't know them clearly yet. I can't look at the sketches I have of my mother or my sister because I know if I do, I will crumble. I need to be a pillar, but that's what I tried to be for my sister, and it didn't matter. Amaya and Zatook have told me that it meant something— that I didn't fail. That I'm not a curse to those around me. I want to believe them; I'm trying to believe them. Everyone has been supportive and encouraging— understanding as best they can. I'm trying to let myself take moments when I need them, but some days it feels like all the time in the world won't be enough." Tristan stopped as he shook his head. "And here I am venting when you have your own sorrows and troubles." He straightened as he attempted to refocus on what he could do in the present instead of what he couldn't do in the past. "You said that if the king died, you would have your magic back. How did he take it from you?" Despite the brave face he presented now, Tristan felt every bit like a child, scared and alone even while surrounded by people willing to help and protect.

"Even pillars have foundations. Locking away your grief isn't strength, Tristan. It's building a dam and ignoring the leaks. Grieve. And trust that your friends want to support you as much as you do them. Outside of Traiborn's audience, Andor is a refuge for you for now. Especially in here." She hesitated with talk of her magic. "I do not fully understand," she confessed. "In the same moment, he sealed away my true husband." She reached up, unclasping the locket she wore around her neck and handing it to Tristan. "If anyone can learn how it opens, surely the Children can."

Holding the locket with care, Tristan studied it for a moment. He wasn't sure what his own Child powers would allow him to do, but perhaps Captain could discern something when she felt up to it. Still, he focused more intently on the locket, his eyes sharpening as he tried to see the essence of the locket. The first thing he could tell was that the locket had two, both entwined closely together and both sealed behind some form of magic— but the type of magic eluded him. It was only then that he looked back at the queen and realized he could not sense her essence. Somehow, Traiborn had sealed it away in the locket.

Considering his own pendant, Tristan wondered if Traiborn did something similar. "I see the magic, but I can't discern anything about it. The Moon Child might be able to use her Sight on the locket once she's rested a bit." He looked up at Corianne. "Would you know what might influence her abilities as the Moon Child? We wondered if it had something to do with my grandmother, or if she might know what is causing it."

"I do not know the extent of her powers, but it may have more to do with the spells binding Aria's abilities than Aria herself— or even the orb. If I get a chance to visit the oracle's chamber, I can ask."

Tristan gave her a grateful nod. "Hopefully, we can learn something in our research and investigations. Though, we're trying to tread carefully." He gave her a wry smirk considering where he currently was. Then more seriously, he added, "My companions are worried for Captain. I am as well, though I don't understand her powers any more than I really understand my own." He thought of the other members in their group with powers and abilities. He hadn't gotten to see Amaya's powers yet, and Tristan had only seen some of Zatook's shadow abilities. The train of thought made something occur to Tristan. "Zatook's voice, he can speak in his other form but not in his usual one. I tried to ask him about it, but he wanted me to focus on training. He's been helping me overcome my insecurities and hesitations in fighting someone with a similar power to my father's. I haven't had a chance to ask Zatook about his voice since, and I didn't want to push too much."

Corianne's gaze saddened, falling to stare at her hands. "Zatook does not speak because of old scars along his throat," she explained softly. "If you have seen his other form, then you know that none of his scars carry over when he transforms. Like many of his scars, they are the result of the king's actions." She stood, moving to the balcony and staring out across the palace and capital city. "It was one of his first punishments under the king." It wasn't her story to tell, yet it was so rare Zatook would confide in others. What if the Children of Legend could truly help him? "He was just a child. Children do not understand when they shouldn't speak. But Traiborn has never believed in a gentle rebuke when it comes to the son of his greatest enemy. So he sealed me to my chair and then forced Zatook to swallow burning coals." She sighed. "I only tell you now because he likely will not. Nor is he apt to explain why he will not allow you to heal them." She turned to face Tristan, leaning against the balcony's railing. "His aversion to being healed is not stubbornness. Zatook cannot be healed. Healing magics cause him pain, and potions make him ill. It is something he inherited from his father… the only magic that could heal *him* was from Lady Rin herself or her guardian Cerberus."

The more he learned of King Traiborn, the more Tristan's blood boiled and his heart broke on Zatook's behalf. Holding up his hand, Tristan studied the gauntlet covering his Sun Child mark. "One of my abilities as the Sun Child is the gift of healing. I might be able to heal Zatook's voice or at least try. I've never tried to heal a wound that's been a scar for so long or that was caused by so grievous an injury, but since my healing power comes from Shaddai, I would like to try if Zatook would let me. I want to believe that the One powerful enough to overturn death is powerful enough to heal any wound." Tristan joined Corianne on the balcony, stepping past the doorway with uncertainty. From what he could see, the tower was the highest central tower, so even if people saw him, they wouldn't be able to make out details. Tristan gently touched Corianne's shoulder, trying to give some semblance of comfort. Recalling Arianna's gift made his heart ache, and yet his hand glowed with warmth and light. Tristan didn't have his sister's empathic abilities, but he tried to replicate the sensation of when Arianna would give him encouragement and reassurance.

Corianne touched her hand to his gratefully, managing a soft smile. "I cannot speak for what Zatook would agree to. But I am sure he would appreciate the offer all the same." She lowered her hand. "Unfortunately, I do not know when you will have the chance."

Tristan inclined his head in understanding. Rubbing the locket between his fingers, he stared at it, contemplating. His hand glowed as he tried using his Child powers on the piece of jewelry. Nothing happened. Releasing his power, Tristan's thoughts wandered to the conversation his group had back in the inn and then at dinner with the royal family. "Lancelot mentioned that he was a sealbreaker. I wonder if he might be able to break the seal on the locket and hopefully give you back your magic," explained Tristan.

Corianne paused to consider. "He would have to come here to try. I am unsure what would happen were I to be separated from the locket. And yet... If he were to succeed, Traiborn would know immediately. I would not be against the attempt, but you must ensure your friends are ready for the fallout."

"I'm sorry," Tristan spoke softly, lowering his gaze in guilt. "I feel like we're causing more problems for you and your family even as we try to help." Tristan thought of Zatook willingly getting in trouble to take Tristan to see the oracle. Despite Corianne claiming he was not at fault, Tristan couldn't help feeling like he'd brought this on Zatook. "I know it was his decision, but I'm sorry Zatook is suffering on my account. I'm the Sun Child, but instead of helping people, I keep bringing them pain." Tristan shook his head. He needed to keep moving forward. The best way to help Zatook would be to do something about the queen's power and do something about the king. Tristan handed the locket back to Corianne as he said, "Are there certain days or times that we need to avoid being here?"

"It is the first time in a long time Zatook has suffered by his own choice," she noted gently. "As much as I dislike his having to suffer at all, his decision attests to the influence your group has had on him." She straightened from the railing and turned to gaze over the city again as she thought. Finally, she said, "Traiborn does not keep to a strict schedule, truly." She turned to face Tristan again. "I could create a talisman that would warn you when he is near to you, however. Should it activate when you near the tower, you would know not to risk the entrance."

"The warning would be appreciated," Tristan agreed. He hesitated as he considered their earlier conversation. "If you don't mind my asking, how did you meet the king?"

Corianne moved to her chest of drawers, fetching a strip of parchment and an ink quill. Rune crafting, at least, she could still do relatively well. As she worked on the calligraphy, she answered: "He was one of my mother's knights. Quite famous, really."

"Would you be willing to tell me the story? Or is that too personal? I don't want to cause you pain, but I am curious," Tristan admitted softly. "And sometimes it helps with the pain to talk to someone. From what little I've seen, you don't have many people to talk to."

Corianne gave a light laugh. "I will not say I mind the tale, simply that it is a long one depending on how I tell it," she teased, finishing the runes and moving back to her seat. She handed the strip of paper to Tristan before plucking up an unfinished cross-stitch to work on while she spoke. "Oh, I lose track of the years. Five hundred, perhaps? No, a little over. He is a few years older than I, having already achieved quite the reputation by the time I became the high priestess in my mother's place. The princess takes over once she turns fourteen, though the queen is often still involved with the temple. Traiborn was one of our best knights at the time, so he was either in the throne room or the temple on any given day. Protecting either the royal family or the priestesses is the highest honor a knight can achieve in Andor, you see. So, we had interacted a few times, but it was when I turned sixteen that we were rather forced into proximity."

"There had been a sickness spreading through the kingdoms, so the priestesses such as myself were out among the people far more often than is usual. Even my mother was ill. Being both royal and a priestess, I was assigned Traiborn as my escort. Surprisingly, he was a fairly pleasant man back then. It's hard to imagine now, let alone reconcile with what he has become. But I digress."

Tristan sat in one of the chairs again and listened intently, imagining the events unfolding and the people the queen described. "It's not that strange," he commented in regard to her mention of Traiborn being different back then. "From what I understand, my father wasn't always like he is now either." He fell silent so she could continue.

Corianne nodded to his comment before continuing

her tale. "One of the days we had been out healing, we returned to the temple to find it ransacked. Thieves had been taking advantage of the sickness, and they had finally grown brave enough to target the temple. Many artifacts and tomes and spell materials were stolen, but none so precious as the…" She paused. "Well. I cannot say the name as part of my seal, unfortunately, but it's the very blade you see hanging from Traiborn's hip these days. Andor had been gifted both the blade and the oracle to guard, and we had always kept them apart so that if something happened to the one, it would not the other." She shook her head. "My father was furious. I do not entirely remember why he was so angry at me. True, I was High Priestess at the time. But I had not been in charge of the temple that day. Still, he held me responsible for the blade's theft. I was not to return home until I had found it. My younger sister took my place in charge of the temple through my absence, and I left. The story would be longer still were I to tell it in full, but I made many friends on my journey. Reina was there. As was your aunt, Amaya, and Rin's son, Dia." She chuckled. "Oh, the adventures we had. I hate to say it, but the blade became a bit of a side quest. And then we met Zex." She lowered her cross stitch, staring at it and yet through it.

"Oh, he was a beast to begin. But it wasn't entirely his fault. He was collared, you see." She paused, considering. "I think your people call them the Forsaken. Celestials charged with crimes by the court and sentenced. Stripped of titles and freedom. Unfortunately, one of the largest Celestial prisons, the Twilight Realm, has the tendency to drive one mad." She shook her head. "But I digress again. Zex was becoming a thorn in our side because of his handlers, but at first we didn't know any better. We thought he was a monster. But the more we faced him, the more we got a glimpse of things under the surface."

She chuckled slightly, taking up her stitching once more. "Once we figured out he wasn't acting fully under his own power, I decided we should help him. It sort of became my new mission; I'm not really sure why. There was just something about him that spoke to me, even then. So we did just that. But he was still suffering from the effects of being in that prison realm. So rather than fully release him, we kept him collared. Since I was a priestess, they let me be his new handler. Little by little, I tried to find ways to help him. We learned fairly quickly that I could not use healing magic on him, but Dia could use his own power to heal any physical wounds."

"Well, one thing led to another, and we found ourselves rather smitten. He was never what one might call 'normal', but I never minded. He was himself, quirks and all." She smiled at the memory. "Once he was well enough, we removed the collar for good. He could have left, but he stayed to travel with us. Eventually, I no longer desired to return home: I was happy with my current life. And we had yet to find the sword. I figured it was long gone. Amaya was going to speak with Hoshiko on the matter, but humans were not allowed in the Celestial Realm, so Zex and I decided to just…settle. If the sword was found, of course we would take it back. But it was no longer my life's mission, if that makes sense. I had found myself while I was traveling. I did not wish to be queen. I was happy to let any of my sisters take my place." She was quiet for a moment, thoughtful. "Zex shared his immortality with me. A boon Shaddai grants the ageless who fall in love with a mortal: they can share their life, whether through immortality or mortality. We chose immortality; most of our friends were immortal by that point; it just made sense." Her gaze saddened.

"The sword was found shortly after Zatook turned four."

Tristan's heart went out to Corianne. He understood finding a life outside the expected politics. After they defeated his father, Tristan would still be the heir to House Shadow Veil, but he wasn't sure he wanted to take his place as the head of the house. Then again, his status would depend on who was the king by then. He doubted Jeremiah would let Tristan take over the house. Those were concerns for another time. "Who found the sword?" Tristan asked.

"Hoshiko had a vision, so she sent Amaya to retrieve it. The blade had been hidden by powerful magic, but from what we could tell, the current owner had discovered the enchantments and removed them," she explained. "We had to bring it back to Andor, of course. I offered to go alone, but Zex... Well, he was still getting comfortable with being a father. He was not sure he could manage on his own. So we decided to make it a trip. Meet the family, that sort of thing— I had not left them in the dark, of course. I sent letters, even though they went unanswered. I would have visited if my father had not banished me until I found the darn thing." She shook her head. "So we returned and...everything was different. My mother had passed in the plague. My father a while after. My sister was on the throne, and she was pleased as petals to learn we had crossed through. She sent an escort for us immediately, with a letter. From what I read..." She paused. "They never heard from me. They thought me dead until the Wall alerted my arrival. Zex and I assumed something happened to the couriers through the years, though it was odd that not a single letter had made it through."

"I wrote back offering to settle in Andor. I explained I had no wish to disturb the order of things or be queen. When her reply was in agreement and a wish to see us, we let the guards take their leave while we traveled to the capital. TekCarriages did not exist back then, so we planned to fly. Granted, introducing my husband by having him fly his six-winged self to the palace may have been pressing my luck a bit, but we could not know the people's opinion was already swayed. I should have seen the signs. Looking back, they were glaring. The soldiers and servants only stared when we landed. No greetings or surprise. No priestesses to meet us and collect the sword. I figured perhaps our arrival method had stunned them, so we walked ourselves inside." She sighed, sitting back in her seat and setting the cross stitch in her lap. "You have probably guessed it was a trap," she noted dryly to Tristan. "Not my sister's doing, bless her. She had no reason to believe Traiborn was lying— he had managed to convince every last person in Andor that I was bewitched. That I had been stolen by a monster, and he had come up with a clever plan to save me, to seal the monster and reinstate the rightful queen." Corianne resumed her stitching.

"It took years to piece together everything," she noted softly. "It would seem Traiborn had always been ambitious, even rising as a knight. He had kept his sorcery secret as a political advantage, and planned to rise as high as possible. He had not considered kingship until the plague. Apparently, he had fallen for me when assigned my escort. He had approached my father to discuss a potential marriage, and it was under consideration. When the blade was stolen, suddenly I was gone. So when the chance came, he 'reclaimed' me." She scowled. "He intercepted every letter. Noted every detail. His trap was the culmination of years of obsession." She couldn't help a dark chuckle. "He even found the sword himself and ensorceled it to keep it hidden. He was the one to point out the magic to the last owner and suggest its removal." She had stopped stitching again, just idly rolling the needle back and forth between her fingers.

"Our last warning was the look on my sister's face when she saw Zatook. She told me later, no one knew we had a child. But before she could question, stop things, Traiborn had approached us. He snatched the blade from my hands and cast the spells that ruined our lives."

"I'm sorry," whispered Tristan sincerely. Even as he sat stoic as he could, his eyes appeared glossy— memories of his own parents' final fight interposing with the narrative playing across his imagination. "And Traiborn sealed Zex in the locket along with your powers?" Tristan had heard his mother talk about Forsaken, and how if he ever encountered one he should leave them be. It sounded like this Zex person had changed from how he had been, though. Tristan felt a stronger urge now to reunite Zatook with the father who was trying to be a good man— Zatook's real father. "If you got your powers back, and we managed to free Zex and Zatook, what then? Would you be able to take control of the throne fully? I imagine we'd have to try to do something about Traiborn. If we even can."

Corianne reached up a hand to tap her chin thoughtfully. "It would take some time to fully regain the people's trust," she noted calmly. "They have spent generations with Traiborn's truth. But there are many things in our favor, including the involvement of the Children of Legend and a member of the Order, as well as my birthright as queen. And Traiborn has not been able to hide me as often, because the people have come to know me and respect me, even if I cannot tell them everything. So, yes, I would regain control of the kingdom. And keep it, should Collette decide not to ascend in my place when she comes of age. But not forever, I think. Simply until a descendent wishes to claim their birthright or, barring that, Shaddai guides me to choose someone for the throne."

Tristan looked down, hanging his head slightly, when she mentioned the Chosen Children. He still felt unworthy of the title, and it felt strange for anyone to put any weight into it. "I'm sorry all this happened to you," he told her sympathetically. "I'm not sure how much good we'll be able to do. Not until we've figured out what is causing issues with Captain's powers. And I'm not my aunt. I don't know what I can do against a king who bested a Celestial more powerful and experienced than me." Not to mention, he was a liability waiting to happen. With the Talisman's seal weakening, Tristan couldn't help questioning the wisdom of him staying in Andor. And yet, where else would be safer? "I think once we help Captain, she'll be better suited to helping bring down the king."

"The Chosen are a team assembled by Shaddai Himself, Tristan. Even if we do not see how or why, if it is your fate to right the wrongs here, then you shall. And if it is not, then He will bring another way." She set a hand on his knee. "You are not Amaya. You are not Reina. You are Tristan, with your own gifts and your own purpose." She pulled her hand back and resumed stitching. "I will see if Traiborn will let me visit the oracle. If I bring it up as a way to help your group find your path, he may agree." She couldn't help a subtle smirk. "He likely wants you on your way before you start causing trouble," she teased before sobering. "Especially considering your connection to Zatook."

"We would appreciate all the help we can get," Tristan answered with a sigh. He continued to stare at the floor. While he wanted to take her words of encouragement to heart, the constant dull ache in his chest reminded him of his own shortcomings and his danger to others. Tristan had helped a little when he healed Jabez, but really, what good had he done? Tristan was the dangerous one that kept getting people killed or nearly killed. He considered if he should reveal his concerns about the Talisman— to warn the queen if nothing else. Tristan wanted to trust Corianne, but he also wanted to avoid adding to her burden by telling her something she would need to keep from the king. "I know it's not about what we deserve, but I don't feel deserving of the title Sun Child. I don't really know what it means to be a Chosen Child of Legend other than something about us facing calamity and righting the world or some such. I'm afraid that instead of protecting it, I'm going to end up breaking the world. People keep getting hurt trying to protect me, and I haven't been able to do anything for them." Tristan ducked his head a little more. "I'm sorry. I don't mean to keep making this about me and my insecurities. You've got so much going on already. I can't even imagine being in your situation. Or Zatook's. Though, I understand to a point, so I think that's what makes me want to help in any way I can. I just… I keep making things worse." Tristan stood so he could leave. "I'll stop bothering you. Thank you for telling me your story. I hope we can figure out how to help you and your family."

Corianne had begun to move before he hit the point of leaving. So as he stood, she simply wrapped her arms around him and pulled him into a hug. "Do not compare your pain to that of others. We all face our trials, we all have our pain— these do not diminish each other, but teach us empathy. Encourage us to help each other. No man is an island, Tristan; even the sturdiest pillar has a support, a base to keep it firm. Every sheltering room is held aloft by other structures. You have much on your shoulders; let yourself feel the weight that you may come to understand and accept it. I was not so different at the start of my own quest. These doubts, these uncertainties in dark times are things we must learn to overcome. When all else fails, rest in the knowledge that Shaddai is with us."

At first, Tristan hesitated to return the embrace, but then gradually he allowed himself to sink into the warmth of another person— Corianne had told him not to worry about formalities. Slowly, Tristan wrapped his arms around her in return, clinging to her a little. "Everyone keeps trying to encourage me and comfort me. I hear their words and understand. It helps, but the pain isn't gone. I'm trying to move forward and not let myself go in circles, but it's like trying to wade into the ocean," Tristan confessed, feeling a little proud that his voice remained steady for now. Yet, there was something about Corianne. Perhaps because she knew his mother or even that Corianne was a mother herself, Tristan felt safe. He had broken down in front of the others, but despite their assurances he still tried to be strong. As Tristan leaned into the embrace he felt himself begin to shake as the emotions and memories— everything he had experienced and been experiencing —came to the surface. "I miss my mother," he confessed in a thick voice. "I miss her so much. I can't help feeling that she would know what to do. That she would have been able to protect Arianna. She wouldn't have let Arianna die." Tristan's eyes stung as his tears flowed once more. "It feels like there's a void where

Arianna used to be. I can't shake the feeling that she's supposed to still be here. I miss her. I miss Almas and Clovestein. I even miss my father— who he was before everything went so wrong." Tristan's grip on Corianne tightened as he sobbed. Between breaths, he told her, "I've cried with my friends, but they're going through things, too. And I'm supposed to be…supposed to help people…I still try to hold back…" he trailed off as his legs gave out with the grief crushing him. Tristan managed to angle himself to at least sit on the sofa as he went down, loosening his hold on the queen so he wouldn't take her with him despite how much he didn't want to let go yet.

He needn't have worried; Corianne sank to the sofa with him, gently rubbing his back and just letting him vent. "I am sorry, Tristan. I wish I could take the pain away. But you will carry that pain. It may feel smaller, it may tuck itself away in the deepest corner of your heart, but loss will always be with us. It is always rawest in the beginning, but it never truly leaves. We simply learn to coexist. To give the pain its time and due and then let it rest again." She reached for one of her spare kerchiefs in case he needed one. "Grief is often like the ocean. The waves will calm or even lie still for a while, but they can rise again with provocation. A scent, a place, a memory, a dream. And the waves will crash over us again. But sailors do not flee the waves, Tristan. They respect the wind and the rain, and they learn to sail with them. It takes time."

Tristan took the kerchief and let himself cry. He sobbed and shook as he curled in on himself. He cried for his mother and his sister. He cried for his kind teachers. Tristan cried for his home and for Rose. He shed tears for Zatook and Jabez for the pain they endured for his sake. He cried for Corianne. Tristan wept for fear of being a failure and a danger to the world he was supposed to protect. He sobbed for his own sake. "I'm drowning in it," Tristan managed to say as he gasped for breath before devolving into quiet wails.

"And so we throw you something to cling to until we can pull you up. Or dive in after you to hold you afloat until you can swim under your own power. Always and always, you are not alone."

Tristan hugged Corianne as he continued to cry. Eventually, he wore himself out; though, he remained awake. A few tears still slipped free, but Tristan managed to breathe a little better. The pain in his chest had intensified at one point and made things worse; however, it had subsided to the now familiar discomfort. Tristan didn't try to speak. What more could he say? He felt so tired from the emotional turmoil as well as the physical.

Corianne had eventually guided him to rest on the couch, his head in her lap as she smoothed his hair. She had resumed humming, choosing an Andorian lullaby in an effort to help soothe him.

Tristan knew he needed to get back to the group and to Jabez waiting patiently for his return, but Tristan felt so tired. The queen's fingers in his hair soothed him further until he barely managed to keep his eyes open. With the warm presence and the safety of the room, despite his fight against the drowsiness, Tristan slowly slipped into slumber.

A little time passed before the magic in the tower alerted the queen to someone's approach. Jabez had figured that Tristan and the queen were simply having a long conversation, but paranoia— and admittedly curiosity — got the better of the ninja. Jabez paused in surprise when the door opened to reveal the queen herself. Before Jabez could speak, Corianne indicated the sleeping young man on her couch. Nodding his understanding, Jabez followed the queen into the tower and then moved to collect his charge. With Corianne's help, Jabez positioned Tristan in a way for the Celestial to remain asleep as Jabez lifted him, carrying Tristan princess-style. Carefully, Jabez gave a slight bow to the queen. He then descended the steps and made his way back to the guest tower, careful not to draw attention as he left the hidden stairway.

20. Follow the Thread

The next morning, Solomon and Jabez were the first up. As Captain came down to breakfast, she found the pair in the training field. Jabez held both of Solomon's scimitars, the Order member having grabbed a set of practice blades to use in their stead. Jabez was picking up the fighting technique quickly. Captain smirked as she sipped her tea and moved to the table. Well, no training her magic or daggers for now. She lifted her mug in greeting when Rose joined her.

"Good morning, Captain," the Half-Drow greeted warmly as she started picking out something to eat. "I see two of our companions went for an early start."

"Oh, aye. Righ' pair o' mornin' birds, those two," Captain joked. "Puttin' t'e rest of us ta shame." She sighed, sipping her tea. "Though I'm nae really sure what ta do wit' meself today. I'm gettin' awful tired o' t'e same stone walls."

Rose joined her in a laugh. "You're used to the open sea; it's no surprise you have no wish to be cooped up all the time, as useful as our learning and training can be. Why not get out for a bit?"

"Tha' requires someone goin' wit' me."

"True, but I doubt you lack in possible companions." Rose poured her own cup of tea as she spoke. "Though I shan't be one of them, I'm afraid. I might have used a bit too much magic yesterday." She glanced up to catch Captain's sheepish look. "No need to look so abashed. I was glad to help hone your ability. I simply do not have the stamina I did alive and shall be taking today to rest and read."

"I s'pose." Captain sighed, leaning back in her chair. "Sol and Jabie seem like t'ey'll be occupied fer a bit. I could ask Nai if'n he's feelin' as cooped up as I be…"

Rose hid a smirk. Shocker, that Alconai would be rather high up in the list of options. She was slightly surprised he still came up after Solomon and Jabez, though only just.

As though summoned by the conversation, Alconai joined the ladies in the parlor, retrieving his own cup of tea before he sat at the table. "Good mornin' ta ye, ladies," he greeted cheerily. "What's on t'e docket fer today? I be gettin' a bit sore from all t'e trainin' we been doin'— though, I ken we need to be ready for anythin'."

Rose hid her smile behind her tea.

"Aye, an' I be thinkin' t'e training field is taken," Captain joked. "I was wantin' ta get out an' about fer a bit. Jus' wasnae sure what ta do."

"Why don't the pair of you check out the castle? There is much to see; Tristan and I even found a museum dedicated to Andor's history," Rose suggested. She thought about adding they could be the first to check the city, but she knew Captain was still nervous about her powers flaring. Lancelot had ventured down just in time to hear Rose's suggestion. He smirked.

"Have her home before midnight," he teased, fully ready to duck if Alconai chucked something at him. Captain just stuck out her tongue.

"Pirates donnae 'ave curfews," she quipped.

Alconai rolled his eyes at Lancelot, but the minstrel refused to waste good food by throwing it at the knight. Like the other mornings, breakfast had been waiting for them in the parlor. Alconai left the table long enough to get some sustenance before sitting to eat. "Mayhap we'll find some clues. Or just somethin' interestin'," he agreed with Captain and Rose. "What do ye want ta see, Cap'n?"

"Anythin' that isnae t'e same two rooms," Captain joked. "So far it's mostly been me room, t'is room, an' t'e garden out t'ere."

"I be hearin' ye," said Alconai. "Even with all t'e space, it be feelin' a little crowded." He glanced over when Tristan joined them. Like Alconai, Tristan had already freshened up and dressed for the day. "Good mornin', Tris."

"Good morning," Tristan answered as he gathered his own breakfast and tea. He sat beside Rose, but addressed Lancelot. "We may need your abilities to help the queen regain her magic and free her real husband." Tristan paused when Alconai just stared evenly at him. "What?"

"Ye and yer droppin' big information on us like yer tellin'

us t'e weather be nice," Alconai snarked. "So ye and Jabie did find t'e queen then?"

Tristan gave the group a sheepish grimace. "Sorry. Yes, Jabez and I found the hidden tower. Jabez stood guard while I talked to the queen. She told me…a lot. The main information to know is that when Traiborn took over, he sealed Corianne's magic and her husband in a locket. The queen keeps the locket on her person. Traiborn keeps her trapped in the tower until he needs her. So, Lancelot would have to go to her to look at the locket and unseal it. However, the queen warned me that Traiborn would know as soon as the locket was unsealed, so we would need to be ready for the confrontation that would ensue," explained Tristan.

"So by helpin' t'e queen get her magic and husband back, we be startin' a coup, eh?" Alconai spoke thoughtfully. "Best have everythin' in order best we can then. Be in top shape for what goes down."

Lancelot folded his arms. "And I'll want to find a smaller blade. I haven't been walking around armed, so people might get suspicious."

"Wouldnae a practice sword work?" Captain asked curiously. Lance shook his head.

"Even the metal ones tend to be pretty low quality to prevent serious injury during training," he explained. "The quality of the metal matters for seal breaking, and I imagine anything Traiborn cast would be pretty powerful." He frowned, considering. "Glass or magic-conducive crystal is the strongest you can find for seal breaking, but ordering something like that would draw a lot of attention. Still, a good metal should suffice."

"Perhaps you should visit the forge to see if Tannen could make you something," Rose suggested. "Since you used a sword in Nocis and haven't had one since Keep Shadow Veil, it stands to reason that you would decide to ask after one now."

"What about the crystal I can create with my Celestial powers?" asked Tristan. "I can imbue it with my Child powers, but I don't know if that works the same as magic-conducive crystals. I'm not versed in enchantments or rune work. However, if my crystal could work, I can try making a dagger for you."

Lance rubbed his chin. "I don't honestly know," he confessed. "It would certainly be worth a try."

"It would allow me to train some of my Celestial abilities. I need practice making better blades and smaller, finer items," Tristan commented. "Besides, according to Solomon, we're not to be going anywhere alone anymore. Understandably." He paused when a knock sounded at the entry door for the guest tower. Tristan then watched in surprise when the door opened to reveal Tannen.

"Oi, timin'. We were just talkin' 'bout ye," Alconai greeted with a bright grin.

Tannen laughed. "I thought my ears felt a little toasty," he joked. Stepping inside, Tannen closed the door behind him and approached the group. "Good morning and please excuse the intrusion. I was hoping to catch you all before you dispersed to your activities for the day." The blacksmith wore his simple clothes without his smithing apron, and his blue-green hair was left free from the bandana that usually covered it. Tannen smiled at the group as he added, "Zatook asked that I come to check on you all since he hasn't had the chance lately."

Tristan tilted his head in understanding. "We're doing well. A little stir crazy from being cooped up, but otherwise no worse for wear," he answered. Tristan looked around the group to see if anyone wanted to correct him. "Thank you for looking in on us."

"I had some free time, and it's rare that Zatook asks for anything, so I try not to turn him down if I can help it," Tannen smoothly remarked. He studied Tristan for a moment before adding, "He actually asked another thing of me. Zatook mentioned that he was training you before you reached the capital." Tristan nodded.

"I've been training with Lancelot to get used to fighting opponents with different styles. Especially since we expect we'll have to fight some Nocium soldiers again," Tristan explained. He lowered his gaze with a small sigh. "I don't know if Zatook told you, but he trusts you. I will, too. I'm a Celestial, and we've been at a bit of a loss for training my Celestial powers. Both the best candidates to train me in that regard aren't available."

"Zatook being one of them," Tannen stated. Tristan gave a nod. "Well, my own parents trained me to fight, and I've acted as Zatook's sparring partner over the years. I don't know anything about Celestials, but I do know that dragons can handle some rather powerful opponents. We can give it a go if you like. I don't think you'll hurt me too badly, all things considered," teased the blacksmith, giving Tristan a playful wink. More seriously but just as easily he added, "I would suggest we go away from the capital, though. It looks like your courtyard is in use, and we won't have to worry about anyone seeing or us getting out of hand. I know enough magic to be able to cast some wards so the king can't spy on us."

Tristan hesitated, looking to the rest of the group. His gaze lingered on Rose, his eyes uncertain but curious. "Would that be all right? Should I talk to Jabez and Solomon first?"

Rose smiled. "I think it would be fine. I can let Solomon and Jabez know when they have a moment."

"Aye, an' I donnae t'ink it counts as goin' off on yer own if Tannen goes wit' ye," Captain confirmed.

"Honestly, Jabez and Solomon had considered the idea," Lancelot confessed. "We just all got distracted with everything else and hadn't brought it up yet."

"I'm honored by your trust," Tannen told them sincerely.

Tristan finished his food and tea before setting his plates aside for the servants to clear. "Do we need to get a TekCarriage? How far out of the capital should we go?" he asked, unable to keep some excitement out of his voice. Like everyone else, Tristan had started to feel restless.

Tannen smiled brightly, his eyes twinkling with mischief. "Oh, I have a faster and more direct way of getting out of the city. More fun, too, so long as you don't mind heights," he answered. To the rest of the group Tannen said, "It was nice seeing you all again. I'll have your Sun Child back by lunch. I'm afraid I can't devote more time than that."

"We appreciate what help ye can give," Alconai assured him.

Bowing to them slightly, Tannen motioned for Tristan to follow him to the courtyard. Tristan had an idea what the blacksmith was about to do, the Celestial watching the half-dragon intently. Tannen had Tristan stop before moving farther away. Then Tannen's form began to change, and Tristan recalled watching Jeremiah transition into his dragon form. As his shape grew and morphed, obsidian scales replaced Tannen's clothes and skin. Fingers and toes lengthened into large, sharp talons as Tannen hunched onto all fours, his body taking on the quadrupedal shape. Vibrant blue-green horns sprouted and swept back into sharp points over the crown of Tannen's head. Rather than looking made of bone, the horns appeared more like carved crystal. Spikes of similar material and the same color trailed along the back of Tannen's spine and down along his tail. The main bones of the dragon's wings were black like his scales. More spikes jutted from the joints along the main bones of his massive wings. The spikes from the upper joints matched the horns while the sharp points at the ends of the wings' fingers looked like onyx. The leathery membrane for the wings started as the luminescent blue-green color near the bones, but then the color transitioned into a vibrant purple.

Tristan stared in awed fascination as Tannen stood tall and massive. Now that Tristan could get a good look at a dragon without worrying about fearing for his life, he couldn't help staring as he took in every detail. A deep rumble reverberated through the air, Tannen chuckling at Tristan's slack-jawed expression.

"Come on then," Tannen encouraged, keeping his voice lower now that he could project more loudly and farther. He crouched down to give Tristan better access to climb.

Tristan's eyes lit up and he quickly scaled Tannen's leg and shoulder to reach the dragon's back. The spikes started a little farther back above Tannen's shoulders, so Tristan was able to settle without worrying about being cut by the spikes. Leaning forward, Tristan wrapped his arms around Tannen's neck as best he could. Tristan's grip tightened when Tannen stretched his wings out and crouched down, Tristan able to feel the dragon's muscles contracting beneath him. The next moment, Tristan found himself plastered to the scales as the ground rushed away beneath them. As they reached the peak of the jump, there was a moment of suspension before Tannen's strong wings flapped and thrust them higher. Soon, Tannen maneuvered into a smooth glide, clearing the castle walls and soaring over the city.

Back in the parlor, Alconai couldn't help his own grin at seeing a dragon for the first time. And yet, he felt more relief at the sight of Tristan's excitement. "I admit ta feelin' a mite jealous now," Alconai joked.

"Maybe a bit," Lance joked back, taking his plate for seconds.

"Oi yosh, do I send ye ta hang out wit' t'e boys, t'en?" Captain teased, wrinkling her nose at Alconai playfully. Rose just shook her head, returning to her breakfast.

Jabez and Solomon had paused to watch the dragon form and take off, but they had resumed their training after. "Eh, maybe ye can talk 'im inta a ride later."

Alconai laughed. "Donnae ye worry, Cap'n. I still be game for some explorin'. 'Sides, t'e company be better," he told her with a devilish smile. Setting aside his own plates, Alconai offered Captain his arm. "Shall we?"

Captain looped arms with him, giving Lance and Rose a two-fingered salute before setting off. "'S'a mighty big palace, where do we even start?" she joked to Alconai as they set off down the hall from the guest tower.

Alconai winked at Captain. "Mayhap we start in t'e library. Tristan found t'e journal in there. Perhaps yer keen eyes will see somethin' worth investigatin'," he suggested brightly. Alconai did keep a look out for anything that might seem suspicious or even too mundane. At one point he added, "I'm tempted to find me a fiddle and sneak everyone back inta t'e ballroom. Have a party o' our own with better music. Though, I suppose if I be playin', I wouldnae be able ta dance with ye." He suddenly stepped ahead of Captain and pivoted gracefully, his hand catching hers in a dancing pose.

Captain arched an eyebrow even as she took his hand. "Dancin' in t'e middle o' t'e hall, eh?" she teased, clearly all for the idea. "I doubt t'ey would min' us borrowin' t'e room, we could jus' ask instead o' sneak. I'm all fer more dancin' an music."

"Where be the fun in that?" Alconai joked. He stepped easily into a few dance moves, twirling Captain and guiding her until they were in the correct position. As they started moving along the hallway, Alconai hummed a tune for their steps. He proved his skill as his rich voice traveled up and down an impressive range. He smiled at Captain as he spun and glided with her in a peppy but elegant dance.

Captain laughed as they moved, keeping up fairly easily. She kept up a little more easily than she had at the feast, glad to be rid of the sandals and in the clothes she was more used to— especially for dancing.

At some point, the hum became words, Alconai showing off his talent once more by managing to sing while dancing. The song turned out to be a rather lively sea shanty. As the dance continued, Alconai lost track of their surroundings a bit. His focus narrowed to the young pirate captain as his heart lightened to hear her laugh. After the recent days of seeing her out of sorts, Alconai felt happy that he managed to bring a smile to her face. He twirled her and danced with her as they made their way through the palace.

Captain had closed her eyes, losing the sight of the hall swirling around them and finding herself out at sea with Alconai, her boys laughing and making music for them to match the man's song. Amaya was there as well, watching in amusement and— by the looks of it —teasing Jabez about his brother taking to his surrogate sister. It wasn't a vision. Not this time. She realized fairly quickly that it was a wish. Some day, when all of this was done, she wanted them all back on the *Effervescence.* Sol, Jabez, Amaya, and Alconai. Rose and Tristan would certainly be welcome, as well, but she specifically wanted her family and…well, whatever Alconai was at this point. Friend? More? She wasn't really certain. With her luck, he was probably just a crush.

"Are ye back on yer ship? Andor be interestin', but it be a long way from t'e sea," Alconai inquired fondly even as he continued to dance with Captain. He resumed humming while he waited for her answer. As long as he could help her escape to happier memories and places, Alconai was happy. The Chosen Children had so much weight to carry for being so young. He wasn't much older, but he'd seen his fair share of hardships. And losing his brother for thirteen years had given Alconai the drive to grow up sooner so he could bring his brother home. Already, the three Children had seen more and endured more than Alconai thought they should. He wasn't Shaddai or the Scareds— Alconai couldn't know Their plans and ways. He only hoped that he could help the Chosen Children keep some happiness and let them be kids for stolen moments. He had a feeling that Captain's jovial and sometimes childish antics acted as a mask she wore for similar reasons. She'd endured hardship that brought a lot of darkness into her life, but Captain seemed to want to bring joy in other's lives rather than be consumed by sorrow.

"Oh, aye, an' it's a grand ol' party there," Captain confessed. "Nae havin' ta worry about t'e hoity-toities at a ball or steppin' on anyone's toes… May'ap steppin' on a few toes on purpose." She opened her eye to grin at him.

"I be hopin' that I be in yer good graces enough for ye ta show me toes mercy," remarked Alconai with a bright smile. "A party on yer ship sounds like a pleasant time all right. T'e sun on yer face, t'e wind in yer hair, and jovial pirates beltin' off key ta some newly made up tune." Alconai winked at her. Gradually, he slowed the dance so as not to tire them out too much. He also checked their surroundings for anything of interest. "Thank ye fer lookin' after me bruddeh," Alconai told her sincerely.

"Oi, oi, he looks af'er me more of'n than nae," Captain noted with a slight laugh, brushing out her skirt as she gazed around the hall. She paused, tilting her head slightly when she caught sight of… well, it wasn't really a thread. Patterns and colors always whirled around her, but this one was different. It was more like a ribbon: wide, red, and glossy. And it actually had an end. She had never seen a thread— or ribbon? —with an end before; they generally stretched into oblivion or joined with others. Yet this didn't wind with any of the others around it, formed no patterns or connections. It was simply there.

Captain reached out to catch the end of the ribbon, gently running her thumb over it. Usually if something like this piqued her interest, she would then use her Sight to see where it led, who it belonged to, but she was trying not to use that power. What if she could do something similar just through her Weaving? As she held the thread, however, she noticed another oddity: sound. Something like a whisper played at the edge of her hearing; that was not typical of her magic, either. Suddenly remembering Alconai, she held up a finger. "Do ye hear tha'?"

Alconai gave her a curious look. "I donnae hear anythin'," he answered, confused. He looked around and listened more closely. "What do ye hear?"

Captain frowned as she examined the ribbon again, chewing her bottom lip. "Nae sure ye'," she murmured. The tip of the ribbon curled upward, almost beckoning. "But I t'ink I need ta fin' out." She reached down, starting to wind the ribbon around her fingers and moving to follow it. "Long story, trust t'e magic," she called over her shoulder with a grin before continuing to gather the ribbon.

Alconai cocked his head in intrigue but followed Captain. Interesting that whatever was disrupting her Child powers didn't seem to have an effect on her other ability. Then again, what would Alconai know? He'd heard stories and talked with Solomon, but beyond that he had very little knowledge of the Doran people and their gifts.

Captain continued to wind the ribbon around her hand as she followed, noting with curiosity that it seemed to shorten as it went— the wrap around her fingers never got any thicker. She had never seen anything like this. She followed the ribbon all the way up to a large pair of double doors, pausing and stepping back to look up.

"Well, whad'ya ken. We woun' up at t'e library anyway," she noted in surprise.

Alconai laughed softly. "Of course, it be right under our noses," he commented cheekily. "Tris found a surprise here, so I suppose we shouldnae be surprised. Mayhap, we just didnae find t'e right book ta pull." He gave Captain a grin before opening the door for her. "Lead t'e way, Captain." He gave her a sweeping bow.

Captain snickered, sauntering into the library. Even though they had been to the grand library a few times now, she couldn't help turning a slow circle to admire the tomes and imagining the scholars at Ben-Gal drooling at the number of shelves. She turned her attention back to the ribbon, winding her way through shelves of books.

Even with all of the group's browsing, some of them were still sadly dusty. She couldn't imagine leaving these things to sit. Finally, she made her way to the very back corner, and then frowned. The ribbon disappeared through the shelf.

This had to be warded. Traiborn was too suspicious to leave secret tunnels unguarded, right? She let go of the ribbon, leaving it to hang in the air as she stepped back and peered suspiciously at the shelf. How would she even test for wards? Some would show up with Weaving, but not most. Normally, she would Look, but that was a bad idea right now. And yet the ribbon kept swaying in a nonexistent breeze, beckoning her.

Alconai had followed Captain inside and closed the doors behind them. He surveyed the treasure trove of knowledge with just as much appreciation as Captain. "T'e stories I could tell with just a few o' these," murmured the minstrel. "A secret could be anywhere in here." Alconai failed to suppress a grin when Captain began staring down a bookshelf, guessing she had found the secret. "T'is be t'e one, ye think?" asked Alconai. Giving the shelves a quick glance, he considered what he might be working with. As an entertainer, most people never really gave thought to him knowing how to unravel magic. That was how he liked it. Alconai had learned from a few different sources and from his own experience how to recognize magic and its effects as well as how to dismantle it. Lightly tracing his fingertips over the wood, Alconai studied the way the books were set up while he felt for any grooves that might be strange. After a moment, he retracted his hands. "Well, I found t'e anchor points for t'e runes makin' t'e wards. Tricky part is dismantlin' them once ye find them. I could always get

Lance." Even as he spoke, Alconai checked the anchor points more thoroughly, noting the barely there sigils surrounding what appeared to be some kind of crystals at each point. "Either way, we be alertin' t'e king no matter who does t'e dismantilin'." He glanced at Captain. "Ye sure ye want to do this now?"

Captain gave him a grin. "Since when do pirates care abou' breakin' a few rules?" she teased before turning her gaze back to the shelf and sobering slightly. "Somethin' or someone be tryin' ta get my attention. An' I t'ink I ken who. If she be callin' us, t'en surely it'll be fine, aye?"

Alconai gave her a cheeky wink. Taking a small but sturdy book from a nearby shelf, he reached into his boot and retrieved a tiny metal pick. Deciding on an anchor point, Alconai touched the pick just beside one of the crystals. Using the book like a hammer, he gave the pick a solid tap. The runes glowed for a moment with being tampered with, but then the crystal shifted just enough out of its place that the runes went dark again. He repeated the action with the other points, disconnecting the runes from their power sources. "That should do it," he announced.

Captain watched curiously as he worked, snickering slightly. "So ye be pickin' more'n jus' prison locks, eh?" she teased, reaching up and pulling out the dusty volume that the ribbon vanished through. Her guess was on point, as the bookshelf slid away to reveal the stone hall spiraling down. "Whelp. Guess we be goin' down." She glanced around, noticing the torch on the wall inside the passage and gesturing towards it. "Can ye carry tha'? I got me hands a bit full." She started to hold up the ribbon to show him, but then remembered he couldn't see it.

"Ye learn a thing or two travelin' 'round. 'Sides, magic has always fascinated me," Alconai told her. He grabbed the torch per her request and used the flint and steel he brought to light it. Holding the torch out before them, Alconai surveyed the corridor. "Nice and spooky for a secret passage," he joked. "Shall we?" He knew they needed to get moving before they were caught.

Captain grinned, wrinkling her nose at him before starting down the stairs. She kept wrapping the ribbon with one hand, but the other she set against the stone wall to keep her balance on the stairs. It wound up being solid wall the whole way down, so she made her way along fairly easily. Eventually, the pair reached the cavern of the oracle. Captain didn't even pause to look; her gaze was on that orb. The ribbon led straight to it. She was right, then. The Celestial of Time was calling. She didn't even bother letting Alconai check for wards, just walking straight over the bridge and to the gazebo. The whisper was louder now. She could hear a voice, but she didn't understand the language spoken. She let the ribbon go as the red fabric vanished and reached for the smoky sphere.

And as far as Alconai could see, she vanished.

Alconai stared in shock. "What? Wait!" He glanced around frantically. He crossed the bridge quickly but resisted the urge to touch the orb. "Captain!" Alconai called to the room as though she might reappear at the sound of her name. "Captain Isabella! Right, Nai, she's more like ta answer ta her full name," he dryly chastised himself. He studied the gazebo and the surrounding area. "Oi yosh. Never mind Sol— Jabie's gonna kill me."

As Alconai turned back towards the orb, he noticed a

change within the smoky depths. Thin red lines spiraled into existence before spelling a message: *Calm yourself, Alconai FoxFeet.*

Alconai stared at the orb. He wasn't surprised the orb was magic— that seemed like a given considering where he was. Still, he hadn't expected the orb to start talking to him. Slowly, hesitantly, he reached a hand out. For Alconai, this whole scenario felt like something Solomon or Jabez should be tackling considering their experience with the Moon Child. Finally, Alconai's hand gently gripped the orb.

The orb felt cool and smooth. The red unraveled for a moment before tracing his fingers, and the cavern seemed to fade away. He found himself in a garden with a brook and gazebo matching those of the cave, except the gazebo held a table and wrought iron chairs. Captain and another woman sat there. The Celestial of Time was calmly drinking her tea, whereas Captain was holding her cup and staring at the other woman. She looked just like Captain's visions. Pale, with one golden eye and one green, and a thin red line detailing intricate patterns along her skin.

"Have a seat, then," the Celestial of Time, Tristan's grandmother Aria, invited Alconai as she waved a hand and caused another chair to appear at the table. "All for the best, so you will not be out there by yourself when the king arrives."

Thunderstruck, Alconai gingerly took the seat. He certainly felt grateful to be inside the orb rather than outside facing the king's wrath. "Were ye sealed in t'e orb or be we someplace else, milady?" asked Alconai politely.

Aria gave a light laugh. "This little pocket of mine is within the orb, yes. It was here long before I was cursed; my sanctuary turned prison. The king of Celestials merely sealed me within. I am cursed in more ways than just the seal, but our colorful friend here can help."

Captain set down her untouched tea cup. "Ye mean ta tell me I can ge' you outta here? But…how? I mean, I teleported Jabie wit' me magic once, bu' I wound up 'alfway across Nocis."

"Yes, I'm aware."

"An I havenae been able ta use t'e Child 'alf of me powers since gettin' into Andor proper."

"Indeed." Aria took a sip of her tea.

"An' we're still in t'e palace, so I ainae teleportin' ye between places."

"'Am nae', dear, but yes."

Captain stared at her, mouth agape. "An' yer very calm abou' all t'ese issues."

"Yes. Because I already know you succeed." Aria gently set down her tea cup, folding her hands on her lap. "Your powers have issues because of the very spells which currently bind me; as you notice, I am free to do as I please in here— so are you. Additionally, by getting me back into the physical realm, you'll break the more problematic enchantments. I will not be fully free, mind you— there are more powerful beings than Traiborn that saw to that —but I will be out of this musty cavern and able to more easily assist your party. And that includes helping you with your Weaving and Sight."

Captain looked at a loss for words. She grabbed her teacup and took a long drink.

Alconai listened to the exchange. "How can she get ye out o' here? And what's ta keep t'e king from sealin' ye back in here?" he inquired.

"By combining her abilities with mine," Aria explained. "Some of my abilities work the same as Weaving because I gifted the ability of Weaving to the Doran. If two Weavers wish to combine their magic, they can do so by accessing each other's threads and twining them together. The type of link details how the powers will combine. There are specific knots for allowing both Weavers equal access or letting one Weaver handle all of the casting. In this case, I would twine myself to Captain here, putting her in control, and then instruct her."

Captain drained her teacup. "Oi, yosh. Ye make it soun' so simple."

"Isabella, look at me."

Captain's eye twitched slightly, but she did as instructed.

"I will not be useless in this simply because I allow you to manage the casting; I will keep things safe. It sounds simple to me because it is. Do not let doubt complicate matters." Aria turned back to Alconai. "Traiborn is not the one who did this enchantment in the first place, though he has added layers. My original seal was courtesy of the King of Celestials, but he…" she paused, pursing her lips. "Let us just say he has other things to concern himself with, for now. I will still be bound to Andor, and I will likely stay even should that binding be broken."

Alconai touched Captain's hand gently. "Ye can do it," he encouraged with a confident smile. "Ye be comin' inta yer own, aye? And we be here. Who better t'e help ye than yer own patron Celestial, eh?"

Captain looked between the pair of them before holding up her hands. "All right, all right! I'll stop me belly-achin'," she promised with a light laugh. "I guess we be doin' t'is, then." She dropped her hands to her lap, twisting one of the colorful strips of her skirt in her hands. "So… wha' am I doin'?"

Aria took a moment to finish her tea before setting down the cup. As sure as it had been there, the table and all that was on it was gone. "Focus on the threads, to start, and find mine. I've stopped hiding it." Captain nodded, taking a deep breath and focusing on the threads around them. She was slightly surprised to find that even though they were within the orb's own little world, the pattern was still full and vibrant around them. Her eyes skipped between the colors before she forced herself to focus on Aria. The woman across from her had already reached out to pluck something from the air; Captain couldn't see it at first, but once Aria had the thread in her hands, she could.

"Can we nae usually see our own, t'en?" she asked curiously, even as she identified the threads spinning from Aria's heart and reached for them.

"No, only under certain circumstances that call for it. Think of it like being aware of your own nose. It is always there, in the center of your face, but you are rarely aware of it in the corner of your eyes unless you need it or it begs your attention. You do not typically notice what you cannot see, so you do not always notice you cannot see it."

"Oi, tha' was a bit—"

"Repetitive, yes. But true."

Aria waited until Captain had the threads twined around her fingers. "Now, watch closely. I am going to tie the knot," she instructed. Captain nodded, watching as Aria gently gathered the threads from the lass's hands and started twisting them around Captain's thread. "This is the knot you use when granting full power, remember," the Celestial murmured, eyes intent on her task. "Be sure you fully trust any Weaver you give this power over your abilities." Captain nodded again but didn't interrupt. Aria finished the intricate design before sitting back and pulling a few other threads. "Now, take these. Good. And watch my movements." Though her hands were empty, Aria mimicked the Weaving Captain would need to perform. Captain watched closely before slowly, carefully starting to copy. "Take your time, Captain. Speed comes with practice."

Alconai watched the two Weavers with fascination. He refrained from commenting, not wanting to distract them from their task. Really, he barely dared to breathe lest that cause one or both of them to make a mistake. As they worked, Alconai committed what he saw to memory as he tended to do with his experiences.

As the pair worked, the air around them started to react. A soft wind stirred, and flashes of rainbow traced along lines Alconai couldn't see. "That does it," Aria murmured. "Start tapping in. You will need them both." Captain took a steadying breath but did not stop. Soon the flashes were happening more often, tracing shapes as well as lines. Captain could see them now. More than just threads, there were sigils in the air, runes. Magic. Her eyes and fingertips carried a rainbow glow as she worked, her Sight revealing the spells and her Weaving working against them. Oddly, she felt no fear from her own power. She felt no overwhelming pull. She wasn't sure how Aria was keeping it stable, but she was. So Captain focused on her task, following Aria's instruction until she found her footing. At that point, Aria stopped leading her and watched, calm and resolute.

And then the first loud *crack* split the air. The serene, rounded sky around them didn't shatter, but something did. Soft particles like glitter fell from the air. Then another crack, and another deluge of sparkles as the sigils shattered and the magic scattered.

Then, with a final crack and a rainbow flash, the trio were in the cavern. Captain staggered as her feet found ground and she was suddenly standing, but Aria caught her shoulders.

"<Well done,>" she murmured before frowning, touching a hand to her lips as Celesi replaced Common. "...<Oh dear. That is unexpected.>" Captain stared at her blankly.

"<Indeed.>" The king's voice was a low growl. One look at his face, and the pair knew he was livid, but Aria seemed unperturbed.

"<Ah, there you are.>" She stood to her full height, passing the swaying Captain towards Alconai as she stepped between them. Her eyes flashed with a surprising ferocity.

"S'i' jus' me, or can ye nae un'erstand a word t'ey be sayin'?" Captain asked Alconai groggily as she leaned against him.

Something tugged at the back of Alconai's memory. He recognized the lilt and the sounds of the words though not the words themselves. It felt like grasping for a memory he barely realized he had. "I donnae ken what they be speakin'," he confessed. He wrapped an arm around Captain to steady her. If not for the king's presence, Alconai would have scooped her up so the pirate wouldn't have to worry about standing.

Captain managed to regain her landlegs, touching a hand to Alconai's to let him know she was steady. Aria was staring down the king calmly, seeming not the least bit concerned that he was there and angry. It struck Captain that Aria was taller than she had realized, standing a good few inches higher than the king.

"<Are you going to make me ask?>" The king ground out his words, shoulders stiff.

"<Do you need to? I summoned the Moon Child here for her assistance, and she succeeded.>" Aria turned away, walking to the gazebo and gently reclaiming her orb. "<I do not need to be stuck in that tiny little pocket dimension to serve the kingdom, nor would you have let me serve my duty training the Moon Child unless something drastic were to occur. Considering

the potential paths ahead of Andor, I chose the least confrontational.>" She turned her gaze back to the king, eyes steel. "<We're leaving the chamber now. You can test your spells if you wish, but I've only broken the ones that needed it.>" She nodded to Captain and Alconai, gesturing them towards the stairs. The guards hesitated, glancing at Traiborn, but he was still glaring at Aria. Finally, he sighed.

"Let them pass, but keep her safe. Two guards at all times." The group saluted before stepping to the sides. Aria lifted her chin and walked right past them once she was sure Captain and Alconai would follow.

Alconai kept his shoulders back and his gait light as though the king and his guards gave the entertainer no cause for concern. Really, it was out of Alconai's hands.

Aria led them briskly from the library and all the way to the guest quarters. She sat herself in the parlor, helping herself to some of the leftover tea. One of the guards offered to fetch some hot water, so she nodded gratefully. Captain sat across from her, watching her carefully.

"Why can we nae understand you anymore?" she asked cautiously. Aria rolled her eyes with a sigh before lifting a hand and grasping her wrist. "Another enchan'ment?" Aria nodded. "Can we break tha' one, too?" Aria shook her head. "Oi, yosh…Can anyone wit' us speak wha'ever ye're speaking?" Her eyebrows shot up when Aria nodded. "Wh— well, no, wait, tha' makes sense. It's Tris, righ'?" Aria smirked. "Ok. So…uhm…are ye goin' ta stay in t'e tower wit' us?" Aria paused to consider before raising her hand and shaking it side to side. "Some o' t'e time?" Aria nodded.

Alconai sat with the women, curious of the Celestial. "I take it she be speakin' something only Celestials would ken?" Alconai asked Captain since she seemed to have deciphered some of Aria's communication. "Of course, our only Celestial be gone trainin' right now," remarked Alconai, smiling despite his wry tone. "He should be back soon."

Captain nodded. "Aye, an' hopefully we can figure somethin' out fer t'e rest of us." She stood and stretched. "Well. Thanks fer keepin' us outta jail, I guess. I think I need ta take a nap fer now." She patted Alconai's shoulder before heading back towards her room.

21. *Trials and Time*

While Captain and Alconai discovered Aria, Tristan found himself immensely enjoying his flight. Tristan smiled brightly as the capital blurred below him in a collection of smeared colors and shapes. Considering the lack of screams from the inhabitants, he surmised that Tannen had used this form of travel previously. The half-dragon Half-Drow cut through the air with practiced ease and bird-like grace. Tristan held onto Tannen's neck tightly to keep balance on the dragon's back, the Celestial's legs gripping as well. As the wind whipped his brown hair and ruffled his clothes, Tristan felt exhilaration bubbling inside him, making him giddy. He had never been this high before even at the top of the tallest tree in Nikko Mori. Gazing out at Andor stretching in each direction, Tristan tried to take in every detail he could see. He felt a little disappointed when Tannen started to glide over a meadow a little ways outside the capital.

"Hold on tight, youngling," Tannen's voice reached Tristan over the wind. Tristan quickly tightened his grips as the dragon dipped and then surged upwards into a steep climb. Once they reached the apex, Tannen suddenly twisted into a dive. Laughter erupted from Tristan as the duo sped towards the earth. Just before the point of no return, Tannen pulled up and flapped his wings in one mighty downstroke. Vibrations wracked Tristan's body when Tannen dropped to the ground in a sturdy landing.

Tristan continued laughing, smiling wide.

"That was amazing!" proclaimed the Sun Child. Nimbly Tristan leapt from Tannen's back to his foreleg and then to the ground. Tristan watched as Tannen reverted to his humanoid form, the blacksmith smiling warmly.

"I'm glad you enjoyed it," said Tannen. "With everything that's been going on, I figured you could use some fun. We'll start training once you're sure you're steady on your feet. Flying on the back of a dragon can be a bit like riding a horse for the first time. Except bigger."

Tristan laughed again, genuinely amused. It felt good to laugh and to do something exciting and new. He walked around a little to make sure he could keep his feet. Tristan watched Tannen quickly carve magic runes at different points on the ground and imbue them with magic, Tristan deducing they would create a barrier to hide the duo from magical means of spying.

Once the blacksmith finished, Tristan spoke, "Well, Zatook was training me on swords and fighting someone more equal to my power. Part of my Celestial ability is producing a type of crystal. So far, I've managed to make the crystal strong enough to cut into dragon hide." Tristan recalled his fight with Jeremiah when Rose first came to Nikko Mori. That encounter felt so long ago in the face of everything now.

Tannen tilted his head in interest at the mention of the crystal. "Please, show me," he instructed politely. Tristan quickly materialized a crystal dagger in his hand to show the blacksmith. Tannen studied the weapon for a moment before getting permission and taking the dagger.

Inspecting it more closely, the blacksmith tested the balance and make with critical curiosity.

"I don't know that this would cut into a dragon, but I used one of my elven blades and coated it with the crystal to strengthen both. It's easier than making a new weapon in the heat of battle," Tristan explained.

"I imagine," Tannen commented easily. "Given the density and makeup, you might manage to cut me with this. However, I'm not inclined to test that theory on myself." He gave Tristan a teasing smirk. More seriously, Tannen added, "However, as an Earth dragon, I can form constructs out of earthen materials: metal, gems, and the like. It's a nice advantage to being a blacksmith. My favorite, though, is working with rare materials that aren't in raw earthen form. It's why Halia and I make a good team. She heats the materials to the required temperature, and I'm able to withstand the heat to work the material. I wonder if we could do something similar with your crystal. Then again, it wouldn't be very lucrative since I suspect this crystal is unique to you and can't be created by other means."

"I honestly have no idea," Tristan admitted. "I've certainly never seen anything else made from it that I didn't make myself. I haven't experimented with it much other than making blades and shields. I have used the crystal to amplify my other powers. Like using glass or crystals to conduct and concentrate light."

"While I can't recreate your crystal, I can help you learn to control the density and form. Even the color," assured Tannen. "Why don't we work on that for now? We can test it against various metals and minerals." He handed back Tristan's new crystal dagger. Tannen then got to work explaining how he manipulated his own materials to create durable, sharp blades and sturdy shields. Tannen had Tristan experiment with the newly formed dagger and then test it against a column that Tannen created, using the minerals in the earth to change the construct's make depending on the test. Tannen also had Tristan practice making the crystal magic-conducive for Lancelot's task.

As the morning began to shift closer to midday, Tannen called a halt to the training. Tristan shook out his hands and allowed himself to relax. He was used to using his powers, but he still felt some strain with trying the different forms. There was one thing he wanted to try, though.

"Before we go back, I want to try to shift into my Celestial form," Tristan announced. "If you don't mind." Tristan felt unease worm its way into his stomach when Tannen gave him a hesitant look. Tristan pressed, "The whole point in coming out here and training is for me to get better at my Celestial powers. I'm going to have to learn eventually, and it would be better to learn it here where my father and others can't interfere."

"I don't know," Tannen remarked, uncertain. "As I said, I don't know anything about Celestials. It might be better for you to wait until you can have one present just in case."

"It's just my other form. All Celestials can do it; though, the circumstances surrounding their transformations vary. My parents told me enough for me to know that some Celestials can make their first transformation at will. Others, it happens through intense circumstances or emotions," Tristan explained. "I don't know that it'll even work, but this is the best place for me to try."

"Do you even know how to start?" challenged Tannen softly, gently.

"I just have to will it to happen," Tristan countered. He relaxed a little when Tannen released a heavy sigh.

"Just be careful," the blacksmith implored. "I won't know what to do if things go wrong."

Tristan nodded. He stepped away from Tannen to keep the man hopefully out of potential danger. Truthfully, Tristan had no idea what to expect. The only time he had seen a Celestial go into their Celestial form was when both his parents transformed into their full power during their final altercation. Those images haunted Tristan's memories even as they filled him with awe. Closing his eyes, Tristan concentrated, reaching for his core as a Celestial. Focusing, he tried to imagine himself changed even as he tapped into the essence of his being. Feeling his power flow through him and his body beginning to change, Tristan forced himself to relax and let it happen.

Ice.

A nauseatingly familiar ice shot through Tristan's veins, freezing his blood. A shockwave of pure agony wracked him next. The source seared in Tristan's chest like someone stabbed him dead center, the pain lancing outwards through the rest of his body. A scream ripped from Tristan's throat.

Tannen watched in absolute horror. This…this was so much worse than he could have imagined. Even as unfamiliar as Tannen was with Celestials, after working with the lad for the last few hours, Tannen knew this power wasn't Tristan's. Not fully. Lost on how to help, Tannen stared as Tristan crumpled to his knees, shrieking in pain. Red and black lines followed along Tristan's veins, glowing even through his clothes. Tristan's eyes turned bloodshot red as tears spilled down the young man's face. Along the lines, Tristan's skin began to turn black in places. Suddenly, Tristan hunched over as his purple and magenta crystal spread over his back and shoulders before shooting out behind him to form large, beautiful wings. Instantly, the red and black lines spiderwebbed up and along the wings. A sickening crack shot through the air as the corrupting power cracked the crystal and even shattered portions of it, creating jagged spikes in a mockery of the original wings. More crystal tried to form along Tristan's form, but the same result occurred. The red and black made the cracks look burned and bleeding despite the lack of liquid seeping from them— like cauterized wounds. Tristan's voice gave out with the continued anguish. His brown hair turned black with streaks of red.

Tristan felt drool spilling down his chin from his mouth hanging open in a continuous, silent scream. *Please, help me. Make it stop, please,* he pleaded to the Sacreds, to Tannen— anyone. Why did the Talisman ruin this? He felt the corrosive influence searing and freezing through him, splitting and burning his flesh and Celestial powers. Corrupting him. So lost in pain, Tristan missed the newest arrival to the meadow.

Zatook dropped from the sky like a rock, wrapping his

arms around Tristan as he took on his gargoyle shape. Tannen hadn't even seen him coming, but he was used to Zatook's speed. The latter pulled the boy close as he let his own power wrap around them, isolating them in old magic. If the Talisman truly spiraled, he doubted he could contain it for long— but they would have another problem then, in the form of the king. For now, he had to trust that it was just reacting to Tristan, to his unlocked power. "Breathe, Tristan," Zatook encouraged, wrapping his wings around them to shield the boy from the outside world. "First, breathe. Ground yourself in what's around you." Softly, calmly, he started guiding Tristan in how to focus past the pain.

Tristan whimpered and whined as Zatook moved him, the motion causing more pain. Zatook's instructions barely reached through the haze in Tristan's mind. Focusing through the agony like he had so many times before, Tristan concentrated on getting one breath in and letting it out. And then another. And another. As he let Zatook guide him, Tristan focused on the feel of the man's strong arms around him, the safety Tristan felt in the hold. He took in the darkness around him in the shadow of Zatook's wings. Tristan smelled the sweat from his own body. As he absorbed each detail, Tristan slowly brought his breathing under control. The pain remained, but he bore it better. Almost subconsciously, he felt inward to see if the seal was still intact, his fear spiking for a moment. However, Tristan found the seal still there— weak but not broken. The tears continued to spill down Tristan's cheeks, stinging the split skin. He curled more into Zatook's hold. "I'm sorry," Tristan rasped. "I didn't mean...I didn't know..." he trailed off as speaking became too painful.

"You have no need to apologize," Zatook assured him. "We could not begin to fathom the effects a weakening seal would have, let alone that it would corrupt your transformation to this extent."

Tristan shuddered in Zatook's arms. "I...I don't...I'm afraid to try to shift back. What if that makes it worse?" whispered Tristan. "But I know...I can't stay like this. It hurts... so bad. And I can't let the king...see this. He'll question."

Zatook was quiet for a moment. "I cannot say for certain, but we shall not know until you try. And you are correct: the king will question." He paused. "There have been...instances where a Celestial's transformation was corrupted by fell magics. Not to this extent, mind. If this is similar, however, it is likely the pain will not follow you back into your original form."

Swallowing to wet his dry throat, Tristan closed his eyes once more. As he tried to will his body back to his first form, the pain caused him to reach out blindly, desperate for an anchor. A large hand enveloped his, the grip gentle despite the size. Tristan slit his eyes open to see Zatook's hand holding his. Gratefully, Tristan weakly squeezed his grip. Focusing on the feel and sight of Zatook's hand, Tristan pushed for his transformation to reverse. The crystal dissipated and the lines began to recede. Tristan's hair turned back to its medium brown color, and his eyes returned to their sapphire blue. The tears subsided, but Tristan's eyes remained clouded with pain. Even though the greater overall agony decreased, the pain persisted beyond the familiar dull ache. The burns remained. Shakily, Tristan used his sleeve to wipe the tears and drool from his face. Weariness weighed down his body as the young man breathed heavily.

Zatook waited patiently, letting Tristan grip his hand as tightly as needed. After a moment, he asked: "Any better?"

"A little," replied Tristan hoarsely. He pulled his hand back and shakily rolled up one of his sleeves, revealing the burns along his arm. He felt them pocked all over his body, hot and painful. "Looks like these transitioned between my forms." He wasn't familiar with the aftermath from the Talisman. Tiredly, he recalled his conversation with Queen Corianne about healing Zatook's throat scars. Were the burns wounds that Tristan could heal? Tristan leaned a bit more into Zatook's hold to steady himself. Then he focused once more, pushing through the pain and fatigue. He reached for his Sun Child healing and let the warm light wash over him. Slowly, steadily the pain lessened. His skin softened where the burns had made the flesh stiff. Gradually, the burns disappeared and the pain returned to the uncomfortable ache in his chest. Once he withdrew his power, Tristan slumped in Zatook's hold, exhausted and nearly unconscious.

Zatook hesitated. If Tristan could heal the burns, then he should tell him about Amaya. But the lad was exhausted and upset; was now really the best time? "Rest, Tristan." He shifted back into his own human form, cradling the young Celestial to him. He glanced around to find Tannen. He would leave a message for Tristan about Amaya's burns, but for now they should get him back to the palace.

Tannen had moved off a little to give the two space. At Zatook's glance, the blacksmith joined him. Sighing heavily, Tannen studied Tristan's relaxed expression, the young Celestial having slipped unconscious. "I feel bad for just standing there. I had no idea what I could do to help," Tannen admitted. He moved around the area and dragged his boot across the runic markings, disabling them. "Will you be all right to carry him back or do you need a ride?" inquired Tannen as he looked at Zatook.

Zatook shifted Tristan slightly to clap Tannen's shoulder before nodding towards the palace. He was fine to carry the lad.

Taking the cue, Tannen deconstructed the training column he had made and then shifted back to his dragon form. He took off to the capital and back to the castle, aiming to land in the guest courtyard. He reverted to being a Drow and inclined his head when he found Jabez watching him.

Zatook landed just behind him. He nodded to Jabez and then to Tristan to ask which room he should take the lad to. Once they had Tristan settled comfortably and Zatook had written a note to leave on the lad's end table, they returned downstairs. Solomon was in the parlor now, currently learning from Tannen what had happened. He glanced over when Zatook and Jabez rejoined them. "Will the king have sensed what happened, as you did?" he asked Zatook in concern. The warrior hesitated before signing.

"I am unsure. I was on my way to see him, however, so I shall learn soon enough." When Solomon nodded, Zatook continued, "Tristan should take it easy the rest of today and tomorrow. Broth and tea to help him recover. He was able to heal the damage from the Talisman, but his body will be tired from the corrupted transformation. And he should not attempt to transform again until we find a way to reinstate the seal."

"Poor lad cannae catch a break," commented Alconai sympathetically.

Jabez spoke, "I'm glad he was able to transform back, and that you two were there for him. Thank you both."

Tannen shook his head. "I wasn't able to help with the transformation, but I think he made good progress on the rest of his training," the blacksmith told them. "I'll check in on him in a couple days to see if he feels up to picking up where we left off." Tannen glanced at Zatook. "Sans the transformation."

Zatook didn't notice the glance, frowning at the fluffy white cat currently curled up sleeping on a chair in the parlor. The trouble was, he didn't remember seeing it before. The castle had plenty of cats around, and he had thought he met them all. Now that the cat had caught his attention, he was more alert, and he sensed the two guards out in the hall. The creature lifted its head, opening her mismatched eyes— one green, one golden — to watch him.

In truth, only Alconai knew the cat to be Aria. The woman had taken to her cat form shortly after Captain went to take her nap, asking Alconai to keep her presence to himself for now until she was ready to introduce herself to the others. But now, she knew Zatook was focused on her. A cat he hadn't met that did not feel like a cat. The boy was powerful enough that she knew he could sense her through her Weavings. She didn't exactly want to spring herself onto the others, especially while they fretted over her grandson, but she wasn't sure the young halfling would give her a choice.

Tannen followed Zatook's gaze and arched an eyebrow at his friend's interest in the random cat. However, Tannen patted Zatook's shoulder and took his leave, figuring Zatook would tell him later if the cat was important. Since Zatook hadn't attacked it outright, Tannen figured the feline wasn't dangerous.

"Are you going to introduce us to your new friend, Nai?" asked Jabez once Tannen was gone.

Alconai shrugged. "Just a cat that followed me and Cap'n. I'll let her introduce herself," he answered nonchalantly, though there was a twinkle in his eye.

Zatook turned his gaze to Alconai at that, frowning. It sounded like the man knew who, or possibly what, the cat was. And truly, he didn't sense any hostility from her. And yet if he walked away from an unknown variable and Traiborn found out… Zatook sighed.

"Am I to assume that you are aware she is not, in fact, a cat?" he signed in question. "And that the guards outside indicate the king is aware of her presence?"

"Oh aye, t'e king kens," Alconai assured easily. "And I be told nae ta say."

Jabez stared at Alconai now, curious and perplexed. Then he watched the cat for a moment. "Are you able to take on another form or speak to us?" the ninja asked the feline.

The cat actually sighed. "<I can speak, though only a few

of you will understand what it is I say,>" she explained calmly. Zatook was staring at her again. "<I had planned to formally introduce myself when you were all together. The guards, Zatook, are for my protection per the king's orders.>"

"<I take it Captain and Alconai found and freed the Celestial of Time?>" asked Jabez, speaking Celesi fluently. He almost flinched with how fast Alconai whipped around to look at him. Ignoring his brother for the moment, Jabez added, "<I'm glad to make your acquaintance; I'm Jabez ShadowDancer.>"

"Oi, oi, where did ye learn ta speak— whatever ye be speakin'?" Alconai questioned incredulously. "Another skill ye picked up o'er t'e years?"

Jabez nodded. "I spent a lot of time with the Order's scholars and sometimes helped them with their transcription and translation work. It gave me something quiet to occupy my mind, and they were eager to share their knowledge," he explained.

"So, of course, he chose to learn one of the most rare languages," Solomon noted in a gentle tease. "Would I be correct in guessing Zatook can understand our guest as well?" The dark warrior nodded. "Then that makes at least two of our current party." He didn't miss Zatook turning to stare at him next. But the warrior didn't say anything, just shaking his head and lifting a hand as he moved for the door out of the guest tower. He did need to go give his report, after all. And the new Celestial was known and apparently friendly.

"Well, t'e Chosen Children be restin' after their eventful

mornin'," Alconai commented. "Lunch be here soon, but we be needin' them ta bring somethin' lighter for our Sun Child."

Jabez sat on one of the sofas. "We'll wake them for lunch, or we can leave it sit under the enchanted serving lids and let the trio wake on their own," he remarked. "Hopefully, we can make introductions then."

"<Zatook plans to inform the kitchens on his way to see the king,>" Aria noted calmly, somehow speaking clearly while cleaning her paw. She hesitated a moment. "<I shall need to speak with Tristan in private, when he wakes.>"

Alconai asked, "Have ye heard o' Celestial transformations goin' so poorly before?"

"<Yes. Generally when fell magics or other corrupting forces are involved, in this case the Talisman.>"

Once Jabez translated, Alconai added, "Be there a way ta keep it from happenin' again? We donnae ken how ta seal t'e Talisman yet. Or do ye ken a way?"

Aria considered for a moment. "<The way shall be made clear in time, but it is not my place to reveal. Until then, Tristan should not try to transform again.>"

"No end o' frustration fer t'e Chosen then. At least ye be able ta help with Captain's powers, aye? What was makin' them flare and what nae?" inquired Alconai, once more waiting for Jabez to translate before asking.

Aria relaxed back down into the chair, curling her tail

around herself. "<Having to endure a while longer and having no end are quite different,>" Aria corrected calmly. "<And yes, I will help with her Weaving. Though as for the curse on her Child powers, I do not yet know. Its source has been hidden even to my eyes, so it will take time to discover.>"

"A curse. If such a spell is hidden even from the Celestial of Time, then I guess there might be no point in looking through the archives or King Zetta's journal for how to lift it," Jabez mused. "I know curses can be tricky and ugly to deal with."

"<Someone very powerful must have found her,>" noted Aria. "<Though I would hazard a guess they could not withstand her powers when they went out of control, and then Amaya arrived before they could return.>"

"I can't help but wonder who would be strong enough to put that kind of curse on one of the Chosen Children, and what would be the intention behind such a feat," murmured Jabez thoughtfully. "As for Amaya, if not for the wards around Andor set by the king, she would be with us."

"<Yes. Those.>" Aria closed her eyes. "<Enduring versus never-ending,>" she murmured almost to herself as she returned to her nap.

***

When lunch arrived from the kitchens, Aria's words rang true: alongside the food was broth for Tristan, as well as a refresh of tea for the parlor. Captain came down a little after the meal arrived, yawning behind her hand, and Rose was not far behind. Lancelot took a little longer, having lost himself in a scroll from the Archives and not noticing the time— Alconai wound up fetching him. They left the broth under an enchanted lid for now since Tristan was still sleeping.

Alconai helped himself to food and settled to eat. For now, he said nothing about the newest addition to their parlor, figuring Aria would introduce herself when she was ready. Alconai frowned slightly when Jabez didn't move to retrieve any food. Catching his brother's gaze, Alconai subtly indicated for Jabez to eat.

"I'll eat later," assured Jabez quietly.

Aria was watching the group from her perch. Solomon had started to turn to Jabez when a soft knock sounded at the door before Princess Collette stuck her head in. Lancelot was still in the habit of standing and bowing, no matter the times she had waved off such formalities in the guest tower. This time, she held up a note as she entered.

"I received your note asking me to join you all for lunch," she explained brightly, though she paused at the confused looks cast between Rose and Captain. The latter, however, turned to the fluffy white cat on a nearby chair.

"<Yes, let Captain know I invited her. She should be included in this,>" Aria explained to Jabez, standing and stretching. She now had Lancelot, Rose, *and* Collette's full attention, the knight having choked on his coffee when she spoke. Aria lightly leapt from the chair and transformed into her human-like form. "<I would rather have liked to include her brother and the blacksmith as

well, but it was not to be.>"

Jabez did as Aria asked, relaying the woman's words to the rest of the group. He considered seeing if Tristan was awake but decided against it. After the young man's ordeal during training, Jabez wanted to let Tristan sleep as long as possible.

Captain was now looking between Jabez and Aria. "Oi, ye can speak wha'ever tha' is?" she asked incredulously, echoing Alconai's earlier surprise.

After a quick curtsy to the oracle, Collette lifted her hand slightly in response to Captain. "Lady Aria is speaking Celesi," she supplied. "It's the language of the Celestials. I have yet to learn it, but Mother and Father use it. I believe my brother understands it, as well." She joined them at the table, nodding in thanks as Lancelot pulled her chair free for her.

"<Yes, Zatook understands it. The language comes naturally to full-blooded and halflings alike as a blessing of Shaddai.>" Aria was seating herself at the table as well, calmly smoothing her skirts. Solomon hesitated when Jabez translated. Well, that confirmed one of his suspicions about the man. Lancelot had managed to regain his knightly demeanor after the first surprise, so he didn't really react to the news except for his own pause before finishing his bite of food. "<The queen speaks it because Andor has a very close history with Celestials.>" Aria's gaze turned fond for a moment before she returned to the conversation. "<But that is only relevant because of my remaining restrictions. Before we discuss more, let's get through the formalities. I am Aria, Celestial of Time and Oracle of Andor. Also, yes, Tristan's grandmother and

Amaya's mother.>"

Jabez refrained from commenting for now since he was acting as the translator. He felt his own surprise with the revelation regarding Zatook, but like with Amaya and Tristan, the confirmation cleared some of the mystery surrounding the man. For his part, Alconai shook his head in incredulousness, simply taking the surprises in stride at this point. Shaddai only knew what else the group would learn and run into before their adventure was over.

Solomon leaned back in his chair. "Considering how much you already know of us, it is likely you know our names. However, I do tend to be one for formalities." He smiled subtly as he touched his hand to his head, his heart, and his mouth before gesturing outward. "I am Solomon SealKeeper of the Order."

"And I am Rose, the Star Child," Rose followed, touching a hand to her heart and bowing before turning to Lance beside her.

"I...well, I don't really have a formal introduction right now," he confessed as he rubbed the back of his head. Being a deserter and all, he didn't feel right calling himself a knight of Nocis. "For now, I am simply Lancelot."

Aria smirked at him. "<Do not balk from your status as a sealbreaker or that of a protector of the Chosen Children. It may not be your planned path, but it is the one before you— and an honorable one at that.>" Lancelot hesitated, glancing at Jabez. When her words were translated, the tips of his ears turned red.

"<The Daughter of Andor and I have met more than once, even if she could not see me,>" Aria continued, smiling softly at Collette. "<Alconai, Captain, and I made introductions while within my sanctuary. And Jabez introduced himself earlier. So that is covered. Onto more important matters.>" She turned to Jabez. "<That paper you have, depicting the sword. Please place it on the table where the others can see.>"

Jabez pulled out the diagram and laid the paper on the table, using a few utensils to weigh the corners to keep the parchment from curling.

"<This is the Etherium Runesaber. Traiborn has unlocked enough of its secrets to know it is dangerous and to make it dangerous, but he has yet to learn everything about my old sword. Especially how powerful it is in the hands of sealbreakers.>" She turned to look at Lancelot. "<It will allow you to break more than just seals,>" she explained. "<Barriers and spells will also fall before you, if you bear that blade. However, attempting to just take it from the king would be quite disastrous.>"

"About as disastrous as unsealing the queen's locket?"

Her eyes glimmered with mirth. "<Oh, yes. But there is more for which you must prepare than fighting a king.>" She gestured that Jabez could put the paper away for now. "<Until Captain and I are certain my enchantments are no longer interfering with her Sight, I will be using my gifts as oracle to aid you. There are many things I will not reveal immediately. This includes the answer to Tristan's woes with the Talisman of Ruin—>" When Jabez translated that, it was Collette's turn to choke on her drink, "<—or when you should expect things to come to a head with the king. But there are things I can tell you to help you prepare.>"

She turned to Collette first. "<The balm your brother requested for his friend— have two more batches prepared and send one with him when he leaves tomorrow. There is a way to heal the wounds, but it will be a while before that can take place.>" Next, she turned to Captain. "<You should stock up at the apothecary and brew up a few potions. There will be a lot happening at once, and we should not overtax our healers— especially given some of what they will face. I will also be attempting to get to the bottom of the issues you have with your other ability.>" Next, she turned to Rose. "<I am aware that Tristan found Zetta's notes, so you know of your ability to heal Celesbane. With a little help from the princess, we are going to practice.>" Back to Collette, who looked innocently confused. "<I will need you to steal from your father; we shall discuss those details later.>"

Rose and Collette both hesitated, the princess burying herself in her tea as the Star Child asked. "How…might one practice that? Exactly?"

Aria met her gaze levelly.

"Oh."

The Celestial shrugged a shoulder. "<It will hardly be the first time I have been stabbed with the nonsense.>" She turned her gaze back across the group, deadly serious. "<You have been granted a time of rest and preparation by Shaddai, but it is coming to an end. Much is going to happen, and quickly, once Nocis breaches Daisuke.>" There was hesitation and more than a few blank looks.

Aria sighed. Right, they wouldn't know that name. "<Daisuke is the Wall of Andor,>" she explained. Now the silence was stunned rather than confused. She turned to Collette. "<I will be informing your parents, as well,>" she assured her. "<But the priestesses will need to be ready for the coming war, and you will need to be ready for what you feel.>" Collette nodded, clasping her hands in her lap. While she processed the information, Solomon explained for the others:

"The royal line has a connection to the Wall, a sort of genetically bound enchantment," he explained. "Those with stronger connections can often feel from the Wall, as it will let them know if something is happening or someone has come to visit."

"My mother has always had the strongest connection, but I am not far behind," Collette added softly. "Which likely means if the Wall— Daisuke? —is breached, we will feel pain."

"The Wall...feels pain?" Rose asked hesitantly. "And has a name?"

Aria nodded. "<Daisuke is tied very deeply to the realm's inherent magic,>" she explained. "<He is to the realm like an elder tree to the forest. Old, wise, and alive in his own way.>"

"Of course," Alconai muttered. Shaking his head, he inquired, "Is there any way ta keep Daisuke from gettin' wounded, or is this somethin' that has ta happen?"

"<This must be... and it will be only the beginning. Once

Daisuke is wounded, much more will come to pass. You must be ready.>"

"Are we helpin' wit' t'e war, then?" Captain asked curiously. Aria hesitated.

"<You will have your own path,>" she explained carefully. "<Though some of your efforts will affect things here.>"

"What should t'e rest o' us be doin' ta help in t'e meantime?" Alconai questioned.

"<Training and preparing for a journey.>"

"And remember, no going out alone," Solomon noted calmly. "That means someone should go with Captain to the apothecary."

"If you need anything from the smithy, I can take your order to Tannen," Collette volunteered. Aria nodded before turning back to Jabez.

"<And you should practice more with the Glyphseal Sentinels. Until I can get to the bottom of Captain's curse, at least, there will be many events that risk her seal.>" She paused when Rose raised her hand in question.

"This is more for the table," she confessed, "but does anyone else speak draconic?"

"Uh, actually, I do," Lance confessed. "King Arden requested the High Houses and upper officers and knights learn. I'm not really sure why, though."

"I can read and speak draconic, as well," Jabez offered.

Alconai smirked at Jabez. "Well, this be one language I ken outside Common," said Alconai. "We be a well-traveled group." To Rose he added, "Why be ye askin'?"

"I happen to know a part of your path lies in the Valley of Dragons," she explained with a shrug. "I have not heard many tales of people going to their lands, so I thought it would suit you to have someone who knew the language."

"Didn't you learn it, as well?" Lance asked curiously. Rose hesitated.

"<The Star Child will not be with you,>" Aria explained calmly. "<But the entrance to the Underworld lies in the Valley— well, moves around it.>"

Rose caught onto at least Lance's hesitation. "Lady Rin offered Tristan a chance, but we do not know anything beyond that."

"So Lady Death will come to collect you," Jabez remarked, his gaze steady but concerned. He wasn't surprised the information had slipped between the cracks. Tristan had a lot he was dealing with, and the group had been focusing on things they needed to figure out for their next steps. To Aria, Jabez inquired, "Tristan told us of visions you had shown him. Is there anything more we need to know from them?"

"<Most have had their truths revealed. You have found the queen, Tristan has learned of his mentor's travels, I have spoken on the sword and the war…>" She thought back to remember what he was shown. "<When he came to me, there were forty-five days before the Lady came… The woman with King Jeremiah is his wife, Rajani… And the last image involved the creation of the Talisman of Ruin.>"

All eyes were on Aria, forks and cups forgotten.

"The creation?" Rose was the one to ask, furrowing her brow.

"<Yes. Though the exact process is unknown, it was made with strong fell magics and the blood of the oldest Celestial.>" Her gaze softened somewhat. "<Innovation's powers are formidable, and the Talisman corrupts them into pure destruction.>"

"Is she a friend o' yers?" Captain asked curiously, noting the change in Aria's demeanor.

"<An old one, yes. I met her during the Purge, though she did not reveal who she was at first. She has always preferred it that way.>" Aria sat back, folding her hands on her lap. "<Innovation is the last living Original. The Celestials hand-crafted by Shaddai. She is old, and she is powerful, but she gets tired of being treated as such. So she does not tell you who she is unless it matters in a bid to be treated as a peer.>"

"An' yer sayin' some'ne got t'e best of her a' some point?"

"<Oh, there have been a few times. But one of those was at the hands of someone who…>" Aria paused, something seeming to dawn before her eyes. "<…is hidden even from my gaze.>" Her eyes narrowed. "<Curiouser and curiouser.>"

"How common is it that someone can hide from the Celestial of Time?" Lancelot asked hesitantly.

"<Not. It is more common, though still rare, to be able to hide from the Sight. But my abilities should press past such spells. So the fact I have run into it twice now...>" She trailed off, Jabez pausing in his translation.

"Indicates a shared source?" supplied Solomon. Aria nodded.

"Wha' was t'e second t'ing?" Captain asked, confused.

"It happened earlier, while you were asleep," Solomon informed her. "Jabez and Alconai had been speaking with Aria about training your powers, and she mentioned not being able to see what caused the curse on your ability."

"Wai', I'm *cursed?*" Captain looked between them before holding up her hand to examine. "Huh. Makes sense, I guess." She paused, eyes snapping to Aria. "Hol' up, are ye sayin' I go' cursed by t'e same guy wha' made t'e Talisman o' Ruin?!"

"<Or that he was in some way involved, yes>."

"Seems yer thread was twinin' with Tristan's a long time ago," Alconai remarked with a teasing smile. Still, the information was a lot to process. "We cannae lift yer curse; we cannae seal t'e Talisman. And both be causin' problems. Best nae let t'e king get wind o' either." He swung his gaze teasingly to Collette, but Alconai knew she wouldn't tell.

"<He already knows about the Talisman,>" Aria noted dryly, "<though not full details, such as how it is kept or the weakening seal. He was attempting to goad you into telling him about that and about Tsukuyomi's true nature in an attempt to gauge your willingness to let go of such information. Politics, basically.>"

Collette grimaced. "Father often knows more than he lets on, but I can confirm that your first dinner here was the first either of my parents knew of Marilyn's involvement. So he doesn't know everything you're trying to keep quiet." She hesitated. "How 'weak' exactly?"

"<Not enough to involve your parents,>" Aria noted flatly. "<A solution shall present itself in due time.>"

"Until then, Tannen can stick to training Tristan's Celestial powers without Tristan transforming," remarked Jabez. "As anxious as the Talisman makes the Sun Child and us, it's good to know there is a solution. We need to keep patient. We do as Lady Aria suggested and prepare ourselves for whatever is coming."

"For now, let's finish lunch," Solomon suggested calmly. "We'll need to keep our strength up, and it sounds like we have quite a bit to do over the next couple of days. Best start with full bellies."

22. Descending Darkness

Slowly, Tristan came to consciousness, his body heavy as lead and his mind foggy from deep sleep. At first, he simply lay there as he recalled what had happened to put him in such a state. Gradually, he forced his eyes open despite wanting to continue sleeping. He sensed someone in the room. Blearily, Tristan shifted onto his back and looked around his guest room.

He spotted the woman almost immediately. The oracle was in his bedroom, sitting in a chair and calmly reading a book. As he became aware of her, however, Aria calmly closed the small tome and set it aside.

"<Hello, Tristan. It is late in the afternoon. Zatook had a broth delivered for you, which I have set on your end table for when you are ready to eat.>"

Tristan stared at her for a moment, trying to fathom how she was in his room and whether or not he was seeing another vision. "<Good afternoon, Grandmother,>" Tristan greeted hesitantly. He found the bowl of broth as she had said, so Tristan sat up and wearily retrieved the food. "<Thank you for bringing the broth. I take it a lot has happened since I came back from training. Possibly while I was away, too?>" He figured he might as well speak with her in Celesi. He could use the practice anyhow after living with non-Celestials for years.

"<Yes, much has happened. And much more is to come.>" While he ate, she filled him in on what she had discussed with the others. She took her time in explaining, giving him time to process what was said and being careful not to overwhelm him since he had just woken.

The information proved a lot to absorb, but Tristan refrained from complaining, simply listening. More would happen? He felt his cheeks flush with embarrassment over his failed transformation, frustration boiling his blood. Still, at least Tristan knew that the Talisman would be sealed again. Perhaps he could try again when there would be no risk of corruption. Tristan sighed heavily and set aside his bowl once he finished the broth. "<I'm glad Captain was able to free you even if only mostly, and thank you for the help you've already given us,>" said Tristan sincerely.

Aria inclined her head. "<The rest may yet be broken, but for now that is unimportant. As charming as my sanctuary can be, I'd rather not spend the rest of eternity there.>" She smirked slightly. "<And I rather do enjoy having the chance to speak with you, rather than just flash a bunch of pictures through your head.>"

Tristan managed a small smile. "<I'm glad I have the chance to get to know you. I knew you had been sealed away, but my father didn't know where. He was reluctant to talk about you and my grandfather other than to remind me that I'm descended from two powerful Celestials. Takumi and Feray told me about you, though. About your adventures with Uncle Zetta and his sister. I also know that I was named after my grandfather: Trystan ShadowVeil,>" Tristan told Aria. His smile fell as he considered everything that had happened. "<I imagine you

know of my mother's fate? Of my sister, Arianna? And my father's part in both. I can't imagine how heavy that knowledge is for you to bear. And Amaya can't be here because of the king. So, you're free but still separated from your family.>"

"<Most of my family. But Shaddai has graced me with your presence for a time, and I shall not remain separated forever.>" She leaned back in her chair, crossing her legs as she considered. "<I am used to bearing sad tidings, but I am not burdened to See only sad things. I find balance, and I remain patient.>"

"<I'm trying,>" Tristan admitted softly. "<I'm mostly failing. I couldn't even transform right. And...it's just been a lot. But I'm trying to keep moving forward. Nothing good will come of me becoming stagnant. I'm glad, though, that I got to meet you.>"

"<Your transformation's corruption is through no fault of your own,>" Aria noted briskly, twining her fingers together in her lap. "<It is a consequence of carrying a very dangerous item, and there is no guarantee you would not have struggled even if the seal was still intact. You carry an artifact of great destructive power twined within your very essence.>" Her expression softened. "<Not everything has been a failure, Tristan. And even our mistakes Shaddai can turn to His purpose.>"

Tristan averted his gaze, not really believing Aria. Reina had been able to transform while she had the Talisman, so Tristan had thought it would be all right. He hadn't thought about how horribly a Celestial's transformation could go or how the Talisman could influence it. Tannen had tried to warn him. Instead of voicing his thoughts,

Tristan asked softly, "<I know that you were sealed, but I don't really know why. Do you mind telling me?>"

Aria was quiet for a moment, though Tristan could guess by the far-off gaze that she was considering her words. "<A very long time ago, a group of humans grew discontent. Their ire turned to Celestials and other beings they deemed unnatural to the realm, including those who could draw on magic. For example, Drow were safe, as their magic was tied to their being, but mages and wizards were hunted as they learned to manipulate the world around them. Their hatred steadily poisoned other minds and spread. Celestials were not all innocent in this, mind. There were those who despised humans, and there were those with other ambitions who simply took advantage of the chaos. One in particular sought both to bring other races to heel and to take the Celestial throne.>" She paused, gaze lost to memory.

"<Some of his plans succeeded. While he was not able to ascend the throne, he managed to arrange the death of King Pax. When the dust settled, another needed to take his place. King Pax's eldest daughter was the popular choice, but she declined. Eventually another was nominated and ascended...but he was wary of what had happened, and deemed that Celestials should not only hide themselves from humans, but avoid them completely. It was not yet a law so much as a caution.>"

"<His wariness was understandable, but his paranoia only grew over time. He started trying to limit what we could do, who could go where, who could live where. Many of us disagreed with his decisions and attempted to provide counsel, but he would hear nothing of it. He started punishing any who criticized him, even naming some

Forsaken and sealing them away. He stopped admitting visitors outside of his circle.>" She shook her head. "<And then he tried to tell us that we were no longer allowed to be in the Mortal Realm, even if we lived there. He decreed that Celestials were not allowed to love humans, marry them, or remain married to them.>" She sighed. "<It had been eighteen hundred years since the Purge and the war, yet his heart remained hardened to Shaddai and any who disagreed with him. The last straw came when he sealed a dear friend away. Those of us who fought in the Purge did not do so to suffer further under a tyrant king. So we did what was left: we rallied others. We fought. And we lost.>"

Tristan recalled the mention of the Purge from King Zetta's journal. "<King Zetta recorded in his journal about the Purge and the war it started,>" he affirmed. "<I've read through some of it, but it…it was horrible. I can understand the Celestial king's wariness, but from your recounting, he took things too far. And you were sealed as punishment for standing against him?>" Tristan's mind went to what Corianne had told him of her husband. "<Queen Corianne told me about her husband, and how they met. That he's a Forsaken but not really by his own fault. We know he's in the locket that the queen wears, but we're waiting for the right time to try to break the seal.>"

Aria's expression had softened when he mentioned Zetta, but it smoothed to an unreadable calm as he continued. "<Forsakens…>" Aria paused, considering her words carefully. "<The term itself is complicated. A Forsaken can be named such by where they fall in history more so than anything they brought on themselves. I could easily have been named such prior to my sealing, but even our foolhardy king recognized the place I held in our society. Doing so would only have fueled the rebellion rather than

crushed it. Some Forsakens are driven by their own lusts for power or grandeur, whereas others fell on the wrong side of politics. Zex…struggled. He always had a temper, and his rivals knew just how to set it off. He also did not tolerate anything he considered foolish, often taking things in his own hands. But the prison where he was kept…>" Aria sighed. "<It never should have been created. It should never be used. And yet Celestials continue to be sealed there, exposed to the madness. There are some ways to protect against the taint, but Innovation herself is not powerful enough to guard everyone within.>" She shook her head, but when she spoke again it wasn't on the prison she had mentioned. "<Even some Fallens are victims of circumstance, but they threw away their allegiance to Shaddai and cast off His ways. Some accept their newfound role as villain and lose themselves to it. Misguided or no, victims of circumstance or no, they must take accountability for their actions and return to Shaddai before they can be redeemed and Fallen no longer.>"

"<I'm surprised my father hasn't been branded a Fallen or a Forsaken,>" Tristan bitterly remarked. "<Perhaps in his own way, my father believes he's following Shaddai's Will. Though, I can't understand how he believes that killing my mother and my sister would be something Shaddai would want.>" Thoughts of his father turned to thoughts of his aunts. "<I wish I knew how to contact Aunt Hoshiko so she could speak with Captain and offer insight into their similar gifts. Then again, Aunt Hoshiko probably already knows and can't get involved yet. Or maybe she's waiting for us to leave Andor. Aunt Hoshiko told Amaya not to go to Nikko Mori after my mother's death— that Arianna and I were in good hands.>"

"<The king has not yet taken notice of your father or

current events in the Mortal Realm,>" Aria noted. "<There are other forces at work to undermine him, and the man is not as omniscient as he would like. Even Lady Mythril has started skirting his orders more. I think she regrets not taking her father's place, but she also senses the change that is coming.>" She paused. "<I do not know how practiced you are in reaching for telepaths. Considering the great distance, it could be too heavy a strain. Were I not limited, I could reach anyone in Aviyah— perhaps even my friend beyond the Mists. But too much of my curse remains, and I cannot seek out other Celestials; they must come to me in Andor, as you have.>"

"<Aunt Hoshiko reached out to me at Keep Shadow Veil, I think. However, I mostly just had my sister who was an empath not a telepath,>" Tristan replied. He sighed as he thought about everything he had learned. "<I wish I knew more or at least knew what to expect. I wish I could do more for Zatook and for Rose.>"

"<Having a telepath reach out to you will not cause the same strain as attempting to reach one as a non-telepath. Rose and I could help you practice; however, with everything that is about to pass... I believe it would be best to wait. As for Rose and Zatook: you have done much for them both and will have many chances to do more,>" she assured him.

"<I feel like I've just caused more trouble for them both,>" Tristan said softly.

Aria actually snorted. "<The only trouble you're causing Zatook is the good kind,>" she noted flatly. "<The man is actively standing up for himself and caring about people other than his sister. He's five hundred and twelve years

old yet has only actively cared for one person outside of his family before Tannen and Halia came along. And he has yet to risk transforming to speak with those two. As for Rose, she is no stranger to trouble, and she rather actively chose yours to the point she refused to die until she could save you. Zatook is positively doting on you, and Rose adores you. And they're both just as caught up in the trouble they bring. But if you three— no, if your *entire group* keeps letting their respective troubles chase them away from each other, then how do you plan to save each other and face the challenges ahead? There are large and powerful forces at work that threaten you all, and they will happily take advantage of your doubts and concerns to drive you all further apart. Trouble is going to be ever-present for your foreseeable future; you must not let it drag you down or keep you from enjoying the time you have with your friends.>"

Tristan opened his mouth to say something but then decided against it. He pressed his lips into a thin line and looked away, feeling both encouraged and admonished. What more could he do? If his grandmother could See as much as she claimed, then surely she had seen how the group was trying to be there for each other. Trying to find strength in each other and spend time together. Tristan planned to help Rose once he knew what he was supposed to do. And yet it felt like every time he moved one step forward he ended up shoved three steps back.

"<Tristan. Look at me. Zatook has practically adopted you, and Rose has all but married you. Solomon is basically the acting father of the group, and Captain is trying to live up to her title. Lancelot is trying to find his place outside of being a knight. You all bring your own trouble— Captain's curse could send her destructive magic out of control to

devastating effects. Zatook has a parasite for a stepfather who is more concerned with his own little stage play of a kingdom than actually sparing his favorite test subject to help save the world. Jabez is at war with a secret organization, and Rose has a psychopathic family member who wants the worst for her. You guard a dangerous object created from the blood of an Original and some of the fellest magics known to the Realms. You will have setbacks, all of you. But you will also have victories, and you have allies through it all. You need to accept that they are sharing these burdens willingly, just as you wish to share theirs. You want to save Rose as badly as she wanted to save you. You want to save Zatook as badly as he wants to help you reach your full potential. It is not about any of you causing trouble for the others; it is about sharing that trouble and facing it *together*.>"

"<That's exaggerating the sentiments a bit,>" muttered Tristan regarding Aria's comments about Zatook adopting him and Rose wanting to marry him. Tristan blushed profusely and decided not to let himself dwell on the ideas. "<We've been trying to be there for each other. I can tell everyone has been acting outside what makes them comfortable, and we've all been trying to support each other. I don't really know what more we can do.>"

"<I'm not telling you to do more. I'm telling you to stop blaming yourself for the trouble that comes in your wake, same as the others. You have all taken on each others' burdens. It is part of being allies, let alone friends.>"

Tristan sighed heavily as he fiddled with the blanket covering his legs. "<It's hard not to blame myself,>" he admitted. "<I keep trying to remind myself that my father's actions are not my doing even if he is doing them

to get to me.>"

"<You have much to do without bearing the sins of your father,>" Aria noted somewhat more gently.

For a moment, Tristan sat in silence, mulling over her words and his own thoughts. "<You mentioned training Captain. Is there an easier way for you to communicate with her, or will you need a translator? I can help while I'm recovering and later when I'm not training with Tannen,>" he offered quietly.

"<The offer is appreciated, but we shouldn't need words to Weave. I might ask that you do so when Rose and I are practicing with the Celesbane, however.>"

Tristan nodded. He spoke with his grandmother for a long while before, eventually, lying down again to let his body rest.

*****

The next morning, Tristan managed to leave his room to have breakfast with the group. He looked better than he had but still seemed weary. Just freshening up some had taken a lot out of him. Still, Tristan retrieved his food and sat beside Rose, greeting her and the others quietly. Glancing around, Tristan didn't see his grandmother, but Jabez explained that she had gone to see the king and the queen regarding the upcoming war with Nocis.

After a bit, Tristan asked Alconai and Captain, "So you two found the way to the oracle's chamber yesterday? Thank you for freeing my grandmother." He said the last part specifically to Captain.

"Aye, Cap'n found t'e passage and freed Lady Aria," Alconai confirmed. "I was just along fer t'e walk." He winked at Captain. "I'll be headin' back ta t'e library once I be finished with breakfast. I can show Jabie and Sol where the passage be that led ta t'e chamber fer t'e oracle. Nae much ta see, but they might see somethin' I wouldnae consider important. Might as well take another look seein' as we be in deep already."

"Did you get to see where the other passage led?" Tristan asked, curious. He hesitated when Alconai stared at him.

"What other passageway?"

"When Zatook took me to see the oracle, there was a passage that branched off the main one," Tristan explained. "You didn't see it?"

Alconai looked at Captain. "I mean, I was payin' more attention ta what Captain be followin', but I remember t'e corridor we be in was solid all t'e way ta t'e room."

"Solid all t'e way," Captain confirmed, though the look on her face betrayed that she didn't believe her own words. "We've already seen a movin' bookcase, though. An' t'is place be full o' magic." She wrinkled her nose. "I cannae see it bein' too difficult ta fake a wall an' get away wit' it." Rose was watching her now. She could practically see the girl's mind spinning.

"What are you thinking, Captain?"

"Tha' t'e only difference between when Tris wen' down an' when we did was Zatook," Captain answered bluntly before taking a bite of her biscuit. "Though i' coulda jus' been hidden after t'e king foun' ye 'cause he didnae wan' us exploring."

"I be imaginin', t'e king be cursin' takin' us in," commented Alconai with a laugh. "Jabie and I can take a look. See if'n t'e king has any other nasty surprises fer us."

"I could come with. It wouldn't be doing much to stand watch," Tristan offered, but Alconai shook his head.

"Once ye be done with breakfast, ye need ta either be restin' in bed or on t'e couch. And ye already be in hot water with t'e king. Let us handle this for now. If we need ye, we'll fetch ye," the entertainer insisted. "We also donnae want too big a group goin' down there." Reluctantly, Tristan inclined his head in understanding.

"If he ainnae cursin' us yet, 'e will be," Captain grumbled into her breakfast. Rose laughed at that, even as she slid a hand to Tristan's in silent comfort.

Alconai chuckled at the remark. He finished his food and drink before standing to leave. "Rest up, younglings." With a flamboyant bow, Alconai motioned for Jabez and Solomon to follow him as he headed for the library once more. Despite his brother's urging, Jabez took his time to finish his breakfast before he followed with Solomon.

Once they reached the library, Alconai walked straight to the bookcase Captain and he had found the previous day.

Alconai started checking the bookcase to make sure the wards that he took down hadn't been replaced. "Oi yosh, that be what I be afraid of. T'e king's replaced t'e wards I took down before and made sure I cannae do t'e same trick twice," Alcoani told Jabez as the man approached. When Jabez nudged him gently with his hand, Alconai stepped aside so his brother could take a look.

Jabez studied the structure for a moment as Alconai pointed out the wards he had tampered with previously. Digging into a pouch, Jabez pulled out two flat crystal discs. Holding one up to the runes for the ward on the stationary bookshelf, Jabez watched as a rune began to glow on the disc. As he released the crystal, it remained hovering in the air in front of the ward. Then Jabez moved to the ward on the moving bookshelf and did the same with the second disc. "Carefully walk between the discs. They're currently mirroring the ward magic to trick them," the ninja told Alconai and Solomon.

Alconai stared between Jabez and the crystals. "Ye just happen ta have a pair o' crystals what can deflect wardin' magic?" he asked incredulously.

Jabez shrugged as he answered, "When you spend years breaking into magically guarded buildings, you learn quickly or you die."

"I would say somethin' about that bein' harsh, but ye're nae wrong."

Silently, Jabez opened the passage and walked between the crystals into the corridor proper. He pulled out another crystal and cupped it in his hands. As he blew on it, a faint glow illuminated the insides of his hands before becoming bright enough to light the way. Alconai snorted but smiled seeing his brother in his element.

"Ye've picked up a few tricks," commented Alconai appraisingly. Jabez glanced back at him, his eyes twinkling being evidence of a smile beneath his mask. Jabez then moved down the passage while carefully studying the walls for any kind of seam or something amiss with the stonework.

Solomon watched them work in silence. He glanced back out at the library, frowning. "You two go on. I'll stay up here in case anyone comes poking around looking for us, then I can signal you. Goodness knows I am not one for stealth— I could not even sneak through Nikko Mori." He glanced at Jabez and jerked a thumb at the crystal discs. "Do I just pull them down if I need to hide where you have gone?"

"Yeah. Just be careful not to trigger the wards while you move the discs. To put them up again, hold one disc in front of the ward until you see the glyph reflected, then do the same with the other," explained Jabez.

"I'll bring him back in one piece, Papa, donnae ye worry," Alconai joked to Solomon before following Jabez. He found Jabez already stopped partway down the passage, studying a section of the wall. "Found our branch?" Alconai inquired. Jabez nodded.

"I believe so."

"Got anymore o' those fancy crystals or other tools o' t'e trade?"

Jabez snorted before remarking, "They're not that rare or fancy. You can pick them up in most markets that have vendors selling magic items."

"They just be sellin' t'e kind o' crystals to trick wards?"

"No. These are repurposed warding crystals."

Alconai looked at his brother, stunned. "Ye ken how to repurpose wardin' crystals? Ye learn magic or somethin' in yer travels?" he asked.

"*I* don't know how to repurpose them, but you can pay mages to do it. Or nick them from other ninja in a pinch," Jabez remarked nonchalantly.

Now, Alconai stared at his brother as though Jabez had lost all sense. "Ye pinch from other ninjas? What happened ta layin' low so they donnae catch ye?" he questioned.

"What happened to the stealth part of this stealth mission?" Jabez snarked quietly.

"Excuse me, Lord Ninja. I donnae have t'e 'nae' fancy crystals ta trick t'e wards that more than like be waitin' ta trigger here," Alconai remarked in hushed exasperation. Jabez leveled a look at him.

"It's a wonder you and Captain didn't alert the whole castle when you came down here."

"We did. T'e king found us when we left t'e orb after freein' t'e oracle," Alconai spoke with his hands as well as his words, though he managed to keep his voice quiet. He glared when Jabez released a long-suffering sigh.

"All right, all right. Let's keep moving before we alert people with our squabbling." Alconai arched an eyebrow at Jabez's comment.

"Oh, Jabie, if this had been a true squabble, we'd be rolling down t'e passage already, stealth thrown ta t'e four winds."

Jabez rolled his eyes as he pulled out two more crystals. "As if you could catch me in a tackle, *Nai.* I'm still your older brother, and I know how to put you in your place," he countered.

"Oh, that be a challenge if'n I ever heard one. We be sparrin' later for sure," Alconai clapped back. He fell silent for a bit while he watched Jabez's hands pass through the illusion of the wall. Jabez moved carefully to find the right spots for the wards without tripping them. "Ye seem to be gettin' around better. I be glad ye've healed up," the entertainer finally said, his tone more sincere.

Without losing concentration, Jabez answered, "I'm alright. Don't tell Sol I said this, but it felt good to test my mettle and find I can still hold my own."

"Me lips be sealed," Alconai agreed quietly. "Watchin' ye train with Sol, ye can more than hold yer own. I still nae be happy ye went toe ta toe with Shaedra solo, but I respect ye ken how ta handle yerself. Ye been fightin' them a while, aye?"

"This isnae really the time to be talking about my encounters with Shaedra," Jabez returned as he set the crystals.

Alconai grinned at the slip. "Oh, Jabie, I could hug ye."

Embarrassed and pointedly keeping his gaze on the wall, Jabez muttered, "Shut up, Nai." With that, he slipped through the wall and the wards. Alconai followed close behind, grinning all the while.

The passage that stretched before the brothers now was well-used. Not even a single cobweb graced the places where wall met ceiling. At first, it was mostly straight, but after a few minutes it curved sharply to the side and started heading downwards. There were scuff marks in the stone of the downward-slanting floor, worn from years of repetitive motion, and pairs of torches lined the hall— though they were currently unlit.

Jabez moved slowly and gracefully along the corridor. His steps stayed silent, the man practically merging with the shadows despite the light he carried. Jabez imagined that for Alconai the light might as well have been a wisp the minstrel was following. Despite the unlit torches signifying the lack of people in the space, a feeling of dread sank into Jabez's stomach. He felt rather sure he knew what they were about to find.

After the pair had been traveling down the path a while, Jabez spied an opening ahead that led into a large stone room. It was rough and simple, a rectangle stretching before them. The door was cut into one of the short walls, and the opposite was barred into a cell. The rest of the room told a rather bleak tale, from the shackles in the wall to the black stains along the floor. Many tools Jabez recognized all too well hung from the walls or were arranged neatly on a nearby table. A now-familiar purple metal twined with the bars on the cell, the chains in the wall, and even a few of the blades. Crystal lanterns hung from the ceiling, and a fireplace that used enchanted coals was set into the long wall across from the chains.

Jabez fought to keep his breathing silent and steady. He felt a spike of anger as he studied the torture chamber. Given the presence of the Celesbane and from what he had seen in Traiborn's study, Jabez deduced the more specific purpose of the room.

"This is where Traiborn punishes Zatook," Jabez noted, his quiet voice sounding loud in the stillness. He heard Alconai's sharp intake of breath behind him.

"Oh I want ta throttle t'e man, but that would be too light a punishment," Alconai bit out as he moved more into the room.

Jabez forced himself to survey the room further even as another emotion overpowered all else: fear. His hand clenched into a fist against his hip as Jabez felt a cold sweat break out across his skin. In his mind, he pictured gray skies over open seas as he reminded himself that he wasn't *there*. He wasn't safe, but he was free. The crystal in his hand lit the place too dimly and washed it in the wrong color. Shaedra's holding cells glowed in a blue-white luminescence. A hand gripping his shoulder tightly helped to ground Jabez in the present. He glanced back to see Alconai's steely gaze. Jabez figured Alconai's grip was meant to keep the entertainer in check more than to keep Jabez from acting foolishly. Carefully reaching up, Jabez squeezed his brother's hand in understanding. Leaving Alconai's hold, Jabez moved farther into the room, trying to look at things objectively and keep his mind distant from the memories trying to overshadow him.

Jabez paused as he came to the section with chains in the wall. Try as he might, he couldn't escape the phantom feel of shackles around his own wrists, cold metal digging harshly into his skin. As he took in the crystal and the implements of torture and other tools, Jabez knew this chamber wasn't just for punishment. Before he could stop himself, Jabez imagined Zatook chained and bleeding while the king fed the shadow warrior lies about Zatook's worth.

"You are a shadow. A tool. A weapon forged and wielded by our master. When you do walk in the sunlight, you do so only to cast a deeper shadow," whispers echoed through Jabez's mind. Sweat dampened his clothes as cold chills wracked his body. The open room suddenly felt crowded as memories and sensations and emotions flooded Jabez. He leaned heavily against the wall and scrabbled at the stones as though a physical grip would keep him from slipping into the prison of his own mind. Every scar— faded or permanent —ached with the memory of blades cutting and piercing his flesh during his own acts of rebellion. Brands and acid and all manner of torture seared into his soul only to be healed to leave no distinguishing marks. Words filling his ears and mind with poison to crush all embers of hope in his soul. Left in darkness to become the shadow.

Hands gripped his shoulders for a moment, Jabez barely feeling them through the haze clouding his senses. The hands slipped under his arms as strong arms wrapped around his torso and pulled, forcing his feet to move. Jabez's own breathing filled his ears. The golden light from the disc shifted to blue-white illumination, and the air felt colder. He was being marched somewhere. To a holding cell, to the torture rack. To his punishment. He had rebelled again, hadn't he? Jabez had to keep fighting— to hold onto his sense of self —but he was slipping. He couldn't hold out much longer— he knew —but he had to try. For Alconai's sake. For Father's. For Mother. For his own sake.

Alconai all but carried his silent brother back up the stairs and up the passage. Why hadn't he considered what they would find? How it might affect Jabez? The meaning behind his brother's reaction made Alconai's blood boil even as he felt sick. The change had been so subtle, Alconai almost missed it. Jabez had gone so still and silent, Alconai thought he was simply trying to blend in with the shadows. However, his brother's grip nearly crushing Alconai's hand, and then Jabez leaning and scratching against the wall between the chains alerted Alconai to something being wrong. Now, it took everything Alconai had to keep Jabez moving. Jabez alternated wanting to collapse completely to trying to bolt wildly. Alconai kept a firm grip on Jabez to keep him from breaking their cover. As much as it troubled him, Alconai felt grateful that Jabez stayed silent. The minstrel had no idea what he would do if his brother started screaming.

When they reached the entrance to the corridor, Alconai realized another problem. Jabez wasn't lucid enough to retrieve the crystals, and Alconai had his hands full. By the time they reached the main passage, Jabez had stopped trying to bolt, but now the man was barely moving on his own. One look at Jabez's blank expression told Alconai that his brother was too far into his memories. Alconai could only imagine what had happened to Jabez to cause such an extreme reaction.

"Jabie?" Alconai tried because he wasn't sure what else to do. "Jabie, come on, bruddeh. I need ye. I cannae grab t'e crystals and hold on ta ye." Jabez just continued to stare dead-eyed. Alconai's heart broke at the sight. "Oi yosh, Jabie. All right. We be gettin' ye ta Sol, aye? I'll come back fer t'e crystals. Donnae ye worry. Little bruddeh's got ye." He rubbed Jabez's chest soothingly for a moment. Then Alconai shifted them into the main corridor. As he debated how best to get his brother up the stairs, Alconai startled when Jabez reached over to one of the crystals and pulled it away from the ward. "Jabez?" The man lifted his head just enough to acknowledge he'd heard Alconai. He then nudged Alconai to walk him over to the other crystal, retrieving it as well.

Jabez's vision swam, and he felt sick. Moving exhausted him, but with Alconai's help he managed to reach the bookshelf entrance and retrieve the last two crystals. Jabez leaned heavily, shakily against his brother. All he wanted was to let his heavy body collapse. Even with his mind slowly wading out of the amalgamation of memories, Jabez found moving his body and trying to speak impossible tasks.

"Solomon," Alconai called quietly to the pirate. "He be in a bad way. I donnae ken what ta do." The entertainer looked truly at a loss.

Alconai heard a book snap shut, and soon enough he saw Solomon coming around the corner. His expression was solemn as he gently claimed Jabez and picked him up to carry him. "Lead the way back, make sure no one else is coming," he instructed Alconai softly. "I don't think he's in a state to lash out, but I certainly know he would rather not be seen. I've got him." He followed Alconai to the double doors, letting the lad check to see if anyone was coming before following him out into the hall. He spoke softly to Jabez, both working to soothe and encourage as they made their way through the palace. Solomon was rather surprised they didn't run into so much as a servant during their trek, but he was also grateful. The guest parlor was empty as well, though Alconai spied a note from Captain on the table that they had decided to visit the stables for a change in scenery. Once they made their way to Jabez's room, there was a tray of tea waiting for them on the nightstand. Solomon got Jabez situated on the bed and sat beside him, gently stroking his hair.

"I can guess what you found," he noted grimly. "And I would hazard a guess Captain knows as well," he added, gesturing to the tea.

Through all of it, Jabez's breathing grew more and more unsteady. It took everything in him to remember the breathing techniques he'd learned to calm himself. Jabez forced himself to focus on the sensations around him. His hands gripped the soft blanket beneath him. Fresher air from the room entered his lungs. Details came into sharper relief, and Jabez fixated on them to claw his way back to full awareness. Shakily, he reached out and gripped fabric he knew would be there, feeling the familiar thread of Solomon's vest. Jabez was vaguely aware of Alconai's presence. Jabez wanted to reach out for his brother, but he was still having issues getting his body to move like he wanted. A wheeze escaped him as Jabez tried to speak— to explain, to apologize, anything.

Alconai watched his brother from a distance. He wasn't sure how to help or if anything he tried would just make things worse. As Solomon tended to Jabez, Alconai asked, "Should I leave?" He didn't want to leave his brother. The blankness in Jabez's eyes gave way to anguished despair. Alconai wanted nothing more than to hold his brother and chase away the nightmares plaguing him.

"You are welcome to stay. In fact, he may prefer it," Solomon assured him, lifting his other hand to hold the one clasping his vest as he gently hushed Jabez. "It is all right, Jabez. You do not need to explain. We understand," he assured him softly. "You are safe." He nodded for Alconai to pull over the chair in the room if he didn't want to stay standing. "Breathe, Jabez. Close your eyes, and return to Ben-Gal. Your place of peace. Smell the beeswax candles scattered through the libraries. The age-old papers. Listen to the soft scratching of the quills. Soft, yellow light. The warmth of the sun baking through the curtains used to protect the books from the sands."

Slowly Jabez managed a nod and stopped trying to force himself to speak. Instead, he concentrated on getting his breathing under control and letting go of the anxiety squeezing his chest. His grip remained on Solomon's vest as Jabez tried to calm, using the feel of Solomon's hands and his voice as anchors.

Alconai moved closer to the bed but still gave his brother space. He opened his mouth to say something, but then closed it, afraid anything he might say would send Jabez back into the spiral. Alconai sat in the chair and made sure to be in his brother's sight. Silently, Alconai prayed to the Sacreds for his brother.

"The scent of herbs in Mist's clinic," the words Jabez spoke so softly they were almost inaudible. He closed his eyes as he let himself drift into different memories. "Light catching her white hair like sunlight on freshly fallen snow. The warmth and softness of Graphite's fur beneath my hand. The clacking of Graphite's claws on the floor." His breathing evened out, and his face relaxed, the tension gradually leaving his body. Releasing Solomon's vest, Jabez lowered his arm to the bed and continued working to soothe his stressed body. "I'm rather certain we found where the king punishes Zatook, and I think Traiborn experiments on him." Jabez's voice sounded tired but stronger.

From his perch, Alconai silently arched an eyebrow. At any other time, he'd be pressing his brother for details about this Mist and Graphite, but for now the entertainer kept his peace. Relief loosened the knot of anxiety in his chest as he watched Jabez relax.

Solomon sighed. "I wish I could express surprise at the idea," he confessed softly. "But we already knew Traiborn does not view Zatook as a person, and he has always had the mind of a researcher— if not one bound by ethics." He ran his hand down his face. Was there really anything to be done with this information? "For now, at least, we know he is not down there. Traiborn has been keeping him busy watching Nocis; that will likely continue with Aria's warnings."

"I think the king is experimenting on Zatook with the Celesbane. What better way to find out the workings and potential of a bane to Celestials than using one to test it," Jabez ground out. Slowly, carefully, he lifted himself to a sitting position. Jabez shifted and leaned back against the headboard beside Solomon.

"Donnae ye push yerself, Jabie," Alconai gently warned.

"I'm doing better. I'll take it easy for a bit," the ninja assured.

Alconai watched him for a moment before asking, "That wasnae a full relapse, was it?" Jabez shook his head.

"No, and I hope you never see me get that bad." Jabez glanced at Solomon beside him. "Usually, Sol can keep me from causing too much damage." His gaze shifted back to Alconai as he added, "But if for some reason Sol or Amaya aren't around and I completely lose my senses, you take the kids and *run*."

"Ye ken neither them nor I be leavin' ye in that state," Alconai protested, his brow furrowing in confusion and concern.

"I won't know any of you, and I'll attack anyone who tries to get near me. I don't want them to go through that."

"Jabez," Alconai's tone turned sharp. "I nae be makin' any such promise 'cause I nae be leavin' ye when ye need me. Nae again."

"Their safety and sanity are more important than mine."

"Why we even be talkin' hypotheticals— ye came out o' it on yer own. Ye be stronger than ye give yerself credit, and I donnae mean just physically," insisted Alconai. "Ye wouldnae hurt us."

"I'm nae talking physically, Nai," Jabez urged quietly, his dialect coming back slightly in his stress. "I donnae want to put any of you through having to see me crazed. Enough people have seen it as is, and it's an ugly, ugly thing."

Alconai kept his gaze locked with Jabez's as he spoke, "Have a bit more faith in us, aye?"

"You know as well as I that Isabella will not leave you, either," Solomon pointed out. "Do you honestly think she would let Alconai pull her away? All of our allies are fully capable of making their own decision to try and help."

"It be how we be gettin' through all this, Jabie," Alconai agreed, "together. Sharin' our burdens and helpin' each other." Jabez sighed but didn't try to argue.

Jabez leaned his head back against the headboard, his body and mind tired from the ordeal. "There's not much to do with the information we gleaned. We already knew Traiborn was mistreating Zatook, and we are not yet in a position to do anything about it," Jabez mused aloud to get back on track.

"We prepare as best we can, and at least part o' that means goin' shoppin' in town," Alconai agreed. He watched his brother for a moment. "Now then, who be this Mist, eh?" Alconai waggled his eyebrows mischievously.

Jabez rolled his own eyes as he replied, "One of the healers I befriended at Ben-Gal. Or rather she befriended me." Alconai nodded but his smile remained.

"Right," remarked Alconai, "yer friend with white hair that reflects light like sunlight on freshly fallen snow."

"Shut up, Nai," Jabez countered, his face warming under his mask. Alconai's grin just grew.

Solomon had turned to pour them some tea, hiding his own amused expression. "And Graphite is her guardian wolf," he added. "Though, calling her a wolf doesn't really do her justice. She is much larger than what most humans have encountered, and she can speak."

"After everythin' we been seein' and who we been meetin', I nae be surprised ye ken a healer with a large, talkin' wolf," remarked Alconai dryly. He smirked at Jabez as his older brother ignored him. Alconai's smile faded a bit when Jabez held up his hand to decline the tea.

Sol handed the cup to Alconai instead, then poured a spare for Jabez and left it under the heat shield with the kettle before leaning back with his own cup. "You know Captain will try to pour it down your throat if she finds out," he teased. "Though judging by her note, she'll be keeping the others away for a little while. Perhaps the trip to town can help with that, as well."

"I'll drink it later," Jabez told him tiredly.

"When I nae be in t'e room," commented Alconai, though his tone held no accusation. He noted Jabez's wince. "I can look away."

"It's not just you. I don't think I can handle taking the mask off right now even if I was alone," Jabez explained.

"I'm feeling better but not fully stable. I'll be alright, so take Captain into town. Both of you would probably like to see more than just the castle."

Alconai rolled his eyes before answering, "We'll go soon enough." He drank his tea while he continued to sit with Jabez and Solomon.

23. *Promise Among Petals*

The trip to the stables had started off well enough, and it only got better once the stablehands offered to fetch them some tack so they could go riding. Not knowing the first thing about saddling and riding a horse, Captain had almost declined, but Lancelot offered to teach her. There was a small ring within the castle walls for exercising the steeds, which was the perfect site to teach a new rider. Both insisted that Tristan and Rose needn't stay within the castle on their behalf, encouraging them to go for a full ride.

Lancelot tacked a horse for Rose, and Tristan helped her mount. She felt steady on her own, so Tristan had tacked a second horse for himself and the pair had meandered away from the castle. They attempted to explore the city, but the crowds were dense enough that it was difficult to hear each other, so they moved for the fields beyond. Now, their mounts walked at a steady pace alongside each other. The riders kept Petalore in sight, not wanting to wander too far despite enjoying the change of scenery from the castle.

"I must admit, I was getting tired of being surrounded by stone again— even if sung stone is prettier than the usual grey," Rose joked softly.

Tristan gazed out at the fields, taking in their greenery

and feeling the breeze rustling his hair and clothes. He smiled softly as he spoke, "I miss being in nature. The castle— despite being different —holds too many memories that I'm not ready to face. Stone walls remind me of living with my parents. Being surrounded by nature feels like home and freedom. And yet, I can't help seeing my sister everywhere, imagining her curiosity and excitement to see new places and people." He took a deep breath and let it out slowly. His smile remained even though it turned a touch sad. "I'm trying to see everything and take in as many details as I can. Trying to honor her memory by continuing the adventure, I guess. Letting myself feel wonder and excitement. Spending time with new friends and reconnecting with others." Tristan shook his head helplessly. "Sorry. I don't mean to be a downer, or to make our outing about… I want to focus on us and this moment. I just keep getting distracted."

"You have no need to apologize," Rose assured him. "I understand. We have not had much time for stillness, and we know that soon things are going to pick up again. It is hard not to let our minds wander."

Tristan sighed heavily, sounding tired despite his alertness. "I feel a bit like I'm in a tempest. I learned Amaya is my aunt and that Andor's oracle is my grandmother. I don't even know where to begin to process everything," he confessed quietly. "Seeing the way the king treats Zatook reminds me of my recent experience with my own father." He turned to look at Rose. "You've got your own whirlwind of things going on as well. Meeting another Drow whose situation is similar to yours, hearing more about what's become of Jeremiah, and the aftermath of your fight with Marilyn and the fight with my father."

"And whatever Lady Rin has planned for us," Rose added with a light laugh. "One certainly cannot claim our lives are boring." She sighed, closing her eyes and trusting her mount for the moment. "It is nice to meet other Drow-kin— and hear of full Drow, even, who disagree with the Elders. There is no superiority between races. Just people. We have our differences, certainly, and our similarities. A part of me would love to trap my grandmother and Traiborn in a room together and see who comes out on top." She grinned over at him teasingly. "Perhaps they would end each other and rid us of both issues."

Tristan laughed. "I don't really know much about your grandmother, but I imagine that would be a rather intense battle of attrition if nothing else," he commented, still smiling. It felt good to smile after everything, a little weight lifting from him. "I honestly don't know what to make of my own grandmother. Despite being a Celestial, I haven't lived among many of them, so I'm not sure what to expect. I have a bit of a hard time imagining Amaya as Aria's daughter, but I can see some of Aria's temperament in my father. Meeting my grandmother and reading King Zetta's journal makes me wish I could have met my grandfather. He sounded wise, and I can't help wondering what he would have done in our situation. Sometimes I wish there was a way for us to speak with the Chosen Children who came before us. What advice would they give us?" Tristan reached down and stroked his horse's mane. "I don't understand peoples' need to feel superior to others. We're all Shaddai's creation— loved equally by Him. Though, I suppose that wouldn't mean as much to those who aren't Followers. Still, it makes me sad to see people judging each other based on prejudices."

Rose shook her head. "You may as well attempt to

understand why people go to war. It's just the way of things, but that doesn't mean we have to fall into the same darkness." She sighed, opening her eyes once more and gazing out over the meadow. "I hope you never have to meet my grandmother. She's a horrible woman. Yours seems much better, spontaneous transformations aside." She chuckled softly. "I had a feeling that wasn't a regular cat, but I couldn't put my finger on why."

"Grandma Aria told me about that," Tristan remarked with a grin. "It's not uncommon for Celestials to have some kind of creature or animal form," he told Rose. He blushed as his smile grew fond at the same time sheepish. "There is a phase for Celestials where our powers can go a bit weird." He lifted his head to look at Rose. "I hit my phase when I was living in the forest with Arianna. For a few days I was stuck as a tiny owl. Of course, Arianna absolutely loved it. Despite how young she was, she still somehow understood the owl was me. Clovestein stayed with us during that time to take care of Arianna until I could get my new ability under control. In the interim, Arianna spoiled me. With advice from Clo and a few of our elven friends, she cared for me as though I was her child. The faeries thought the whole thing was hilarious, and that I was adorable. I was about their size when they changed into their tiny forms, so they liked getting to snuggle into my feathers and ride on my back when I let them. Arianna always made sure not to let them tire me out, though." Tristan rubbed the back of his head. "So, yeah, I have that ability. Once I got a handle on it, I didn't use it much, though, on account of not wanting to leave my sister unattended while I flew."

Rose couldn't help it: she giggled at the mental image of a tiny owl surrounded by faeries. Her expression softened into a smile as she thought of Arianna. "She had quite the caretaker streak. One of the times the Talisman was paining you, she took me flower picking. Well, you knew about part of that." She gestured toward her hair, where the girl had woven a crown of flowers. "But she also picked several herbs and made sure Solomon prepared them for you."

"That sounds like Arianna," Tristan commented. "She wanted to learn, so I tried to teach her as best as I could. We got help from our elven friends and the faeries, too. They loved her eagerness, and she loved learning about the world around her. More than that, I think she wanted to learn how to help when people or animals were hurting in a physical way." Tristan gazed at the flowers as memories continued to surface. "I would have nightmares of our mother's death and of our father from time to time. Somehow, Arianna always sensed when I was sad. I would wake up from the nightmare to see her standing in her crib while she was watching me. And then she would start insisting that I pick her up, no matter how much I might not want to. When she got older and had her own bed, she would just come to me and hug me tight. Every time, I felt her warmth wash over me. I admit, at first, I just thought it was her presence and physical contact that was soothing me. I figured out later that she had the same effect on other people and animals. She used her feelings to soothe the hurts that couldn't be reached physically." He smiled sadly at the memories. "She would have been a good Sun Child. She would have been better at it than me."

"But that was not her title to bear; it is yours," Rose noted gently. "If I were being honest, I am glad it was not hers. I worry what that sort of pressure would have done to temper her innocence and energy. With luck, she could have been like Captain tries to be. But even our sprightly pirate friend has an ever-present sadness clinging to her like cobwebs." Rose sighed, shaking her head. "Though, Arianna could certainly have livened up the current dour atmosphere. I doubt even King Traiborn could resist those bright eyes and that charming little smile."

Tristan snorted at that. "Arianna certainly knew how to wrap people around her little finger. Although, I don't think she ever wanted anything more than to be friends with people," he said. "She also had an uncanny sense when it came to people, so she might not have wanted anything to do with the king. She would have loved the queen, though. And the princess." He breathed deep and slow when his eyes stung, managing to fight back the tears. "I'm glad she got to live a more carefree life. I'm glad she felt safe enough to be so trusting and open with our group. I'm glad she got to meet you. She could tell you were good and trustworthy. That we should help you. Arianna's part of the reason I got involved with your skirmish with Jeremiah."

Rose chuckled. "I still remember the utter incredulity of running across such a fearsome blue ball in the forest," she teased. "I wasn't surprised to hear people actually lived there, more surprised that I saw someone and they were quite so young and carefree."

"Perhaps I let Arianna be too reckless," Tristan groaned, rolling his eyes at the memory. "Cute, innocent girl greeted you, and then you had to deal with her protective brother who was trying so hard not to panic." He smirked at Rose. "I have no idea why you decided to trust me considering the greeting I gave you." His expression grew a bit more somber as he studied her face. "I'm grateful you came for me; though, I don't fully understand why. Why you wanted me to stay when I truly considered turning back. I think maybe I know, but I don't want to misread things. I know why I stayed, and it wasn't just for Arianna's sake."

"You were protective. It was an understandable greeting," she murmured. Her gaze roamed the meadow without really taking it in when he got to why she wanted him to stay. She remembered that evening, Arianna tucked between them. She remembered everything that followed, right up to why she told Lady Rin she couldn't give in to her embrace. But could she admit as much now, with so little time remaining between them? Would that be too much pressure for him to complete the Lady's challenge, whatever it may be?

Then again, if she didn't tell him before she left...she may not have the chance.

The gentle breeze gusted a little stronger, sending a few flower petals and other things swirling through the air. A contemplative silence stretched between them, broken only by the sounds of the meadow and the horses, their tack jingling slightly with their movements.

"I had planned to continue on quickly," Rose confessed softly. "But the forest started helping to hide me, and I wondered if it wouldn't be better to rest while I could. Perhaps the forest could keep them from finding me, and I could see exactly who was following me and how best to avoid them. I knew Jeremiah would be there; I was his, after all. His slave, his protégé, whatever he thought of me..." She shook her head to clear the distracting thoughts. "Nikko Mori seemed content to let me rest a little while, and I had the strongest feeling that I should do so, despite the urgency I had felt before. The further I walked after meeting you, the more I felt pulled to stay. Perhaps it was Shaddai's guidance, perhaps I was simply tired… but I lingered. When Jeremiah and his men drew near, I decided to risk watching them, and then I noticed you watching them as well." She plucked a few seed wisps that had landed on her sleeve, lay them on her palm, and lifted her hand to release them back into the breeze.

"At first, I felt a little guilty that I had not yet left as I had claimed I would. I was going to leave then and there, head straight through. But then Jeremiah detected you, and…I could not just leave you to whatever happened. I kept telling myself I would leave after we got away from the battle, or I would leave after we spoke over tea, or I would leave after the pair of you were asleep, or I would leave in the morning. And I found I did not want to." She paused, watching the seedlings and petals and other things dance in the air. Her blue-and-red gaze found Tristan's sapphire. The wind's dance had caught his tousled hair, the sun's reflection shimmering along the strands. "The longer we were together, the more I knew I did not want to be apart again," she confessed softly.

Tristan's heartbeat quickened. He held Rose's gaze even as he felt his cheeks warm. Dare he say how he felt when so much uncertainty lay before them? However, if he failed in the Challenge, his and Rose's time in Andor would be his last chance. But wouldn't it be selfish of him to make her departure more difficult? Tristan took in how the sunlight illuminated Rose's hair, shining like silver starlight: brilliant and captivating. A hope and reminder of light beyond the darkness. Finally, Tristan responded, "I'm glad you stayed and that you convinced me to stay. I don't know where I would be right now if I had to face Arianna's passing alone. If you hadn't come for me, I would still be under my father's control being forced to do who knows what. So, thank you." Holding the reins in one hand, he held the other out to Rose. Once she placed her hand in his, Tristan carefully bent even as he lifted her hand. He brushed his lips gently against her knuckles. He let the kiss linger a moment before slowly straightening, still holding her hand and her gaze. "I have something I want to tell you, but I'm going to wait. The moment we're reunited, I'll tell you."

Ever-subtle against her slate-grey skin, Rose blushed with the kiss to her hand. She gently squeezed his hand in response to his words. "Then I shall look forward to it," she promised softly.

***

As the morning slipped away, Tristan and Rose steadily made their way back to the stables so they could return to the guest tower with Lance and Captain for a late lunch. Captain had gotten comfortable enough with the horse that Lancelot had mounted another and was riding around the edge of the ring with her. When they saw the pair returning, Lancelot lifted a hand in greeting as they both turned to return to the stable— Captain was gripping her reins in both hands and concentrating. Lancelot taught Captain how to detack her mount and brush out their coat while Tristan tended his own, but the stable hands insisted on handling Rose and Lancelot's so the group could go eat. Despite it having been her first ride, Captain didn't seem incredibly stiff as they walked back through the halls.

Lunch was waiting under heat shields when they arrived, and Solomon, Jabez, and Alconai looked as though they had only recently come to the table themselves. Aria was there, as well. The oracle had found an updated map of the city and was marking certain shops for Alconai. Captain noted with a subtle glance that Jabez didn't have food in front of him, but she didn't comment; it wasn't unusual for him to eat in his room later when he wanted extra privacy. She would just have to make sure he actually ate later.

Alconai studied the points Aria showed him, memorizing them and noting anything of interest along the roads. He glanced up when the others joined, flashing them a smile in greeting.

"Enjoy yer rides?" he asked conversationally.

"The meadows are beautiful, and it was nice to get outside the castle again," answered Tristan. He sat with Rose after they retrieved their food.

"You went trail riding?" Solomon asked as he glanced up from his current scroll, quirking an eyebrow at Captain.

"Nah, jus' t'e two lovebirds." Rose did *not* choke on her water at Captain's comment. "Lance was 'elpin' me figure out 'ow to stay in a saddle in t'e stable's ring."

"She only touched the ground when she wanted to," Lance joked as he dished out some food.

"Aye, wasnae tha' different from keepin' balance on a ship in some ways," Captain confessed. "I migh' try t'e whole trail ridin' thing later if'n we 'ave t'e time. But me feet work just as well."

"What say ye then, Cap'n? Think ye feel up ta adventurin' inta town with me?" Alconai asked. He couldn't resist a slight smile at Rose's reaction to Captain's jab and noted how Tristan blushed.

"Soun's good ta me," Captain agreed brightly. "I havenae 'ad a chance ta get outta t'e castle grounds yet."

"Ah, so now the *other* pair of lovebirds gets a date," Lance jibed with a smirk.

It was Alconai's turn to blush, and he very pointedly did not look over at Solomon or Jabez. Instead, Alconai grabbed some food and busied himself with eating for a moment. Eventually, he commented, "Gettin' outta t'e castle should be a nice change. Especially gettin' away from these hooligans fer a bit." He winked at Captain.

"Pre'y sure we be t'e hooligans," Captain joked right back.

"Nay, we be t'e lovable chirpers," Alconai teased. "Aria be showin' me where ta find t'e potions and other helpful items. Do ye think we can borrow t'e map just in case we be gettin' distracted by t'e town?" He directed his question to Aria.

Aria nodded in response, folding up the parchment and handing it to him once she had finished.

"If you purchase anything while you are out, you can ask the shop to have it delivered," Solomon noted. "Petalore has dedicated couriers to move goods through the city."

"Hopefully, the king won't get paranoid with us stocking up," Jabez remarked dryly.

"I doubt we be havin' any weapons delivered," said Alconai. "But I ken what ye mean. Even stockin' potions can look ta mean we be expectin' trouble of a sort." He took a few bites, chewing contemplatively for a moment. "Should we be worried about t'e ninjas?" Alconai looked over at Jabez, now noting his brother's lack of food. Alconai refrained from saying anything given how stressed Jabez must have been feeling after finding the chamber.

"No more than usual," Jabez answered. "Until declared otherwise, we are under the Royal Family's protection. Shaedra is smart enough to wait until we leave or fall out of good graces with the king."

"Seems ta be a short fall," snarked Alconai.

"<The king is aware enough of what is to come to understand your preparations,>" Aria assured them calmly. She turned her gaze to Rose. "<One thing the king is *not* aware of is that I managed to procure a sliver of the bane crystal,>" she added with a smirk.

"Bane crystal— do you mean the Celesbane?" Tristan inquired. "I might visit Tannen at some point and see about adding some reinforcements to my armor. With the foes we'll be facing and my change in fighting styles, I'll need a little more than just leather, I think."

Aria nodded in response to his question, before noting, "<I believe the princess is looking into having Tannen assigned to you while the other smiths focus on preparing the army's necessities for the upcoming breach. For efficiency's sake, of course.>" She moved to refresh her tea.

"<Traiborn will be distracted strategizing with his generals, but the soldiers and Shaedra will also be more on edge. I do not believe he has told them specifics, but they know war preparations have increased.>"

"We'll be mindful o' Shaedra and t'e soldiers," Alconai promised. "However, if'n t'e king be busy, we should take this opportunity ta head inta town." He set aside his empty dishes and stood. "Whene'er ye be ready, Cap'n."

Leaving the palace remained uneventful, Captain giving the guards at the palace wall a two-fingered salute as they passed under to reach the gently sloped streets of the sung city. They garnered a few passive looks, some of the city folk giving a double take when they noticed Captain was barefoot. They had gotten a decent look at Petalore when they arrived, but sitting in the TekCarriage wasn't quite the same as walking among the crowds surrounded by the vibrant buildings. The weather was incredibly pleasant, so many stores had propped their doors open or raised the curtains hanging in front of open-faced designs like the dyers. They could see more Tek devices as they wandered: boxes for shops that would track purchases and store money, dye shops with self-mixing vats that could work from a sample to recreate a color, beverage machines that would pour for tavern maidens while they took care of their customers, cooking devices that heated without fire. The air practically hummed with magic and

Tek and the sounds of daily living.

Mixed in with the innovative and flashy was traditional. Instrument shops, selling a variety of hand-carved items such as fiddles and cellos; gazebos where bards could perform or people picnic; fountains surrounded by running, giggling children; tailors with a mix of hand sewn clothes and automatic stitching machines. Cobblers hunched over their stations as they hammered together new shoes. Glass blowers carefully tended their craft in furnaces made of metal and glass that could regulate internal temperatures, while the potters next door used a wheel powered by Tek to help throw clay. Captain marveled as the pair walked down the street, making note of various shops and things to investigate while they were out— they had decided to visit the apothecary first and then take their time exploring.

Alconai stared at the marvels of magic. He'd seen magic used throughout Nocis but nothing as grand as these. His eyes lingered on the music shops, his hands missing the familiar weight of his fiddle. While he could play a plethora of instruments as part of his profession, the fiddle had always been his favorite since it allowed him to sing and speak while he played. Shaking his head, Alconai refocused on finding the apothecary.

"Rather grand spectacle this place be," he remarked casually. "All t'e Tek be impressive for sure. If this be what it be like for t'e shops, I wonder what an average house has."

"T'ings usually hit t'e stores first, but I hear tell tha' runnin' water is standard fer houses instead o' jus' 'ere an' t'ere like Nocis. An ye donnae 'ave ta be at t'e palace ta ge' hot water from t'e faucets. No outhouses 'ere, eit'er." One of Captain's hands idly sorted through threads, though she kept it to her side so as not to draw curious gazes. She paused, sniffing the air. "I smell 'erbs," she murmured, turning down a connecting street.

Letting Captain lead, Alconai remarked, "T'e runnin' water be in Nocis, too, though it be nae standard, aye. Lucky ducks nae havin' t'e deal with filthy, smelly outhouses. Though, I wonder what be keepin' waste from stinkin' up their houses. Probably some other Tek or spell."

"T'ere's undergroun' channel-like t'ings wit' spells that 'andle t'e water, though I donnae ken wha' all t'ey do," Captain noted. "Now if only we could ge' plumbin' on ships." She laughed with that one.

Alconai joined her laughter. "Cannae be any worse than it already be, eh?" he joked. "Though if'n ye think about it, t'e ocean be one big chamber pot fer fish." He winked at her with a smile.

"I'd rather nae, thanks," she teased right back. Her gaze scanned the bright painted signs outside the different businesses until she spied the mortar and pestle of an apothecary. "There t'ey be."

"Nice ta ken that no matter how fancy and innovative a place be, there will always be symbols and pictures what mean t'e same no matter t'e place," Alconai remarked cheekily. He entered the shop with Captain and immediately observed the space. His eyes scanned the shelves and labels for health and healing even as he moved through the aisles with Captain. "What ye be thinkin' fer t'e potions we be needin'? Ye bein' t'e expert mixer and all." He flashed her a mischievous smirk.

Captain was scanning the shelves. With an unspecified timeline, she wouldn't want to use a recipe that needed to simmer. Traditional it was, then. There were little vials, containers, and pouches that she could measure into, and she would be charged by weight. "If'n I use t'e vials, I can reuse 'em for t'e actual potions," she noted before snatching a few and moving between the large barrels of powdered ingredients. As she worked to fill the containers, she let Alconai hang onto the ones that were done.

Alconai studied the vials, reading the labels and any descriptions he could find. "How did ye get inta mixin'? It be more on t'e alchemy side o' healin' than herbalism." He watched Captain as she found her ingredients.

"Ye could say s'in me blood," she noted with a laugh. "Me mum's side o' t'e fam'ly, ta be exact. Went through a bit o' time tryin' ta figure ou' *me*, ya ken? So did some Seein' atop learnin' about t'e Doran."

Alconai glanced at the shop owner as he moved closer to Captain. "Would ye be willin' t'e tell me 'bout yer people?" he asked quietly. "I understand if'n ye'd rather not, but I be curious 'bout t'e mysterious Captain."

The shopkeep simply nodded in acknowledgement, currently assisting a customer up at the front till. Captain snorted. "I'm 'ardly tha' mysterious," she teased. "But I wouldnae be against t'e idea. Wha's mine ta tell, a' least. I ken t'ey nae be tellin' much ta ou'siders, though I donnae ken why. I havenae looked inta tha'. I want to meet an elder an' ask 'em in person, ya ken?"

"Some peoples hold their knowledge and traditions in order to protect their people. Some do it just ta be pompous." Alconai gave her a cheeky smirk to indicate the last line was a joke. His smile slipped a little as his thoughts turned to his brother. "And sometimes t'e knowledge be too painful ta bear."

Captain took a moment to answer, weighing out a few items into the vials. "I wonder, too, if'n t'ere be differences between clans," she confessed. "An' jus' 'ow many clans t'ere be. Fer all I ken, t'ere could be more beyon' t'e Mists or even jus' o'er t'e Jaromír Mountains. I mostly looked inta me own clan so far. I ge' caught between jus' Lookin' ta learn an' wantin' ta meet actual people instead o' jus' watching like some creeper." She flashed him a grin before leaning into a barrel that was almost empty to scrape up some of the remaining powder. She wasn't exactly tall, so she had to lift onto her tiptoes to reach.

"I think it be expected to be curious 'bout yer people and t'e clans affiliated with yers," Alconai reasoned. "Mayhap some day ye can explore and track down t'e other clans. Meet more of yer people. At t'e moment, we donnae ken what we be doin' or where we be goin'."

"Oh, I ken where we be goin'," Captain noted lightly, putting a stopper in the last vial. "We be goin' ta pay." She winked at him as she led the way up to the counter where the shopkeep was finishing up with the other customer. After tallying up their order, she waited patiently for Captain to fish out her coin purse. Setting up the delivery was as simple as Solomon said— Captain just told the woman it needed to go to the guest tower at the palace, and the vials were placed in a special carton with a bright pink sticker. To her credit, the shopkeep didn't even flinch when she processed who had just purchased from her. Captain led the way back out to the street before turning a slow circle. "So, where to next?" she mused before looping arms with Alconai again and heading down the street.

The pair chatted as they shopped and browsed, occasionally stopping to watch a street performer or just take in the life of the city. They purchased all of the supplies on their list first before just wandering and enjoying their time together. Eventually they wound their way back to the main street up to the palace gate, but rather than head straight back, Captain meandered her way towards the music shop they had spied earlier in the day.

When he realized their detour, Alconai gave Captain a side-long smirk. As they neared the shop, they heard a shopkeep calling out to passersby on the street, the man showcasing a new violin. The instrument had a few runes carved into it as well as having some Tek with buttons for different enchantments to enhance or change the sound. Some people glanced at the display, and some stopped, but most kept going. His smile growing, Alconai winked at Captain before approaching the shop owner. Introducing himself as a traveling minstrel in the market for a new instrument, Alconai requested to test the violin and see if it would be a good fit for him. The shopkeeper agreed, delighted to have a violinist interested in the new instrument.

Showing his familiarity with the instrument, Alconai easily took up a starting position. At first, he played a few simple chords to get a feel for the special features and tested what the enchantments would do. Then Alconai met Captain's eyes and grinned. Nimbly, one hand swept the bow along the strings while his other fingers pressed the strings and buttons as Alconai played. He used the enchantments to raise the volume so people up and down the street heard the little concert and experimented with the different sounds to grab more attention. Alconai put his whole self into performing, the song lively and familiar even with the new sounds added. After playing a couple verses, Alconai started the song over. This time, he added his own voice to the mix. Once more, Alconai caught Captain's eyes and gestured with his head for her to join him. His feet moved in time with the music as Alconai danced and sang and played. With the invitation, Captain was quick to jump in and join him. She spun and danced, a whirl of colorful cloth and russet hair and beaded bracelets.

The crowd had gathered as Alconai played, grew as he began to sing, and continued to pack the small area around them. Some of the watchers started clapping in time with Captain, while others cheered them on between verses. Alconai relished the audience as he poured his all into the performance. Careful not to impede her, Alconai joined Captain in twirling about the space, dancing with her even as he played and sang. Eventually, he brought the song to a climactic end, striking a pose with Captain. Breathless, Alconai smiled brightly as the crowd cheered and applauded. He handed the violin back to the shop owner and then took Captain's hand before having her bow with him. As the applause died down, the shopkeeper tried to convince Alconai to purchase the instrument— even offering a deal since Alconai's performance brought more customers to the shop. Instead of taking the special instrument, Alconai persuaded the shop owner to part ways with one of the man's traditional violins at a discount price. Even buying the simpler instrument had Alconai grinning 'til his cheeks hurt. It felt good to have a violin again, and Alconai couldn't wait for the next opportunity to perform.

24. *Shards*

The Nocium army had been camped between Caer Talon and the Wall for weeks, and the soldiers were growing restless. To keep them busy, Jeremiah had the generals running them through drills. But there was nothing to be done for StormShaper or the dragon king's enchantress. The Shaper refused to spar with humans, and Jeremiah could not be spared. At least the warrior had his cat; the little beast had been going everywhere with him since Keep Shadow Veil fell. As for Jeremiah's enchantress... Lillith was still trying to talk him out of this war. Normally, he would send her to stay with his daughter, but the pair were currently at odds over this very issue. Shila fully understood Andor had been left alone for far too long, while Lillith saw no use in the war— only loss. But Shila was in Caer Albright, watching over Nocis with her mother, and Lillith was here. Jeremiah knew he would have use of her abilities, and he knew when the time came she would follow his command. But she seemed committed to fighting him right up until the battles began. If the girl were an actual soldier rather than his ward, he would have her face a stricter discipline than simply sending her to her chambers in Caer Talon.

Still. It had been a while. What was Marilyn waiting for? Jeremiah frowned as he oversaw the current set of drills. The sorceress had shut herself away in her tent almost as soon as she arrived, warning him not to interrupt her if he wanted to see the Wall fall. But his patience was wearing thin. Armies were expensive, and right now they only had Nocium supplies to keep things running. He did not appreciate wasted labor. If the woman needed this long, why had she told him to bring the entire army? The incident with Andor's demon and LightningRider had helped calm matters after news of Cryso and Lancelot's desertion had spread, but drills could only keep up the nationalism for so long. He needed *something.* At least a report or some sign of progress.

Even as he thought it, the blood mage did him one better: she stepped outside. The woman had taken to wearing a glamor while they were around the soldiers, looking all the realm like a voluptuous red-headed elven sorceress. She crooked her finger at him even as she stepped out into the path towards the Wall. Jeremiah signaled the generals to wrap up before moving to follow. He stopped when Marilyn held her hand up, the woman crossing the rest of the expanse alone. Jeremiah could hear his men forming up behind him, but he only had eyes for the witch and the Wall. He didn't even look when StormShaper bolted to his side, that long-haired calico of his curled around his shoulders. Jeremiah wasn't worried about the cat if the Wall fell; StormShaper had someone in camp who could take care of it when he was busy, some servant or other in Tsukuyomi's employ that had come along with the warlord's soldiers.

"Has she figured it out, then?"

"Well, she was smiling," Jeremiah noted. StormShaper nodded.

Marilyn had reached the Wall at this point, the metal

solid to her. She smirked as she slid her hand along the smooth surface, her expression widening to a grin when the structure turned bitter cold in an effort to get her to remove her touch. Instead, she crooked her fingers and drove her nails into the metal. Small, spiderweb cracks appeared around her nails; the metal shuddered. She did the same with her other hand, and then she called on her master's magic. The crimson and black lines started small as they filled the cracks, but they gradually spread. Soon, to the soldiers behind Jeremiah, it looked like thick red vines had spread like veins from the mage's hands to cling to the wall. But StormShaper tensed as he sensed the magic she was using. He recognized how it felt. It was the same power that Nightshade had used to shatter the keep, yet the woman seemed to wield it freely.

The entire Wall was shaking now. Ripples danced across its surface as the metal fought the magic, attempting to free itself. But it wasn't going to be enough. "Nothing can withstand my master," Marilyn whispered to the Wall before laughing, a trickle of red slipping from the corner of her mouth. "See how I struggle to contain this power, even as he aids me?" She dug her hands in further, feeling the vines of magic force their roots into the metal in much the same way. Then she braced herself, waited for the magic, and *pulled*.

The Wall exploded outward, chunks of metal shooting across the gap. The ground was covered in pieces, some larger than most boulders and others as small as dust. The metal appearance seemed to melt away, leaving stone in its wake. The Wall quickly moved to try and meld back together, but thick red vines of Ruin wrapped around the jagged edges to keep it from mending. On the other side, the people of Stonewillow were in the street, having been preparing to evacuate before stopping to stare wide-eyed, but they were not undefended. Andorian soldiers had been waiting behind the Wall, standing ready to defend the townsfolk. The sorceress stood in a clear patch of grass, laughing as Jeremiah's men swarmed past her through the Wall's Breach, StormShaper at their lead, his cat safe and sound at camp.

***

Back in Andor, Corianne felt Daisuke's pain immediately. Momentarily forgetting the current audience, she stood and took a step forward, hand lifting to her locket. The chamber stilled as the queen moved, Traiborn raising a hand to pause the current petitioner and watching her. Corianne returned his gaze and nodded. Now Traiborn stood as well, digging into his pocket and pulling out a small coin. He tossed the metal piece into the air, but rather than reach a peak and return, it continued to climb. Once it reached the roof, the metal stuck, and a strange brown energy-like substance seemed to drip from it. It arced away, falling in the shape of a dome around the audience chamber. Anything beyond the dome suddenly took on a sepia hue and seemed to stop moving.

There wasn't so much as a whisper. Many in attendance had only heard of the spell in legend, but they all knew its import. Something was happening, and rapt attention was required.

"The Wall has been breached." Traiborn wasted no time in the announcement. "Generals, priestesses, hasten the preparation and transport of the soldiers. The men at the line should be able to hold for a little while, but we had best provide reinforcements as quickly as we can manage." He turned to the side, snapping his fingers. In a whisk of shadows, Zatook appeared before him. "Go ahead of the others and hold the Wall." The Shadow bowed at the waist before vanishing again. Traiborn turned to the guild representatives. "Merchants. Pass the news to your compatriots: per contracts with the palace, begin sending a portion of your stock to our front lines. Track all expenses for proper reimbursement." Next, his gaze found the representatives of the noble houses. "Nobles. We are officially in wartime operations. Prepare your spare grounds for refugees; speak with palace staff if you need more supplies, and they will put you in touch with the proper resources." His gaze swept the crowds. "My people, do not panic. We knew the dark sorcery was coming, and we have been in preparation. Now, we must come together and face those who would dare darken our threshold with their violence. We all have our roles to play in the coming weeks, and I know you will play them to your best experience. See to your tasks as soon as the veil falls. My queen shall continue seeing to petitioners, but I must adjourn with our generals." Solemn gazes and simple nods met his words, but the instant he snapped again and the brown coloring faded, there was a flurry of movement.

Corianne returned to her throne, steeling herself in the face of the commotion and praying for her son's safety. Once the hall had settled once more, now noticeably more empty, the gentle smile returned to her face as she heard the needs of her people.

***

Zatook wasted no time in reaching the Wall. The soldiers they had managed to prepare thanks to Aria's warning had already engaged Jeremiah's forces. For now, the dragon king was letting humans fight humans; Marilyn was behind the lines with him, as was Lillith. StormShaper, however, was in the thick of it. Zatook quickly adjusted his path, bursting up out of the ground to meet the lightning-wielder's blade and push him away from the Andorian forces. At the sight of the dark warrior, the Andorian forces let out a roar— their king was already aware of what was happening. They would not be alone long.

Jeremiah frowned as he watched Zatook and StormShaper battle. The pair were still rather evenly matched, but StormShaper's preoccupation meant his men had stalled in their advance. Jeremiah himself was waiting to engage, saving his energy for the sorcerer king, but he was not the only trump card in the Nocium army. And they needed to send a message; not just to the hidden king, but to a certain group of refugees Andor was currently harboring.

The presence swept through the troops like a whispering breeze. While the Nocium forces felt bolstered, fear tore through the Andorian soldiers— a familiar power affecting the battlefield. No announcement precluded his arrival. Zatook's blade clashed with another. StormShaper and Zatook found a new fighter between them, a silver mask peering at Zatook with black, eyeless sockets. The man stood tall even as he held a battle stance against the famed Demon of Andor. Sunlight glinted off reflective, silver armor and blazed along the gleaming steel of a katana. Black fabric peeked out from beneath the armor, tattered sleeves and swaths of tunic swaying like shadows. The man wore a black, hooded cloak over the armor with the hood pulled forward. A sigil of a sword with a scarf loosely wrapped around it from hilt to point adorned the man's breastplate: the crest of House Shadow Veil. The man was another of High Lord Tsukuyomi's great warriors whom the lord would send out for battles of great significance. The warrior simply called himself Void.

"StormShaper, command your men and keep pressing the attack," Void ordered in a deep voice. The silver mask's gaze remained on Zatook. The black fabric beneath the armor billowed and lengthened into actual shadows as Void's power manifested. In the reflective surface of the mask Zatook's face held his transformed features.

StormShaper had checked his blade the moment he felt Void arrive. If he held the same complaints at being interrupted in fighting Zatook as he had when Marilyn and Shila were there, he did not voice them. He simply bolted back into the fray to rejoin his soldiers. Zatook frowned at the mask, more so the man than the reflection. While he found it odd that his reflection didn't match his current form, the fact did not seem worth dwelling on. If Void was powerful enough to have command over StormShaper— or at least be equal with him in rank —then Zatook couldn't afford to take him lightly. No distractions. His gaze was calculating as he pushed his sword against Void's to get some space between them. He had yet to ever meet the warrior, so he knew nothing of his abilities. But the mere fact the man was able to hold off his large blade with a katana spoke volumes. Zatook slid his feet back into a fighting stance, letting his shadows wrap about his ankles and wrists. He wouldn't use his powers to attack yet, but he would brace himself for a bit of extra sturdiness.

Void held his stance, only shifting enough to be ready to

attack or defend. "The boy will return to his rightful place. You will fail him, Demon," stated Void coldly. Soldiers' shadows sprung at Zatook, ignoring any attempts the warrior made to control them and landing cuts along his limbs. Void appeared before him with his blade arcing down to slash Zatook across the chest.

Zatook showed no outward response to the taunt, though his frown deepened when Void took the shadows away. He didn't pay too much mind to the cuts for the moment, focusing on stopping the man's blade from dealing a more serious injury. So, his initial assessment had been correct— StormShaper was outranked. And considering the stops he had pulled to face the Shaper before… The shadows along his wrists and ankles stretched to shield him from the ones that were attacking as he and Void started fighting in earnest. He needed to change. His other form had more strength and would be harder to cut, even if Void was able to best him in shadow control. Then, he needed to find a way to get both StormShaper and Void back beyond the border. He had let Amaya know the Wall was breached, and if she was able to come she could either take StormShaper or help him against Void.

Zatook didn't even flinch as a massive volley of magical attacks swept past them to the left; Andorian mages had arrived and were unleashing both their own magic and stored Tek spells to double their impact. Zatook risked a check through his own shadows and noted that several priestesses had arrived as well, some to fight and some to heal. Good. He returned his focus to Void. He leapt back, flaring his wings for some extra distance. The fighting factions had split around the two powerhouses, so he wasn't worried about hitting any soldiers as he shifted into his gargoyle form. He barely got his sword up in time to block Void, the man charging after him to give no quarter.

In his transformed state, Zatook had a better time fending off the man's attacks, so he was able to switch from pure defense to actually fighting back. His own shadows rose to wrangle the ones Void controlled while their blades clashed. The power of their blows led to the armies making an even wider berth around them to try and avoid the aftershocks. Zatook quickly gauged the space from where they were fighting to the Wall. He didn't know exactly where Traiborn would have placed the wards to keep out Amaya, so he wasn't sure how far he would need to push. Then again, at this rate, Void would be determining where they fought— it was all he could do to keep up with the man. Zatook's brow furrowed as he caught his reflection in Void's armor again. It was his human form this time, but not as he was; instead, his coverings were gone, his scars on display. As Void shifted, the image in his armor changed, and Zatook saw himself cradling Aditi's lifeless body.

Red painted his gaze, and the purple in his irises gleamed. He suddenly surged forward with a newfound strength. Purple runes gleamed along his blade, and ribbons of purple light wrapped around his wrists. Zatook didn't hold back the power. He didn't care that it wasn't his to wield. He was getting this man out of his country, past the borders, and he was going to make the journey as painful as possible.

Ribbons of power and runes shot through the shadows while others whipped towards Void. Spells of all manner lashed at the man— ribbons that felt like fire, ribbons that felt like ice, ribbons that would try and crush his bones if they caught hold. Zatook knew he wouldn't be able to keep it up long, so he tried to pour as much power into the blows and spells as possible. Even more ribbons rose like tentacles throughout the battlefield, whisking up Nocium soldiers and throwing them back towards the border. A wave of force was sweeping through the enemy soldiers, pushing them back, back.

The shadows deflected and, in some cases, absorbed the spells. Void proved nimble as well as powerful, keeping pace with Zatook and seeming unfazed by the flare of power. Even so, Zatook gradually forced Void back toward the breach and toward the border. At times, Void's armor reflected the spells back, the damage striking Zatook and any nearby Andorian soldiers. Still, little by little, the Demon of Andor pushed Void back. As soon as Void's backside shifted past the crumpled section of the wall— officially out of Andor —hands gripped his belt through his cloak. He hurled through the air and into the trees. Void flipped and slammed his feet into a tree trunk, rebounding back to the Wall. He landed a few paces away, as between Void and the Wall stood Amaya.

Hair draping her shoulders in wavy, ebony tresses, Amaya's silver gaze flashed with fury. In addition to her usual dark attire, she now wore a black jacket. Despite standing tall, sweat dampened her face already, her hair and clothes clinging to her. Her hands trembled, and her jaw clenched. Amaya held a determined stance even as she fought to choke down the pain coursing through her body. She had felt the power despite being far from Andor. Whatever magic breached the Wall resonated with the wounds marring her body. Hoshiko had begged Amaya not to join the fight, but Amaya couldn't ignore the implications of the power she had felt or Zatook's message. She knew who would be at the breach.

"Hiyah, Tsuk," Amaya greeted her brother coldly. Void regarded her with his masked gaze.

"Amaya, I'm genuinely glad you didn't fail my expectations," greeted Tsukuyomi, his voice changing just slightly from the one he used as Void. "You have always been a protector, dear sister, even when you are barely standing. I'm curious, how do you expect to beat me?"

Amaya flashed him a dogged smirk with the question. "With sheer damn determination," she answered. Her blades glinted when she snatched the daggers from their sheaths. She launched.

Amaya strobed in and out of sight as she raced at Tsukuyomi from several angles, her speed making her movements nigh impossible to track. And yet, after having witnessed Amaya's fight with Shila and Marilyn, Zatook knew Amaya wasn't moving as fast in this battle. Amaya and Tsukuyomi danced around each other, steel clashing and ringing. Sparks of fire and electricity burst against the shadows fast enough to parry the attacks before the magic could be absorbed. Despite her skill and speed, cuts tore Amaya's jacket and the bandages beneath, revealing blackened skin before blood filled the gaps. As shadows sprang at Amaya from Tsukuyomi's sword, Amaya's electricity arced around her as a shield. More shadows wrapped up her legs from where the light of the lightning cast her silhouette on the ground. Tsukuyomi's power overwhelmed the electricity. Amaya twisted to the side but sucked in a sharp inhale as her brother's blade managed to cut through her jacket and her corset across her side.

As Tsukuyomi moved to follow up the attack, Zatook rejoined them, his own blade blocking the katana from reaching Amaya again. While Amaya had kept Tsukuyomi's attention, Zatook had managed to push the Nocium soldiers back across the Wall so the priestesses could raise barriers. He wasn't sure how long they would hold the breach, but hopefully it would be enough time to finish evacuations. He had directed a group of magi, Andorian soldiers who used magic as they fought, to keep StormShaper occupied. Now, he had come to help Amaya.

He was still in his gargoyle form, but the purple ribbons of magic no longer accompanied him. He wrapped his own shadows over his skin and Amaya's in an effort to dull the effects of Tsukuyomi's magic and attacks. He paid no more attention to his reflection in the man's armor.

Disengaging the blades, Tsukuyomi pressed his attack, fighting both Celestials ruthlessly. Amaya continued to use her electricity and fire to thwart the shadows, but even with Zatook's magic acting as a second armor, some of Tsukuyomi's attacks managed to land.

Tsukuyomi didn't stick with just shadows. He attacked with spells as well, showcasing his knowledge of magics outside his own and his years of experience in combat. His ice spells clashed with Amaya's fire. Tsukuyomi refrained from using spells with a base of fire or lightning since Amaya would be able to use her own abilities to redirect or absorb them outright. Still, the tricky part was that Tsukuyomi knew how to conceal the spells in his shadows, so it became difficult to know what was just shadow and what was a spell about to hit Amaya and Zatook.

As the battle progressed, Amaya breathed heavily, sweat pouring down her face and her gaze tired and pained though determined. As long as she could stay standing, she would keep fighting.

Around them, the war raged in full. Andor's forces were proving formidable, such that even StormShaper's presence made little headway. Jeremiah had finally sent Lillith in as well, but Marilyn had disappeared somewhere rather than join the fight. Jeremiah continued to wait, though not for much longer.

The whole field knew when Traiborn arrived. Even those without magic could feel the force of his presence before powerful spells ripped through the ranks. Such was his skill that none of his spells harmed the Andorians, no matter how near they were to the effect or the enemy. Great green vines erupted from the ground, entangling Nocium soldiers and hampering their movement. Stakes of ice fell from the sky, and the earth turned to sand and mud beneath enemy boots while firming under allies. Traiborn did not call on lightning, keeping an eye on the spark-wielder facing his magi, but he pulled on all the other elements of magic— light, dark, fire, air, earth, water, and ice.

As his spells raged, Triborn stepped out from the new barriers. He held one hand aloft, a floating book gleaming above his palm; his other hand held the Etherium Runesaber unsheathed, revealing the silver-blue blade in all of its glory.

Jeremiah growled, his pupils turning to slits. He shrugged off his waistcoat and tossed it to his attendant before taking a running leap. Black scales encased his skin, and leathery wings sprang from his back. Yet he drew his sword and met Traiborn blade-to-blade rather than fully shifting. Despite grasping his hilt in both hands and pouring all of his might into the strike, the dragon's blow barely shifted a hair on Traiborn's head. The King of Andor met Jeremiah's gaze levelly as he parried the strike. Magic coated the Runesaber, making the light blue metal gleam. Jeremiah sneered.

"Magic against a dragon? A sorcerer should know better."

"Such arrogance is unbefitting a king so newly crowned." Traiborn's blade met Jeremiah's again and again, the sorcerer not moving from where he stood despite the array of attacks. Finally he shifted, pivoting and spinning low to slice at Jeremiah's leg. He only managed to nick the skin as Jeremiah dodged, but the dragon was surprised to feel the magic lash out and wrap around his scales— and even more surprised to feel them burn with pain. Traiborn smirked as he stood. "I would advise you hold nothing back if you wish to keep that crown."

Jeremiah lunged, swinging his blade as Traiborn raised a shield of ice. The dragon struck through the frozen crystals, shattering them, before dodging to avoid a spear of the substance flying from behind the shield. Now that he knew the man's magic could harm him, he needed to be more defensive. But that didn't mean he wouldn't press his opportunities.

Elsewhere on the field, Zatook and Amaya were managing to hold against Tsukuyomi. Zatook let Amaya focus on the tendrils of shadow in an effort to mitigate Tsukuyomi's attacks while he pressed the physical battle. He felt a pang of regret for contacting her— she hardly seemed fit to fight —but he recognized that she had made her own decision to come, and he was grateful all the same. Still, he did his best to keep Tsukuyomi's attacks away from her and used the shadows under his control to try and lessen the damage from any that slipped through. He was keenly aware of the king's arrival, but he did not let that distract him. He could not afford to lose focus, hardly even minding his own pain. The effects of having wielded so much of his forbidden power did not escape his notice, but he would not let himself feel the consequences. Not yet. Andor could not afford for him to let Tsukuyomi through. He wouldn't leave Amaya to face her brother alone, either. Too many people were counting on him to keep the man at bay, if not drive him off.

Amaya doggedly kept her focus on her brother even when she felt Traiborn join the battle. She also felt the toll her own fight was taking, agony wracking her body and compounding her fatigue. Damn that magic— whatever the hell it was —that brought down the Wall. So far, Amaya refrained from transforming— partially because she didn't have Tsukuyomi's luxury of making hers look like armor and because she wanted to avoid displaying her wounds that showed up in both her forms. Amaya knew she wouldn't beat Tsukuyomi as she was, and her brother knew it too. Amaya wasn't the real threat in this battle. Tsukuyomi focused his attacks largely on Zatook since the Andorian used shadows as well and was shielding the duo with them. Amaya moved to intervene time and again to keep Zatook from being overwhelmed.

At one point, Tsukuyomi's shadows threaded through Amaya's defenses enough to reach her. Instead of trying to pierce through the shadows shielding her, the black tendrils wrapped around Amaya, restraining her.

Tsukuyomi appeared before his sister as Amaya used her lightning to shred the shadows holding her captive. More shadows speared towards her. As they neared, the shadows transformed into mirror shards in the forms of blades, their surfaces reflecting the light from the lightning to cut through Zatook's shadows meant to protect Amaya. More shadows coalesced around Amaya, this time to protect her from the onslaught. Zatook bolstered the shield of darkness against the light with the shadows he'd been using on himself. Tsukuyomi's form shattered into shards of glass. The man seemingly reappeared in front of Zatook as Tsukuyomi's katana pierced Zatook's chest. The shadows lacing Tsukuyomi's blade delved into Zatook's body through the sword wound and the other cuts marring the younger Celestial's form. Slicing inside and out, the shadows exacted ruthless agony. As the pain shook him, Zatook's mental fortitude faltered. He met the eyeless gaze of the mask, and the abyss swallowed him.

"<Monsters do not question their Masters.>"

His earliest memory. The first of many painful lessons. He could feel the burning coals ripping, tearing, searing.

"<Monsters do not have friends.>"

The second lesson. Zatook had dared to befriend a palace ward, and Traiborn's punishment was swift and fierce— for him and the other boy. It would be a hundred years before he first forgot this lesson.

"<Monsters are tools.>"

Once he was ten, the king started making him useful. He began to forge his shadowed blade. Anything Traiborn wanted, he sent Zatook to get. Enemies, dead. Artifacts, recovered. Magic tomes, stolen.

Failure met swift retribution, and then he would be sent again.

"<Monsters do not shy from pain.>"

And Traiborn reveled in being the cause. If he didn't have something for Zatook to do, the warrior was chained in his cell. Sometimes the king would experiment, testing Zatook's abilities or toying with his blood. Other times he would take his anger out on Zatook, his frustrations from the day. Traiborn tested new spells, new instruments, new ways to cause pain.

He never tried to discover how to heal Zatook.

"<Monsters serve their Masters in all things.>"

He was fifteen when Traiborn learned the spell to force his transformation. Of all the things the king had done to him, that was the most excruciating.

"<Monsters do not love.>"

Aditi. He never should have dared.

"<Monsters have only what their Masters allow.>"

Befriending Tristan and the others had been temporary.

Traiborn could have forced him to return at any time. His friendship with Tannen hinged on Zatook's usefulness to the king. The time he got to spend with his sister could be and often was taken away at the slightest provocation. He could only visit his mother when the king allowed. Everything was Traiborn's to control.

"<Monsters may dream of freedom, but they are only dreams.>"

Zatook's was a life of pain and servitude. He was not allowed anything else. Every broken bone, every wound, every burn— all of these served as reminders, because they had been caused by his master first. Any pain brought by his enemies was nothing compared to what waited for him should he fail or the king become bored. He was a symbol: Traiborn's monster, the King's Shadow. He was meant to be feared, reviled, abhorred. He was meant to keep others in line. He was meant to dirty his hands so the king's remained clean. Zatook was nothing unless the king called for him. He was a shadow, a sword, a tool, and no more.

"<How dare you forget.>"

Traiborn's voice rang clear in his mind. Centuries of lessons, of punishment, of pain revisited. He could feel every slice, every burn, every spell piling atop each other to cause nothing but agony. He could feel the king's bindings flare along his wrists and neck, feel every feather plucked from his wings and regrown, feel his body ripped apart and reshaped to match the king's will. Each a reminder of what Traiborn could do to him.

He could see everyone he had ever hurt or killed. He could see the fear and revulsion whenever he was in the cities or the villages. The children whisked into their homes or behind their mother's skirts, the blood draining from the faces around him. Even in the capital, the side eyes and sucked-in breaths. And so he stopped looking.

"Zatook…"

He could hear the whispers. The rumors. The names. The things said about the few who dared to care about him. He could hear his mother, the pain in her voice as she was forced to watch while he suffered. The fear when she told him only to use his ancestor's power in the most dire of circumstances. He could see the pain and sadness in her gaze, and so he stopped meeting it.

"Zatook."

To be Zatook was to suffer. To love Zatook was to suffer.

"Zatook!"

Agony pounded through his body with every heartbeat. He could hear the battle around them, though it was dulled by the rush of blood in his ears. He could feel his body sluggishly attempting to catch up with what Tsukuyomi had done to him even as he could feel the tortures of his past. Amaya was beside him, bloodied and bruised. He never should have sent that message. He should have faced what came himself, no matter the consequence. Perhaps things would be better if Void had managed to kill him.

Groggily, Zatook's mind caught up. Amaya was practically dragging him back to the Wall, to the breach and the barrier. He could still sense Tsukuyomi, but something was keeping him at bay. The king, perhaps? Or something Amaya had done? He couldn't tell. He could barely think. He dreaded what his master would do once he healed. If he healed.

Amaya's body glowed softly as her powers flared behind her, keeping Tsukuyomi at bay for a short time. As she shouldered as much of Zatook's weight as she could, Amaya felt her own body screaming in agony. She pushed through the pain. If she went down now, Tsukuyomi would take the chance to get through the breach and make his way to Tristan.

Amaya held Zatook steady, not repulsed by him in the slightest despite the black blood seeping into her clothes and sticking to her hair, mixing with her own crimson blood. Once she sensed the barrier before them, Amaya met Zatook's gaze, fondness and relief glimmering in her own eyes.

"Hey, Shadow," Amaya greeted gently. "I can't take you through, so you're on your own from here. Go get healed. And, Shadow?" She gave him a small, tired smile. "Take care of the others, aye?" With that, Amaya shifted his weight and helped him step across the barrier, her touch staying with him until it came upon the wards banning her entry. Amaya watched Zatook a moment longer before she turned to face Tsukuyomi.

The light around her flared as Amaya called back her powers. Her silver eyes flashed blue, and neon markings curved and swirled across her clothes, Amaya shifting into a partial transformation in the hopes of holding her own a little longer. In a flash, she launched into the shadows surrounding Tsukuyomi.

It was the last thing Zatook saw. He felt arms wrap around him and pull him through the barrier; magic coursed through him, and then everything went dark.

25. *Sunlight and Shadow*

The parlor of the guest tower was filled with an earthy smell. Captain had rustled up a cauldron from the staff and was working to mix some basic healing potions. Everyone knew the war had started in earnest. Even if the renewed activity in the palace hadn't told them, Aria had straight up said so. Zatook and Collette were gone, Traiborn had challenged Jeremiah, and Corianne was managing things in the palace. Captain's hands itched to grab a thread and go; she didn't like sitting idly by while others were fighting. But they had their own tasks to prepare for, and Aria had been firm— this wasn't their fight. At least not yet.

To pass the time, Solomon had pulled Jabez, Alconai, and Lancelot into the training area. Tannen had crafted a new sword for the knight, and Solomon had a new set of matching scimitars as back up should he ever need to lend Jabez the Sentinels. Tristan watched them from the garden; he had mostly recovered after a sudden, powerful spike from the Talisman of Ruin, but Aria had insisted he continue to rest. Said Celestial was curled beside him in her cat form, resting under the sun. She had been training Rose in removing Celesbane for the better part of the day but had finally sent the Half-Drow upstairs to sleep and recover some energy.

The cat peeked open her green and golden eyes. "<You

should see to your visitor,>" she murmured to Tristan just as her guards outside the guest tower knocked on the door and opened it to let Halia in.

Captain had started to smile and wave, but she hesitated at the look on the faerie's face. Tristan moved to the parlor, concerned. His sense of dread only grew when he saw Halia's ashen face. As soon as she spied Tristan, the faerie ran to him and took his hand.

"Tannen sent me. Collette had Zatook sent to Tannen from the battlefield," Halia explained, her eyes desperate. "Zatook's in bad shape— bad enough there's nothing Tannen can do to ease the pain or get Zatook on his feet again. Tannen thought maybe you could help."

As he listened, Tristan recalled his conversation with Queen Corianne about his Child powers having the potential to heal Zatook. It seemed Tannen thought the same.

"I can try," answered Tristan gently. He gave Halia's hand a reassuring squeeze before letting go. He then headed to the courtyard to tell the men what was happening.

Jabez looked to Solomon, Alconai, and Lancelot as he spoke, "I'll go with him. We'll fill everyone in once we return." He followed Tristan back to Halia, and the trio set out for Tannen's abode.

Halia kept glancing back to make sure the men were staying with her, fear and concern in her eyes. If Collette usually sent Zatook to be patched up by Tannen, Tristan wondered in what states the forge duo had seen the shadow-wielder. It also made his stomach twist in knots to think what the trio would see this time. Halia kept going when they reached her and Tannen's apartment, the faerie ushering Jabez and Tristan inside. She led them to a spare room where Tannen had gotten Zatook settled. The blacksmith looked up and inclined his head to them. Beside Tannen on a cot, Zatook lay motionless. A cloth covered the lower part of Zatook's face, but the rest of his body lay bare save for the bandages. The linens almost looked like Zatook's clothes with how stained black they were. Tannen did have a portion of the sheet covering Zatook's extremities to give the man privacy while he was tended. Gashes, bruising, cuts, a stab wound, the injuries seemed endless. Despite feeling mortified by Zatook's condition, Tristan pushed down his unease. His friend needed him.

Tristan barely heard Tannen say, "Thank you for coming. I've done what I can, but he's in terrible condition. I'm concerned that without healing…well. And normal remedies and healing magic won't work. Even my bloodline healing does nothing for him."

"We came as soon as Halia reached us," Jabez assured Tannen. "Do I need to stand guard or help in any way?"

"Zatook always came to me when he needed help patching himself up. It got to the point that the queen and the princess convinced the king to send Zatook to me whenever he needed help with his injuries," explained Tannen. "So, the king knows this is where Zatook likely is and shouldn't bother us. As for helping, I'll leave that to the Sun Child to advise. Do you need anything, lad?"

Running a hand through his hair, Tristan let out a

steadying breath. "This…is a lot. I don't know how wiped I'll be once I'm done, but I don't want to heal him partially if the king is going to send Zatook back out to the battlefield," he answered, eyeing Tannen to see if his assumption was correct. Tannen confirmed with a nod. "Just keep him from thrashing so he doesn't injure himself more or injure me."

Refocusing on Zatook, Tristan knelt beside the cot. He waited until Jabez and Tannen had positioned themselves to hold down Zatook's shoulders and legs. Feeling the pressure of possibly being the only one to be able to heal Zatook, Tristan took another steadying breath. Once more he recalled his lessons with Almas and Clovestein. Tristan thought of when he healed Jabez, recalling Solomon's words of encouragement. Above all, Tristan reminded himself that his Sun Child power wasn't his own. He was merely the vessel. Trusting in Shaddai and the Sacreds and sending up a prayer for Their guidance and power, Tristan gently placed his hands over the stab wound— the worst injury. The sun marking appeared on his hand as the flame markings coiling up his arm glowed golden. White-gold light illuminated Tristan's hands. A warm, comforting, and immense presence filled the room, spilling out into the rest of the abode— fathomless and uncontainable. Tristan felt peace. As the light touched and filled the wound, the injury closed, and the flesh knit back together until not even a scar remained. Once satisfied, Tristan moved to the next injury. One by one, Tristan used his Sun Child powers to heal each wound. True to his word, he kept going until Zatook lay fully healed.

Releasing the power, Tristan breathed heavily as he sat back on his heels. He barely registered Jabez moving beside him and guiding Tristan to lean against the man's legs. Tristan mumbled his gratitude, exhausted and weak but elated. Relief washed over him as he whispered a prayer of gratitude to the Sacreds as well. Keeping his eyes open, Tristan watched Zatook— though he wasn't sure if the man would wake right away. Tristan blushed when he felt a hand gently ruffle his hair, wearily lifting his gaze to see Tannen smiling brightly at him. Halia hugged Tristan before softly taking Zatook's hand and watching the warrior eagerly.

Despite their concerns, Zatook had not so much as flinched while Tristan healed him. He had, however, slowly relaxed as the pain abated. His breathing had eased, his brow unfurrowed. And yet, as much as his body begged for it now that the pain was gone, he would not stay resting. His hand twitched in Halia's as he forced himself to rouse, opened his eyes. At first, everything was bleary, but a couple of blinks cleared what he could see.

He was at Tannen's. For a moment, he couldn't remember why, and then the fight came trickling back. But he wasn't in pain. How long had he been unconscious? How long had he been away from the battlefield? How long had Amaya...? Amaya. His eyes widened and he sat up, but then he hesitated when he saw the others. His gaze took in Tristan's exhaustion and the blackened bandages that had been discarded nearby. Those...were fresh. The group could actually see surprise flash behind his gaze as he found Tristan again.

Tristan smiled tiredly as he met Zatook's gaze. "I guess I shouldn't be surprised you'd be awake already," the young man teased softly. "Seems your mother and I were right. Thankfully, Tannen had a similar theory and sent Halia to get me. Just like with my transformation, my Sun Child powers healed you."

Halia watched Zatook with wet eyes. "I went as fast as I could when Tannen sent me. I even shrunk down and flew most of the way to get to them faster. You scared us," she told Zatook. A couple of tears slipped down her cheeks. "You've looked bad before, but that was the worst. Who… what happened?"

"Easy, Halia. He just woke up," Tannen soothed the faerie, reaching down to stroke her hair gently. To Zatook he said, "I'm glad to see you whole, my friend. I thought of Tristan's transformation and how his Child abilities allowed him to heal the damage. Who is a greater healer than Shaddai Himself?"

As he listened to Tannen and Halia talk to Zatook, Tristan's smile faded. The same question kept circling in his mind: who would be strong enough to put Zatook in such bad shape? The man's bouts with StormShaper never seemed to hurt Zatook to that extent, and given how strong Zatook was, Tristan had a hard time believing Jeremiah to be responsible. Perhaps Marilyn? Or…

"Was," Tristan started quietly but felt his mouth run dry. Averting his gaze as dread sank like a stone in his stomach, Tristan forced himself to ask, "Was it my father?" The question came as a whisper, and Tristan deliberately raised his gaze so he could see Zatook's answer.

Zatook's groggy gaze shifted to each as they spoke, taking in their expressions and concern. A part of him knew he shouldn't be surprised, yet another part of him wished they weren't concerned for him. They were getting too close. And now he could be healed. His master... it was hard to imagine how the king would react. Would he be angry? Or would he take advantage of the fact that Zatook could now instantly recover? Would he try to keep Tristan here, or force the group to leave?

And then Tristan asked about his father, and Zatook's mind flashed to Amaya once more. If it really had been mere moments, she was still out there. Did she need help? Should he tell Tristan and hope the group could make it in time to help her?

"Take care of the others." And who was going to take care of her?

The hesitation was the only real answer Tristan needed about his father's involvement, but Zatook started to lift a hand to write with shadows when the summons came. It was something Tannen and Halia had seen before. Vibrant red runes scrawled quickly around Zatook's neck, wrists, and ankles, burning his skin. The burns would only deepen the longer he took to respond. His master was back, and he wanted to see Zatook. He must have already sensed that he was healed; why else would he summon him? He needed to go, quickly, or his master would be even more angry. But if the king had returned, perhaps that meant that Amaya had managed to drive Tsukuyomi off after all? Why would Traiborn leave if any of the major threats were still on the field? The sooner Zatook answered the summons, the sooner he might know. Assuming his master was willing to tell him. More than likely, they would be...discussing...his own failure. Zatook stared at the runes on the wrist he had raised. Tannen had seen him roll his eyes at the summons before, let out a sharp sigh, growl, any number of things. But this time, he just stared dully at his wrist.

"He's being summoned by the king," Tannen explained upon seeing Tristan and Jabez's perplexed looks.

"Summoned? No, he just got back, just got healed," Tristan spoke softly but fervently. Turning back to Zatook, Tristan touched the markings on Zatook's wrist, calling on his Child powers once more. Maybe he could undo the magic Traiborn was using to summon Zatook? Before the power could even try, Jabez gripped Tristan's hands and forced them back while Zatook pulled his arm away from Tristan. Tannen held a hand between Tristan and Zatook, ready to be a barrier if the need arose.

"Tristan," Jabez spoke in a gentle but firm voice, "Tampering with the magic will only make things worse for Zatook. And we're on thin ice as it is."

"Maybe the ice should be broken then. I can't...I can't just stand back anymore," Tristan said sorrowfully, bitterly. When he felt a hand gently ruffle his hair, Tristan looked up to meet Zatook's gaze, noting the warrior was the one touching Tristan's hair this time. "You just got healed," the Sun Child insisted again.

As Zatook pulled his hand away from Tristan's head, Jabez guided the younger Celestial back to give Zatook room to get dressed. Tannen helped his friend, his own expression grave. The blacksmith had thought something similar to Tristan's words several times over the years, but Tannen knew that trying to intervene could just make things worse. It often had.

While Zatook readied himself to return to the king, Halia stood off to the side, refusing to watch him go. She had seen this scene so many times, and it never not hurt. So many times she had curled up in Tannen's arms while they both worried for their friend.

Tristan stared dully at the ground as he fought back the tears stinging his eyes. He let Jabez hold him, the man using his grip on Tristan's hands to wrap the young man in a hug. Tristan barely registered the gentle rumble of Jabez's voice in his ear, the man trying to soothe Tristan and reason with him not to do something reckless. Once Zatook left, Jabez coaxed Tristan to stand before releasing the young Celestial. After checking to see if Tannen and Halia needed anything, Jabez put his arm around Tristan's shoulders and started leading him back toward the guest tower.

Tristan walked in silence, taking what comfort he could in Jabez's hold. However, his mind kept going back to the markings shackling Zatook, and then Tristan's thoughts sank into memories of enduring his own torture at the hands of the man who was supposed to be his father. Even as horrible as Tsukuyomi had been in recent years, he hadn't been like Traiborn. At least, not to Tristan's knowledge. He couldn't imagine what Zatook had endured and was still willing to endure. Well, not so much willing, but Zatook was alive. Despite Zatook having told him that Tristan was strong, Tristan couldn't help thinking that he wouldn't have survived as long. At one point in their trek, Jabez squeezed Tristan's shoulder and guided them down a different route than the one they had taken when they followed Halia.

At Tristan's quizzical look, Jabez answered softly, "I

noticed a couple of figures lurking in the shadows. Shaedra might be trying to pull something while we're away from the rest of the group. Even if they aren't, I'd rather avoid them just in case." Tristan nodded his understanding.

The two men decided to skirt around the throne room as well since Jabez knew Traiborn kept a few Shaedra agents as guards in the area. Instead, Tristan and Jabez followed a hallway that led past a chamber connected to the back of the throne room. A door led from the hallway to the chamber which acted as a war room. The group had come across the room during their explorations of the palace. As they neared the door leading into the hallway, Tristan found his thoughts interrupted by a wave of magic, the young Celestial sensing the aura. He jerked his head up in the direction he felt the pulse— the chamber behind the throne room. Ducking from Jabez's hold, Tristan moved to the door and quietly opened it just enough to peer inside. He sensed Jabez joining him, but Tristan kept his focus on the interior of the war room.

The first thing he saw was Traiborn standing at the large table within, hands on the edges as though he had been leaning over the map. Now, however, his scrutinizing gaze was on Zatook. Tristan could just see the man through the crack in the door, down on one knee with his gaze lowered. If he hadn't felt the magic or noticed the warrior's white-knuckled fist, he might have thought the scene rather typical of a soldier reporting to his king.

"<...had you not performed so abysmally, you might already know,>" Traiborn was mid-sentence, his voice a growl as he straightened from the table and walked towards Zatook. He wound his hand through the man's hair and pressed him downwards, forcing Zatook to shift into a full kneeling position. Tristan felt more magic, and Zatook's hand curled tighter. "<Monsters do not question their masters. I will decide what you need to know from the field, and you will follow what I say and leave the rest. Am I clear?>"

Blood boiling, Tristan clenched his own fist. Zatook had just been healed, and Traiborn was torturing him already. He felt Jabez's hand squeeze his shoulder and try to lead him away. Despite trying to keep his emotions in check, Tristan stayed rooted behind the door, his gaze locked onto the scene.

Traiborn's hand left Zatook's hair, but as the latter tried to lift his face from the ground, he felt Traiborn's boot take its place and press him back down. "<I have rather had it with you, creature. It would seem your punishment upon your return was not enough to quell this rebellious streak of yours. Need I remind you what happens when you get these wild ideas?>" Zatook's hand slowly uncurled, shifting as if he were going to form words, but Traiborn moved his boot to step on it and grind it into the floor.

"<Do not make matters worse by attempting to speak,>" he growled, turning and stalking back to the table. One of his hands gripped the dagger sheathed by his sword, tapping along the handle thoughtfully. "<By the time I am done with you, boy, you're going to wish that lightning witch had let you die. Now sit up.>" Despite the magic still searing through him, Zatook obeyed. He stayed on his knees, sitting back on his legs, and kept his dulled gaze on the floor. Traiborn made a few adjustments to the map before returning to stand in front of Zatook. "<Face and

torso bare,>" he ordered coldly. Zatook obeyed, peeling off his shirts, mask, gloves. The x-shaped scars across his torso burned angry reds and oranges, testament to at least part of what Traiborn's magic was doing. "<I will not ask again. How are you healed?>"

Zatook did not move, staring at the floor. Traiborn held his hand to the side, and his tome appeared, hovering in the air above it. Runes swirled along his palm and up into the pages. Zatook flinched as the pages began to turn rapidly; Tristan saw him take a deep breath as the pages slowed.

"<Monsters do not shy from pain.>"

The spell hit, and Zatook was forced back into agony. As Tristan watched, wound after wound rewrote itself across his skin, but they weren't wounds he had healed. Traiborn wasn't calling the memories of pain from the battlefield. His sword needed to be resharpened, his monster retrained. This was simply a faster way to revisit certain lessons.

Tristan wrenched from Jabez's grip and barged into the room. Righteous fury blazed in his chest as Tristan called on his Sun Child powers, the golden light wrapping around Zatook and dispelling the magic hurting him. Placing himself between Zatook and Traiborn, Tristan stared down the king.

"You may be a good king to your people, but as a person you are the monster," growled the young Celestial. "You are a spiteful, jealous *beast*. You resent Zatook because he doesn't have to force people to love him. You hate him because you know he's the furthest from being the monster you claim he is, and you know that you are the closest."

Tristan kept his gaze locked with Traiborn even as Jabez joined him and eased the young man behind him. Jabez inwardly sighed. Well, this was about to go all kinds of horrible. Despite his fury with the king's treatment of Zatook and the painful memories that tried to resurface of his own torture and brainwashing, Jabez knew the situation was dangerous. He kept note of where Traiborn had the Celesbane blade.

"You want him to fight on the battlefield, then isn't torturing him counterproductive?" Tristan pressed.

The only movement Traiborn had made was to quirk an eyebrow at Tristan's little tirade. He waited for the boy to stop talking. "What I do to that which belongs to me is none of your concern." His voice was ice as his grip on his dagger tightened. "Do not speak to me of wars and monsters when you have not set a foot on the field of battle to protect the place that offers you shelter. You are young, naïve, and wearing on my patience, Child of the Sun. This is your final warning. Get out. Go back to your tower, finish your preparations, and either put Andor behind you or go fight on the battlefield you seem so concerned with. Relieve yourself of concern for this one and be on your way with whatever mission has you hidden away behind our walls." His eyes narrowed. "Or you can dare to contradict me again, and I can have you stripped of your protected status. I will allow my comrades to reclaim their own shadow," his gaze flicked to Jabez and back to Tristan, "and you will die. Whether by my hand or *his*, I have yet to decide." His gaze traveled to Zatook behind them. "<Get up.>"

The warrior flinched. Tristan had only used enough magic to dispel Traiborn's magic, not having healed him yet. Still, Zatook rose to his feet and clenched his hands at his sides. He kept his eyes on the floor, but his mind was racing. To say this was bad would be an understatement, but he daren't try and speak to sway Tristan. The boy needed to take the chance and leave. Zatook wasn't worth this. He couldn't be responsible for them being hurt. For hurting them. Jabez being taken. Tristan killed. He was only meant to be a temporary companion, a shield loaned from the queen until the king recalled him. A tool from the shadows, returned to his master.

He risked it. Shadows swirled in the air just behind his master, over the man's shoulder where Tristan could see them. *Go.* With his gaze lowered, he didn't see Traiborn's nostrils flare or his jaw clench. But the king didn't move. Yet.

Memories of his father fighting his mother and killing his sister haunted Tristan's mind and fueled his fury. The situation felt similar to when Tristan faced his father's ultimatum, being claimed as a possession and used as a tool.

Jabez stood firm between Celestial Child and sorcerer king. "Are you willing to risk the potential backlash of killing one of the Chosen? Revered as they are, your people will not stand for it, especially after such a public display of allyship. And then there are those outside Andor who would rally against you for such an act. You know you would bring ruin on your kingdom, Your Majesty," Jabez countered evenly. He knew there was a possibility that Traiborn would make good on his threat, but Jabez had a feeling the man was aiming to intimidate rather than truly threaten— at least for now. Hoping to keep the situation from escalating further, Jabez reached back and nudged Tristan to move for the door. Jabez planned to stay between his charge and the king just in case. However, Tristan refused to budge.

"As a member of the Order, Zatook is my guardian and my ally," Tristan kept his voice calm despite his emotions. "Furthermore, as the Sun Child it is my sacred duty to protect and help those who need it. To give hope and to heal. If Zatook is the monster— the demon —you claim him to be, then this will have the opposite effect." With that, Tristan turned to Zatook and placed his hands on the man's shoulders. The sun and flame markings appeared once more as golden light spread over Zatook, healing the new damage and relieving the pain.

Inwardly, Jabez cursed. He kept his eyes on Traiborn and the dagger, anticipating the king's reaction. There was no time to reach through his connection with Captain to alert the group. The sinking feeling in Jabez's stomach only heightened when he noted movement in the shadows.

"*Enough.*" Traiborn's hand lashed out, shoving Jabez aside. "You are no longer guests here," he growled, reaching for Tristan. Zatook was faster. While he had initially tried to step away when Tristan reached for him, concern and a hint of panic breaking through his dulled gaze, now he grabbed Tristan and Jabez and shifted into shadows. He grimaced when he discovered Traiborn had warded the chamber against his escape, though he had left open the path to the throne room. At least that would give them more space. He reformed in the center of the room, keeping himself between Traiborn and the pair.

But Traiborn was not their only concern. Agents of Shaedra were already flanking the main and side doors, with more moving forward to surround them in a half circle opposite Traiborn; the king was now walking through the door behind the thrones. "My people trust their king," he proclaimed, drawing his dagger. "I have extended every offer of grace, and you continue to spit in my face. No more. The status of Chosen only extends so far. Perhaps I will not kill you, but you shall never again be free."

Zatook's eyes didn't leave Traiborn as he reached to the side and summoned his sword; his other hand was stretched back to keep Tristan behind him. The king paused at the top of the steps leading to the thrones. "You have already damned yourself twice today," Traiborn growled, his voice dripping with ice. "Do not dare to turn your blade against me." His eyes narrowed as Zatook continued to stand his ground. He took a step down, and a pulse of magic filled the air. Runes once more scrawled across Zatook's neck and wrists, the man still exposed. But now they were brighter, harsher. Zatook tensed, but he didn't move. He couldn't let Traiborn have control. Not this time. Not with Tristan right behind him. He wouldn't do it again. He wouldn't kill someone he actually cared about *again*.

Traiborn met his gaze for a solid minute, slowly walking down the stairs and across the carpet. Magic had also snaked up and around Tristan and Jabez's legs, immobilizing them while the king fought to regain his shadow. Tristan called on his powers again, managing to break the spell just as the Shaedra agents closed the distance, grabbing both to pull them back from the king's demon.

Using his Celestial strength, Tristan threw off his attackers. Crystal spikes burst through the floor to create a barrier between Tristan and the Shaedra agents. His attention snapped to Jabez reaching his side in time to parry a chain that had been flying towards Tristan's neck.

"You'll not have him," growled ShadowDancer to the ninjas. Blades drawn, Jabez stood ready to attack or defend.

While Jabez focused on the Shaedra agents, Tristan turned his attention back to Zatook and Traiborn. Trusting Jabez, Tristan moved back toward Zatook, planning to use his Child powers to release the magic controlling the man. Tristan felt his body protesting, growing increasingly exhausted after multiple intense healings and using his Celestial abilities. Still, he wanted to free Zatook— damn the political ramifications. Traiborn was stalking towards Zatook. As the king approached, he lifted the dagger, intent on bringing the man to heel. The image of Amaya's scar flashed through Tristan's mind as did her warning to stay away from the blade. Zatook had already been wounded several times, and even with healing magic, the stress took a toll on the body. As he moved, Tristan thought about his lessons with Tannen, conjuring a crystal sword to parry the dagger. He didn't have enough time or practice to create armor for himself, but Tristan managed to form a half-chest piece with his crystal to cover his left shoulder and over his heart. He knew there were other areas just as fatal if pierced, but this would have to do.

As Traiborn brought the dagger down, Tristan appeared between him and Zatook, sword at the ready. Traiborn adjusted quickly, magic flaring around his wrists to switch the dagger with his tome. The thick book snapped shut around Tristan's blade, holding it in a vice grip as the king's dagger instead found Tristan's right shoulder. Zatook actually let out a roar of anger, the sound pressing past his scars as he snapped free of the immobilization and surged forward. Traiborn released Tristan's sword from the book and shoved the lad at Zatook, causing the warrior to stumble as he caught him. And then Traiborn was behind him, the dagger in the small of Zatook's back.

26. To Challenge a King

Tristan choked on his screams, the agony lancing through him knocking the air from his lungs. Warmth and strength rapidly drained from his body with the blood spilling down his torso, leaving cold and weakness in their wake. Cracking filled his ears as the crystal protecting his left shoulder crumbled and hit the ground in shards, shattering further. Tristan's sight blurred. Unable to keep his feet, Tristan collapsed in Zatook's arms, the younger man shaking like a newborn fawn. Was this what Amaya felt when Traiborn stabbed her? The cold left by Arianna's absence grew as Tristan felt his powers diminish before vanishing altogether. Would he be seeing his sister and his mother soon? Weakly Tristan gripped Zatook's arm and tilted his head back to find the man's face. Tears of pain and fear stung Tristan's eyes as he felt himself fading into agony and darkness.

Behind them, Jabez tried to reach both Celestials, his worst fear playing out before his eyes. Arms wrapped around his arms and twisted them, locking his wrists behind his back in vice-like hands. The agents dragged Jabez back and towards the closest door. Getting his feet under him, Jabez drove his heel into one of his captor's knees, snapping the bone. As the ninja crumpled, Jabez jabbed his second captor in the throat and pushed the man away while he choked for air. Jabez made it only a few steps before a chain wrapped around his neck.

Grabbing the length of the chain, Jabez loosened the hold around his neck and pulled his assailant to him and right into his fist. Wresting the chain from his attacker, Jabez started using the weapon to fend off the other agents, once more showcasing his prowess as a fighter. All the while, Jabez's thoughts stayed on Zatook and Tristan and the need to reach them. He would not lose them. Silently, he sent a prayer to Shaddai for help.

The next pulse of power didn't come from the king. Nor did it come from either of the wounded warriors. As Zatook sank to his knees, eyes going dull as Traiborn's spell took full effect, the audience chamber was suddenly filled with rainbow light. As the burst faded, light gave way to movement. Another flash of rainbow saw Tristan disappear and then reappear between the thrones, where Rose was on her knees waiting. Captain flopped down on the stairs beside them, panting heavily. With Aria's training, she hadn't lost a single thread, but moving so many had taken a toll and she wasn't ready to fight yet.

Solomon had lowered his shoulder and started running as Captain teleported them, using the momentum from his run and the tug to slam into Traiborn and get him away from Zatook. He had the Glyphseal Sentinels drawn, quickly diverting the fire spell that Traiborn threw in response. Tannen was behind him, moving towards Zatook. He slowed when the shadowed warrior stood.

Unlike a full-blooded Celestial, the dagger did not steal Zatook's powers, merely weakening them. As Tannen watched, shadows wrapped around the dagger and it vanished, only to reappear in its sheath at Traiborn's hip, free of blood. And then Zatook turned to face Tannen, and the blacksmith knew. His friend was no longer in control of himself. Empty eyes met Tannen's gaze as Zatook gripped his sword. At first it seemed he might resist further, might not move, but all it took was a hissed order from the king, and Zatook surged towards Tannen.

Lancelot and Alconai appeared beside Jabez. The knight caught a blade on his gauntlets before shoving it away and following up with his own sword. Alconai's yo-yo wrapped around an attacker's arm and pulled to counter the man's strike. Alconai felt a tad dizzy from the teleporting, but he found his rhythm quickly, aiding Lancelot and Jabez as they fought back the Shaedra ninjas.

"Go help the others with Traiborn," growled Jabez, the venom in his voice directed at his opponents even as he spoke to his allies, "I have this."

Chancing a look at his brother, Alconai saw a coldness in Jabez's eyes that struck the minstrel as foreign, but Alconai believed his brother's statement. Catching Lancelot's gaze, Alconai jerked his head to indicate the other end of the throne room. Before parting, Alconai squeezed Jabez's arm.

"Stay safe, Jabie," requested Alconai. He released Jabez and moved with Lancelot to help Solomon.

Lancelot turned with Alconai, hesitating as he noticed there were two battles beyond: Zatook was squaring up with Tannen to one side while Traiborn's spells blasted against the Sentinels on the other. Jabez had said Traiborn, but now the knight wondered which battle they should join. "So, crazy ageless king or mind-controlled shadow wielder?" he called to Alconai as they ran.

"Jabez said ta help Sol with t'e ageless king, so that be what I be doin'," answered Alconai as he ran. "'Sides, I donnae fancy bein' thrown through a wall by a Half-Celestial." Dodging a spell, Alconai whipped his yo-yo line around Traiborn's legs to hopefully trip the man. Alconai knew the group needed to get Traiborn's sword, but with the king throwing around spells and demonstrating his power there weren't going to be many opportunities to try.

***

For his part, Tannen sorrowfully met Zatook's gaze. As his friend advanced, Tannen's body shifted into a partial transformation. His wings sprouted from his back and his fingernails elongated into talons, scales stretching over his fingers and hands as they changed to be more dragon-like. Blue green, crystalline horns twisted from his brow and back over his head. His tail swept behind him as Tannen anticipated needing to dodge and parry. Gray skin turned black as scales covered his body. A deep growl reverberated from within Tannen's chest when Zatook charged and the warriors clashed.

"Zatook, friend, fight it," urged the dragon hybrid. "You don't have to let him control you. There are people here you care about— people who want to help you break free of the king's control." Tannen knew he might be wasting his breath, but he had to try.

At first, Zatook's reactions seemed sluggish, weaker than what Tannen knew he was capable of. But the longer they fought, the longer the spell delved into the crevices of Zatook's control, the stronger his blows came. Traiborn knew his shadow had reached a limit, and he was pushing him past it. Zatook's eyes were bloodshot, his skin paling, and still he fought. He didn't try to use his shadows or transform, but neither did he respond to his friend's words.

Tannen clashed with Zatook again and again, talons against the man's blade. At one point, Tannen managed to divert his friend's strike, moving the blade to the side. Taking the opening, Tannen attempted to tackle Zatook, one taloned hand locked around Zatook's sword hand's wrist. Tannen wrapped his other arm around Zatook's torso, attempting to grapple the man.

"Zatook, they need you. You're stronger than Traiborn and that's why he fears you. Look around. Traiborn is going after people you care about. He's going to kill them, imprison them, torture them. You've been there," urged Tannen, his voice slightly strained as he fought against his friend's strength. "Tristan needs you. Traiborn means to hurt him in ways only you understand. You don't want your lad to go through what you have. So fight for him. Fight for all of them. These people are battling to free you because they care. Fight for yourself— to be free of the king. You know there is a stronger power than him, so call to Them."

***

Captain sat on the stairs and watched the three battles unfold. Rose was wholly concentrated on healing Tristan, working to filter the poison from his blood. Tristan lay with his head in Rose's lap, the young man wheezing in pain and weakness. Sweat plastered his hair to his head and his clothes to his body.

Captain leaned back on her hands, taking stock of the situation and considering what their actions should be. They hadn't really known what they were getting into— Aria had simply informed them Tristan and Zatook had been stabbed and to take Tannen for aid. The rest was up to them. So how were they meant to handle this?

She wasn't exactly known for strategy. See enemy, stab enemy. See enemy, distract enemy, get away. That was about the extent. When that didn't work, she would use her Sight, either to read enemy movements or pick the best course of action. But she couldn't rely on that right now, and frankly, she didn't want to rely on it for everything. It should be a tool, not a crutch. Yet daggers wouldn't do much against a sorcerer as powerful as Traiborn, and she wasn't about to stab Zatook if she could help it. That left her Weaving. Captain sighed as she sat up straight. She had caught her breath from teleporting everyone, and she didn't want to just sit around while they fought. She focused her gaze and started searching through the threads. Her fingers slid through the air as she sorted through colors, looking to see who was who and what could be done. As Tannen managed to halt Zatook's movement, Captain was able to find the shadow warrior's threads. They were frayed and dulled, but there. Yet when she tried to reach them, her fingers passed through them almost like a shadow. Burning cold stung her hands where she had tried. That…was new. She had touched Zatook's threads before. Curious, she cast about through the room and found the pattern winding around the king. His threads had a similar sensation. It must have been something his magic was doing; she wasn't surprised he would have defenses against Weaving. She just needed to find a way around them.

With Rose working to remove the Celesbane, Tristan managed to fight his way back to consciousness enough to slit his eyes open. Blearily, he focused on Zatook locked in battle with Tannen. Tristan's hand shook as he reached for his mentor. Tannen holding Zatook in one place helped Tristan aim his Child power, but there were still other combatants between Zatook and the Sun Child, and the distance felt like miles with the lack of strength in Tristan's body. Pushing through the weakness and doubt, Tristan felt the warmth of his Sun Child power radiating from his shoulder down to the tips of his fingers. He pictured shooting his arrows in Nikko Mori, threading around the tree trunks and branches to reach his intended targets. On the other side of the room, a familiar power— weak but there —spread over the runes shackling Zatook to Traiborn's will. The Sun Child's power tugged, but the runes held. Exhausted as he felt, Tristan refused to give up now that he had a hold. He ignored the strength draining more from his body and the darkness threatening the edges of his vision. He was at his limit, but Tristan refused to let go.

***

As Alconai pulled tight on the wire, he saw Traiborn's boots crease beneath the pressure, but the man's legs didn't budge. Rather, he took a step, pulling the wire further apart and almost seeming to ignore it— at least until he dealt with Solomon. A well placed parry and a concussive blast knocked the guardian away and into Lance to interrupt the knight's charge towards them, buying time to glance down at the wire. Orange, burning runes wrapped around the metal line and began to race to its source, the metal starting to glow from the intense heat of the spell and yet not melt. Grateful for his gloves,

Alconai released the wire from Traiborn and retracted it back into his yo-yo, careful of the heated metal.

The king took another step forward, and power pulsed from him. Several runes lit to life on the ground before lightning flashed through the air, forcing the trio to focus on dodging the symbols. Traiborn raised the Runesaber, and the lightning struck faster and in more places. Lancelot frowned. A spell that showed where it would land seemed a bit simplistic for such a fabled sorcerer, regardless of how many spells he was simulcasting. Was controlling Zatook straining him that much, or…? The knight's eyes narrowed as he caught sight of the tome in Traiborn's other hand. He hadn't noticed at first with all the flashy spellwork, but energy was gathering above the pages. Traiborn was planning something big and trying to keep them occupied. Unfortunately, the knight didn't recognize the spell, but he didn't necessarily need to know what it was to channel against it. He dashed past a rune of lightning and drifted slightly along the tile floor, lowering a hand to keep his balance before taking off in a new direction without losing any speed. He channeled into his armor and felt it liquify and rise up to cover his face, leaving only a protected space from which to see. More glyphs shimmered among the metal before fading, and he turned his path to the king.

He didn't dodge the lightning anymore. Running a straight line to Traiborn, his boot crossed a rune just as it flashed, but the strike hit his armor. While the strange armor was able to resist some of it, he also channeled the energy of the magic to ground out the rest. It was jarring, painful even, but he didn't stop. Based on the strike, he could withstand one more; that meant he couldn't waste his movement.

Traiborn had lowered the blade now, several more area spells flashing through the air to try and keep space between them. He lifted the tome, and the book began to… well, Lance wouldn't describe it as 'glowing'. The opposite, really. It seemed to suck in all the light around it, yet the book was still eerily well-defined in the darkness. Dark flames ringed the area in which the four were fighting. Solomon grabbed Alconai and pulled him close so that he could use the Sentinels to divert whatever spell was about to be unleashed. Alconai stayed close to Solomon as the man defended them, but he couldn't help a smirk of pride despite his concern as he watched Lancelot maneuver. Lancelot had made it to within a few feet of the king. Solomon and Alconai just saw him step through another lightning bolt as the spell from the book suddenly concussed outward.

Rings of dark energy pulsed out from the king in rapid succession at varying heights and times. Lancelot jumped over the first and slid below the next. A sphere of dark fire had surrounded the tome and was growing with every pulse that created the rings. The book was rising higher into the air, which complicated things.

Lance, how 'igh d'ye need? Captain's voice cut through his concerns.

Very.

He felt the ever-more-familiar tug, and soon he was at the room's zenith. The feeling didn't completely leave; Captain kept her grip, gaze focused. The knight would need her to keep him from splatting on the floor when he was done with whatever he was trying to do. Trusting his safety to Captain, Lance positioned his sword in a point and let gravity drive his momentum.

Sealbreaker magic was strange. He couldn't draw on the magical energies of the world, the nine elemental magics, like a mage could. He couldn't draw and empower runes or cast spells like Traiborn. It was more reactionary. What he could do was cut through spells and, with enough channeling of the energies given off, potentially shatter foci like tomes and rods. He wasn't sure how much Traiborn needed the tome, but he *was* sure it was casting a hell of a spell right now. He was slightly surprised that Traiborn wasn't casting anything new his way to stop him, but the king's attention had snapped to Zatook.

Lancelot's sword tip met the sphere around the tome just as Tristan's power broke through the first few runes.

***

Tristan felt hope flicker in his heart as the first of the runes gave. However, there were still more. Ignoring the spells and the fighting, Tristan poured every ounce of determination into keeping his hold on the magic controlling Zatook. White flame spiraled from Tristan's shoulder down his arm, across his hand, and along his fingers to their tips. The Sun Child markings glowed brilliantly, clearly visible despite his clothing. The power gathered even as Tristan's body waned, his eyes alight with resolve. Thinking of the arrows flying through the forest, of Zatook's shadows weaving through enemies, of Captain's threads, Tristan focused on the lines of magic connecting his Child power to the runes along Zatook's body. Once he felt sure of the trajectory, Tristan chanced one look at Traiborn.

"He's not yours," declared the Sun Child quietly.

Light raced over the runes of magic, weaving into every layer and tracing every magical shackle. Tristan poured everything he had and more, blood trickling from his nose with the effort. He hoped. He prayed. He believed. The runes flared with white golden light and shattered. Tristan felt his arm— heavy and limp —hit the dais just before darkness swallowed his vision.

***

As Tristan freed Zatook, Lancelot pushed through the sphere to the tome. The room filled with blinding light and the sound of shattering glass. Tannen felt the weight in his arms grow heavier, and Rose shifted from stabilizing Tristan so he could use his powers without killing himself to working to heal him again. Captain closed her eye against the brightness, but it snapped open again when Lancelot's thread phased through her fingers.

The room started to shake. Tendrils of dark flame licked across a few surfaces as magic energy filled the room uncontained. Traiborn stood at its epicenter, eyes murderous. As Lancelot had pierced through his focus, the king had taken notice, stepping to the side and snapping a spell that would stop the Doran from saving him. Rather than just letting the knight hit the ground, which would have been entirely too unsatisfying, Traiborn had caught Lancelot's wrist and slammed the sealbreaker into the ground himself. Less fatal, still painful. He twirled the Etherium Runesaber and pointed it down; Alconai and Solomon had taken off at a run, the more spry entertainer outpacing the guardian in concern for his friend, but neither made it before the blade broke through Lance's armor.

As the knight gasped and choked, dark cracks spread from the point of the blade along the tiles of the floor.

"I have had enough."

Traiborn's voice sounded deeper. It reverberated through the room, the very air shuddering under the weight of his words. He jerked his sword out of the floor and Lancelot's back as the cracks spread and widened. Dark flames licked from the openings and then lashed out for anyone nearby, whipping at them, wrapping around their limbs to burn them, flashing through the air. Rose threw a shield around the three Children, but she couldn't reach the others *and* keep healing Tristan. The room continued to shake, cracks starting to form along the walls and ceiling. Traiborn turned to Alconai and stalked forward. Lance had stopped moving.

True to his name, Alconai FoxFeet nimbly dodged the flames trying to wrap around him, but they kept him from his goal. Despite trying to keep his cool, the sight of his friend lying motionless gripped Alconai with panic. Fear skittered along his bones with the powerful display from the king. Oi yosh, he was really in it now. Suddenly, fighting a controlled Half-Celestial sounded so much better than an ageless sorcerer king, and the king was moving right for Alconai. Mind racing and feet still moving, Alconai drew the short sword he had picked up at the smithies when he had started training with the group. Armed with the blade and his yo-yo, Alconai wondered what he could really do in this fight against a man who almost killed a Celestial and kept a Half-Celestial as a slave for centuries.

***

Captain had snapped out her hand, quickly winding her fingers through Lancelot's threads to hold them together. She coughed as she braced herself, the power suddenly pulling through her. She wouldn't be able to hold him long, but shifting him with this grip would mean she swapped with him instead of just transporting him. She glanced at the fight on the floor below. If someone else could get to him, stabilize him, she could adjust her grip. She shakily reached her other hand for another familiar thread. She grit her teeth and reached across the other connection. *Jabie.* It would take more than one person to distract the king, and someone needed to get Lance. As she focused, something else caught her eye: Traiborn's threads were flickering in and out of phase, almost like a flame.

***

Tannen shifted Zatook over his shoulders and used his own wings to give him a boost to the dais. Laying Zatook beside Tristan, Tannen allowed his body to take on more of his dragon shape, growing larger even as metal formed over his scales. He stopped when he could crouch over the Chosen and Zatook without impeding Rose and Captain's sight.

Rose cast Tannen a grateful glance; she didn't drop her own shield, but she returned her focus to Tristan. If Traiborn aimed for them, Tannen could buy her enough time to firm the shield around all of them rather than trying to just keep it up in case. But the king didn't seem to be paying them any mind for the moment.

He was more concerned with the ants scurrying about in front of him. He steadily picked up speed until he planted one foot and pushed off, closing the remaining distance in a blink. As Alconai lifted his sword to defend, the king batted it away as one would a fly before coming in with his other hand to sock Alconai hard enough to knock him off his feet and to the ground. Before Traiborn could follow up with his sword, Solomon reached them, catching the Runesaber between the Sentinels. Alconai could see Sol's knees buckling even as Traiborn lifted a boot and kicked the man's abdomen to knock him away; Nai was pretty sure he heard something snap, but Solomon just coughed and rolled over to pick himself up. He was moving more sluggishly, most of his energy gone from having held off the earlier spells. Traiborn turned his attention back to the minstrel. Alconai gripped his sword, ready to defend from his place on the ground. He stared for a moment when a shadow sailed over him.

The heel of a boot crunched into Traiborn's face with enough force to stagger the man back a step. Jabez landed gracefully in front of Traiborn and followed up his kick with a swipe of a dagger aiming for the king's throat. The Runesaber blocked the smaller weapon, and over the locked blades Jabez leveled the king with cold lividness.

"'A powerful mage is not immune to harm'," Jabez echoed Traiborn's own advice back at the man. "'All mages have their weaknesses'." Cuts tattered Jabez's clothes but none of his wounds proved serious. The same couldn't be said for the Shaedra agents he'd left sprawled at the other end of the throne room.

While Jabez had the king distracted, Alconai regained his feet and forced himself to move. Here he was faltering, and his brother literally leapt into the king's personal space like the sorcerer was any other opponent. Alconai joined his brother and slashed his short sword at the king to aid Jabez in disengaging with Traiborn. As soon as he pulled free, Jabez quickly dodged around the king to avoid squaring off with him. Now the brothers flanked the man as they considered their next moves. Alconai caught Jabez's gaze and noted the ninja using his eyes to indicate Traiborn's sword. Alconai gave his brother an imperceptible nod.

Traiborn reached his free hand up to his face, rubbing his thumb across his cheek. "I should have expected such audacity, considering who has helped train you," he growled. "I daresay you're the first person to land a blow on my face since LightningRider herself." Before Jabez could respond, a sharp and practiced whistle caught his attention before Sol tossed up the Sentinels. A rainbow flash surrounded them, and they appeared upright in the air in front of Jabez's ready hands. The ninja quickly grabbed the hilts and shifted his stance. Traiborn's eyes flashed to Solomon as the man started to move around them, but Jabez took the brief opening to reengage him. Traiborn stepped back to avoid the blow. He lifted his free hand to fire a spell at Alconai even as the Runesaber swiped at Jabez. The brothers danced around the king's blows, primarily defending to keep his attention, but they knew they couldn't defend forever. Eventually the pair would tire, and then Traiborn would strike them down.

While the pair kept the king occupied, Solomon made his way to Lancelot. He pulled off his vest but hesitated; he couldn't get the armor off. How was he supposed to help? For now, he wrapped the cloth around Lance's midsection and tied it taut. That seemed to be enough, as Captain shifted her grip and then pulled them both behind the shield. Tristan was stable, the Celesbane out of his system, so Rose quickly moved to stabilize Lancelot next. Captain was watching the trio below. They couldn't let the pair fight Traiborn alone for long, but what were they supposed to do? Rose wasn't in any shape to fight, and the man's magic was going haywire. Spells of all forms were crashing against Tannen's metal and scales, and while they mostly rolled off the half-dragon, it would be dangerous for the others. She could tell Solomon was more worn than he was letting on, and Lancelot and Zatook were both out cold. Frankly, she'd be surprised if Zatook woke up that *week*, but that was a worry for another time. First, Traiborn.

Captain narrowed her eyes as she watched the spells flaring around and examined the man's thread. With all of the fluctuation, perhaps other spells had suffered as well. Captain closed her eye and took a deep breath before opening both. No headache assailed her, and she grinned. She reached out, twining one hand through Jabez's threads and the other through Nai's so she could talk to them directly. Rather than reach out immediately, her hands started weaving through the threads almost on instinct.

It willnae las' long, but ye can talk ta each ot'er now, her voice whispered through the brothers' minds. *Some o' Traiborn's spells are slippin'. I migh' be able ta start affecting 'is magic, too, wit' a bit more time.*

We need to get the sword away from him, answered Jabez. The brothers kept moving as they fought the king. Since he wasn't the true wielder of the scimitars, Jabez couldn't fully activate the Sentinels' abilities, but the enchantments still diverted Traiborn's spells and magical effects to a degree. *Nai, I'm going to get him in another lock. When I do, use your yo-yo to pull the sword out of his grip,* Jabez instructed his brother.

That puts ye right up close, Jabie, Alconai protested.

Jabez tightened his grip on the Sentinels and insisted, *It's a gamble we'll have to take.*

Jabez closed the distance to Traiborn. Once more the ninja forced Traiborn into a lock with their swords, but this time Jabez positioned his second sword on the opposite side and end of Runesaber. Jabez stepped off to the side at the same time he pivoted his swords around Runesaber and used their positions to wrench Traiborn's sword lower to the ground. Traiborn's iron grip kept Jabez from forcing Runesaber out of the king's hand; however, Alconai's yo-yo wrapped around the blade and yanked. Between the force and speed of Jabez's maneuver and the compromising position the move put the king's wrist in, Traiborn failed to keep his grip when Alconai pulled, the sword flying to the minstrel. Alconai caught Runesaber, having sheathed his own sword when Jabez first stepped in close to the king again.

Rather than immediately step after the sword, Traiborn's palm came flat against Jabez's chest. He cast as he stood, a bolt of lightning-based magic shooting through the ninja, across the air, and into his brother. Traiborn's gaze was downright murderous as he held the grip, intent on electrocuting them both, regardless of any protections in their clothing. He would sear through them—

Or he would have, if that pirate witch hadn't pulled them

away and taken their place. Captain's gaze was just as dark, a dagger in each hand and both eyes open as she ran at him. He had no sword to help him now, no focus to allow his magics to be divided and controlled through the room. She had his attention, and she was going to keep it. She could see his thread more clearly now. It hadn't snapped back into reality quite yet, but it was slowly solidifying.

Captain wasn't the strongest fighter. She wasn't the best strategist. But she was quick, and she was angry. She didn't even bother bantering, leaping up with a spin and going straight for Traiborn's jugular. When he lifted a hand to stop her, she tweaked the fingers around her hilts and suddenly vanished to appear behind him, crouching and slashing at his ankles. She just nicked his boots as he jumped away, and she pressed up in a leap to follow, slashing again. Traiborn brought both hands together, palms out, and a ball of fire leapt from his hands, but she could see the weave within the magic. And she could See something she had never thought to try before.

She didn't halt her jump or move to dodge; she simply changed the target of her dagger from the king to the weave. By wrapping a bit of her power around the blade, not enough to set off anything dangerous, she managed to sever the threads. The fire dissipated into nothing, barely-warm embers tickling her face as she chained her leap to strike at the king again.

Surprise had flickered across his gaze, but he was catching on to her movement. He started firing more spells and dodging her strikes, and she kept cutting through his weaves or using the threads around to help her movement.

What would it take to wear this man down? How did he still have so much energy, so much stamina for magic? Even without his tome or his sword, he had yet to so much as need an extra breath. Sure, she had managed to surprise him, but that advantage was already gone. Even with her Sight, he was matching her movements, guessing where she would appear, shifting his spells to trace instead of just flare. The pair were constantly moving, attacking, dodging. Since the throne room was no longer filled with lightning and fire and other large spells, the battle seemed eerily quiet. The sounds of boots and feet against tile, the swish of cloth and slice of metal, the sounds of spells. There was no banter, no glib remarks. Just two furious fighters brought to a similar power level because one was at her peak and the other had been brought down several pegs.

Rage fueled her movements, and something more. This man had hurt her friends. He had almost killed Tristan, done unspeakable things to Zatook, almost killed Lance, and hurt her brother and…well, whatever Nai was at this point. Were they a thing? Now really wasn't the time to think about it. But she also knew she couldn't afford to let her anger get the best of her. She couldn't afford to lose. She was one of the few party members still upright, and they would all be damned to Traiborn's wrath should she fall. This needed to end. She needed to win. But the question again became 'how'. What did she have that could truly overcome a man who had been alive for centuries, who had bested even Celestials?

Captain spun her grip on the daggers, throwing them. As they flew, she drew more from within the strips of cloth that made her skirt and threw and threw and threw. As Traiborn worked to dodge or blast them away,

Captain reached out and found the threads that filled the air around them. Her daggers suddenly seemed to be enchanted, staying in the air and flying at the king from multiple directions. One scraped past his cheek, one sliced against his glove, a third cut his waistcoat. And yet she couldn't land a solid hit. Captain growled, grasping a handful of threads and pulling herself around to another area in the room as Traiborn leveled several spells at where she had been standing. She didn't stop, sliding a bit before taking off in a run to continue avoiding the barrage. She dropped to the ground and slid the last few paces to get behind a pillar. She sat for a second, breathing heavily.

"Are you quite done?" His voice was quiet yet firm. "Is hiding all you have left?" A spell with decent force slammed against the pillar to taunt her, actually shaking the stone. "Shall the spider finish the little gnat?" Captain closed her eyes, leaning her head back against the pillar as she caught her breath. She could hear his boots crossing the room. There had to be something she could do. An edge from her powers, something in the Weaves, anything. "Did you honestly think your little rabble could do what myriads more powerful than you have attempted and failed? You could not even protect one little girl."

Captain's eyes snapped open. She stood, brushing off her skirts, and stepped out from behind the pillar.

"There you— "

Her hand lashed out, wrapping around the pattern connected to Traiborn. The king stopped mid-step, his mouth twisted into a sneer. Her hand started to burn like it had when she tried to help Zatook, but this time the threads didn't slip free. She wouldn't let them, rainbow sparkles swirling around her hand as an oil-like shimmer coated the threads. It still faded to ash as it got away from her. She could feel the destructive energies building up within her, fighting to be free. But she wouldn't give it the time to. She twisted her other hand to summon a dagger to her grip, and moved to cut.

Everything stopped. Even the lights from the crystals throughout the room held their shine in the exact position. Captain's hair hovered in the air from her movements, her blade inches from Traiborn's threads.

"Isabella."

She was free. Captain straightened, not releasing her grip on the threads just in case, and turned to face Aria. Only, the woman did not appear as before. Instead, Captain found herself facing a beast of legend. The fierce cat was taller than the Doran girl, with pure white fur. Red danced through the strands in runes, shapes, and patterns too fast for her to watch unaided. A red sash of ribbon wrapped around Aria's foreleg, hovered in the air over her shoulders, and came down to wrap around the other foreleg. Saberteeth gleamed in the light of the throne room, and her heterochromatic eyes were focused on Captain. She sat down.

"What you are about to do—"

"Donnae ye dare tell me nae ta kill 'im," Captain interrupted with a growl. Aria paused, then tilted her head slightly.

"I will not. But I cannot let you proceed without a word of warning. Severing a life from the Pattern comes with a heavy toll. With great power comes great cost— thus is the balance of most magics. And this magic, in particular, is mine. I did not gift it to make death simple."

Captain frowned. "So, wha'? Life fer a life or somethin'?"

"I cannot tell you the cost. You have felt the toll of learning, of transporting, seeing, controlling. I can only tell you that the cost is there. Shaddai alone knows the price you will pay."

Captain turned to the threads in her hand, considering. What was she willing to pay to kill this man? He had hurt her friends, hurt Zatook. He would do even worse if he survived this fight. "If t'ere be a cost, then I'll pay it. Even if I die, I cannae let 'im escape our fight."

"You would die for the pride of victory?" There was no accusation, more like a prodding.

"No. I would die ta save me frien's an' ta free Andor, even if t'ey donnae ken t'ey need savin'." To punctuate her statement, Captain brought her dagger up and severed Traiborn's connection to the Pattern.

For the others, no time had passed between Captain snatching the air and then swinging her dagger. A brilliant flash of rainbow filled the space, shining to pure white for a few seconds before finally fading. As the room came back into focus, both Traiborn and Captain were lying on the floor.

27. Afterimage

In darkness, Tristan first noticed the warmth wrapped around his body. Instead of hard flooring, he felt softness cocooning him, trapping the heat and keeping the cold in his body bearable. As the darkness faded, Tristan saw faint light glowing through his eyelids. Slowly, he forced his eyes open, the lids feeling heavy. It took a couple of tries for him to keep them open and to focus, but finally he recognized the interior of his guest room. Tristan's chest rose and fell with a heavy sigh as he worked his way to full wakefulness. His gaze landed on Rose. She was reading while sitting at his bedside. Despite his body feeling heavier than lead, Tristan pulled his arm free of the blankets and reached for her. He barely managed to lift his hand enough to lightly brush his fingers along the back of her hand. Rose's eyes glanced up from her pages at the movement, and her hand found his as she set the book aside with a soft smile.

"I would say good morning, but I do believe we are closer to afternoon by now," she greeted gently. "Do you think you can drink? I have some water for you, and there's a health potion."

His voice felt stuck in his throat, so Tristan simply gave a small nod. The sooner he found his voice the sooner he could ask questions. What happened after he passed out? Were the others okay? Had they lost anyone? His mind flashed to Zatook and the man's state the last Tristan had seen him. Pushing through the dryness in his mouth and throat, Tristan barely rasped, "Z-Zatook?"

"Alive. Asleep." Rose released his hand to fetch the water first. The potion was a little thicker, so a wet throat would make it easier to swallow. "You managed to break the runes binding him, and in the moment of distraction, Lancelot was able to destroy Traiborn's tome." She helped him sit up so he could drink. "We did not lose any of our own," she assured him softly. "Though, most of you were heavily wounded. Jabez and Solomon are up and recovering. Alconai has woken a few times. Now you. That leaves Captain, Lancelot, and Zatook who have yet to at least regain consciousness."

Tristan lightly touched Rose's hand holding the cup to his lips. He sipped the water until his tongue felt looser and his words easier. "What happened to Captain?" he asked, concerned. Even with the worry for his surrogate cousin, Tristan felt relief with the knowledge everyone in their group lived. Still feeling weak, he gratefully accepted Rose's help with drinking the potion. A little more strength and warmth spread through his body and chased away the cold that tried to set in now that he wasn't fully beneath the bedcovers.

Rose considered. "I...am not entirely certain." After helping him settle back into bed, she told him of the battle. How Traiborn had taken Lance down for destroying his tome and aimed for Alconai next. Jabez's daring intervention, and the brothers retrieving the Runesaber. Then she told him of Captain's fight. "I do not fully understand what happened at the end," she confessed. "She came out from the pillar, caught something in her hands, and then there was a brilliant light and they were both on the ground. Traiborn was dead, and she unresponsive. I had hoped to ask Aria, but she has been with the queen. 'Damage control', as she put it." Rose leaned back in her chair and folded her hands. "The city knows the king is dead. I do not think they know how or why as of yet, but I am uncertain. The presence of the queen and the oracle have helped to quell the panic for now, but they have much to do. Corianne's magic is still sealed, as well."

"I want to get up and check to see if there is anything I can do to help our friends recover," Tristan murmured. He sighed as he sunk back into the mattress. "However, I still feel weak." He was glad to feel his connection to his Celestial abilities, but he knew he would need more rest. He had pushed himself. "How long has it been? Has anyone contacted Aunt Amaya? Zatook had left me a note saying that she was wounded with injuries like the ones I sustained when I tried transforming. Burns from the Talisman. However, at the time, she couldn't come here, and it was too dangerous for me to go to her. Amaya would want to know about Captain, and with the king dead, the barriers keeping her out should be gone, right?"

"We are not yet sure," Rose confessed. "Since the king tied off the spell sealing the locket, it is possible those wards are also still in effect. And we do not yet have a way to reach out to Amaya. We looked through Zatook's things for the crystal he had told us about, but we could not find it. He had likely hidden it before reporting to the king." She sighed, reaching up to brush some loose hairs away from her face. "It has been several days."

Tristan felt little surprise with how much time had

passed. He half expected that he had been out for days considering getting stabbed with the Celesbane dagger had nearly killed Amaya in her fight with Traiborn. Then Tristan exacerbated his condition by using his Sun Child power. He felt more concerned for Zatook, Lancelot, and Captain and their prolonged unconsciousness. Lancelot, he knew, most likely just needed rest.

"I want to look at Captain and Zatook. Maybe I can discern something with my Sun Child healing," said Tristan. "I also want to go find Amaya or find a way to contact her. However, I know I should wait and see just how recovered I really am. I get the feeling if it was serious enough Aria would have told us. Or so I hope." Tristan gave Rose a sincere look. "I remember you treating me in the throne room. Thank you. Getting stabbed with that dagger felt… well…horrible." He shivered as the memory sent chills down his spine.

"The healers are taking good care of Captain, and Tannen has Zatook," Rose assured him. "There is no rush for you to see to them." She leaned forward, reaching for his hand. "I owe your grandmother a great deal for training me in how to do so. I am glad I learned in time." She gently squeezed it.

Tristan returned the squeeze weakly. "I'm grateful to you both. For saving me and, I'm assuming, watching over me in the aftermath," he told Rose. "I'm sorry for what it put everyone else through, but I don't regret standing up for Zatook. I'm glad it worked out, and that I was able to do something to help. Especially given I'm the one who pissed off the king in the first place." Tristan gave Rose's hand a small, playful tug. "You keep saving me. I suppose there are worse things than being in your debt forever."

He gave her a weary smile.

Rose chuckled. "We knew it was likely a matter of time before we ruffled his feathers," she assured him. "Jabez told me what happened. I cannot say I would have been able to keep myself back, either." She sat up, sliding her hand away. "Now that you are awake, however, you should eat. There is some broth in warmers downstairs." She activated the TekChair and moved to the door. She paused on her way out, turning to face him. "I shall add this to your tab," she teased with a smirk before closing the door.

Tristan smiled at her tease. Once he was alone, he shifted his gaze to the window and let his mind wander. While he felt relief, he also felt trepidation for the changes his actions had caused. There probably had been a better way to handle things with the king, but in the moment, all Tristan could think of was his own torture at his father's hands and Arianna's death. Seeing Zatook's mistreatment firsthand had been the spark to ignite Tristan into action. What kind of Sun Child— what kind of person — would he be if he had just walked away? Yet, his actions pushed the group to commit regicide, and three of theirs lay unconscious with the others recovering once more. Tristan closed his eyes. Nothing for it now. They were alive. They would recover. Then they would figure out their next steps.

***

Jabez surveyed the king's study. He moved to the worktable where Traiborn had had the notes about the Celesbane dagger and the vial of Zatook's blood. Despite the disapproving glances from Solomon, Jabez hadn't been able to stay still. Thanks to his training and precautions with the leather in his normal outfit, Jabez had been one of the ones to regain consciousness first. Still, he had taken the brunt of the lightning spell and Traiborn's fury in the king's attack. Healing potions and rest helped immensely to speed up the group's recovery, but the healers were busy with healing soldiers fighting in the war still waging at Andor's border. So, the Chosen Children and their companions were left largely to heal on their own.

Considering the state of their group, slipping away from Solomon's even more watchful eye had been a bit difficult for Jabez, especially with his own body still healing. Jabez couldn't help feeling some exasperation at being back in a state of recovery, but that was the price he paid for fighting an ageless sorcerer king. Jabez planned to take it easy, but he wanted to help even if only a little. With Tristan out of commission, they needed another way to extract the Celesbane from Zatook, so the man could regain his Celestial healing. Thus, Jabez's return to Traiborn's study. This time he dismantled the wards completely— the king wouldn't hear them anyway. Looking over the notes, Jabez saw the same cipher he had noticed during his previous venture. Since signs in the torture chamber and in the study pointed to Traiborn using Zatook to test the Celesbane, Jabez deduced the king had a way to remove the Celesbane when he was done. With the king gone, Jabez now had time to study the cipher and see if he could discover the king's removal method.

With a sense of nauseating familiarity, Jabez spun around when he sensed a presence behind him. Stiff and sore his body moved slower, and a hand wrapped around his throat, cutting off his air with a crushing grip. Jabez's back hit the bookshelf as his attacker bodily pinned him, ignoring a few books raining down on the pair. A fist slammed into Jabez's sternum, knocking the remaining air from his lungs and making him see stars, but the grip on his neck kept Jabez firmly pinned, the shelves digging into his back and shoulders.

"With the king dead, I thought you might return here," Rugan's voice spoke against Jabez's ear. "It was only a matter of time before you would slip up and fall into Shaedra's grasp again. And now here you are." Jabez choked as Rugan squeezed to punctuate his point. His vision clearing, Jabez glared at the man despite the fear pounding his heart against his ribcage. Air suddenly filled his lungs again when a hand wrenched Rugan's from Jabez's throat. In the same move, the newcomer shoved Rugan away from Jabez.

Gulping down air and leaning against the shelves, Jabez observed the second ninja now standing between Rugan and him. The newcomer's physique appeared masculine in Shaedra's uniform with the man standing a tad shorter than Jabez and with an agile build similar to Tristan. Jabez recalled the ally within Shaedra that Solomon had mentioned. Was this that person?

"Eclipse," Rugan growled. "Explain yourself. You're already on thin ice with Shroud due to your failure last time you guarded this room."

"I got a reprimand, true enough," Eclipse replied evenly, "However, as I understand it, Shroud deemed you the main one responsible for letting the Order member interrupt the king. In a lapse of judgment, you left your post. Now, you demonstrate your poor decision making by attacking Phoenix while the palace is on higher alert due to the king's death and Shaedra's recent attempt in absconding with our rogue agent. Phoenix's comrades will notice if harm comes to one of their own or if one goes missing, especially since they know we look to reclaim him."

"Don't lecture me, boy," spat Rugan quietly. "I know you let that Order member get the better of you. For Shroud's pet, you went down too easily."

Eclipse shrugged and splayed his hands helplessly as he nonchalantly countered. "I'm not infallible. As Shroud saw it, my fault was fully putting my trust in my then superior's judgement. The Order member shouldn't have even known about the study, but he found it after you left. What does that say about your skills in keeping to the shadows, Rugan?" Rugan growled with the taunt. However, Eclipse's demeanor changed as he shifted his weight into a relaxed but ready stance. "Leave Phoenix be, Rugan. By Shroud's orders we are to vacate the palace and lay low. We'll have other chances, and you wouldn't want to embarrass yourself again by disregarding Shroud's orders, would you?"

"I will put you in your place, *child*. Or perhaps I should report you to your handlers," Rugan threatened. "They know best how to teach you to respect your betters."

"My handlers know I pay respect to my superiors when I am in the presence of one," countered Eclipse coolly.

The tension hung thick in the air as the two Shaedra agents stared each other down. However, Rugan finally retreated from the study, his very presence radiating animosity. After waiting several seconds once the door closed, Eclipse turned to Jabez, stepping back some to give the man more room.

"Why?" Jabez asked simply. "Why are you risking yourself for me? I don't recognize your moniker as being one I knew in my time at Shaedra."

"You don't know me, but I know of you," Eclipse supplied. "Shroud speaks highly of you despite your defection. Actually, I would say he speaks highly of you because you managed to defect and stay defected. You are a trophy as much as a thorn to him."

"That's not all that comforting. I don't really understand why he would want me back alive. He has better subordinates than me now, and I know secrets that would be cause enough to kill any other deserters," mused Jabez.

"You have attested to your skills by remaining beyond Shroud's reach. I can't fully speak to the man's designs and motives, but I can speculate that he sees what an asset you could be if he managed to bring you back into the fold. And the threat you pose if he fails," Eclipse answered. "My interest lies in the latter. The moniker Shroud gave you is a bit on the nose but accurate. No matter how much or how many times people try to crush you into the ground, you always push yourself back to standing. You haven't let Shaedra crush you, and you got out and stayed out. I want to keep it that way. So know, ShadowDancer, that you have an ally in the shadows."

"If you are looking to take down Shroud, I'm afraid I won't be much help," Jabez told the man. "My escape took its toll, and I'm still paying the price."

Jabez felt Eclipse's eyes regarding him even without seeing them behind the mask. "All the same, you give me hope, and something to aspire to," the man said. "I hope perhaps we can help each other when circumstances allow. Such as now." He produced a piece of paper from one of his pouches and set it on the desk. "A token of my goodwill: the key to the king's cipher. It's only a partial one since one of the languages used has been difficult to obtain. Given whom you travel with, I get the feeling someone from the Order might be able to help with it."

"Why would Shroud have any key to the king's cipher?" asked Jabez. He straightened from the shelves as he watched his supposed ally.

"The king hired Shaedra, but Sir Jeremiah employed us first. Shroud decided what better way to glean information about Andor for Nocis than to infiltrate under the guise of taking King Traiborn's request," replied Eclipse.

"Playing both sides does sound like Shroud," Jabez remarked dryly. Then he added, "You are called Eclipse?"

"Yes. However," the man said, "my true name is Seradin." Reaching up, the man pulled off his full-head mask. Ebony hair plastered to his head from having the cloth covering it. Aquamarine eyes regarded Jabez with a keen, intellectual gaze. The man appeared young, not much older than Tristan in human years. However, the most striking things about him were the silver markings curving and swirling across part of Seradin's face and disappearing beneath the fabric of his shirt, almost invisible due to the young man's pale complexion.

"A Sylvarin," breathed Jabez. "Can't say I was expecting that. I can see why Shroud had you in Andor, though. You could easily pass for a visitor from Sylva Arae."

"That was the idea," Seradin confirmed. "Now, you have a face to both names, so you'll know me without my mask." Replacing his mask, Seradin inclined his head to Jabez. "Stay safe, ShadowDancer. Stay free." With that, the young man left the study.

Jabez watched where his alleged ally retreated for a moment. While he felt hesitant to trust the Sylvarin, Jabez also understood how much the young man risked with what he had already done for Jabez and shared with him. Retrieving the paper from the desk, Jabez glanced over it. Well, this would make studying a lot easier if it was real. Gathering the king's notes and the key to the cipher, Jabez headed back to the guest tower.

Jabez spent the next several hours poring over the cipher. It was a complex mesh of runes and glyphs from different magics plus words and letters from various languages. Between what Shaedra had and what he had learned on his own at the Order, he was able to make up a complete key. He wrote down extra copies before turning to the notes. When Solomon came down at one point to check on him, he took a copy of the key and a set of papers to look over, as well. The older man didn't pester Jabez about wandering the castle; with Traiborn's demise, Aria was now free to speak with them in Common. She had already assured them that she would convey any important information if needed.

Aside from a power-hungry fantasy-building egomaniac, Traiborn had been a meticulous researcher. His notes spanned all manner of subjects, from the natural to the supernatural. Jabez found notes on ancient magics, runic combinations, and powerful artifacts. There were detailed studies on the anatomy of all manner of races and creatures, and diatribes on how certain magics affected them. He found research on various plant life and tonics, animal husbandry, even Tek engineering. It would be easy to get lost in the notes, but Jabez had a goal. He started skimming the various papers for any mention of Celesbane or Zatook.

It hadn't taken long for him to find once he realized Traiborn wouldn't write about Zatook by name. As soon as he identified the chosen moniker, the papers started to pile up.

Jabez refused to let the revelation distract him. The king was dead; retribution had. Instead, he found the sections regarding the king's methods for getting Zatook back to function after the sessions using Celesbane against the Half-Celestial. Jabez looked for ways the group could apply the practice since the palace's healers were busy. Tristan needed to rest, and Rose was looking after her beau. That left Solomon and Jabez and Tannen to handle the extraction of the Celesbane.

For all the experiments and research notations, there was little in the way of learning what could heal Zatook. His own healing was sufficient for Traiborn's purposes; however, he ran into the unique predicament that Celesbane prevented Zatook from healing on his own. He *had* to find a way to remove it, or his sword would be useless.

"The creature's blood presents a unique problem,"

read the notes. "It is one of the few types that cannot be touched by blood magics of any form. Healing does naught but harm it. Records exist of various magics that might be harnessed to rid the bane, but while the temptation exists to pursue more systems of magic, the current need renders the solution impractical.

It is in the arts of Andor that I find my inspiration. Infused runecrafting, combining the marvel of science and the natural world with magics to obtain a desired result. Tekkers have found a way to use magic to remove contaminants from water to make it safer to consume; the priestesses have been investigating a way in which to apply the concept to healing, to remove harmful substances from the bloodstream when magic is unavailable. If I were to combine this concept to what I have learnt of the bane and the blood, I may find a simple solution."

He went on to discuss his various attempts, rune combinations and their results when exposed to infected blood. Then he went on to trying different tools.

"The spell itself is simple now, a matter of memory. But with all things, a single method should not suffice. Were the creature to need purging in my absence, particularly for an urgent mission, then it must have a way to do so itself. The tool must be something simple, so even the creature cannot misunderstand its application and need not pester another for aid."

Now came more diagrams, more attempts to create something that could hold the spell and remove the bane. The first devices proved too large, too cumbersome. Later ones had no way to remove the bane once it was separate from the blood. New runecrafting came into play, something to adhere the bane to metal so it could be pulled from a wound. Finally, there was a finished diagram: a long metal apparatus shaped like a thorn, with a hollow interior. Halfway up the thorn, magic-conducting crystal crawled like vines to the end point, where it gathered in a small ball. According to Traiborn's notes, the thorn would draw the bane from the blood and gather it in crystalline form in a separate space. Once all of the bane had been removed, the crystal globe would shine to let the user know the process was complete.

Jabez considered the information. There were two places the king might have kept the apparatus, and Jabez doubted Traiborn would let Zatook enter the study in the king's absence. That left the torture chamber Jabez had found with Alconai. His blood running cold, Jabez leaned his arms heavily on the table. Was it smart for him to go to the chamber after what happened last time and so soon after another encounter with Shaedra? Pressing his palms against his eyes, Jabez rubbed them with a tired groan. After a moment, he pressed his hands flat on the tabletop and pushed himself to his feet. This time he had Solomon follow him just in case.

They walked the now familiar path to the library, to the bookcase, and down into the passage. Jabez moved slowly due to trepidation and his own continued recovery. Once they reached the chamber, Jabez's feet refused to move into the room. Staring into the space meant for punishment and brainwashing, Jabez felt a cold sweat break out over his body. He felt Rugan's knuckles digging into his sternum and the man's fingers around his throat, the areas aching still from the encounter. Jabez forced himself to take a deep breath and slowly release it. He breathed again. Through the pain trying to surface. Pushing out the memories attempting to drown him. His resolve steeling, Jabez deliberately stepped into the chamber proper. His goal giving him clarity and focus, Jabez searched the room until he found the apparatus. His hand remained steady as he plucked the instrument from among the other tools. Making one sweep around the room to make sure he hadn't missed anything, Jabez had Solomon follow him back up to the library and then to where he knew Tannen was tending Zatook.

Traiborn's meticulous notes served them well in using the tool to remove the Celesbane from the Half-Celestial's blood. Though he continued to sleep, already they could see signs of his naturally accelerated healing at work. Now all they had to do— all they really could do —was wait.

True to his stubborn nature, even with everything that had happened, that his body had been through, Zatook did not make them wait long. Come the next morning, when Tannen awoke and moved to change Zatook's bandages, he found the warrior staring blearily at the ceiling.

Seeing his friend awake, Tannen let out a sigh of relief as well as a slight chuckle. "Of course, you're awake already. Not like you came from the battlefield half dead and then endured being healed and tortured again all within the span of a few hours," the blacksmith snarked. However, he settled beside Zatook and got to work changing the bandages. Even if the man wasn't fully lucid for a conversation, Tannen continued speaking to give his friend a focal point. "Tristan is alive. They all are. The king is dead, and you are free. Jabez found Traiborn's notes and learned about the king's methods for extracting

Celesbane from you. Now, you're on the mend."

Zatook didn't respond at first, his muddled mind working to catch up. So. Tristan healing him hadn't been a dream, or his confronting the king an elaborate nightmare. But they were alive. And his master... Zatook blinked. The king was dead. Traiborn was dead? A million things crossed his mind, yet he didn't have the concentration to pick just one. What would Andor do with their king gone in the middle of a war? Was his mother free now? His father? How did they manage it? Did the man not have some hidden trick up his sleeve to make it only appear as though he had died? Were the wards keeping Amaya out— Amaya. Suddenly the sight of her standing in the Breach, facing the oncoming army, filled his mind. If Traiborn had left, if Traiborn was dead, was she still holding the Wall? He quickly tried to sit up, but Tannen's hand on his shoulder stopped him. Rather than fight it, Zatook lifted his hand and called the crystal. There were no messages from Amaya, so instead he tried to send her one. To see where she was, if she could pass the border now.

She didn't respond, and he tried to sit up again.

Since Zatook insisted, Tannen helped him sit up but kept his hands on the man's shoulders. He glanced at the crystal and had a sneaking suspicion regarding its purpose.

"What are you trying to do? I can get the others to help. Jabez and Solomon are recovered enough to help look after everyone," Tannen offered.

Zatook ran a hand through his hair to push it away from his face. He lowered his hand, palm up. *I need to find*

Amaya, he explained, before hastily conveying why and where she had been.

Tannen hesitated. He didn't know anything about the goings on at the Wall or the battles waging. However, if Zatook had come back in as bad a shape as he did, then there was a possibility that this Amaya was no longer alive. It had been days since Zatook's return.

Before Tannen could voice his concerns or make any suggestions, a consciousness touched Zatook's mind. The touch felt gentle and patient, warm. It waited for Zatook's invitation before a voice spoke, *Amaya is in Nikko Mori. Seek out Clovestein in the cabin by the sea.* The voice sounded soft but strained with effort— distracted but desperate. *Please, Zatook. I know you and Tristan need rest, but please take my sister to the Sun Child. Amaya is dying, and I cannot go to her.*

As though to confirm the voice's urgency, the messaging crystal flickered as the connection to its twin wavered.

Tannen's grip did nothing to dissuade Zatook standing now. He was already spelling out the request to have Tristan ready for his arrival even as he summoned fresh clothes. He was gone before Tannen could finish reading, setting the shadows to stay for a bit so the message would last. He did not tarry, even to gauge the battle at the Breach. He dove deep underground and sped through the darkest depths to beneath the blessed forest. Since the voice told him to seek Clovestein, he guessed correctly that the forest would let him enter. It was mere moments before he appeared along the coast.

Even standing on the coast, he could sense powerful

magic. Music permeated the air, a gentle, soothing melody that seemed to come from everywhere rather than just the cabin. Zatook did not pause to marvel, though the magic in the air had him wary. He walked right up to the door and knocked. It wouldn't do to barge in on strangers; they would be on edge, from Amaya's state and Tsukuyomi's last attack.

The door opened almost before he finished knocking. Instead of Clovestein, a short, elven woman stood in the doorway. Her wavy, silvery white hair cascaded about her shoulders and down her back, framing her face as her bright green eyes peered at him with relief rather than alarm.

"Well met, son of Queen Corianne. I am Feray. Hoshiko told us to expect you," the woman explained. Due to her eleven heritage, she appeared rather young. The fabric of her simple purple frock with a teal bodice and overlay swished as she stood back and ushered Zatook into the cozy abode. The aroma of herbs and woodsmoke filled the air, giving the space a homey feel. Natural light lit the spaces. As they passed a room, a glance inside revealed a tidy desk with papers and books and writing utensils. A table stood near the desk with different instruments for herbalism, runecrafting, and alchemy. Feray led Zatook to a guest room toward the back of the cabin. Clovestein sat beside the bed. Despite Zatook's arrival, the Drow kept his gaze on his patient. His hands hovered and glowed as he poured healing magic into his charge.

Amaya lay still— far too still for the energy she usually radiated. She was dressed in a sleeveless blouse for comfort, a thick blanket hiding the rest of her outfit farther down. Bandages wrapped around her arms and peeked out from under the neckline of her shirt. The dreadfully familiar burns now covered her arms completely and crept across her shoulders and clavicle like black, spindly fingers reaching sickeningly for her throat and heart. The burns contrasted sharply with the porcelain pallor of Amaya's complexion. Her ebony tresses stuck to Amaya's face and shoulders and neck, damp with perspiration. Bruises and cuts marred Amaya's face, her expression pained. Breaths wheezed between Amaya's parted lips. In one hand, she weakly grasped the messaging crystal. As though sensing his presence, Amaya's eyes slit open to reveal her glassy, silver gaze.

"Sh-Shadow?" she slurred, the words barely pushing past her lips.

"He's here, Amaya. He's going to take you with him," Feray told her. Then to Zatook, she added, "She's been out of it for days. Shaddai only knows how she managed to get herself to us. We've done what we can with healing magic and runic wards around her vital organs. This corrosive magic is beyond us, and it's keeping her exhausted enough that her other wounds are healing slower than they should even with help."

Amaya's voice rasped again, "Came...f'r...me?"

Zatook crossed the room quickly, taking in everything around him yet ignoring it for Amaya. He gently brushed some of her hair away from her face; he wasn't sure she was lucid enough to see him signing, but at least she would know he really was there.

Another stranger lounged in an armchair nearby, dressed all in blue. He would have looked perfectly in place on

Captain's ship with his loose-fitting trousers, trimmed and shaped coat, and wide-brimmed hat with a plume of feathers. Like Zatook, a stretch of cloth reached up to cover the lower portion of his face. Sitting almost sideways, with one foot up on the edge and the other dangling, he seemed completely relaxed despite the atmosphere. He was the source of the music, a lute propped across his lap. A myriad of other instruments filled the cabin; even with his quick glance, Zatook picked out a lyre, a shamisen, a sitar, a flute. And yet he could sense there was more than just music to the man. Crystal clear water, filled with the same energy as the notes in the air, coiled around what he could see of Amaya, joining with Clovestein's magic. The man didn't move from the chair to greet Zatook. The wide-brimmed hat and his ebony hair shaded his face aside from one shockingly vibrant blue eye watching their visitor. Despite the man's languid pose and carefree music, the gaze was as sharp and cool as ice.

"I daresay you can flirt later, Amaya. You have somewhere to be." The sharp gaze softened with the tease. "You should take her through the shadows, lad. Flying will be rougher than magic."

Zatook nodded, turning to look at them. "I am grateful for what you have done. On your word, I will take her," he signed to Feray.

The water that was coiling Amaya's limbs shimmered, reflecting a myriad of colors and lights before spreading to cover her in a thin barrier. The magic would help hold Amaya steady until the young prince could get her to the Sun Child. Amaya fell silent aside from her labored breathing, her eyes glazed. However, she leaned weakly into Zatook's touch. Clovestein released his own magic and sat back.

"Be well, Princess of the Sea," Clovestein said in farewell and smiled softly at Amaya. "Return soon to regale us with your adventures of seafaring. We have missed you, lass."

Feray bowed her head in acknowledgement to Zatook's gratitude. "Amaya insisted on holding the crystal even though she had not the strength to use it," the woman told him, a twinkle in her eye. She stepped over to the musician and touched his shoulders, her fingertips glowing as she bolstered his magic with her own.

Zatook's gaze dropped to the crystal, but he did not allow the idea to distract him. At the man's signal, he left. Rather than lift her and risk deepening her pain, Zatook let his shadows wrap around Amaya and shift her into the darkness. Once more he sped without delay, straight to Petalore and then into the palace. He could sense Tannen with Tristan in the parlor of the guest tower, but he took Amaya to the infirmary instead. While he shifted her out of the shadows onto one of the beds, Tannen and Tristan felt something brush against their ankles before the shadows rose up and wrapped around them. When the darkness fell away, the pair were in the infirmary near Amaya's bed. The shimmering water still wrapped around her, lights dancing within. Zatook didn't leave her side.

Tristan staggered in surprise upon arrival, but the sight of Amaya caught his attention. Quickly Tristan knelt at Amaya's bedside, his eyes wide at the foreign magic and the severity of the Talisman's damage. However, something about the magic seemed familiar. Gently,

Tristan touched the water. It took him a moment since it had been so long since he last felt it, but Tristan recognized the magic. As he poured his own healing into Amaya, Tristan encountered the runes, but instead of pushing him back, they welcomed him like an old friend.

"She was with Takumi and Feray," Tristan murmured more to himself than to the other men. Instead of focusing on that revelation, Tristan gathered his power and concentrated as he worked to heal Amaya.

Tristan focused on removing the burns from the Talisman since that was the bigger threat and the hardest to mend. Guilt gnawed at him, but he refused to give in to the distraction, not while his aunt's life was at stake. The power washed over Amaya in a white gold glow, but tongues of golden flame also swirled around her body, healing instead of burning. Slowly, the burns receded until they vanished altogether. Tristan knew he needed to stop; he wasn't fully recovered from over-exerting himself in the previous battle. However, he hated to leave Amaya in a state of pain and injury. Even as he debated with himself, Tristan pushed to heal the worst of her wounds. Tired and weak as he felt, he needed to get Amaya to where she would be safe to heal on her own. And yet, he should do more. She was in this state because of him. They all were.

After a little time passed, Tristan barely registered Tannen touching Amaya's shoulder, presumably to check on her. When Tannen's other hand touched Tristan's, the young Celestial continued healing anyway.

"Tristan, you're going pale and starting to shake," Tannen spoke gently but firmly. "She's all right to heal on her own now. You've done enough."

It was true Tristan felt tremors wracking his body, and color slowly returned to Amaya's cheeks. Still, Tristan hesitated to pull away. He barely managed to keep his hands in place when Tannen used a little more strength to push against them.

"Enough, lad," the dragon softly ordered. "There's no reason to run yourself ragged. You won't be any good to anyone then."

"She's like this because of me. It's my fault," Tristan insisted, his words tinged with bitter remorse. "It's all my fault. Everything is my fault." He jerked and weakly thrashed when he felt a pair of hands pull him away from Amaya and Tannen. Tristan quickly found himself enveloped in strong arms and sheltering wings even as he pushed against Zatook.

Zatook didn't let go. He wrapped around Tristan in a firm but gentle embrace. He was all too familiar with the type of guilt plaguing the lad, and even more familiar with the kind of damage one could do to themselves if they pushed beyond their means. Amaya was safe. Amaya was in Andor.

Amaya was in Andor. The king really was dead. He still couldn't quite fathom it. Some small part of his mind felt he should be glad, but another was terrified. And yet, neither was at the front of his mind. He was worried about his mother. Worried about Andor and the war. Worried about the others. Worried about Amaya. Worried about Tristan. But most of all, he was *tired.* He couldn't think of any way to reassure Tristan other than to hold him and try to calm him, so for now, that was what he did.

Gradually, Tristan became too weak to fight. He slumped in Zatook's hold and released shuddering breaths. He didn't cry, but it was a near thing. Unknowingly, he shared Zatook's sentiment with feeling tired.

"You should rest. You just woke up, right?" asked the Sun Child quietly.

"Both of you should rest. I'll stay with Amaya for now, and I'll send word to the queen," Tannen interjected. "Either go to your rooms if you can, or lay on the cots in here."

"The wounded…soldiers need the cots," Tristan argued. Even as he spoke, he rested his head against Zatook's shoulder. "I do feel tired. Everything…feels like so much."

"As it does when one is exhausted; the smallest hill can feel like a mountain," commented Tannen sagely.

Now, Tristan pushed lightly against Zatook more to urge him than to escape him. "Can you make it to Tannen's abode or do you want to sleep in the guest quarters?"

Zatook slowly let go, lifting a hand to ruffle Tristan's hair. He slid his hand down to the lad's shoulder, and the shadows reached up and wrapped around the lad before whisking him back to bed. Zatook gave Tannen a grateful look before shifting himself to the blacksmith's home and all-but dropping onto the bed. He stared at the ceiling, his mind a whirl. Amaya was in Andor. Traiborn was dead. There was still a war going on. His mother needed him, but he would need to be at his full strength. That meant letting himself rest. As he closed his eyes, he thought back to the voice that had called to him, and the strangers in the forest. Takumi and Feray; Tristan knew them, and yet something sounded familiar about the names even to him. Before he could dwell much further, sleep claimed him.

28. Timeless Starlight

Amaya heaved a deep sigh. She recognized the heaviness of waking from a very deep sleep and also the lack of excruciating pain in her body. Even the soft bed at Takumi and Feray's had felt agonizing against her skin. Now, the bed felt like any old cot. Not sensing the presence of her caretakers, Amaya's attention caught on one in particular: as familiar as a distant memory. Forcing her eyes open, Amaya took in her surroundings. An infirmary. Amaya still felt bandages around her torso and arms, so she wasn't fully healed, but the burns were gone. Then her eyes landed on the figure sitting beside her. Amaya stared. For several seconds, Amaya wondered if she was seeing things, her gaze stuck on the woman's face.

"Mum?" rasped Amaya. Tears stung her eyes. She hadn't dreamt about her mother in years, and it had been even longer since she had seen the woman.

Aria smiled, squeezing Amaya's hand gently. "Welcome back, Little Spark." She reached her other hand forward to smooth some of Amaya's hair from her face. "And welcome to Andor."

Once the sight had fully sunk in, Amaya pushed herself up, ignoring the pain and stiffness of her injuries, and wrapped her arms around her mother's shoulders. Amaya felt the sting of tears intensify before the droplets began spilling down her cheeks. Soft sobs shook Amaya's frame as she held her mother tightly, overcome with relief that the woman was real. This wasn't a dream or a hallucination.

"Mum," sobbed Amaya quietly, "I missed you. Over five hundred years, how are you out? Is this for good?"

Aria slid from the chair to sit on the edge of the bed so Amaya didn't have to reach so far, wrapping her arms around her in turn. "I missed you. I Watched you as often as I could. I have been so proud of you." She shifted to kiss Amaya's temple. "I do not yet know for certain, but for now, at least, I am free to wander the palace. There are many potential futures ahead of us."

Amaya tucked her face in the crook of her mother's neck and shoulder. "You said that this is Andor?" she asked wetly. "So, I wasn't dreaming. I was with Feray and Takumi last I knew. They were looking after me with Clo. And then…I remember Shadow— Zatook —but I think I drifted off again. Now I'm here. How did anyone convince Traiborn to let me in? Was that your doing? Where's Coco? And the others? There should be a group here—" Amaya trailed off when Aria gently hushed her.

"Traiborn is dead, Corianne is currently in a meeting with her generals, and your friends are in the guest tower. Much has happened, Little Spark. And I will fill you in on all of it, once you are lying back down and resting. While the worst of your wounds have been healed by the Sun Child, you still need to heal." Aria gently smoothed Amaya's hair, but she didn't move to force her back down yet. Five hundred and seventy-five years was a very long time, and she had missed her daughter.

Amaya let the information soak into her mind as she simply cherished the warm, solid feel of her mother. "Sounds like everyone had fun without me," Amaya softly joked. Then her tone turned serious as she added, "I was fighting Tsukuyomi at the Wall breach. I knew…I couldn't beat him— not in my state at the time —but I couldn't let him into Andor or he would have gone after Tristan. After I got Zatook back behind the border, I tried to fight. I almost…he would have…I guess I shouldn't be surprised given what happened to Reina and little Arianna, but it still hurt more than the physical wound. Hoshiko intervened. She got me away, but she stayed to fight Tsukuyomi. Hoshiko used her powers to help me get to the borders of Nikko Mori, and Clovestein found me trudging my way to the coast. I don't remember much past getting to Aunt Feray and Uncle Tak's."

"Hoshiko has kept your brother occupied since," Aria confessed softly. "It was she who told Zatook where to find you." She couldn't help a soft smile. "I rather hope to get the chance to thank those two in person. It has been an age since I saw them last, and they have taken such good care of my family."

"Yeah. I just hope the next time I visit will be under better circumstances. Hopefully, then I'll remember more of it," Amaya teased. As weariness dragged at her muscles and her wounds throbbed, Amaya finally pulled away. She imagined that she looked and sounded as tired as she felt. "Recovery is both the worst and the best. Just woke up, but I still feel exhausted." Frowning, Amaya recalled something. She looked around until she found the messaging crystal on a nightstand beside her cot. Instead of grabbing it, she left the crystal, relieved to see she hadn't lost it. "Zatook was probably glad I wasn't sending him messages everyday anymore. I kept sending him jokes and nonsensical remarks about whatever I was dealing with at the time. I was hoping to give him something to brighten his day, even if it just annoyed him. Though, I hope I didn't get him in trouble. I just…" Amaya sighed and shrugged. "I guess in a way I was also trying to stay connected to everyone even if I could only be here in spirit."

"He only really put it away when he was in the palace," Aria noted absently, helping Amaya get comfortable. "It was never found, so he was never in trouble for it." She fussed with Amaya's covers to hide her smirk. "When you sent Zatook away, Tristan discovered he can heal him. But then the king summoned him. And you know the first two things that man did? He hid the crystal and then asked Traiborn if you were all right. I think it is rather safe to assume he enjoyed your messages."

"I'm the annoying comrade that people somehow can't live without," Amaya joked. She allowed herself to sink into the cot and get comfortable under the covers. "I'm glad Zatook is all right. I doubt Traiborn told him of my well-being. The king was probably hoping I would be slain on the battlefield. Joke's on him. I'm the thorn no one can get rid of."

Aria was fixing her daughter with a flat look. "We may be ageless, but we can die like any other. He almost got that wish; would have, were Zatook indisposed a moment longer. He barely got you to Tristan in time."

Amaya felt a bit guilty for the trouble people had gone through to save her, but she also knew that by the time Traiborn was no longer an issue and the barriers against her were gone, she hadn't been in traveling condition. "I'll be sure to thank him. Both of them. I didn't say anything before they came to Andor because Tristan had just woken and was still recovering. I didn't want them to worry while they were stuck here," Amaya explained softly. "I'm glad I'm alive to see you again. And them. I'm a bit surprised the Moon Child isn't glued to my side at the moment. Then again, if they fought Traiborn, Captain probably went and wore herself out with the rest of the group."

Aria visibly hesitated before sitting back in her chair and smoothing her skirts. "Well, I can assure you she has not died; neither has she woken." She lifted a hand to pause questions. "And now I'll tell you everything that happened," she promised. Aria was not one to hide details or put things gently. When she said she would tell Amaya everything, she meant it, down to the last detail. From the group's arrival to the feast, to Captain freeing her and Tristan's corrupted transformation. All the way to the end of the fight with Traiborn and getting everyone tended. She ended with a recount of Zatook going to find Amaya the moment he had woken and who in the group had at least regained consciousness.

Amaya listened solemnly, taking in everything her mother told her. Some of it warmed her heart while other details left her feeling concerned. "Could I go to Captain's room? I might be able to make it if I'm careful, or I wouldn't mind help. I just want her to know I'm here even if she's not awake to know consciously," she asked softly.

"The priestess on duty might have a fit if we tried to move you," Aria teased. Then she shook her head. "Let's get some food in you first. I shall see if there is a spare

TekChair or a certain stubborn shadow prince available to get you up there." She smirked at Amaya as she stood. "For now, rest. I shall see that the kitchens send you some broth."

As Aria stood, Amaya weakly caught her mother's hand and gave a slight squeeze. "Hopefully, we'll get a chance to catch up. Perhaps once I'm strong enough that conversation doesn't exhaust me," she joked tiredly. Releasing Aria's hand, Amaya settled under the covers once more.

***

Zatook was growing steadily restless. He had been a model patient for Halia (and Tannen), actually resting and letting himself heal. But there was too much on his mind to keep sitting still. He needed to be doing something, needed to be useful. He didn't walk openly through the palace, but he did make his way through the shadows towards where he sensed his mother.

Corianne was in the war room. Zatook hesitated. He hadn't been in the room since his last report to Traiborn. The queen was currently standing over the table, but she wasn't leaning against it like Traiborn used to. She had one arm crossed and holding the opposite elbow; she held her chin as she gazed at the map before her. Zatook glanced at the table, noting the rumpled parchments bearing Collette's thin scrawl. Until Zatook could return, or Corianne leave the palace, it was up to Collette to hold the army. Zatook felt guilt weigh heavier on his shoulders. He steeled himself and stepped from the shadows.

Corianne was back to wearing the royal waistcoat with

pants and high boots. Though she had taken to wearing her crown at all times, she had stopped spending the effort to twist her hair up; instead it was gathered in a low ponytail, the thick curly strands free to puff out behind her. She turned to smile at Zatook, instantly stepping up to him and pulling him into a hug. He hesitated before awkwardly returning the gesture.

"I'm glad to see you are up, Zatook." She pulled back, lifting a hand to cup his face. "But should you be? How are you feeling?"

"I'm fine," he assured her, stepping out of her hold a bit as he signed. If she was surprised by the skill, she did not show it.

"Fine does not mean well," she prompted gently.

"How fares Collette?"

Corianne sighed, but she turned back towards the map. "Hoshiko has kept Tsukuyomi away from the field, but Jeremiah has stepped in a few times. Collette is doing her best to hold the line, but they've had to give some ground." She slid her hand over the map, and the topography shifted and then zoomed towards the Wall, showing the breach. The Nocium forces had pushed past the first village, but the army had not given any more ground. Zatook nodded, lifting his hands. He had just started to express his intent to return, but Corianne gently caught his hands to interrupt him. "Absolutely not." She met his gaze. "Zatook, you haven't had a real rest in ages. Do not think I missed how much of your ancestor's power you drew on. I understand why, but it takes a powerful toll. You almost died. Your friends are still recovering from fighting the king. They worry for you. Let them see you heal before you go chasing danger again." A coy twinkle entered her gaze. "You haven't even been to see Amaya since she woke."

Zatook pulled his hands away and folded his arms, returning to stare at the table.

"Zatook." He did not turn at his mother's gentle tone. "Zatook. You do not have to spend your entire life in battle." She touched a hand to his arm. "You do not need to avoid those you care for anymore. Traiborn is *dead*. No remnant of his lifeforce clings to his items, his focus was destroyed, and the Runesaber is clean of his influence. He isn't coming back. You do not have to follow his rules."

He did not respond at first. She could see the conflict in his gaze, and where others might not catch it, she sensed his uncertainty. That which he had deemed impossible had come to pass, and now he had no idea how to deal with this new truth. Zatook had been under Traiborn's heel for so long, he didn't really know any other way to be. And yet, had he not had a taste when traveling with the Children and their entourage? He hesitated when he felt his mother's hand shift, but he let her turn him and pull him into another hug. She was so small compared to him. Slight. She still felt frail, though the shadows under her eyes were fading. She only met his height thanks to the heels in her boots. Zatook steadily slid his arms around her in turn, curling around her slightly.

"It's OK, Zatook. Traiborn is gone. Really and truly. He cannot harm you. He cannot stop you from coming to see me. He cannot stop you from having friends, or helping their quest. He cannot harm the ones you love anymore."

His sister was even smaller. She had yet to fully come into her magic, and yet she could command the respect of an entire army. They were beloved. He was a shadow in their brilliance, a stain.

"And they do love you, Zatook. As do I. As does your sister."

Zatook started to pull away, to protest, but Corianne would not let go. He wasn't meant to be loved. He was a tool, a sword in the shadows. A monster for a master.

"We *love* you. We care about you. We worry about you."

His mind thought back to Amaya in the cabin, wounded and burned. The crystal he kept on him whenever he could. The little messages, the jokes. He had never known how to respond, but he had read them all. I wish I knew how to break your chains, Shadow.

His mind went to Tristan. How the lad had barely contained himself until he could no longer. How he had stepped between Zatook and the king, more than once.

To Tannen, who had stayed beside him despite the danger and the costs. Who cared for him whenever he was wounded, who did whatever he could to support him.

To Halia, who always welcomed him with laughter and light. Who shed the tears he never could.

To Jabez, who faced down his own darkness to learn more of Zatook's so they could find a way to help him heal.

Slim and frail as his mother may be, Corianne could show her strength when it mattered. And as her son slowly curled farther into her hold, as he lost his grip on his stoic mask, she held him. She rubbed his back and smoothed his hair, whispered encouragement and love to chase away the darkness. She knew this wouldn't be enough. Traiborn's wounds ran deep. But with Shaddai's blessing and guidance, she would see them healed.

***

The day had slowly slipped past. Zatook had stayed with his mother for some time, first finding comfort and then quietly supporting her through her tasks. As dinner neared, however, she gently pushed him towards the kitchens. "Go take your friends something to eat," she had urged him. "I am sure they would love to see you."

He was almost to the kitchens when he met Aria. "There you are. Turn around, you are coming with me." When he hesitated, she rolled her eyes. "I will handle the food, then. *You* will handle getting Amaya to the guest tower." She nudged him towards the infirmary. "Go on. There aren't any spare chairs, and you can carry her the most comfortably." To his credit, he didn't stumble at her choice of words or when she pushed him the first couple of steps. Aria smirked at his back as he moved towards the infirmary. He seemed a bit stunned at the sudden change in orders, but he went. She nodded in satisfaction before turning to finish the trek to the kitchens.

Zatook paused outside the door. He had barely been convinced to face everyone for a meal, and now he had to face Amaya alone. What if his mother was wrong? What if Amaya was angry with him? He had called her there and then left her to fight alone. She had almost died. But she hadn't been mad when he arrived at the cabin, right? Zatook closed his eyes and took a breath before opening them and walking through the door.

The infirmary was quiet. A few of the more heavily wounded soldiers had been transported home. Curtains were pulled around the filled cots, and a priestess was making her way between them to check on the wounded and help sit up the ones who could for when dinner would arrive.

Amaya's cot was not partitioned off. Since she was getting ready to move to the guest tower, the curtain had been pulled away.

Zatook found Amaya sitting up on her own with her back resting against the headboard. However, her position belied her weariness as her eyes were shut when Zatook first entered. The burns were gone, and while some bandages still peeked out from under her sleeveless shirt, her complexion had regained a healthier color. Similar to his arrival in the cabin, Amaya seemed to sense him and blinked her eyes open.

"Hey, Shadow," she greeted him with a smile. "I'm guessing my mother sent you to cart me to a new room. I know she's not awake, but I'd like to be with Captain." She shifted upright a little more, failing to hold back a slight wince. She stopped and simply sat. "Oi yosh, I'm stiff as a board and my body's groaning like an old tree. Still, feeling pain means I'm alive to feel it. I understand I have you and Tristan to thank for that. Thank you for going to get me. I'm glad you seem to be doing better. You're up and around at least. Though, if you're as stubborn as the rest of us, you probably should be in bed."

"I have healed," he assured her, moving over to her cot. He hesitated with her thanks. "I apparently make for good transport," he signed sheepishly. "I merely carried you, as I shall do now."

"Nothing merely about it, Shadow. You carried me all the way from the *coast* of Nikko Mori to Andor. After nearly dying. After going through hell thanks to that donkey's arse of a king," Amaya countered flatly. Her cheeks tinted a light pink even as she reached up and wrapped her arms around his neck. The blush deepened slightly when the move brought her face closer to his. For a moment, Amaya felt torn between suddenly being shy and self-conscious or doing as she normally did and plowing through the awkwardness. She ended up doing a little of both, shifting her arms to hang on better and lowering her gaze to his shoulder. "I'm glad you're free. You didn't deserve that man's hatred," she said, her voice softer.

Zatook lifted her easily. He used the shadows to adjust her position slightly so she would be comfortable as he cradled her. Once he was sure he wasn't hurting her, he started walking. Having his arms full gave him an excuse not to answer her. What could he say? To any of them, really. He had wished for freedom, long ago. He had eventually lost all hope. And now... Everything he had been trained to believe no longer applied. He was free, and he had no idea what to do. How to be. Who to be.

Shadows wrapped up and around the door, and he stepped through them and out the other side. They saw few palace staff; though the pair caught sight of a few more ducking back around corners when they saw the

King's Shadow. Despite the queen's assurances, they were more frightened of him than before. Now that the king no longer held his leash, they thought a monster walked among them. Were they wrong? Zatook stopped watching the intersections, eyes on the path he walked. He was tempted to step through the shadows. Get Amaya to the tower within moments. But he wasn't sure if they were ready for her; perhaps they were still preparing Captain's room for an additional occupant. He also didn't want Amaya to think he was trying to be rid of her.

Noting Zatook's unease and the looks of fear from the staff, Amaya felt exasperation flare in her. She knew it would take more than a few days to change the picture painted of Zatook over the last few centuries. Ignoring her own trepidation, Amaya tightened her hold and settled more comfortably in Zatook's arms, demonstrating how relaxed she felt in his presence and displaying her trust in him. She doubted anyone would take note— no one knew her, after all.

"One good thing that came out of the battle against my brother," Amaya suddenly said, "I got to see your Celestial form again. I've encountered scary monsters and beasts before, but I'm sorry to say, Shadow, you're just plain old cool." Even though Zatook wasn't looking at her, Amaya gave him a smile and a wink. "At least you look intimidating and strong. I just look like a giant will-o-wisp."

Zatook's gaze actually snapped to her in surprise. His foot caught on the carpet, but he managed to not actually trip. Though hard to see with his coverings, he even blushed. He quickly averted his gaze, but he couldn't justify not responding now. Shadows curled in the air where she could see them. *Yours was ethereal.* Now he pointedly wasn't looking at her.

Amaya's blush brightened, and it took everything in her not to avert her gaze as well. Was he calling her— no. He was just giving her a compliment, stating a fact. Still, Amaya felt her heartbeat quicken. "Thank you. A bit ironic, I suppose, since I've helped Lady Rin ferry souls sometimes. Fits with the role," she remarked shyly. Turning her head, she rested her chin on her arm draped over his shoulder. Musing to herself, she suddenly asked Zatook, "Does it bother you when I call you Shadow? I can change to calling you Zatook or something else if you would rather. I realized I don't know what kind of names Traiborn might have had for you, and I don't want to stir up negative memories or emotions. You were just so quiet and followed us around at first. Like a shadow. Still, I want you to know that despite your title, I have never thought of you as a monster or a demon."

It took a moment for him to respond. He wasn't entirely sure how to articulate the things running through his mind, so he started with the simplest: *I do not mind the name.* 'The King's Shadow' was one of the titles the people had given him, but he had never minded that, either. He had rather preferred that to being the Demon of Andor.

"All right. I don't want to do anything that would make you uncomfortable— well, no more than some good natured ribbing once in a while," Amaya said. She shifted to look at him again. "I'm…actually glad you have shadow powers. Seeing and feeling yours helps me to associate them with someone other than my brother. Knowing I have a friend in the dark helps me not to be afraid of it." Her gaze drifted to the middle distance as memories of her last battle overtook her thoughts, her voice sounding a bit quieter. Shifting to rest her chin on her arm again, Amaya attempted to hide her face from Zatook as her eyes stung. Taking a deep breath, Amaya released the air slowly as she fought back the tears and emotions.

Zatook kept his gaze ahead to give her at least a semblance of privacy. He felt as though he should do more, say something, but he had no idea what. Amaya was confiding in him. She was not the first to do so, and yet he struggled to know how to respond. Comforting Tristan had come much more naturally; he had spent years helping his sister with her concerns. So why was he hesitating now? Why was he weighing every thought?

Zatook's steps had slowed to a halt, lost in the deluge of thoughts that refused to form anything coherent to say to her.

In the past, he might have protested the idea that she found him a friend in the darkness. That she confided in him, trusted him. But without Traiborn binding him…why wouldn't she? Why wouldn't any of them? He was allowed to have friends now. To care. His trustworthiness was his to determine, to keep.

So why couldn't he come up with something to say?

Despite her tumultuous emotions, Amaya kept her voice steady as she spoke, "I wasn't surprised— not really, not after what Tsukuyomi did to his own wife and daughter —but knowing is different from having reality bearing down on me. If not for my sister, I would be dead by my brother's hands." Amaya's voice grew quieter towards the end as she wavered. "You probably wish I would stop talking. All I do is talk your ear off even when using a communication crystal." The laugh she released sounded a bit tremulous.

Zatook mentally shook himself. Here Amaya needed him, and he was gaping like a fish on dry land. *I do not mind listening,* he promised, his feet moving again. *Nor did I mind the messages.* He hesitated a moment before writing, *I have never been good at conversation. I often cannot find the words to respond. But I am very good at listening.*

"We're the perfect pair then," Amaya commented teasingly. However, she reached up to wipe her eyes, her other hand tightening a little on his shoulder. "It's less being afraid of the dark and shadows. Those haven't bothered me in a while, but it helps to have the reminder that my brother doesn't own the shadows and darkness." She turned to him, ignoring how her eyes still felt a bit glossy. "I want you to know that I don't regret going to the breach. I knew I would have to fight my brother at some point, and I couldn't ignore a friend. I'm glad I was there to help. I confess, I was worried you wouldn't be able to heal, but I trusted Shaddai. I trusted you. I trust you, Shadow."

I shall endeavor to remain worthy of such trust. He didn't say anything for a moment before adding, *You may not regret coming, but I am sorry I asked all the same. I caused you pain, even if indirectly. Had I realized how severe the burns had become...* He hesitated, not finishing the sentence. What would he have done? What could he have done? And what would have been the consequences?

"The magic used to breach the Wall resonated with the remnants of the Talisman's magic in the burns— like when I fought Marilyn. I don't know if it's the same or just similar enough," Amaya explained. "I wasn't that close to Andor when I was afflicted, but I knew something had happened. Your message just confirmed it. If I felt it from that distance, I can only imagine the pain Tristan suffered when the Wall fell." Amaya thought about what Aria had told her— about Zatook hiding the crystal and asking after Amaya's wellbeing. "I appreciate what you risked in asking after me to the king. Given our history, I imagine Traiborn wasn't pleased. I'm sorry for adding to your pain, but I am glad I could help against my brother." Her hand lightly touched Zatook's neck. "I'm glad you're free of your chains, Shadow. After centuries, it'll take time for you not to feel like you need to constantly look over your shoulder. But I've got your back. If there's anything I can do to help remind you of your freedom, just let me know."

Zatook frowned. The concept of freedom had his mind stirring again, whirling through what that would even mean. About his chains, figurative and literal, and how long he had been bound by them. Was still bound by some. *I do not know how to be without them,* he confessed.

"You've got friends to help you figure that out. Give yourself time. Maybe start by seeing what it's like being a mentor without the worry of the king's shadow. From what my mother told me, you have practically adopted my nephew, and Shaddai knows he could use an adult Celestial who can teach him and who actually cares about him," encouraged Amaya, "I'm around now, but I know it's not the same as having another man he can turn to. Maybe start by picking up Tristan's training again. Spend time with your mother and your sister when you can. Actually hang out with your dragon-kin friend and your fae friend. Take it one step at a time and before you know it, you'll be walking like a natural."

I can only do so many things at once, he teased before writing more seriously, *and there is a war. Comradery may need to wait, at least until Daisuke is repaired or Zex freed.* It felt odd considering his father, let alone being able to write his name again. He didn't really have any memories of the man; most of what he knew, Corianne had taught him. Had Zex been aware of what happened beyond his prison? Had time passed for him at all? Would meeting him be like welcoming a father instead of a stranger?

"Hopefully Daisuke can be repaired. I don't think I've ever seen the Wall breached before. As for Zex, well, he's a bit predictable in his unpredictability," Amaya agreed. "I imagine Coco is waiting for the right time, and for the rest of our group to heal. From what my mother has told me, Lancelot should be able to free Zex."

Mother believes Daisuke can be repaired, though we must first find a way to remove the vines of magic. She can still sense the spirit within, though he is struggling to speak with her. He hesitated at the nickname for his mother, but it wasn't the first time he had heard it. *Lancelot and Tristan both,* he confirmed. *Lancelot to do the unsealing, Tristan to create the crystal he can channel through. Though Lancelot may be able to use the Runesaber.*

"The irony of using Traiborn's beloved sword to unseal his rival," Amaya commented with a smirk. She shifted her arm so she could rest her head on his shoulder, getting comfortable as her energy waned. "Thank you for looking after everyone, Shadow."

Zatook didn't respond, rounding the corner into the corridor that would end at the entrance to the guest tower. Had he done well enough to be thanked? Many of their problems in Andor had stemmed from their relationship with him. And between Traiborn's training and missions, he had not had much chance to be near them during their stay. Now Captain was unconscious, and the others injured or exhausted. He tried to push the guilt away as they neared the tower. Two guards still flanked the doorway, though now more for actually securing the guest quarters and guarding the injured than following Aria around or attempting to spy for the king. They had also been joined by two errand runners so that Solomon, Jabez, and Rose could send for things instead of leaving their charges. One of the runners hesitated when he saw Zatook approaching, but when he noticed the man was carrying someone, he still ran to open the door, knocking first. Zatook nodded in appreciation as he carried Amaya through.

True to Aria's word, a meal had already arrived. Zatook was mildly surprised to see a rather full table. Jabez he had expected, but Tristan was a surprise. Since the lad had insisted on eating with whoever else made it to the parlor, Rose had joined him. Then there was Alconai, and beside him Lancelot. A hint of guilt wormed between Zatook's shoulders for not having known the knight had woken, but it was quickly replaced by concern over whether he should have made it all the way down to the parlor instead of eating in his room.

Rose was the first to spot them, smiling. "Amaya, it is good to see you are awake."

"Mostly awake, aye," Amaya agreed. She lifted her head

from Zatook's shoulder and took stock of the people in the room. "I heard you all had quite the time under Traiborn's hospitality. Glad to see you all alive and more or less in one piece." She gave them a wink.

Tristan left his seat and approached Zatook, relief shining in the young man's eyes as he looked over both of them. "It's good to see you both. I'm glad you're on the mend. If you need more healing, let me know. I can at least help ease the pain," he told them. He blushed when Amaya reached down and wrapped her arm around his shoulders. The angle made the hug slightly awkward, but Amaya insisted.

"Thank you, Tristan. You can rest now and let nature do the rest," Amaya told him sincerely.

Returning the embrace, Tristan whispered, "I'm so sorry. It's my fault. Why didn't you tell me before we left for Andor?"

"There wasn't time," Amaya answered softly. "You were still weak from the altercation with your father, and we had no way of knowing if you could heal me; nor did we have the time to try. Once you were inside, you couldn't leave Andor without risking being attacked, and I couldn't go inside to reach you. So, I said nothing to save you the worry. I was looked after, though. Our friends helped me."

"Takumi and Feray?" Tristan guessed.

"And Clo. They miss you," Amaya told him. She released the hug and righted herself, holding back a wince. She tousled Tristan's hair. "Zatook is taking me up to

Captain's room, so I can be with her. Get back to your food. We'll talk more when I've a bit more energy, aye?" Tristan nodded.

"Glad ta have ye with us again, milady," Alconai greeted with a grin.

Amaya gave him a flat look. "Oi, if I could, I would throw something at you. However, in the spirit of recovery, I'll settle for giving you a dirty look. Just call me Amaya," she snarked. Her gaze slid to Jabez, noting the man not eating. He didn't look gaunt around his mask, though, so she figured he hadn't fallen back into old habits too badly. She inclined her head when Jabez gave her a tired but genuine two-fingered salute.

"Solomon is upstairs with Captain," Rose chimed in. "Since we knew you were coming, he took your meal up. Rest well, Amaya. We'll be here if you need anything." Lancelot gave his own weary wave; he was glad to see her as well, but it was taking most of his energy to stay awake and eat, and he didn't really have anything to add.

Amaya nodded. "I'll let you know if we need anything. In the meantime, rest up all of you. You've more than earned it," she told them, giving Zatook a look to let him know she was including him in her comment.

With the parting words, whether or not Zatook took them to heart, the shadow prince nodded to the others and continued towards the stairs. Solomon must have heard them coming, for when they reached the level that led to Captain's room, he was standing with the door open.

"Amaya," he greeted in warm relief, but he moved aside to let Zatook carry her in. Captain lay to one side of the bed, russet hair freshly combed and an empty bowl of broth nearby. She could easily be mistaken as simply sleeping if not for the fact she had been down so long and the small bandage wound around her hand. The only sign of outward injury had been a blackish-purple mark akin to frostbite where she had wound first Lancelot's and later the king's threads. Zatook moved to the other side of the bed, gently lowering Amaya and then helping her get comfortable.

"Hey, Sol. It's good to see you," greeted Amaya. Once on the bed, Amaya shifted with Zatook's help until she could easily reach Captain. Brushing back some of the girl's hair, Amaya softly said, "I'm here, Moon Sprite." Her fingers combed through some of the strands as Amaya gently kissed Captain's brow. Sighing, Amaya settled against the headboard so she could eat before resting again. "Thank you, Zatook. And thank you, Sol, for looking after her."

Zatook gave a slight bow before slipping from the room. Solomon sighed.

"As best I could, at least."

"Like I do anything else?" responded Amaya lightly. "Aria told me what all happened. Sounds like everyone has been through the wringer. Do we know what's keeping Captain asleep or what can be done to help her if anything?"

He shook his head. "Aria has told us it is the cost of something she did with her magic. The priestesses could find nothing to heal aside from the mark on her hand. We likely will not know more until she wakes." He hesitated before adding, "Aria mentioned there may be lingering effects even then. But even she hasn't Seen for certain."

"And there's no knowing when she'll wake," Amaya mused softly. She looked down at her surrogate daughter. "Why in the world did you decide to take after me, Moon Sprite?" She reached down and gently held Captain's hand. Amaya then used her free hand to eat the food Solomon had brought.

***

As the days of recovery continued, the group felt the passage of time more distinctly. With each sunset and sunrise, Rose's time became one less day. And then the morning came. With Tristan on the mend, Rose alternated spending her time with him and checking on the others. Tristan often made the rounds with her or even went on his own when Rose decided to rest. That day, he chose to stay with her no matter what she ended up doing. All morning and afternoon, Tristan put on a brave face, but inside his heart ached. He couldn't decide if the waiting made Rose's eventual departure worse. He felt glad to be able to spend time with her, but he disliked the anticipation of the inevitable.

The rest of the group largely left the couple alone together, but everyone who could made a point to eat lunch together. As afternoon crept into evening, Tristan invited Rose to ride with him to the meadow again. This time, he took only one horse, wanting Rose close and not willing to risk wearing her out by having her ride alone. He brought a pack with him. It was still light when they stopped in the meadow the couple had visited previously. Tristan helped Rose dismount before he got to work pulling items out of the pack. Spreading out a large blanket, Tristan set out a couple of small lanterns with illumination crystals for later. He then proceeded to produce a few dishes of food for them, still warm thanks to the enchanted containers. He finished by placing another folded blanket at the edge of the spread-out blanket. Once Tristan was sure the horse was watered and wouldn't run off, he helped Rose sit on the picnic blanket.

"I wanted us to have a chance to get away from the palace for a bit," Tristan confessed. "I also just miss being in nature."

"I certainly have no complaints," Rose assured him with a soft smile. "I had rather hoped for some time under the stars." She tried not to mention the impending deadline. In truth, she was at peace with the Lady coming. And while she had faith in Tristan, she didn't want to pressure him with reminders of his upcoming trials. She just wanted to focus on the present.

Tristan returned her smile with one of his own. He served the food he had brought for their dinner. "I'm glad I could provide," said Tristan. As they ate, Tristan engaged Rose in conversation, talking about the food and making jokes. He told her stories of his time in Nikko Mori and even some of his life at Keep Shadow Veil. He asked after her life as a champion of Nocis. Soon, the vibrant, burning colors of sunset faded into twilight before the light surrendered completely to the stars. As the sun disappeared, Tristan activated the crystals in the two lanterns. He also grabbed the extra blanket and wrapped it around Rose and him to ward away the night's chill, keeping an arm around Rose as well. Gradually, fireflies flitted in and out of sight like sparks winking in and out of existence.

"I'm glad we met," Tristan softly told Rose. "I'm glad and thankful that you rescued me, and that we are able to have this time together."

Rose leaned against him, watching the various lights around them. "As am I. Bless the Lady for letting us have this extra time. And a chance for more." She couldn't help a slight chuckle. "Our little party has a penchant for trouble; I am curious to see where time will take them. Us."

Tristan rested his head atop hers as he commented, "It'll depend on the Trials, and what they entail. After that, I'll have to contend with my father at some point or other. Perhaps, we can gather allies to fight him. I can't spend my life running away from him." He squeezed Rose a little closer. "If everything turns out well, what do you picture yourself doing once all this is over?"

Rose was quiet for a moment as she considered. "I need to find out what happened to Jeremiah," she confessed softly. "The man who stands there now is nothing like I remember during my training. And yet I still cannot pinpoint when or how he started to change. Perhaps I will find a way to solidify my memories, to investigate them for some manner of sign."

"I remember you said that he was strict but good. It was strange for him to kill King Arden or have anything to do with the king's death. And we think Marilyn is involved, but we're not sure how since you didn't sense blood magic at work around him," Tristan recalled. He rubbed her shoulder. "Aside from that, though. If we answered all the questions and accomplished all our goals, what would you like to do for the rest of your life? Would you ever consider settling down? Having a family? Is there anywhere you have always wanted to go but never had the chance?"

The pause stretched longer this time. "I…don't really know." She closed her eyes, enjoying the warmth building between them and the softness of the night. "I haven't really had the time to even consider. Before, I was a slave, with little choice over my future. Then a deserter headed for war, and then a Chosen caught up in adventure. Everything has happened so quickly, I have not considered what may be after."

"I sympathize," Tristan confessed quietly. "I think I would like to go back to Nikko Mori and see Clovestein as well as Feray and Takumi. Feray and Takumi used to help take care of Arianna when Clovestein and I needed to protect the forest. I miss them. I miss all of them." He looked at Rose as he added, "I'd like to introduce you to them and show you more of Nikko Mori if you would like."

"I would." She opened her eyes, meeting his gaze. "I would like to see more of your home, your friends. And then, perhaps, see more places. Jeremiah used to sail beyond the Jaromír Mountains on trading voyages, but I was never taken along. Sailing to rescue Captain was my first time on anything more than a rowboat."

Tristan chuckled. "Mine as well," he reminded her. "I would like to see more of the world too. Perhaps we can travel together? Maybe we could come back to Andor when things have calmed down and get to experience the kingdom fully. Being Chosen, I would also like to visit Ben-

Gal and meet the Order."

"I think that sounds like a wonderful plan." She leaned against his shoulder again, staring up at the stars. A soft breeze stirred through the night, but it wasn't cool enough to disturb them, simply playing with their hair and the edges of the blanket.

Tristan took in the sight of Rose: mysterious and beautiful backlit by fireflies. She made him think of the stories he read to Arianna about brave, magical princesses. Was he the prince? A knight? He felt more like a commoner reaching for the literal stars. And yet, here she sat in his arms: Starlight Princess Comsom Cryso, brave, selfless, and brilliant.

Ignoring the pain in his heart, Tristan dropped the blanket and stood. He held his hand out to Rose and helped her to her feet when she took it. Guiding them off the blanket, Tristan held Rose close as he started to sway with her in a makeshift slow dance. He led them carefully and gently as he kept his gaze locked with Rose's. Touching his forehead to hers, Tristan cherished the feel of Rose in his arms.

"I was just thinking that you look like a mysterious, beautiful princess of the stars," he told her. "I'm glad you find me worthy of your presence, my lady."

Rose felt her cheeks warm. "Considering the time we have spent among royalty, I hardly feel fit for the title," she demurred. Then her voice turned to a soft tease as she added, "Besides, as I recall, *you* are nobility. I am but a simple soldier."

Tristan snorted even as he blushed. "And yet we met on equal ground as warriors in a forest. Dirty with travel and labor and both hiding from those who would control us for ill gains," he remarked softly. "Here, outside castle walls and beyond battlegrounds— no armor or courts —we are Comson Cryso and Luadril. Rose and Tristan." Tristan lifted his hand to lightly brush the backs of his knuckles along her cheek, his thumb caressing her jawline. Slowly, he tilted his face closer, giving her time to pull away if she chose. Their lips touched. Gentle and sweet, everything felt right. Tristan slipped his arms around Rose and held her close. Once they felt more comfortable, he deepened the kiss, cherishing the moment.

Rose slid her arms up and around his neck, leaning fully into the embrace. Around them, the symphony of the night rang, an orchestra for their dance, their embrace, their kiss. And yet she hardly heard it, all of her senses tuned to Tristan. The feel of his heart beating through their chests, his lips pressed to hers, his arms…his scent of meadow and sunlight. She took in all that she could bear, wished the moment could last forever. Slowly she sank against him as her energy waned, and his strong arms held her safe. Finally, somewhat regretfully, their lips parted. "I never want tonight to end," Rose confessed, "And yet I should not test the Lady's patience."

Tristan held her a little tighter. "We should probably go back, but I want to stall as long as I can even if my efforts amount to nothing," he admitted. Tristan touched their foreheads together once more. "May I stay with you? I want to be with you for as long as I can."

"You may." Despite their words, they did not move for

a moment longer. As Rose's energy continued to wane, they returned to the blanket and lay beneath the stars a while longer. As the night darkened, loathe as Tristan was to let her go, the pair returned to the palace and Rose's room. They curled in the darkness, occasionally speaking softly but mostly just resting against each other as a hushed stillness fell across the castle. Slowly yet surely, sleep claimed the inhabitants— for those who had not fallen asleep naturally, the Lady's spell took hold. As her presence filled the room, Rose quietly slipped from Tristan's arms. She paused at the edge of the bed, turning and bending to gently kiss his temple. "Good luck," she whispered, "and thank you." As she stood to face the Lady, she felt the weariness in her bones melt away. Lady Rin smiled softly and offered her hand.

As the pair slipped away, a small scroll appeared beside Tristan's head.

To Be Continued

Glossary and Pronunciation

People

Aditi /uh-DYE-tee/—Deceased. Aditi was Solomon's daughter. She fell in love with Zatook; furious, King Traiborn forced Zatook to kill her.

Arden /Ahr-den/— Deceased. As King of Nocis, Arden often butted heads with King Traiborn of Andor. After years of strained diplomacy, he had concocted a plan to use Rose's abilities to breach Andor's borders and start a war. He was betrayed by Jeremiah and slain by Marilyn.

Arianna /ar-EE-AN-na/—Deceased. A young girl of only seven, Arianna had a keen sense for the joys and sorrows of others. She instantly took to Rose and Solomon, and she loved getting to know Amaya and the rest of Captain's crew. Arianna was murdered by her father, Tsukuyomi, in an attempt to control Tristan.

Alconai FoxFeet /Al-conneye/—Alconai worked as a traveling minstrel, telling tales and singing songs throughout all of Nocis while attempting to find his missing brother, Jabez. He let Arden's soldiers catch him singing about the Sacreds in order to find Lancelot. Alongside his ensorcelled friend, he also met Captain and discovered she knew his brother.

Amaya LightningRider /uh-MY-uh/—First Mate of the *Effervescence* and Captain's surrogate mother. Recently revealed to be Celestial, she bears the title of Wanderlust.

Aria /AR-ee-uh/—The Oracle of Andor, able to peer into

the past, present, and future.

Clovestein /CLOH-veh-stine/—The guardian of Nikko Mori, he is tasked with keeping the forest and its inhabitants safe. When Reina passed away, he took Tristan under his wing and helped raise Arianna.

Collette /COH-lett/—Princess and High Priestess of Andor, Daughter-Heir to Corianne. A gifted mage, especially in the art of healing.

Corianne /COR-ee-ahn/— The Queen of Andor and a member of the Order. Despite being all that stood between King Arden and King Traiborn in diplomacy, the queen has been mostly out of the public eye and unreachable by the Order.

Feray /fear-EYE/—One of the residents of Nikko Mori, married to Takumi and surrogate mother of Clovestein.

Halia /HALL-ee-uh/—A fire faerie who helps Tannen in the forge. One of the few friends Zatook dares to keep.

Hoshiko StarSeer /HO-shee-ko/—A healer from Jabez's childhood, she was the first to find him after his escape from Shaedra.

Jabez ShadowDancer /j-AI-b-eh-z/—When Jabez was younger, he was kidnapped from his home and conscripted into the shadowy ranks of Shaedra. There, he was honed into a weapon. Jabez constantly resisted and received brutal punishments. Eventually, his mind shattered. He was taken in by Hoshiko and, as he recovered, found sanctuary at the Order. He never dared to reunite with his family, constantly hunted by Shaedra and fearful of their safety.

Jeremiah /JERE-uh-my-uh/—Once a popular knight of Nocis, Jeremiah worked with Tsukuyomi and Marilyn to secretly arrange the death of King Arden and take his place. No one currently knows the dragon's end goal, though he seemed keen to recapture Rose.

Keeshe /KEE-sh/—Rose's grandmother, an elder

matriarch among the Drow. For reasons unknown, she has worked with Marilyn in the past despite her deep hatred of humans and other races.

Lancelot /LAN-sa-laht/—One of the most famous knights of Nocis, Lancelot had lost touch with his childhood best friend Alconai. When the minstrel found him, he was under the control of a blood mage named Finnegan. Once freed, he helped Captain and her current crew overtake Keep Shadow Veil.

Lilith /lih-LITH/— Jeremiah's ward, a formidable enchantress. Though they did not know her name, Tristan and Amaya encountered her abilities during the journey to rescue Captain: The Lady in Red.

Marilyn /mare-ih-LIN/—A powerful blood witch with strange, unnatural features. She helped Tsukuyomi capture Tristan and also arranged the death of King Arden. During the battle at Keep Shadow Veil, she nearly killed Jabez in battle.

Shaedra /SHAY-druh/—An organization working in the shadows of Aviyah. Shaedra operatives are trained to be weapons and informants at the mercy of Shroud.

Shila /Sheye-luh/— Jeremiah's daughter, the current princess of Nocis.

Solomon /SAHL-uh-muhn/—Member of the revered Order, Solomon has dedicated his life to serving The Sacreds and Their Chosen. While this first culminated in taking Jabez under his wing, he has also become Captain's guardian alongside Amaya. A human, he has no magic abilities, however he has shown a strange ability to soothe Captain's powers when they flare beyond her control.

StormShaper / STORM-shaper /—A powerful warrior who fights for Tsukuyomi. He appears to have powerful magic that can control wind, water, rain, and lightning. A strange spell obscures his features, as though trying to view him through several fragments of distorted glass. He has speed and strength equivalent to elven-kin.

Takumi WaterSong /Tahk-umi/—One of the residents of Nikko Mori, married to Feray and surrogate father of Clovestein.

Tannen /TAN-nen/—A skilled blacksmith in the palace of Andor, Tannen is one of the few friends Zatook dares to keep.

The Chosen Children: Also referred to as the Children of Legend. Individuals Blessed by the Sacreds with incredible abilities to face the trials of their age. There are always three, represented by the Sun, the Moon, and the Stars.

> **Captain Isabella MoonChild** /ih-suh-BEL-luh/— At only 16, Captain is a fierce leader and a loyal friend. Though she has no clan, she still considers herself one of the Doran. She leads a merry band of pirates on the *Effervescence.* Captain bears the title 'Moon Child,' gifted with the magic of Weaving, the power of Sight, and a secret, more destructive power glimpsed only once when channeled through her surrogate brother, Jabez. For reasons unknown, Captain struggles to contain and control her abilities.

> **Rose** /r-OH-z/— Loathed by her grandmother for being Half-Drow, Half-Human, Rose was sold into slavery as a child. She was taken in by the knight Jeremiah, who secretly raised her to be the Scarlet Swordsman, Nocis' most powerful champion. She bears the title of Star Child, gifted with the ability to manipulate stardust into a powerful shield. Her lineage grants her natural abilities in blood magic, and she is telepathic. Drow name: Comson Cryso / COM-son. Cree-soh/

> **Tristan Nightshade** /TRIH-stan/—Born into a noble house of Nocis, Tristan was raised as heir to the family name. His life was upended the day his mother died. From noble heir to forest guardian

protégé, Tristan dedicated himself to raising his sister and helping guard the forest that took them in. Fate found him the day Rose first entered the forest, with Captain and adventure finding them soon after. Tristan bears the title of Sun Child and the gift of light and healing. He has also shown the abilty to create and shape a strange crystal substance. At Reina's death, he was tasked with becoming the temporary guardian of the Talisman of Ruin, which Tsukuyomi has done everything in his power to try and obtain.

The Doran /doe-rahn/—A nomadic people known to travel in clans. They are wary but welcoming of outsiders. The Doran tend to keep to themselves aside from sharing a meal, a fire, or good stories.

The Drow—A secretive race similar to elves. They have skin in varying shades of grey and deep black, and their hair is usually brighter colors like white or silver. Drow have a natural affinity for magic involving blood manipulation. Most Drow look down on other races, believing themselves superior, especially when compared to 'barbaric' humans. Because of this, they tend to keep to themselves and do not welcome outsiders.

The Order: A group dedicated to serving The Sacreds and Their Chosen, however called. The Order welcomes all races and abilities, from warriors to scholars to laborers and more. Though headquartered in the desert nation of Ben-Gal, members are known to travel far and wide and are generally respected.

The Sacreds: Our realm's equivalent to God, an eternal, all-powerful, all-knowing, loving, just, merciful being Who created and preserves all things. As God, Jesus, and the Holy Spirit are three-in-one, so too are the Sacreds.

    Shaddai /Shuh-DIE/—God the Father.

    Elohim /Eh-low-HEEM/—God the Son.

The Counselor—God the Holy Spirit.

Traiborn /TRAY-born/— The King of Andor and Zatook's master. Years ago, he ordered Zatook to kill Solomon's daughter Aditi.

Trystan ShadowVeil / TRIH-stan/—Tristan's grandfather, the former Celestial of Virtue.

Tsukuyomi SoulMirror /su-ku-YOmi/—The High Lord of House Shadow Veil, Tsukuyomi is an ambitious man who betrayed and murdered his wife and later his daughter in pursuit of his goals. He seeks the Talisman of Ruin, revealing to Tristan that he plans to use its power to reshape the world.

Zatook ShadowSword /ZAH-took/— Little is known of the silent shadow who joined the Chosen during the adventures of *Tainted Rose.* Named by Solomon as the Champion of Andor, he was sent to aid their quest on behest of the Queen of Andor, a former member of the Order. He quickly proved to be fiercely loyal despite carrying as many secrets as he has hidden scars.

Zetta Albright /Z-eh-tuh. ALL-bright/— The First King of Andor.

Places

Andor /An-door/—Just north of Nocis, Andor is known for their impressive feats of magic and a beautiful, gentle queen. Magic is sacred, but there is no set religion and people are free to worship as they will.

> Known Locales:
>
> **Cassiana** /cas-SEE-ah-na/
>
> **Lilymere** /LIL-ih-mare/
>
> **Petalore** /PET-AH-lore/—The capital city, a spectacle of sung stone and color.
>
> **Stonewillow**—A border town located where the Wall

meets Nocis.

Aviyah /uh-VIE-uh/—A continent surrounded on all sides by the shimmering Mists.

Ben-Gal /behn-gaul/—A nation tucked away in the deserts north of Andor. Home to the Order.

Jaromír Mountains /JAR-oh-meer/—a rugged mountain range that splits the continent of Aviyah down the middle.

Nocis /NOH-keys/—The southernmost country on the Western half of Aviyah, Nocis is known for being a strict, rugged country that runs on farming and fishing. They have recently started establishing trade beyond the mountains. The people tend to worship the Celestials, with some kings — including Arden — going so far as to outlaw worshiping the Sacreds.

> Known Locales:
>
> **Caer Albright** /CARE ALLbright/—The capital, a fort surrounded by a port city.
>
> **Caer Talon** /CARE tal-on/
>
> **Howsergale** /HOW-zer-gale/
>
> **Keep Shadow Veil**—High Lord Tsukuyomi's stronghold; now destroyed.
>
> **Nikko Mori** /Nee-koh MOR-ee/—A sanctuary forest blessed by Shaddai
>
> **Thorn-Drake**

Regalia /reh-GAL-ee-ya/— a peaceful kingdom to the west of Andor, known for their diplomacy and arts.

Sylva Arae /SIL-vuh. Ar-AE/—A Star Vein sanctuary forest bordering Andor and the Jaromír Mountains.

The Mists— a magical border of fog that completely surrounds Aviyah. Any ships that try to sail through wind up coming back out at the exact same point they entered.

About the Authors

Kimberly Glassco

Kimberly lives in Missouri in a supportive community and her overabundant imagination. From the wildernesses of her childhood backyards to the lined paper of her notebooks, Kimberly loves exploring and storytelling. And now, she's excited to bring others along for the journey. Her inspiration stems from her love of all things Celtic, fantasy, and magic. Just give her a blank piece of paper, some epic music, and a cup of pumpkin spice chai, and she'll have a new tale to tell in no time.

While working a full-time job to pay the bills, Kimberly has constantly felt God's calling for her to write at least on the side if not eventually full-time. To that end, she has been focusing on writing this series with one of her best friends. They have so many stories to tell and so little time in a day to work on them.

Carissa Barker-Stucky

Carissa lives in Missouri with the love of her life and their multitude of pets. Though her characters seem to have a will of their own, somehow she's managed to wrangle them into something resembling proper stories. Nothing inspires her more than a cup of chai or frozen matcha and a purring kitty on her lap.

When Carissa's health changed her life course, she started to focus more on this series with one of her best friends. She also takes any opportunity to encourage awareness regarding Dysautonomia and the illnesses associated, such as her own Postural Orthostatic Tachycardia Syndrome. The curious can find more information from Dysautonomia International, the leading nonprofit resource regarding this health condition.